BLOODLINES

16 JOURNEYS ON THE
DARK STREETS OF URBAN FANTASY

BLOODLINES

EDITED BY
AMANDA PILLAR

Tm
pm Ticonderoga
publications

For Tom,
for all the times I've ignored you
with claims of "I'm busy"

Bloodlines edited by Amanda Pillar

Published by Ticonderoga Publications

Designed and edited by Russell B. Farr
Typeset in Sabon and Bellerose

A Cataloging-in-Publications entry for this title is available from The National Library of Australia.

ISBN 978-1-921857-55-3 (hardcover)
978-1-921857-56-0 (trade paperback)
978-1-925212-38-9 (ebook)

Ticonderoga Publications
PO Box 29 Greenwood
Western Australia 6924
Australia

www.ticonderogapublications.com

10 9 8 7 6 5 4 3 2 1

ACKNOWLEDGMENTS

Firstly, I want to thank Russell B. Farr and Liz Grzyb. This is my second solo project, and without their support, I'd never have made it this far. Secondly, I want to thank all the authors who contributed to this collection, chatted with me about the concept, and of course, those that made it through to final selection. Without your work, this book wouldn't be the vibrant, engaging collection it is.

I would also like to thank the talented Pete Kempshall for his help with proofreading, you have the eyes of a hawk. And of course, I would like to thank my usual support cast of heroes: my husband, family, and of course, my cats, whose snuggles kept me warm over the long nights editing.

CONTENTS

INTRODUCTION

AMANDA PILLAR

BLOOD.

It's such a core part of our physical beings. It's essential to who we are: it defines us. Our DNA is hidden within its red depths, we are categorised by our blood types: A, AB, O, B, negative, positive... even the colour can indicate how healthy we are, or the medications we take. It's sometimes the only clue left at a crime scene to let the world know who was there.

But it's not just the physical nature of blood, it's also the metaphysical elements that tie us together. Our bloodline—ancestors and descendants, and our current relatives. Sayings, "Blood is thicker than water" and "Blood will tell" are still relevant today. It speaks of who we can and can't love, who we owe our loyalty to, and even raises the question of nature versus nurture. Then there's the idea of familial traits, those gifts—or curses, if you believe some of the stories within *Bloodlines*—that are passed down throughout our family trees.

Then, of course, there's the magical element. Humans have believed in magic and religion for as long as we've been around. Blood magic is still alive in some cultures, and you'll find it living deep within the pages of this collection.

Bloodlines is my eighth anthology and the sequel to *Bloodstones*, which was published by Ticonderoga Publications in 2012. Seanan McGuire wrote the introduction to *Bloodstones*, and now has a story within *Bloodlines*. Joanne Anderton, Alan Baxter, Dirk Flinthart, Stephanie Gunn and Pete Kempshall have stories in both collections, and it's this passion for the series that connects these two books in important and palpable ways.

Bloodstones was an amazing collection that took old myths and legends, placed them in an urban fantasy setting and created something remarkable and new. That's the beauty of fantasy of all kinds: urban, high, epic... They take conventional ideas and flip them on their metaphorical ears. *Bloodlines* does this, but the focus is different. I wanted stories about blood, bloodlines and the intangible but very real effects of our blood, and how it defines us.

I love every collection I work on, but *Bloodlines* has a special place in my heart. This anthology had a long gestation period, from discussions at various conventions and award ceremonies with numerous authors—some who are now contributors within these pages—to a final anthology call. In between all of this, my brother was diagnosed with a blood cancer (the irony wasn't lost on me). He kicked cancer's arse and I hope this anthology packs just as powerful a punch.

Despite the delays this caused the overall project, the authors were extraordinarily patient and kept faith in the quality of this book. And their patience has been rewarded. This collection of 16 stories is full of love, hate, betrayal, hope and new beginnings. I invite you to journey through the four parts of this collection: to where the fay walk the streets; where our bloodlines define us; where crimes and criminals need to be solved and caught; and finally, to where even the city is as much a character as the people that populate it.

I invite you to meet new authors, and re-familiarise yourselves with others. I hope you love these stories as much as I do.

September 2015

THE FAY

'The iron tongue of midnight hath told twelve:
Lovers, to bed; 'tis almost fairy time.'
~William Shakespeare, *A Midsummer Nights Dream*

INTO THE GREEN

SEANAN MCGUIRE

ANDREA picked up a deep purple heirloom tomato with emerald lines running through its marbled skin and sniffed the place where it had been broken off the vine. The sharp sweetness of sap and the rich *green* smell of tomato leaves caressed her nose. She smiled and added the tomato to her basket. Today's purchases would be the stars of tonight's meal, and like any director, she believed in the importance of good casting.

At the stall next to her, two people were peeling back the husks on ears of corn and arguing loudly enough that she couldn't help overhearing. Politeness only got you so far in such cramped quarters. The Farmers' Market didn't have much space, and the organisers believed in filling every inch.

"I'm telling you, this corn isn't worth buying. Telltale Farms have opened their produce stand for the season. Why are we even looking at this?" The man sounded irritated, like the existence of substandard corn was somehow a personal slight.

"Because it's here," said his companion. She sounded less frustrated and more amused: this was a joke to her, one whose punchline was yet to be revealed. "An ear in the hand is worth two on the stalk."

"That is where we'll have to disagree." There was a thump, as of someone throwing an ear of corn down in disgust. Andrea turned in time to see two well-dressed people walk away from the corn vendor, who was glaring after them in mute frustration.

She paid for her tomatoes and went home thoughtful.

◆

HER BUSINESS PARTNER was doing the dishes when she unlocked the door. "Tom, I'm home," she called, and was rewarded with a vague noise of greeting from the direction of the kitchen. Andrea walked across the living room and stopped in the doorway, her basket slung jauntily over her arm. She was aware of the picture she presented: pioneer princess, home from a hard day of gathering food to feed her family.

She had everything but the corn.

"Hey, Tom, you ever hear of a place called 'Telltale Farms'?" she asked.

Tom dropped the plate he had been drying. It shattered into sharp white shards when it hit the floor. Andrea yelped, hurrying to put her basket down on the counter, and for a few minutes, both of them were preoccupied with cleaning up the mess.

Only when the offending plate had been deposited in the trash did Andrea look at Tom and frown. "You're not usually such a butterfingers."

"Sorry," he said, cheeks reddening. "You just—I was distracted. What were we talking about?"

"Telltale Farms," Andrea prompted.

"No such place," said Tom.

Andrea's frown deepened. "So the name startled you into dropping a plate because you're surprised when I talk nonsense? Come on, Tom. I know when you're keeping secrets. This is one of those 'you're not really a local until you've lived here for twenty years' things, isn't it?"

"No, really, there's no such thing," said Tom. "*Taitale* Farms is out near the old highway. They grow corn, mostly. Corn, wheat, pumpkins, and sometimes sunflowers, when the weather's right. They're strictly small potatoes. Heck, they don't even grow potatoes." He laughed at his own joke until he realised that Andrea wasn't laughing: Andrea was looking at him coldly, her eyebrows lifted almost to her hairline.

Tom sighed. "Aw, c'mon, Andy. They're weird. They're a weird little family farm. They grow good produce, but they're not worth dealing with."

"That's not what I heard," Andrea said. "The people at the Farmers' Market said that anybody else's corn wasn't worth buying."

"Who are you going to listen to?" Tom asked. "A couple of local snobs, or your dedicated business partner?"

Andrea's cold look turned withering. "Our Table to Yours is dedicated to using locally sourced ingredients, and showcasing the best in local business," she said. She had fallen automatically into using the slightly sing-song voice she used for media inquiries and local news outlets. Somehow, Tom didn't think that pointing that out was going to help his case. "If there's a local farm growing corn that's better than anything at the Market, we owe it to our customers and to ourselves to get our hands on it. As the local member of this partnership, you should have brought it to my attention. I shouldn't have to rely on Farmers' Market gossip."

Tom swallowed a sigh. There was no point in arguing: once Andy got herself worked up about the restaurant, the only thing to do was wait for her to come back down of her own accord. "Fine," he said. "I'll take you there."

Andrea smiled. "There, see? That wasn't so hard."

Tom didn't say anything.

◆

TAITALE FARMS WAS located nearly fifteen miles outside of town, tucked off beside the road like an afterthought. "A hop, skip, and a jump from nowhere," as the locals would have put it, if they had been willing to talk about the place at all. Remote, on a stretch of road that led from nowhere good to no place better, and surrounded by nothing but fruitless fields and empty, crumbling barns, it was easy to let Taitale slip from everyday thought. It didn't matter in the day to day course of things.

Andrea thought differently. "Tom, look at the *corn!*" she squealed, pointing at the towering green stalks with a shaking hand. "It's like something out of a picture book! Have you ever seen corn this high? Or this green?"

"Yes," said Tom, who had been to Taitale Farms before. "Look, their sign isn't out. They're probably not selling right now. We should come back later."

Andrea sniffed. "We're not just here for a few ears of corn, Tom. We're here to offer them a major opportunity to move their produce through an ethical local restaurant, and make a lot of money in the process. Most people don't turn you away when you're offering to back the money truck up to their front doors."

Tom had gone to school with some members of the Taitale family, and thought that she might well be surprised. Still, there was no point in arguing with her: this had been his last attempt. Clenching his hands on the wheel, he turned off the road and onto the narrow gravel driveway leading up to the farm.

The Taitales hadn't made any effort to make it easy to reach them. Unlike most of the independent fruit and produce stands, they didn't set up on the road itself: people who wanted to buy their corn had to be willing to turn down the driveway blind, knowing that another car could easily be coming toward them. The driveway was curved, meaning that people at one end couldn't see the other, no matter how hard they tried. Worse yet, it ended at a gravel parking lot roughly the size of a small front yard, with no defined parking spaces. When the 'Fresh Corn' sign was out, it turned into something out of Thunderdome every time.

Driving along the gravel road was like diving into a world gone green. Corn towered on every side, straining toward the sun in an unbroken wall. Andrea gasped and cooed at the sight of heavy ears clinging to the stalks, topped with wisps of golden silk like a promise of deliciousness within. Tom kept his eyes on the road. He had been here before, and he knew that the price of carelessness could be a fender bender or worse.

Then they came around the curve, and the house appeared in front of them: two-story, painted white, with a little porch swing in front and a big red barn behind, it was a perfect snapshot of a Norman Rockwell America that had never really existed outside of the magazines. Andrea whistled.

"This should be on our menus," she said. "Just this farm. It's *perfect*. How could you think I wouldn't be interested?"

Tom didn't answer.

There was a small produce stand off to one side of the lot, situated in a perfect cut-out from the corn. It was open, and a pair of teenagers had settled behind the counter. They didn't pay any attention as Tom parked the car, probably because all their attention was reserved for each other. The boy had his hands in the pockets of the girl's cut-off shorts, and she was sitting on his lap so that her legs were almost wrapped around his waist. Tom snorted faintly.

"Well, there you go," he said. "Your future farmers of America."

Andrea shook her head. "It's unprofessional. Someone should have a word with their parents."

"Now, Andy. They didn't have the sign out. We should leave them in peace."

"Like hell. I came here for corn, and I'm not leaving without it." Before Tom realised what she was going to do, she had leaned across him and slammed her hand down on the horn. The sound echoed through the cornfield, sending crows flying for the sun.

The horn's effect on the teenagers was even more dramatic. The girl yanked backward, and only the boy's hands on her behind kept her from toppling clear off the stool. He grimaced with the effort of keeping her in place. Both of them turned, looking utterly stunned, to stare at the car.

"Andy—" Tom began.

Too late. She was already in motion, unbuckling her belt and opening the door, her big, salesperson smile in place. "Hello!" she called, waving to the startled teens. "I'm Andrea Paulson, and the man in the car is my partner, Tom Ryan. You have a beautiful farm here. Are your parents around?"

The girl blinked slowly, revealing sparkly green eye shadow the colour of the corn stalks. "Are you implying that Evan's my brother? Because that's just sick. Where are you people from?"

The aforementioned Evan pulled his hands out of the girl's back pockets, allowing her to slide off his lap. "I'm not a Taitale, ma'am. Is this police business?"

"What? Oh, no." Andrea laughed, sounding so patently artificial that Tom winced. "We're restaurateurs. We own Our Table to Yours downtown. Isn't that right, Tom?"

"That's right," said Tom, closing the driver's side door. "Afternoon, Jill."

"Mr Ryan," said the girl with the green eye shadow. "Not like you to come by without calling first."

"Sorry," he said.

Andrea turned to him, looking stunned. "I thought you said you'd never been here."

"I never said that," he said. "I just said that it wasn't worth making the trip. There's a difference."

"I beg to differ. Smell that corn!" She inhaled exaggeratedly. "It's like breathing summer. Where are your parents, Jill? I want to discuss a business opportunity with them."

"We don't need more business," said Jill. "We have enough. Can sell you a sixer if you wanted one, though. There's some left over from this week's orders."

"A sixer?" asked Andrea.

"Six ears of corn. It'll cost you a dollar." Jill fished around behind the counter before coming up with a paper bag. The sides bulged. "Just picked today. Didn't mean to come up with extras, but sometimes things happen, you know?"

"Jill?" A rustling in the corn accompanied the voice, followed by the appearance of a second teenage boy, this one a year or so older than Jill's boyfriend. He stopped at the edge of the field, looking suspiciously at the visitors. "We've got company?"

"Tom's new friend owns a restaurant," said Jill, hand still resting on the paper bag.

"You must be Jill's brother," said Andrea. "I'm Andrea."

"Jack," said the boy.

The two teens looked similar enough that there was no question as to their relationship. Both had the same corn silk yellow hair, tanned skin, and freckles; their eyes slanted very slightly upward at the tips, giving them a questioning air, like they were on the verge of announcing some great and bewildering discovery. Jill was thin and wiry, but her arms were corded with muscle, while Jack was all classic American farm boy, broad at the shoulders and narrow at the hips, built to carry bales of hay and hoe rows of potatoes.

No, wait, they don't grow potatoes, thought Andrea, almost nonsensically. Aloud, she said, "It's a pleasure to meet you. Are your parents around? I learned about your corn today, and I just had to come out and see if it was as good as everyone said."

The first flicker of real interest lit in Jill's eyes. "Really? People were talking about our corn? What people? Do you remember their names?"

"Well, Tom wasn't among them," said Andrea, forcing a laugh. Something about the way the girl was looking at her made her profoundly uncomfortable. Teenage girls weren't supposed to stare at you that way. "He left me to find out about you from strangers. The best-kept local secrets, hmm? So, your parents?"

"They're in the fields," said Jack. "They're always in the fields."

"Oh, harvest time, huh? I would have expected them to make you play free labour, while they lounged around selling corn to strangers." Andrea produced a card from her pocket, holding it out for Jack to take. Frowning, he did. "Let them know that we came by, and that we're really interested in exploring a partnership with your farm. If you have the best corn in the area, then we want it for our menu."

"Thank you, ma'am," said Jack.

"It's really beautiful out here," said Andrea. She reached for her wallet. "Now about that sixer . . . "

♠

JACK AND JILL stood side by side at the mouth of the driveway, watching as the stranger woman and Tom Ryan drove away. Evan was back at the produce stand. He had been dating Jill Taitale for the better part of a year: more than long enough to know that when the siblings closed ranks like that, he was best served by backing up and letting them do what they felt needed to be done. Dating a Taitale was a little more complicated than dating a cheerleader, but he was willing to put up with the complications in exchange for the benefits. Like Jill herself.

At the moment, all Jill's attention was focused on the receding taillights of Tom's Lexus. "I don't like strangers showing up here," she said. "It's not right, and especially not this close to the end of the season. She could confuse things."

"Or she could solve them," said Jack. He glanced her way. "What if this is the solution to our supply problems? We could let her have some corn for her restaurant. We have plenty."

"But she's not from around here," said Jill. "We don't supply strangers. That's counter to the corn, and you know it."

"If her restaurant is in town, we're supplying a stranger to feed the locals," said Jack. He shrugged. "It's not perfect, but it's liveable. The corn will forgive us. The corn forgives a lot of things."

Jill sighed. "I'm not going to like it. You know that, right? The corn forgives a lot of things, but it doesn't forget much of anything. I don't want to get caught out in a season because the corn remembers that we went and supplied a stranger."

"Aren't you the one who offered her a sixer?" asked Jack.

"That was different!" Jill protested. "She was here, and she wasn't going to go away empty handed. Six ears is placating. Sixty is supplying."

"Then we supply, and we see what happens," said Jack. He looked out over the fields, growing green and seeming to glow in the afternoon light. He sighed. "I should go out and tell the folks what's going on. You good to hold down the fort for the rest of the day?"

Jill glanced to the produce stand, where Evan was waiting for her. He had pulled a book out of his backpack and was reading, studiously ignoring the conversation happening on the other side of the lot. "I suppose I can find something to distract myself," she said.

"Just take your tongue out of his mouth if one of our regulars shows up, all right? We have orders to fill."

Jill hit her brother, who laughed, and kept laughing as he vanished back into the corn.

♦

TOM AND ANDREA had been quiet for the drive back to the house, both of them lost in thoughts of the Taitale Farm. Andrea was dreaming of menus emblazoned with pictures of that amazing American house, while Tom thought about the siblings, Jack and Jill with their corn silk hair, and about the Taitale kids who had been in his class back in high school. That pair had been named John and Jenny. They had been a year apart but still essentially joined at the hip: where John went, Jenny followed, and vice-versa. Neither of them had gone off to college. So far as Tom remembered, they had graduated and then gone back to work on the family farm.

Neither of them had ever mentioned younger siblings that he could remember, and neither of them was old enough to have been a parent to both those teens. Maybe the younger one, if John had gotten a girl pregnant straight out of high school, but both of them? There was just no way. And even if neither of them was the parent of the teens he'd seen today, where were they? They should have been there.

Maybe they had been out in the fields with their parents. Farm families tended to be large, and it wasn't entirely outside the realm of possibility that Jack and Jill were just the result of carefully timed pregnancies. After all, what better way was there to make sure that you would always have farmhands than to breed them for yourself?

When they reached the house, Tom parked, still feeling a little uncomfortable about their trip to the farm, and watched Andrea walk inside with the bag of corn in her arms. He'd never been *told* to keep strangers and newcomers away from Taitale Farms, exactly: it was a whispered admonition, passed back and forth by people who had lived in town much longer than Tom had, who had seen generations of Taitale children come and go.

Did all of them have names that sounded like something out of a nursery rhyme? Did all of them come in pairs, and stand side by side like they were preparing to shut the entire world out? What was he *missing*?

"This corn is *amazing*!" Andrea's voice drifted back through the open garage door. Tom sighed and finally got out of the car. Whatever he was or was not missing, his partner was waiting to deliver her I-told-you-so about the visit to the farm. It was better to get it over with.

Andrea was in the kitchen, a pot of water on the stove and six ears of corn, expertly shucked, gleaming like something out of a painting on the counter in front of her. There were no bad kernels, no marks left by invading cornworms or caterpillars: each ear was as perfect as the next, pale as sweet buttermilk, and scenting the air with the faint, earthy smell of fresh-picked corn.

"Taste this," commanded Andrea, thrusting her palm toward him. There were three pale kernels at the centre of it, clearly plucked from the base of the ears, where they would have been less tightly packed together. "You have to taste this."

"Yes, dear," said Tom mechanically, and plucked one of the kernels from her palm. He rolled it between his fingers before popping it into his mouth. His eyes widened.

"Well?" said Andrea.

"I forgot," he said weakly.

That single kernel tasted more like the ideal of corn than all the ears he had prepared, sampled, or consumed over the previous three months. It was a cascade of sweetness, tinted with that faint, ineffable bite that marked really good sweet corn, but couldn't be defined using any word he knew. He thought of the concept of umami, and how it described a taste combination that had previously been outside the realm of simple sweet, sour, and savoury. Really good corn was like that. It had a flavour that didn't have a name, and couldn't be given one without rewriting the language so that the word 'corny' ceased to mean 'ridiculous' and began to mean 'sublime'.

"If it's that good raw, what's it going to be like once it's cooked?" asked Andrea. "We could make *anything* with this corn, Tom. Relishes. Ice creams. Cornbread that will bring the Food Network to our doorstep. We could have locked in their entire harvest. We could have been serving this to our customers for *months*. And you just forgot to mention that they were there."

"Sorry," said Tom. He was aware of how weak his voice sounded. He had no excuses. Yes, he was a local, but he was also a small business owner. He should have been thinking of the restaurant first, and of the vague prohibitions he remembered from his youth later. "I really am sorry. This is amazing."

"It's more than amazing. It's perfect." Andrea turned to check her water. "We're going to need more. A lot more. We have to go back."

"Yeah," agreed Tom. "I think you're right."

◆

THE SECOND TIME they came to Taitale Farms, the 'Fresh Produce' sign was out, and the parking lot was packed. Tom managed to wedge the car into a narrow space at the very edge of the lot, forcing Andrea to squeeze her way out between the Lexus and the pickup truck in the next space over. Tom stepped out of the car and straight into the corn, which grew right up to the edge of the lot.

The world went green. He breathed deep and tasted the growing world on his tongue before stepping out again.

Andrea was gazing in dismay at the large crowd surrounding the produce stand. Jack, Jill, and Evan were all there, forking over paper bags as fast as their arms could sustain. Six ears for a dollar, a dollar a bag ... "They might as well be giving it away for free," she said, sounding pained. "Don't they understand what a goldmine this is?"

"I guess they're more interested in feeding people," said Tom.

"We feed people," said Andrea, and waded into the crowd.

Tom stayed where he was, watching her go and wishing that he knew exactly how to feel about all this. She was right about the corn: it was some of the best he'd ever tasted, if not the very best. It seemed to have a depth of flavour that was missing from all the other farms in the area, although it was grown in the same soil and watered from the same aquifers. If they could secure even a portion of the harvest for Our Table to Yours, they would be able to attract a whole new class of customers. The Internet reviews alone would explode with delight. And yet . . .

And yet.

Taitale Farms had always been a local secret. Not in the sense of 'people discover it for themselves': in the sense of *secret*. Everyone who met the Taitales knew that they were strange, and that they grew the best corn in the county, maybe in the state. Maybe in the *world*. But no one told strangers about them. It wasn't done. Something about the family discouraged that sort of casual sharing.

Andrea had worked her way up to the front of the crowd and was talking to Jack, gesticulating wildly as she tried to get her point across. She was probably asking if he'd passed her card along to his parents like she'd asked, since no one had called to discuss providing corn to the restaurant. Tom walked across the parking lot to join her, cringing a little at the looks he received from the people who were waiting for their corn. Some of them looked scornful; others were looking at Andrea, and hence at him, with expressions of pity and regret, like he was committing some incredible crime by standing in this place, at this time, with this woman.

Jack shook his head. "They haven't had time, ma'am. This is our busy time."

"That's exactly why we're here," said Andrea. "Your busy time could be a lot simpler if you'd just agree to supply us with a certain number of ears daily. We could buy enough to make it possible for you to hire more help. Less corn to move and extra hands to move it. What could be better?"

"Not having strangers sniffing around the farm every time we turn around," said Jill, dropping a bag of corn on the produce stand counter. She snatched a dollar bill out of an outstretched hand and shoved the corn over to its owner. "We don't need a restaurant to save our farm. Our farm's doing just fine."

Andrea frowned. "Where are your parents?"

"We told you, ma'am: they're in the corn," said Jack. He folded his arms. "If you're here to buy something, we're happy to sell it to you. But we're not going to agree to something without talking to our parents, and we can't rush them. You're going to have to wait."

"Fine," said Andrea, rolling her eyes. She reached into her purse, producing her wallet. "It's a dollar for six ears?"

"Yes, ma'am."

"All right, then." She produced two twenties, ignoring the groans from the crowd around her. Looking almost feral now, she smiled, and said, "I'll take forty bags."

The drive back to town was somewhat cramped.

♦

"THEY'RE GOING TO keep coming around here, you know they are," said Jill, twisting a piece of corn husk between her fingers as she watched her brother count out the day's take. "Tom Ryan's a decent fellow, but he can't keep that restaurant woman away. She's going to keep coming. Have the folks said what to do yet?" There was a soft wistfulness in her tone as she asked the question. Unlike her brother, she hadn't gone into the heart of the green for months. Her parents were out there somewhere, and she missed them, even if it wasn't their time.

Jack replied gently, "They said to let her keep coming back. Season's almost done. We'll keep giving the city people corn, and they'll keep coming back, and then come end of the season, we'll take care of things. It'll be easier this way. We don't make a fuss, so they don't raise a bunch of questions we'd rather not answer, and we don't have to choose. The choice is already made."

"I don't like this," said Jill. "It has too many moving parts. The old way works. Why are we doing something new?"

"Because the stranger is something new," said Jack. He looked at the corn doll taking shape in Jill's hands, and then up to her face. "Evan is something new, and you like him."

"Evan's different," said Jill, defensively. "He's from around here. He understands."

"Not everything."

Jill didn't have an answer to that. No one understood everything. If they had, the Taitales would have been driven out years ago, not allowed to keep quietly planting and harvesting their fields.

"Hey." Jack sighed, forcing his expression to gentle. "It's all right. We're done here for the day. I'm going to get dinner on; why don't you go see Evan? Maybe he'd like to join us."

"All right," said Jill. She slid off her stool, pressed a kiss to her brother's cheek, and was gone, plunging into the green like a diver slipping into the sea. He watched the corn stalks rustle for a few seconds. Then she was too deep to track visually, and everything was still, and he looked away.

No one understood everything.

◆

THE SHOWPIECE OF the menu at Our Table to Yours the night after their second visit to Taitale Farms was corn. Corn chowder and relish; roast corn and boiled corn and baked corn; corn ice cream and cornbread pudding. It was a symphony of harvest flavours, and the reviews they got from that night were better than anything they had seen before. Of the two hundred and forty ears of corn they had purchased, they went through over a hundred and fifty by closing time.

The next night was all about the secondary uses: corn in stew, corn in soup, corn as garnish for other things. It was less focal, but it uplifted everything it touched, imbuing simple dishes with a complexity that had previously seemed impossible. The corn ice cream was sold out by eight o'clock. The corn sorbet sold out shortly thereafter. They finished the night with three uncooked ears in the pantry.

The morning of the third day, Andrea turned to Tom and said, "We have to go back. We need more corn. People *want* more corn. We have so many reservations for tonight that I'm not sure we'll be taking any walk-ins. That's never happened."

"I don't think we can just keep rolling up and driving away with two hundred ears of corn," protested Tom. "For one thing, we're not paying nearly enough. I feel like we're committing some sort of crime by buying that much, that cheaply."

"If they want us to pay more, they'll start treating us like a supplier, and charging by the case," said Andrea stubbornly. "This is going to make our name in the culinary world."

"It still seems dishonest," said Tom.

The phone rang.

Both of them turned to look at it, surprised. Almost no one called the house line. People knew they were living together to save on rent, but all business calls went to the restaurant office, while personal calls went to their respective mobiles. The phone rang again.

Andrea leaned over and picked it up. "Hello?" As Tom watched, her expression slid from surprise into wonder, and finally into joy. None of that came through in her voice, however, as she said, "Yes, we would be delighted. This afternoon, you say? Would two o'clock be all right? We own and operate a restaurant here in town, and we'll need time to prepare for the dinner rush. Yes, that would be fine. Thank you. Thank you so much."

She delicately replaced the phone in its cradle. By the time she turned to Tom, she was beaming.

"That was Mr Taitale," she said. "He got my card from Jack, and he'd like us to come by this afternoon to discuss supplying Our Table to Yours with corn for the rest of the season."

Tom blinked. Then, slowly, he began to grin.

"I guess you did it," he said.

"I guess I did," Andrea agreed.

◆

ONCE AGAIN, THE sign was down when they reached the turnoff for the farm: either the day's supply of corn had already sold, or the teens had simply decided not to open the produce stand. Privately, Andrea hoped for the latter. She wanted as much corn as she could get her hands on, especially with the dinner rush coming up in just a few hours.

The produce stand was closed and shuttered. Jack was standing in front of it. Jill and Evan were nowhere to be seen. Tom parked the car; Andrea was out of it before he had turned the engine off, making a beeline for the elder of the Taitale children.

"Hello," she said. "Your parents called. We're supposed to be meeting them here. Did they send you to wait for us?"

"Yes, ma'am, they did," he said. "They're out in the corn, but they're looking forward to your little talk. Today's the official end of the season."

"What?" Andrea looked alarmed. "But the corn—"

"Oh, we'll have corn for weeks yet. Today's the day the last stalk puts out the last ear. It won't ripen for a while. Nothing's ever quite as sharply delineated as folks want it to be, especially not city folks. Nature moves at her own pace." Jack's eyes flicked to Tom. "John and Jenny say hello."

Tom raised an eyebrow. "They remember me? Where are they, anyway? I expected to see them when we started coming by."

"They're in the corn," said Jack. "You'll see them soon."

"Oh," said Tom. "Well, uh. Lead the way."

Jack nodded, once, before he turned and walked toward the wall of green. Andrea and Tom exchanged a glance, and followed.

Walking through the corn was a little bit like wading. The air seemed thicker, scented with chlorophyll and petrichor and the ineffable scent of things growing, ripening, swimming in the green world. Several times, Tom thought he had lost the others, only to glimpse them again through the waving stalks up ahead.

The heavy air was surprisingly easy to breathe, once he had adjusted to the difference. After the first ten yards or so, it was as if he was really breathing for the first time in years. Memories started to tickle the back of his mind. Kissing John Taitale behind the auto shop while his sister filed her nails and made disgusted noises. Holding hands when no one else was around to see, especially not the other members of the football team, who would never have been able to understand. Hell, he wasn't sure *he'd* been able to understand. It had been a school romance, and while it had led him to realise that he was gay, he'd forgotten it almost as soon as the graduation bell had rung.

Shouldn't that have seemed strange? Didn't most people remember their first loves for as long as they lived, replaying every kiss and every caress like a favourite film? But here he was, chasing that long-ago love's little brother through the corn, and only now was he remembering what he had put aside.

Then they broke out of the corn into a clearing, and everything fell away.

Someone had crafted a throne, of sorts, from woven corn husks and tall, dried-out stalks: it stood easily eight feet high, and was still shorter than the corn itself, which towered twelve and thirteen feet around them. The corn shouldn't have been that tall, should it? But facts couldn't deny reality, and the corn was everywhere, and infinite.

Two people sat on the throne, a man and a woman, and they were older versions of Jack and Jill, golden-haired and green eyed and tan. They lifted their heads, and Tom's heart stopped.

He would have known those eyes anywhere.

"Johnny?" he whispered. His voice was dry as chaff, and seemed to catch in his throat.

The man on the throne smiled, but there was sadness behind his eyes. "Hello, Tom," he said. "You came to the corn. I never expected that."

"But . . . you can't be . . . "

"I can, I am, and it's complicated." John slid off the throne. Jenny didn't move, but watched Tom with wary, disapproving eyes. "I wish you hadn't come. You should have stayed away."

"This is . . . a little odd, but hey, we're modern people, we can roll with the changes," said Andrea. She sounded uncertain, like she didn't quite understand what was going on. Of course she didn't. She wasn't from town.

Even Tom barely understood. He had been away too long.

"I wanted to talk to you about your corn," said Andrea. "I've never tasted anything like it. I very much want to secure a supply for our restaurant. We serve only the finest locally sourced foods, and your corn would be a centrepiece of our fall menu. We're happy to pay you much more handsomely than your current customers. A dollar for six ears is almost an insult."

"A dollar for six ears is a token," said John. "It's a way to honour the harvest. We don't need the money. If we needed the money, we would have come to you, rather than expecting you to come to us."

Jack and Jill, who stood near the edge of the clearing, were silent. Tom looked from John to Jack and back again, and it was hard to tell them apart. They could have been the same man, just twenty years removed. The same could be said of Jenny and Jill. "Where are your parents?" asked Tom. "You can't . . . Jenny's your sister, and you're . . . "

"We're not their parents," said Jenny. "They're our siblings. Get your head out of the gutter, Ryan. You weren't good enough for my brother when we were in high school, and you're not good enough for the corn now."

"But we came here to meet your parents," said Tom.

"Well, yes," said John. "And you will. You—" He stopped as there was a rustling from the corn. All of the Taitales turned to watch as Evan emerged into the clearing, moving at a rapid trot. He didn't seem to notice the throne of corn. His attention was on Jill.

"Jill, there's a car in front of the produce stand, I think those people are back, I think they came back...again..." Evan trotted to a stop, blinking at the sight of Andrea and Tom. "Oh. They're here. They're here?" He turned back to Jill. "Why are there strangers in the corn?"

"You're a stranger in the corn, if you want to get technical," said Jill. She sounded frustrated but fond, like this was a conversation they had had before. "Go back to the yard, Evan. I'll be there soon."

The wind rustled through the corn. Jill's face fell.

"What?" she whispered.

"What?" echoed Evan. His eyes widened, confusion transitioning into alarm. "No, wait. I didn't—I helped all season, I helped you sell the corn. I worked the farm. I did what you asked."

"Jack?" Jill turned to her brother. "No. Please, tell it no. Tell it that this isn't right."

"I'm starting to feel like I've wandered into a family dispute," said Andrea, taking a step backward. "I'll tell you what: tell your parents that we would really like to discuss supplying our restaurant, but that we're done playing games with you. If they want to have a business meeting, they can come to our offices, like normal people."

"Oh, no." Jenny was suddenly there, taking Andrea's elbow. Tom hadn't even seen her move from the corn throne. "See, you came to us. Three times, you came to us. You ate our corn. You bound yourself to us. You *volunteered*. We appreciate the power of a willing sacrifice."

"What are you talking about?" Andrea tried to pull her elbow away. Jenny didn't let go. "Take your hands off me!"

"Jack, *please*," keened Jill.

"I'm sorry," said Jack.

"What's going on?" asked Tom. Jack was holding Evan now, and Jenny was holding Andrea. Jill was crying, fat tears like sap rolling down her cheeks. Only John was empty-handed and calm.

He looked at Tom. "I told you once, when we were younger," he said. "I told you about the corn. You broke up with me the next morning, but you never told anyone. I should thank you for that, but I doubt it was your choice. It so rarely is."

And there was something, wasn't there? Something in the back of Tom's mind, something about the corn... "I don't remember," he whispered.

"I know, sweetheart; I know." John looked toward Jack and the struggling Andrea. "You have to feed the corn. That's what it all comes down to. You tend your land, you feed your crops, and your crops feed you. If you want to thrive, you have to be willing to make sacrifices. You have to reap so you can sow."

Something about the corn.

Tom stumbled backward, remembering hot summer nights and the smell of the corn, John's hand on his chest and the sound of screaming. But it was far away, the screaming was far away, and John was right there, kissing him, and he didn't know whether it was in the past or in the violent present. He just knew that he had been unkissed for too long, and that John could protect him from the green. The green, which took what it wanted. The green, which was parent and purpose for the Taitales, who always came in twos, who were never old enough, or young enough, for the generations to line up.

"I'm sorry," John whispered, and Tom fell down, into the green, and everything was silence, and the scent of blood on the corn.

♦

TOM RYAN WOKE alone in a green world. The clearing was gone. There was no corn throne; there were no bodies. He thought he could remember screaming, but it was far away, in another lifetime, like a boy whose kisses always tasted like the corn.

He picked himself up out of the loam, bits of soil and rotten leaves clinging to his clothing. His mouth tasted like a copper penny, all brightness and bleeding. Slowly, he staggered toward what he hoped would be the road. He didn't know how long he walked, only that he kept going until his legs were tired and his head spun from the thick air between the stalks. The corn seemed to be never-ending, all-encompassing and unforgiving.

Something tickled his lip. He wiped at it, and the back of his hand came away dark with blood, red and filled with secrets. Tom kept walking.

Somewhere in the back of his mind, Andrea screamed, and kept on screaming, until the scythe came down and the blood flowed free.

He just kept walking.

When the corn gave way, he stumbled, almost falling out into the openness of the parking lot. The sky was bruised purple and streaked with orange and red, like a ratatouille spread out across the horizon. All four of the Taitales were there, standing in front of his car, barring him from leaving the property. All four of them had red hands, deep, bright, arterial red at the fingertips, shading up to a dark burgundy at the wrists. He knew what that meant. He didn't want to know.

Jill's eyes were puffy, and she glared at him like he had committed some crime by coming out of the corn alive.

"I'm sorry," said John, moving to help Tom stand. "I know you cared about her. But she'll keep the parents sleeping for another year. Isn't that important enough to be worth it?"

"The parents?" asked Tom blankly. "Who *are* you people?"

"We're from the green," said John, and kissed him lightly. "We come from the green, and we go back to the green, and we keep the parents sleeping when they're not needed. We give them what they want, and they leave us be."

"You can't keep him, John," said Jenny. She sounded faintly frustrated, like this argument had been going on for hours. "You had your chance."

"The corn didn't want you," said John. "I'm so sorry."

His hands closed around Tom's jaw before Tom could do more than blink. There was a sharp cracking sound, sending the crows scattering into the sky, and Tom's body hit the gravel like a sack of mulch.

"You get rid of the car," said John. "I'll take care of the mess." He picked up Tom's body, slinging it over his shoulder, and vanished into the green. Jenny followed him. Jack and Jill piled into the car and drove it away, and everything was silent at Taitale Farms. Nothing stirred in the fields; nothing woke, nothing walked. There was only the whisper of wind through the green, and the good, sweet smell of corn.

◆　◆　◆

THE TIES OF BLOOD, HAIR AND BONE

NATHAN BURRAGE

BLINK.

Pain: an excruciating spike that runs up his arm and nails the back of his skull to the floor.

Blink.

His right hand, throbbing and bandaged, the little finger gone, severed at the first joint.

Blink.

Police peppering him with questions. Answers eluding his mangled grasp.

Blink.

Jared tries to divide his confusion into pieces that might—in time—be assembled together.

♦

EARLIER . . .

A flashy car was parked in the driveway, its sleek steely blue lines glinting in the autumn sunshine. Jared studied it, the first flickers of rage stirring in the pit of his stomach. A Mercedes E250 Cabriolet.

His dream car.

In his favourite colour.

Fucking Annika.

She must have bought it with money from the settlement, rubbing his nose in the court decision, as if being forced to move to this shit-hole of a rental on the outskirts of Sydney's north-west wasn't bad enough.

Jared uncurled his fingers. His nails, chewed and uneven as they were, had left welts in his palms. Annika was talking to Ellette in the front passenger seat. It wasn't difficult to guess the conversation: Elli would be complaining about having to stay. Annika would be reassuring her that it was only for a few days. Elli would pout, Annika would frown, a tiny crease in her forehead that held all the threat of a thundercloud. Elli would find her composure, adopt that bright smile she had perfected during the separation . . .

. . . and the passenger door opened.

Elli emerged from the Merc. "Hi, Dad." Her long black hair was pulled back into a single ponytail near the crown of her head. While Elli was only eleven, the resemblance to her mother was becoming starker with each passing day. Not only did they share the same hairstyle, Elli's taste in clothing was moving towards black as well.

"Hi, sweetheart." A hesitant smile crept across Jared's face. The boot opened silently and Elli retrieved her bag.

Jared hurried down the steps from his porch. "Here, let me."

"I can do it." Elli tottered under the weight of her backpack. Jared lifted the bag from her protesting grasp.

"Dads like to be useful. At least now and then."

Elli let go, her hazel eyes searching his face. Far too much awareness in that gaze. She was slipping away from him, just like Annika had, and he was powerless to prevent it.

"There's apple juice in the fridge. Why don't you go inside? I'll be with you in a minute."

"Are you sure?" Elli glanced at Annika, concern fluttering across her delicate features.

"Yes, I'm sure." He was pleased that his tone remained level.
"Don't be long."

"I won't." He walked her to the front door and deposited the backpack next to the umbrella stand. Elli slipped inside the house without a backward glance.

The boot closed automatically with a click. Jared walked up to the passenger window and tapped. By now, his rage was well alight. If Elli wasn't here, he might have taken a mattock to the sleek lines of the Cabriolet. Just to make a point.

The window slid down. Annika peered over the top of her sunglasses. He was looking into Elli's eyes, except Annika's lashes were fuller and longer. She hadn't aged since he met her a dozen years ago; no grey strands nestled in her black hair, no blemishes had dared touch her fair skin.

When he and Annika first started dating, his mates had labelled her a stunner, a real catch. His female buddies were notably less enthusiastic, branding her haughty or worse, after a few drinks. Mitch, his oldest mate from primary school, was brutally honest. "Don't chase this one, mate. She's toxic."

He hadn't listened, of course. Annika was beautiful, intelligent and constantly surprising him with her worldliness. Life with her had held so many possibilities.

"Morning, Jared." Annika's voice was light with just a hint of impatience.

Jared grabbed the handle and yanked the door open. Anger was good. It had sustained him this long. He slid into the leather seat and slammed the door.

"Nice car."

Annika sighed. "Do we have to do this every time?"

"Do what?" His nails were digging into his palms again.

Annika thumbed her sunnies back up her nose, retreating behind the dark lenses. "Elli will be watching. Can't you pretend to be civil for her benefit?"

Jared glanced at the living room window. Did the curtains just ripple? Sitting in the Merc, immersed in the cloying smell of new car and Annika's perfume that always made him think of lilies, his anger faltered. At least Elli would get to enjoy this car; lifts to school, shopping excursions, a weekend cruise down the old Pacific Highway. He could choose to be happy for his daughter, couldn't he?

Annika nodded as his mood shifted. She had always understood him, even from the very beginning. He was the ignorant one, the one who always needed more, especially once her 'retreats' became more regular. He'd tried hard to find the bloke who had split them up, but had never succeeded. Now he wondered whether Annika was right; that man was only a mirror away.

"I take it you have something to say." Annika's manicured nails drummed on the soft leather of the steering wheel.

"The new school," Jared muttered.

"Ravens Grammar. What of it?"

"They called me. Said Elli's attendance has been erratic."

Annika's lips thinned to a slash of red lipstick. "I'm sorry, Jared. They should have contacted me. It won't happen again."

"What won't happen again; the school calling, or me having any involvement with my daughter's education?"

Annika *tsked*. Jared detested the sound.

"Why do you have to make everything about you?"

"I'm not. This is about Elli."

"Of course it is, which is why I will visit the school and sort this out."

"We should go together."

Annika finally lifted her hands off the steering wheel. "That's not necessary."

"Why not?"

"It would send the wrong message." A note of irritation had crept into Annika's voice.

"What message would it send, Annika? That I am interested in the welfare of my daughter. Would that be so bad?"

"No. It would suggest we're still together. And that *would* be bad." Annika's gaze flicked to the front door.

Elli was standing in the shadow of the lintel, her arms folded across her chest.

"If you're so worried about Elli, you'll get out of the car and act like everything is fine."

Jared knew he'd taken this as far as he could. At least for now. He climbed out of the Merc meekly, wondering why he let her boss him about.

Because she's out of your league. Always has been.

"Dad? Everything okay?"

"Yes." Jared mounted the steps and gave her a belated hug.

"How would you like pancakes? I've been practising."

"Dad, it's four thirty in the afternoon. You can't have pancakes for dinner!"

"I know that. I just thought you'd like a treat."

"What's for dinner then?" Elli's gaze narrowed in suspicion.

"I don't know yet." Jared shrugged as if it wasn't a big deal. "I'll rustle something up."

"You haven't been shopping, have you?" Suspicion shifted to something far more complicated on such a young face. "If you need money, I can give you one hundred dollars from my savings."

"No!" Jared retrieved Elli's backpack so she wouldn't see the shame that flushed his face. "That's good of you, but I'm fine. Let's just go inside. You can tell me if I'm flipping the pancakes the wrong way, eh?"

Elli rolled her eyes. At least that was normal, Jared thought with a smile.

♦

LATER THAT NIGHT, Jared stopped outside the door to his office. He liked to refer to it as that, rather than the second bedroom, although it was Elli's room when she stayed with him. Having an office reminded him of when he still owned his landscaping business: *Terrace, Lawn and Tree*. A bit like *Surf, Dive and Ski* he used to joke with potential clients. At its zenith, TLT had thirty employees and there had been talk of franchising. The future had been bright before the divorce. He might be clinging to past glories, but there *was* a desk, along with a stack of unpaid bills and a sofa bed.

Jared took a step closer to listen at the door and grazed his bare foot against the doorframe. "Fuck." Bending down to rub the scratch, he noticed a strand of hair wedged between the wall and the skirting board. It was brown and short, so definitely not Elli's. Must be his.

"Bit clumsy, mate. Must have been that last Scotch." Whenever he talked to himself, it was Mitch's voice he heard. Shame he'd moved to Melbourne. Jared placed a steadying hand against the wall.

Elli should be asleep by now. He had no idea what time it was. At least four fingers of Scotch had followed the last quarter of the Swans game he'd been watching. He should check on her. This dump he was renting had its share of draughts and it was chilly outside. Turning the handle slowly, he did his best to slip inside quietly. A sudden chill prickled across the nape of Jared's neck as he entered the room.

Elli was curled up on the fold-out sofa, only a sliver of her face visible between the edge of the doona and her long hair. A rare smile settled over Jared's face. His life might have turned to shit, but he still had Elli.

Edging around the sofa, he adjusted the doona so it wouldn't slide off during the night. Jared's fingers brushed against a hard surface. Peering closer, he saw a book was hidden underneath Elli's pillow. It was a hardback, not one of the thin paperbacks that Elli usually liked to read. Lifting the pillow gently, Jared eased the book out. Elli stirred, but didn't wake. Jared held the cover up, expecting to find a picture of horses or funky urban princesses. Instead, he could just make out the silvery letters: 'My Diary'.

A diary? Wasn't she a little young for that? Then again, maybe not. Girls were more inclined to write about their feelings, weren't they? Jared knew Elli wouldn't want him reading it. And yet he couldn't help wondering what she'd written, especially since the divorce was still fresh. Any insight into her frame of mind would only help him be a better father, right? And he could return it without her ever knowing.

Decision made—even though it weighed on his conscience—he tucked the diary under one arm and retreated to his bedroom. Collapsing into bed, Jared switched on his bedside lamp and studied the diary. The red leather was soft beneath his fingers. Annika had undoubtedly bought it. Had they written something in there together? The thought of them sharing this secret overwhelmed any lingering reluctance.

The first few pages were just sketches: a love heart, a horse, and a surprisingly good castle. The early pictures showed signs of adult help, but as he flicked through the images, Jared could see Elli's technique was improving.

He stopped at an unusual picture. It looked like an arched doorway in an old wall. The blocks of stone were particularly vivid, with shadowing that suggested a light source just above Jared's left shoulder. A faint triangle—so lightly drawn Jared had to squint to make it out—connected three symbols. A tiny bone shape had been etched into the keystone at the top of the arch. The foundation stone to the right of the doorway bore a curling shape, while the image on the left foundation stone was a teardrop. A severed hand lay in front of the archway, the grasping fingers reaching towards whatever lay beyond.

"What the hell?"

Jared shook his head. Annika had always let Elli watch whatever shows she wanted. It was one of many areas where they'd disagreed on parenting. Clearly some of them had affected his daughter.

Jared flicked through the remaining pages. They were all blank, except for the very last one. Elli's large, immature script covered the page. Jared's conscience made a feeble protest. Diaries were meant to be private, yet gaining an insight into Elli's inner thoughts might help him bridge the steadily widening gap between them.

Setting his concerns aside, he began to read:

Dear Diary,

This is my first entry. I'm starting at the back because that's how my life is—all messed up.

I feel funny inside ever since Mum left. Is that normal? I don't know. Maybe.

I am staying with Dad. He gets angry sometimes. When he drinks alkahole. But he doesn't mean to.

I know Dad loves me. But he scares me too. Sometimes he even pretends I'm not there. The school councellor gave me a phone!!! For emergincys trouble. I'm not to tell Dad. But I won't need it.

Mood = Anxious

Elli ☺

Jared closed the book gently and squeezed his eyes shut. He regretted reading the diary now. Things had been difficult over the last few weeks and . . . well, he hadn't always been attentive. But he would never ignore Elli. Sometimes he just lost track of time. Who didn't? As for being afraid of him . . . Jared's mind shied away from pursuing that line of thought.

Closing the diary, he retraced his steps and slipped it back under her pillow. Staring down at the one part of his failed marriage that would last, he silently vowed to do better.

◆

A dark shadow drifted past. Jared jerked awake.

"I can't sleep." Elli stood next to his bed.

Rubbing his eyes, Jared sat up. His head felt stuffed with rocks that shifted painfully every time he moved.

"What time is it?"

Elli glanced at the digital clock on the bedside table. "Three seventeen. In the morning."

Jared peered at her blearily. "What have you got there?"

Elli looked at the purple scissors in her right hand and shrugged. "My Smiggle scissors."

"What for?"

"To cut away the threads of dreams."

That made no sense, but Jared was too tired to debate the matter. "Do you want to sleep in my bed?"

"No. Can I have a glass of water?"

"Sure, then straight back to sleep."

His dreams, when they finally descended, were filled with squealing tyres and a horrible tumbling that refused to end.

◆

HAVING INSISTED ON dropping Elli off at school and enduring the peak hour traffic on his way home, Jared didn't start making calls until ten thirty. That was pretty late for tradies, but hopefully he'd catch them on a break. The first couple of calls rang out and he left brief messages. Finally, someone answered their mobile.

"Yeah, g'day Tom. My name is Jared. I'm an experienced landscaper and was wondering whether you were looking for more crew?"

"Sorry, mate. Business is pretty slow. I'm not looking to take anyone on at the moment."

Jared suppressed a curse. "I understand, but maybe I can leave my number with you in case one of your blokes isn't available? I've got plenty of experience. You just need to point me in the right direction and I'll get on with it."

"Yeah, sure. Your number's come up on my phone. What's your surname?"

"Hills. Jared Hills."

"Wait, like that bloke on the news?" A note of caution had crept into Tom's voice. "He was a landscaper, wasn't he?"

Panic clawed at the insides of Jared's gut. He thumbed the disconnect button and dropped the phone, his breathing fast and shallow.

He mustn't think about the reporters . . . or any of that. Incessant questions and camera flashes snapped behind his eyes.

All he wanted was work. *Focus on that,* Mitch said in his head.

Jared stared at the list of numbers he'd circled in the local directory. He'd already contacted two-thirds of them and either left messages or been palmed off. All his contacts were in the inner west, not up here in the north. Still, the bills were mounting and he was too proud to go on the dole. What would Elli think of him? All he needed was one chance to show what he could do.

Jared marched out of the office, trembling with a restless energy. His feet led him down the hallway and into the kitchen. The half-empty bottle of Scotch was sitting on top of the fridge where he'd left it the night before. He stared at the bottle, torn between the desire to pour a few fingers and to smash it against the wall.

Reaching up, he unscrewed the lid and held the bottle at a slight angle over the sink. He might be in a hole, but he wasn't going to sink any lower. *But what if you do, mate?* Mitch's voice whispered treasonously in his head. Jared trembled, caught between opposing desires. Gritting his teeth, he tipped the bottle over and poured the Scotch down the drain.

Jared marched into his bedroom, stripped down to his trunks and stared at himself in the mirror. His chest and shoulders were still broad and sharply defined, although he'd put on some weight around his middle.

It took a bit of a search, but eventually he located his boxing gloves. The punching bag was stuffed in a storage container under the house. He scratched one shoulder on the head of an old nail retrieving it. A thin trickle of blood ran down his triceps, but Jared ignored it.

Hanging the bag on a hook in the carport, Jared took an experimental swing. The heavy thud and accompanying shudder were deeply satisfying. He threw a few more combinations until the bag was swinging wildly.

"I. Will. Get. Through. This." Each word was punctuated by a punishing blow. This might not be the life he'd imagined, but he'd turn things around. A grin lit Jared's face as he began to sweat.

Dear Diary,

Dad hit me today. He didn't mean to. He said I got in the way of his punching bag.

Dad was very sorry. He cried a lot and couldn't look at me. I told him it was OK, but that made it worse.

It's Mum that makes him angry. I wish she wouldn't, but she refuses to move on. Sometimes I think maybe he sees her, insted of me.

Mum told me that being caught between two worlds is never easy. I think I'm beginning to understand.

Mood = Hurting

Elli ⊗

Jared stared at the page. A dark brown smudge marred the bottom corner. Was that blood? He ran a shaky hand through his hair. He didn't hit Elli, did he? Surely he'd remember something horrible like that. Yes, he'd worked the bag over, but Elli was at school. Doubt flickered through his mind, as it did so often these days.

At least Elli was sleeping peacefully now. A week had passed since her last visit and there had been no more calls from Ravens Grammar, just as Annika had promised. Jared had picked up some casual days of labour digging trenches for the footings of retaining walls. It was hard work, but he'd enjoyed the exercise. The other blokes had been stand-offish, eyeing him and muttering under their breath. Jared didn't care. All that mattered was the cash in hand. Things were finally looking up, but now Elli was making up new stories about him.

What should he do? If Annika saw the diary, she might try to revoke the custody agreement. He could talk to Elli, but she'd realise that he'd read her diary and that could only end badly.

What he needed was sound advice. Jared picked up the phone and dialled Mitch's mobile.

"Hey Mitch, it's Jared."

"Jared? Mate, it's been a long time. It's great to hear from you. Hang on a sec. I'm on night shift and it's bloody noisy." Jared caught the whine of a circular saw in the background.

"There. That's better. So how are things?" Mitch sounded more cautious than Jared remembered.

"Yeah, okay." Jared flopped on the lounge. "Haven't found steady work yet, but I've picked up some casual jobs here and there. It's keeping me going."

"That's good. I wasn't sure if you got my messages." Mitch paused before saying, "Our move to Melbourne was a bit bumpy, but the job is good and the kids are settling. Janine's not entirely happy, but she's met a few mums through school. Reckon it will work out."

"Great. I'm really happy for you."

Mitch laughed. "I know that voice. You never were a good liar."

Jared chuckled. "Look, I know it's been a while. Maybe this isn't the best time."

"Nah, it's fine. What's on your mind?"

Jared sighed. "It's Elli. I found her diary the other day. She's writing stuff in it that's, you know, make believe."

"O-kay. Is that a problem?"

Jared could picture the puzzled expression on Mitch's honest face. "Guess not. But she's said some stuff about me that's not very . . . kind."

Mitch hesitated. "Like what?"

Jared bit the inside of his lip. "Just stuff. Who knows what Annika said to her?"

Silence on the phone. "Look, about this business with Annika—" Mitch began.

"All right, don't start down that road again. I don't need a 'I told you so'. All I wanted to know was whether Tim or Maddy keep diaries and if so," Jared shrugged, "whether they made up shit about you and Janine?"

"Mate, you know that's not what I meant."

Jared hated hearing the hurt in Mitch's voice. The phone trembled against his ear. "Please, just answer the bloody question."

After a long pause, Mitch said, "Well, Tim's always on his Xbox, so I can't imagine him writing anything. Maddy's a bit younger than Elli, of course, but she's beginning to demand a bit of privacy. If she's got a diary though, I've never seen it. Have you thought about talking to Elli about this? She's a pretty mature kid."

"Of course, but I don't want her thinking I've been snooping through her stuff. Things are strained as it is. She might stop talking to me altogether."

"True. How long have you been in your new place?"

"Dunno. Five, maybe six, weeks."

"Well, that's not very long. Give her some time to settle, eh? And if she's using a diary to work through some difficult emotions, well, that's probably healthy, right?"

"I suppose." Mitch had his head screwed on right, but that didn't explain what Elli had written. Or drawn.

"Listen, I need to get back. But we'll catch up properly on the weekend, yeah?"

"Sure, sure," Jared muttered. "Look forward to it."

Mitch disconnected and Jared stared at the blinking digital display. It didn't feel like things were settling. If anything, it felt like his life was tipping over in slow motion.

◆

A PIERCING SCREAM split the night. Jared lurched upright, layers of sleep sloughing away.

"Mum," Elli wailed from the office. Jared rolled out of bed and hurried into the makeshift bedroom. Elli was thrashing about, struggling with her doona. Her pillow had fallen onto the floor, along with her diary.

"Elli. Sweetheart. Daddy's here." Jared gently stroked her forehead. "It's all right. You're just dreaming."

"Noooo," Elli moaned. "I don't want to. I don't want to!"

"Shhh. It's just a dream. You're safe." Jared kept stroking her hair until she drifted into a deep, untroubled sleep. He retrieved the fallen pillow and diary. The book lay face down and Jared noticed a page had been torn out when he picked it up. That was odd. Elli had never ripped a page out before. He turned the pages, a dark suspicion taking root in his mind. The page with the stone archway and the weird triangle had been removed. But why?

Shifting Elli carefully, he placed the pillow under her head. After a moment's hesitation, he slipped the diary under the pillow as well.

Jared padded out of the room and into the kitchen. The glowing display on the microwave told him it was 2:37 in the morning.

Why rip out that page? Had Elli been creeped out by what she'd drawn? Or was there something else at play?

He pulled the plastic garbage bag out of the bin and rummaged through the trash. Fortunately it was only half full. Jared found a scrunched up ball of paper at the bottom, as if it had been deliberately shoved down there.

The torn page *was* the one he remembered, complete with the strange symbols in each corner of the triangle. Only now, written along each side of the triangle was Annika's familiar, cramped script. Jared turned on the fluorescent light over the oven and strained to make out the words: *Our hair marks us. Our blood defines us. Our bones remember.* In the centre of the triangle was a small, bloody fingerprint.

What the hell was going on? Was Annika actually encouraging Elli to indulge in these fantasies?

Jared snatched up his phone and sent a quick text to Annika: *Family conference. 2moro nite. My place. Make time b/c urgent.*

◆

"ONE CUP OF Earl Grey, black, no sugar." Jared passed the steaming cup to Annika. She was particularly pale tonight and Jared wondered if she was unwell. Not that he could remember her ever being sick. As usual, Annika was clad all in black, from her ankle high boots, all the way to her long-sleeved top, which was just transparent enough to reveal her black bra.

"And one hot chocolate."

Elli accepted her mug with a tentative smile. She was dressed in purple pyjamas dotted with Halloween pumpkins.

Jared settled into his chair, one hand clasped around his steaming cup of coffee. After the interrupted night's sleep and a day digging holes for timber posts, he was pretty buggered.

"You said it was urgent," Annika prompted.

Jared glanced at Elli, who was sipping her hot chocolate. He'd spent most of today thinking about how to approach this conversation. Now the moment had arrived, all of the phrases he'd prepared felt awkward or inappropriate. "Look, I know the last few weeks have been difficult."

"Try the last year, Dad."

Had it really been that long since he and Annika announced they were splitting up?

"Fine, Elli. The last year. Still, we have to make the best of the situation." Jared cut Annika off with a warning hand. "I'm not saying that I hope to get back together with your mum. That horse has bolted. But there's no reason to pretend I'm something I'm not."

Elli glanced at Annika. It was impossible to interpret the look that passed between them.

"What are you saying exactly?" Annika's eyes had narrowed and she hadn't touched her tea.

"I'm saying that I'm doing my best." Jared shifted his attention to Elli. "I'm saying that I'm trying hard to be better than I was, and that I need you to give me a chance."

"I *know* that, Dad." At least she didn't roll her eyes.

"Then why are you writing such terrible things about me in your diary?"

Elli's eyes widened and a flush bloomed across the pale skin of her neck. "You read my diary?"

"It fell out of your bed when I was tucking you in after a nightmare," Jared replied, "but that's not the point."

"It's exactly the point," Annika snapped. "You've never respected anyone's privacy."

"Stop changing the subject," Jared fired back. "I want to know why Elli is writing these horrible things about me."

"Show him," Annika said to Elli.

"Mummmm."

"Stop whining and show him."

Elli reluctantly pulled her sleeve back to reveal an ugly bruise on her upper arm. A large Band-Aid, dark with congealed blood, covered a scrape on her elbow.

Jared gaped. "I didn't do that. Elli, who did this to you?"

"Dad, please." Elli's beautiful hazel eyes had filled with tears. "I know it wasn't you. Not really."

Annika pushed away from the table. "You're sick, Jared. You're hurting our child and you can't even admit it."

"No! I'd never do that." Jared reeled at the accusation. He'd lost chunks of time before, but that was just the booze, wasn't it?

"Who was it, Elli?" Jared asked in desperation. "You can tell me. Does it have something to do with this?" Jared pulled the torn page of Elli's diary from his back pocket.

Another swift look passed between mother and daughter.

"What is this?" Jared demanded, shaking the scrap of paper.

"Your father asked you a question." Annika was staring intently at Elli, not him.

Elli glanced miserably between the two of them. "Why are you doing this to me?"

"Doing what? I just want a straight answer." Jared's temper was rising. It was a struggle to hold it in check.

Elli shook her head, unable to voice whatever she was feeling.

"See, even your father wants you to choose."

"Whatever is going on, I deserve to know," Jared said in the calmest voice he could manage.

Elli covered her face with her hands. Annika's expression was cold and remote. Until this moment, Jared had assumed that whatever she'd felt for him had retreated over the last few years. Seeing her now, he wondered if she had ever truly cared for him at all.

"I can't really explain, Dad. I can only show you." Elli glanced at Annika, who nodded deliberately.

"This way."

Jared followed Elli out of the kitchen and down the hallway towards the office, his confusion growing with each step. As Jared passed through the doorway, an invisible skein brushed against his face. At first Jared thought he'd walked into a spider web, but a current suddenly pulsed through his limbs and up his spine. Silver spots flared across his vision and heat prickled through his flesh. He tried to cry out but his jaw was locked.

Elli stared at him, her eyes enormous in her face. "I'm sorry, Dad. This . . . it's the only way."

"Well done, Ellette." Annika walked straight through Jared, a chill crackling through his body.

Jared would have gaped if he wasn't paralysed. Seams were splitting down the sides of his brain and deeply suppressed truths were threatening to spill free. Jared tried to shake his head and failed. The current was running up both feet and exiting through the follicles in his scalp. He remembered the patch of hair he'd found wedged into the skirting board and the same image on the triangle.

What the fuck?

Annika patted Jared's cheek, the tips of her fingers like feathers rimmed with ice. "Poor Jared. You must have so many questions. Yet there's no point answering them. Your memory is so, so unreliable."

"Isn't there another way?" Elli pleaded.

Annika turned slowly, her boots gliding over the carpet. "We've discussed this, Ellette. My time on this plane has ended prematurely thanks to your father. You must complete the invocation if you wish to become a Bride of the Eternal. Fail now and you'll be condemned to the ranks of the mundane just like your father. Is that what you want?"

Elli glanced between them. Jared didn't understand what was happening, but it was clear Annika wanted to take Elli away. He pleaded with his eyes, hoping that she could read the depth of his feelings for her. Whatever he'd done to Elli, whatever sins he'd committed, he was sorry. Tears welled in his eyes.

"No," Elli said heavily. "I want to claim my birthright."

Annika drew up to her full height. "Then fetch the burner."

Elli hurried over to her bag and returned with a small case of burgundy velvet that Jared had never seen before. Opening the case, Elli removed a long, thin blade, a pair of wicked looking tin snips, a capped bottle and a small, iron flask in the shape of a three-sided pyramid.

Sweat beaded across Jared's forehead and his armpits became damp. He tried to break this unnatural paralysis, but his body didn't budge.

Elli left the room and returned with the portable gas burner they used on camping trips. Removing the cap from the pyramid flask, she poured the contents of the glass bottle into it. Setting the flask on the burner, Elli sat back on her haunches.

"I know this is difficult," Annika said, "but this is why I chose your father. His anima is strong. It will help you ascend from the physical plane."

Elli nodded, her gaze on the unused implements. Jared made a Herculean effort to wrench free from the accursed doorway. All he could manage was a hiss of breath through his clenched teeth.

"You won't remember any of this. I promise, Dad." Elli held the thin knife in trembling fingers.

Jared screamed in fear and frustration, but the sound never passed his lips.

"Our hair marks us," Elli said. Standing on her tiptoes, she cut a lock from the back of Jared's head. Elli placed the hair in her mouth and then spat it into the bubbling solution. One face of the pyramid flask turned a dull red.

"Our blood defines us." Elli ran the blade along Jared's little finger and squeezed the cut. Sucking the blood from Jared's wound, she spat it into the pyramid as well. Another side glowed the colour of a cooling ember.

Jared was trying to shout, the fear and anger only echoing inside his skull.

Elli picked up the tin snips. Her face had turned ashen and Jared's blood trickled from the corner of her mouth. Tears leaked from Jared's eyes as he willed her to stop. Elli shuddered and wrenched her gaze from his face. "Our bones remember," Elli said hoarsely. The cutting edges settled around the first knuckle of Jared's little finger. He moaned in his distress and Elli's hands shook.

"Focus," Annika whispered.

Elli took a calming breath and squeezed the handles of the tin snips together with all her strength. Jared howled silently. Even though the edges gleamed, Elli had to squeeze a second time to sever his finger. Blood spurted on the floor and the urge to cradle his injured finger was so strong, Jared's other hand twitched.

With a look of revulsion, Elli popped the severed finger into her mouth and spat it into the flask. She dry retched and beyond his blinding pain, Jared actually felt sorry for her. His little girl didn't want to do this. Annika was forcing her. That much was obvious.

All three sides of the flask now glowed a sullen red.

"Well done," Annika crowed.

Elli turned off the burner and replaced the cap on the pyramid. Taking a paintbrush from her case, she quickly drew a large equilateral triangle on the carpet around the pyramid using the puddle of Jared's blood. Once complete, she said, "Three faces we wear. The first we show the world, and so are ruled by it." With this, she drew the curling symbol inside one corner of the triangle.

"The second face is worn within, and so we must master our inner selves." Elli painted the tear drop in the next corner.

Reaching the final corner, Elli said, "And the third face belongs to the Eternal, from whom we all spring and ultimately return." A quick set of brush strokes produced the stylised image of a bone.

A thin mist coalesced inside the borders of the triangle. The pyramid had dulled to the colour of charcoal and a slow hiss escaped a narrow hole in the cap.

Elli put the brush aside, a look of apprehension tightening her young face. Annika drifted across the carpet. Her body became translucent as she entered the triangle. Lifting the pyramid in both hands, Annika offered it to Elli. "Drink, Bride of the Eternal."

Elli joined her inside the triangle and accepted the pyramid. If it was still hot, she gave no sign. Removing the cap, she drank the contents, gulping it down without pause.

A triumphant smile lit Annika's ethereal features. "You're ready to join us, my Ellette."

Elli's skin turned a shade of ivory and her eyes blazed with a frightening luminosity. "Yes, Mother. I'm ready to be my own person." Elli backed out of the triangle. Annika's eyes bulged in surprise. She flung a hand out towards Elli, but it couldn't pass beyond the border of the blood triangle.

"What are you doing?"

"I'm choosing," Elli replied, "just as you said I must. I'm choosing a mortal existence, but I will be anything but mundane."

"No," Annika cried. "I suffered for you, I debased myself so that you could be made. We only visit this plane once a century. By then, your bones will be leaching into the ground!"

"I'm tired of trying to be like you," Elli replied. "Dad is far from perfect, but at least he loves me in his own way. Tell your sisters . . . tell them that girls today want to be more than just brides. Goodbye, Mother." Elli smudged one corner of the triangle with her shoe. The mist dissipated, taking Annika with it. A faint wail of anger hung in the air, before it too, faded.

Elli looked up at Jared. She appeared taller somehow, although perhaps he'd diminished, Jared thought wildly.

"I'm sorry, Dad. This was the only way for us to escape. And what's the point of eternity if you never care about anything?"

Jared stared, unable to reconcile this self-possessed girl with the child he thought he knew. Annika was gone . . . somewhere . . . wherever she'd come from. He felt no sense of loss, only relief.

Pressing her index finger against his bloody stump, Elli then smeared a horizontal line of blood across Jared's forehead. "When you wake, Dad, you won't remember what you've seen in this room. Nor will you remember what you saw in my diary."

Elli joined the end of the first line to the bridge of Jared's nose. "You'll be free of the veil Mum has drawn across your mind, so you won't drink, you won't neglect me, and you'll never, ever, lash out again in your pain."

She drew the final side of the inverted triangle. "And from now on, you'll see the best in people, including yourself. Three times have I sacrificed, three times are you bound; from without, from within, and from beyond. Now sleep, Dad." Elli pressed her thumb into the centre of his forehead.

Jared's limbs collapsed. He was falling, falling backwards into a darkness that rose up on all sides and swallowed his bewilderment and pain.

◆

BLINK.

"Mr Hills? Can you hear me?"

Jared blinks, trying to focus.

"He's coming around."

Jared is lying on his back. He tries to sit up. No one prevents him. Pain shoots up his arm and two faces swim into view.

"Mr Hills, can you hear me?"

Jared tries to reply. Really, he does. All he can manage is a croak.

"Give him some water."

A bottle is pressed against Jared's lips and he gulps greedily.

"Mr Hills, it's Detective Andrews and Detective Mayberry."

Jared blinks and some of the blurriness retreats. Andrews is in his late forties with a thickening waist and thinning hair. Mayberry is hatchet-faced; her flat eyes and pinched mouth suggesting she's the harder of the two. For some reason, they look vaguely familiar.

"Mr Hills, we received a report that your daughter hasn't attended school in three days and they've been unable to reach you. Can you tell me where your daughter is?"

"Elli?" Jared frowns. "She was just here." Didn't he make her a hot chocolate last night?

Andrews and Mayberry swap a look before Mayberry says, "Why didn't you report her as missing?"

"Have you contacted my wife? I mean, my ex-wife?"

Andrews and Mayberry share a puzzled frown. Slowly, almost gently, Andrews says, "Annika Hills died in a car accident a fortnight ago. We're still investigating the circumstances of her death, as you well know, given you were the driver."

An icy feeling of shock slithers down Jared's spine. "No. That's not what happened. Her car is parked outside. Look!" He struggles to his feet and points at the E250 parked in the driveway. Only it isn't there. His battered 2003 Hilux is sitting there instead.

Connections are forming in his head; memories seeping back in; colours replacing sketchy greys. Elli! She'd been with him ever since they moved here, yet he'd only paid her attention when he thought she was in his custody. And Annika . . . Annika was gone, killed while they'd been arguing as he took her new Merc for a spin.

"Have you taken any medication recently? Or recreational drugs?" Andrews asks.

"What? No, of course not." Jared looks around in bewilderment. Two paramedics are packing up their equipment. Both are listening, but they avoid meeting his gaze.

"Can you tell us what happened to your hand?" Andrews presses.

"My hand? What do you—" He lifts his arm and sees a bandage wrapped around his hand and what remains of his little finger. The sight is accompanied by a deep, stabbing pain. "I—I don't remember."

"And what about the blood in the spare bedroom?" Mayberry is holding an iPhone to capture his responses. Had they been recording the whole time?

"Blood? What blood? Look, I don't understand what's going on."

"On the carpet," Mayberry replies. "Is it your blood, Mr Hills? Or does it belong to someone else?"

"I don't know what you're talking about." Jared glances between the two detectives in confusion. "Where's my daughter? Where's Elli?"

Andrews glances at Mayberry, who nods and pockets her iPhone. "We'd like to know as well. Let's continue this conversation down at the station." Andrews takes Jared by the elbow.

Jared lets them guide him outside. He feels weak and . . . unbalanced. Something precious is missing, yet he can't say what it is. He can only identify it by its absence, like trying to guess an object by its shadow.

They're almost at the squad car when Elli appears at the bottom of the driveway. Tears glisten across her pale cheeks and she's shaking. "Dad!" Elli launches into Jared's arms. He holds her tight, a desperate relief rushing through him. The police are right, he'd almost lost her. Somehow.

"Where have you been, Miss?" Andrews demands.

"I was at the mall," Elli replies. "Dad said he'd come get me, but he never did."

Andrews and Mayberry look unimpressed.

"I had an accident." Jared studies his bandaged hand. He has no memory of the injury, although the pain is real enough.

"I'll look after you," Elli says, squeezing his ribs tight. "After all, it's just us now."

Jared clings to her, still trying to assemble all the scattered pieces in his mind. One thought towers over all else: Elli is the most precious thing in the universe and she deserves the very best he can possibly give. Everything else is just details.

◆ ◆ ◆

IN THE BLOOD

DIRK FLINTHART

"INTERNETS down." Geoff's voice drifted up from the ground floor.
"Do you want to check it? Or shall I go?"

I smoothed my hand through Finn's soft hair. It was a pleasure I
took when I could. He was due for another round of chemotherapy
in less than a month. Soon enough that sweet mop of raven curls
would be gone and we'd be back to knitted caps over the pale egg of
his scalp. "You go," I called. "It's probably just the weather anyway.
Or McGuigan and his damned plough again." The old man down
the road had cut our lines on four occasions already. If he wasn't
such a drunk, I'd swear it was on purpose.

Finn didn't move. He was so pale, there under the eiderdown, just
the fever-spots on his cheeks to show he was more than a corpse.
It nigh broke my heart seeing him that way, but I couldn't bring
myself to leave, though he was fast asleep. "Poor mite," I said, and
touched the silk of his hair again. "Better days will come."

I was still watching him when I heard Geoff's footsteps on the
worn carpet of the landing, and the familiar creak of the floorboards.

"I think you should take a look, Deirdre," he said as he came into the room. He was flushed with exertion or excitement and his eyes glittered behind his glasses. "I think there's a fairy ring down in the hollow."

My chest tightened. "Are you certain?"

Geoff shook his head. "Of course I'm not certain. You're the expert. That's why I want you to go." He looked down at Finn. "How's he doing?"

"About the same," I said. "His temperature is down a little."

"I'll sit with him," Geoff said, and settled into the chair on the far side of Finn's bed.

Expert, he called me. Like anyone could truly understand the Others. Their return had been confirmed less than a decade ago. They were elusive, aloof, and equipped with abilities that made a mockery of our science. What little we knew was a matter of observation and induction: things involving the Others happened in particular ways, and the patterns seemed to repeat themselves. Were they real patterns, or simply artefacts of a limited data sample? We had no way of knowing.

The theory I liked best said that the Others lived in another *brane*—another four-dimensional space-time continuum drifting through a greater universe of seven, eleven or thirteen dimensions, depending on whose math you accepted. And from time to time, their *brane* overlapped ours in places, touching like two silk scarves on a clothesline, blowing in the wind. When the *branes* came together, sometimes it was possible to pass from one to the other. Possible for *them*, anyway. For us, not so much. Maybe the physics was wrong. Nobody knew. But we knew things didn't work quite right around a true Incursion, which was why Geoff got anxious every time the Internet connection fell over.

The sky outside was cool and clear, one of those brisk days you get in early autumn. We kept the house warm for Finn's sake, but I preferred the crispness of the air off the Burren—all those acres of limestone and meadow, blackberry and hawthorn. Some folk held that our house, so close to that wonderful desolation, was a lonely place to live, but I loved it. Coming here to the land of my ancestors after generations in exile—there was no real reason it should be so, but it felt like a homecoming. I fell in love with the old house the moment we saw it. That it was a hotspot in local fairy lore made it perfect.

I took my stick with me down to the hollow. It was seasoned blackthorn, what the old ones would call a *shillelagh*. Not all the Fay were friendly. Nor were they all vulnerable to the weapons that we understand best. But if I stayed outside the ring, a metre of tough blackthorn bound in iron would offer a measure of security. I also carried salt, a pocketful of iron nails made by a blacksmith, and a Glock 9 mm semi-automatic pistol with custom loads. I have dealt with the Others before, which is why some people think of me as an expert.

The instant I broke through the mass of wind-sculpted hawthorns and blackberry bramble, I stopped. The air seemed heavier and warmer, and the breeze was gone. The hollow was a queer place at any time—a tiny, perfect circle of meadowland amidst the wildness—but today the wide ring of orange-capped toadstools made a clear warning: *stay back!* I did not ignore that warning, dropping to one knee to peer through my hand-glass at one of the fungi.

My belly did a flip-flop. Geoff had been right.

There are many fungi which produce so-called fairy rings. They are nothing more than the fruiting bodies of a dispersed, largely underground organism. There is only one species which is known to depend on whatever magic it is that comes from the place where the Fay live: *Amanita fata*, from the Latin for 'Fate', the goddess who gave her name to our word for the Others. *A. fata* is slightly toxic, wildly psychoactive, and grows only at the site of an active Incursion. The ring in the hollow was among the largest I had ever encountered, perhaps twenty metres across. I took one of the smaller toadstools from the outer edge, and tucked it into my satchel. The science boys in the labs at Limerick would want to check the DNA, but I was already certain.

I brought the news back to Geoff. "It's a fairy ring all right," I told him, and his face sagged with relief. "Don't get your hopes up," I admonished. "We don't know if we'll get a visitor. And if we do, we don't know what kind. Lesser sprites, flower fay—it might not even be able to help."

"But there *is* hope," Geoff said. His hand fell on Finn's brow. Finn murmured in his sleep, and rolled onto his side, and my heart ached for him.

"Other people have had luck," I agreed. It was true, as in the old stories: luck and the Others went hand–in–hand. But just as in the old stories, there was a price. "We need one of those who can handle blood magic. They're a difficult, dangerous lot."

"I know," said Geoff. "Still, any hope is something."

I slipped behind him and put my arms round his chest, resting my head against his neck. "I'll take a bowl of milk to the edge of the ring," I murmured. "I don't know if it will be any use, but it may help them understand we're well-disposed to visitors."

That night the weather closed in, with rain and fog. Geoff and I sat, moodily taking turns to build up the fire in the wood-stove, until tiredness overcame him and he went off to bed. I waited until the birds sang dawn into the sky, then fell asleep in my chair.

◆

"THE MILK DIDN'T work," Geoff told me when I awoke, stiff and groggy. "Any other ideas?"

I yawned, tasting the foulness of unbrushed teeth. "How do you know it didn't work?" I said. "Some of them are quite small. All of them are good at remaining unseen. They may have come."

Geoff made a snorting sound, and stalked off to the kitchen. I heard him rattling around for a moment, and then he returned with an old plastic ice-cream bucket. In the bottom were the jagged remains of the blue-flowered ceramic bowl which I had filled with milk and left by the fairy ring. "I didn't bother collecting all of it," he said. "It was pretty thoroughly crushed."

I pushed the pieces round with my fingertip. There wasn't a single piece even so large as a pound coin in there. "I'd call that a rejection," I said. "Not all of them like milk, Geoff." I glanced over his shoulder at the liquor cabinet. "*Uisce beatha*," I said. "Water of Life. Or so I'm told."

He followed my gaze. "You think they might like whiskey?"

I nodded. So far as the stories went, some of the Others had a taste for spirits. What I did not say to Geoff was that most of those were wild ones, unpredictable and dangerous. Bargaining with any of those would be fraught. But my son lay in his bed upstairs, his blood poisoned with cancer. I would bargain with the Devil himself if there was hope in it. "We'll leave them a bottle tonight," I said. "A whole bottle, still sealed."

"Drunken fairies," he said sourly. "Is that a thing?"

"Sometimes," I said. "I'll take a shower. Then I'll go into town and get a bottle."

Geoff shook his head. "You stay here. Finn needs his mother. Besides, I know you didn't sleep worth a damn last night. You'd probably put the Land Rover into a hedge."

I hesitated. "He needs his father, too. But you're right about the Land Rover." Pulling myself out of the overstuffed chair, I leaned into Geoff until he hugged me properly, the roughness of his beard scratching pleasantly at my forehead. "Make sure it's good whiskey," I said. "The best we can afford. I don't know if they can tell the difference, but I don't think we should take the chance."

He held me at arm's length, and looked at me. "Thank you," he said. "I know you don't like the . . . the Others. And I know the stories, too. Everyone does. But Finn . . . "

I shushed him with a fingertip. "I know," I said. "Me, too."

◆

THE DAY LASTED too long. The Others are liminal creatures, seen most often by dusk or in the first light of dawn. To ease the waiting, I sat with Finn and read to him. He wanted fairy tales, those hoary myths made popular again by the mysterious return of the creatures that spawned them so long ago. I chose the gentlest and most innocuous that I could: the tale of the cobbler and the elves that make shoes from his scrap leather. Finn fell asleep before I was half through, but I finished reading the story anyway. It was comforting: the kindly shoemaker and his wife, the cheerful, diligent little elves, and the easy bargain they made. Prosperity for the shoemaker, new shoes and clothes for the elves.

I glanced at Finn, pale and drawn in his bed. I would gladly stitch a thousand little suits of clothing and count it the greatest of good luck, if it meant a cure for him. But even if Geoff and I could strike a bargain with a wild Fay, it was almost certain the price would be much higher. They used to say such Others came from the Unseelie Courts, and the tales concerning them did not end with prosperity and new shoes.

Geoff returned with a bottle of something I didn't recognise, and had no hope of pronouncing. My family had kept to its Irish roots down the long decades in America, proudly marching on St Paddy's day, cheering for the Fighting Irish at the football, and singing the old songs at family gatherings. Even my name—Deirdre—is one of those ancient Irish names, but I know hardly a word of the old tongue. I have promised myself I will study it properly one of these days, but there's never enough time. I held the bottle up to the light, admiring the rich, red-brown of the contents. "It's good, then?" I asked.

"Better be," Geoff answered. "We're two hundred pounds the lighter for it."

"If it works," I said, "It'll be money well spent. We'll buy another and share it to celebrate."

He smiled at that, the little crinkles showing at the corners of his grey-blue eyes. I kissed him, and sent him off to watch over Finn. As he climbed the stairs, I called to him: "I'll place the bottle now, and get ready. Remember, if we have a visitor tonight, you must leave the bargaining to me. You understand?"

He nodded, and went up to our son.

You can study the Others. There are scientists all over the world working day and night to unlock their secrets. What little we have gleaned can be learned in courses at the world's universities: names, types, abilities, histories . . . All of it *caveat emptor,* and subject to change without notice. They are what they are. No two are entirely alike, and even the abilities of individuals vary. There are things they can do within the confines of a fairy ring which seem to be impossible for them outside. Some claim to be stronger during certain phases of the moon. Most can be turned by iron, and some by salt.

None of these things can be relied on. Personally, I think the courses are useless. What good is it to know that a spriggan is a tree-sprite whose flesh resembles gnarled wood? Those are words. The reality is something altogether more. Studying the Others doesn't prepare you for actual magic.

Experience helps. I don't know if it's possible to get used to the Others, but I know that one can learn to control oneself around them. The glamour that many possess—the ability to mask their appearance, to seem as something or someone else—is as variable as so much else about them, but almost all use it to impress, seduce, or even to frighten and overwhelm. At first, the influence of Fay glamour is nigh irresistible, but with repeated exposure, you can learn to deal with it. Those university courses—they'll tell you to use mirrors, to splash fresh water into your eyes, or even to look cross-eyed to see through the enchantment. I suppose some of those things work, for some people, with some of the Others. But familiarity is the real teacher.

Family can help. There are bloodlines. People of different races, different ethnic stock, whose families have a historic connection with the Others. It's hard to sort out the truth here, because nobody wants to be watched, poked, prodded, interrogated and studied. The suspicion is that perhaps at some time in the past there was some genetic exchange between humankind and the Others. The old stories mention such things: selkie-children; Morgana le Fay, half-sister to the legendary King Arthur. The few samples that the scientists have taken from the Others confirm that they have cells and DNA much as we do. There are differences, but not so great as to make the old stories of changelings and half-breeds completely impossible.

What is certain is that some families have more luck in their dealings with the Others. My family is one such. So is Geoffrey's. For this reason, we were successful when we petitioned the government for permission to buy the old house. If we could strike the right bargain, perhaps we might do more than just cure Finn. Maybe we could buy a cure for all children like him.

It was another couple like Geoff and I who acquired the secret of Fay-silver, the alloy of mercury and silver that can flow like liquid yet transform in an instant to something harder than steel. Ivan and Katinka Bruloff, in the north of Russia traded the complete works of Beethoven and a CD player in exchange for Fay-silver. Now they are impossibly wealthy.

I would be happy if my little boy could run, and play in the sun.

◆

NOT LONG AFTER twilight, the wind changed. All day the breeze had come from the west. Now it swirled, tossing the hawthorns, spinning the old iron weathercock on the roof to exhaustion. A raven called nearby, once, twice, three times. I looked at Geoff. He nodded.

A knock came at the wooden door, the back one that gave into the kitchen. I took a deep breath. "Who's there?"

"A traveller," said a deep voice. It was coarse and gruff. "The night's cold. I'd welcome the hospitality o' your home."

"Enter, then, if you can," I said, and waited.

The door flew open, though neither Geoff nor I had unlocked it. Framed against the night I saw what seemed a small man, hairy and naked save for a pair of heavy boots and a sagging cloth cap of red. That was not what he wanted me to see, I knew. My eyes swam and watered. Sometimes I caught a glimpse of a tall, handsome man in a dark suit with a red tie, but I knew that the short, hairy naked vision was closer to the truth.

"Redcap," I said, between my teeth. Geoff glanced at me, puzzlement in his eyes. I waved him to silence.

My vision stopped wavering. The hairy little man—he was no taller than my waist—grinned at me. "Ye know my kin, eh, lassie? Wull enough. I hae yer leave tae enter?" He affected a Scots accent, of sorts. Maybe he'd learned his English there.

"If you can," I repeated.

He grinned more widely, showing big, yellow teeth and bobbed his head, but he didn't move. "Eh, twas you as brought the wee bottle, no? Tha' was a fine gift, like. I'm awful sorry aboat yer milk, an' all. I was took by surprise there. The bottle makes us square. I come as a guest, lass. No harm to ye or any under yer roof."

Geoff took my hand. I knew what he was thinking. He wanted me to take the iron horseshoe from above the door so our visitor could enter. But I knew Redcaps. Or at least, I knew the stories. "Your word?" I said. "You mean us no harm? You'll act as a proper guest should?"

"My word, lass," he said, and I knew I'd get no more assurance than that. With my *shillelagh*, I knocked loose the horseshoe. It fell with a clatter to the slate floor. "Eh, there's a thing," said the Redcap. "Never did like the look o' such." He glanced around the kitchen, then stepped inside. The nails in his heavy boots clacked against the floor. "Would ye have such thing as bite o' supper about the place? I'm verra partial tae teacake, if ye have any."

"Teacake," Geoff said. I didn't like the sound of his voice. He was trying to repress a laugh, I could see. I squeezed his hand sharply. He winced, and set his jaw. "Yes. I think we have a teacake in the pantry. It's only a store-bought one, mind. Neither Deirdre nor I can bake."

Those bright little eyes beneath their dark and craggy brows settled on me. "Deirdre, is it? There's a fine old name. And who would yer man be, then?"

"My husband is Geoffrey," I replied. "And now you've the knowing of us, and we've none of you." I squeezed Geoff's hand again, and he scurried off to the pantry, returning with a slab of teacake still wrapped in plastic.

"Rory," said the Redcap, though I think an Irishman or a Scotsman might have spelled it differently to me. "And the truth is, I'm plain famished. I dinna wish tae be rude, but I'd be much obliged if we could set a while, and eat."

"This way, Rory," I said, and together we went to the dining room.

Rory ate his way through the teacake in one sitting. He chatted about the weather, and about the doings of some Lord Scroop he'd known hundreds of years ago. I listened, and answered politely when it seemed right. When Rory leaned back from the table, wistfully eyeing the last few crumbs of teacake, I nudged Geoff, and he brought out the cupcakes we'd been saving for the weekend. Then it was the scones that Mrs McGuigan gave us, with the last of the wild blackberry jam, and half a loaf of toast with butter and honey. At last he pushed his chair back from the table and burped, holding his hand up to his lips.

"Tha's a grand feast," he declared. "Yer a mighty host, Geoffrey." His eyes glittered as he looked at the pair of us and the dark, wood-panelled room in which we sat. "Ye've a bairn," he said, gesturing at Finn's football, sitting sad and half-deflated on the toy-box. "Tha's guid. A couple such as ye I'd wish many fine, happy, bouncing babbies."

"We have a son," I said. "But he's sick. He can't come down from his room."

"Is tha' right?" Rory affected concern. "Eh, now. We cannae be having with tha', can we? Ye've been such fine hosts an' all, I'm inclined as I might take a look at the wee lad. I know summat o' the healing ways."

"His blood is sick," Geoff said, and I shot him a look but his face was white behind his glasses, and I could see his fists balled on his knees under the table. "He's going to die."

Rory's face fell. "Aww, nay, nay. An' him but a lad? Take us tae the wee feller, eh?"

"You want to help him?" I put in before Geoff could speak.

The Redcap waggled his head. "Happens I may. If I can, tha' is. An' if ye'll have ma help."

I grabbed Geoff's arm under the table. "We'll take you to see the boy, Rory. We can talk once you know whether you can help him."

Finn did not awaken when we switched on the lamp in his room. Geoff went to his bedside, and Rory went with him, but I hung back by the door. With my jacket partly open, I could reach my Glock quickly. Whether I was quick enough to match a Redcap was an open question. I was counting on his guest-oath to protect Finn—to protect us all. The Others take hospitality very seriously, in my experience; even brutes like the Redcaps, whose cloth caps are scarlet because they are regularly dipped in fresh blood.

Normally I would never have let something like Rory anywhere near my house. But Redcaps know blood, perhaps best of all the Others. I would have been happier dealing with a Fay Queen, or a lordling. Capricious though they are, there's something of kindness in them. Redcaps are killers, pure and simple. Yet they do know blood, and blood magic, and since science had given up on my son, magic—the impossible talent of the Others—was all that remained to Geoff and I, and to Finn most of all. So I held myself very still, and I breathed as evenly as I could, though my heart pounded in my chest, and I let the monster approach my sick, sleeping son.

The Redcap sniffed the air like a dog, his long nose twitching. "Aye, he's sick right enough," he said, and looked directly at me. "Might I touch the lad?" he asked, and I wondered how he knew to speak to me, though he had named Geoff as his host.

I wanted desperately to remind the Redcap of his guest-oath, but even more, I did not want him insulted or angered. Not trusting my voice, I nodded.

"I may touch him?" Rory asked again. Clearly, he was waiting for my word.

"You may touch him," I said, and folded my arms, sliding one hand under my jacket as I did.

The Redcap lay his hand, all hairy and long-fingered like a great, pink spider, on Finn's forehead. He frowned, and leaned over, sniffing once more. Then he straightened, and broke into a beaming smile. "Eh, now, an' I'm sure ye said it was a serious matter," he said to Geoff, his gruff voice light. "This is the Eating Sickness. Back home, not e'en the bairns suffer this. Takes only a few moments tae cleanse blood an' bone, an' they're right for all time. How've ye not fixed the lad already?"

"We don't know how," said Geoff simply, but I saw the tears forming in his eyes. "They told us he's going to die."

"Aww, nae need fer all tha'," said Rory, and folded his heavy arms across his broad chest. "Like as not I kin fix him up here and now, if ye'll have it."

"Yes," said Geoff, before I could speak. "Please. Yes. Save my son."

Then we were all talking at once: I was asking the cost, and Rory was saying it was more than a simple guesting-gift and there would be a price, and Geoff, poor lovely Geoff, he wouldn't shut up and he wouldn't stop saying yes, anything, yes, take whatever you will have if you will save my son.

And I could not unsay the words for him.

A chill washed over me. My heart raced. Rory glanced my way, but I stood as still as the stones of the house. He looked at Geoff, and nodded. "Let it be so," he said, and lay his hand once more upon my poor boy's fevered brow. At his touch, Finn cried out. Geoff moved then, but I lunged across the room and grabbed him before he could interfere.

"It's too late," I hissed. "You've agreed. Now we take what comes."

On the bed, Finn tossed and writhed, his little body bouncing and struggling, but the Redcap's hand never shifted. Though I can't swear to it, I believe I saw something moving, something that came out of the Redcap's palm and went into Finn, and something that fled Finn in his breath—a rank steam, a fog, a miasma that flowed from his nose and mouth into the night air. Then the Redcap took a pace back from the bed and grinned.

"Tha's done," he announced. "The laddie will be right as ever, soon's ye can get some o' tha' fine food intae him for his strength. And now," he said, his voice dropping lower. "The matter o' my price. Blood for blood, an' a life for a life. I'll have your blood for my cap, my lad," he said to Geoff. "I cannae take it here beneath yer roof as I've sworn, so ye maun come down the ring at dawn. An' mind yer no' late, or I cannae vouch for the consequences tae the wee one there," he said, with a nod at Finn. Then he laughed loud and long, a harsh, braying cackle that followed him down the stairs and out into the night.

Oh, and what a long and angry night it was.

Come the first hint of grey in the east, I stood with Geoff, shivering at the edge of the ring in the hollow. Finn was safe enough. His fever gone, he was in the care of the doctors in Innis. The tests were not yet returned, but I knew he would be cleared, the cancer vanished. I knew also that if Geoff did not appear at the ring by dawn, there would likely be far worse in store for our son.

"You're a fool," I told him gently, for the hundredth time. "You were supposed to let me bargain."

Geoff shook his head. His face was pale, and there were dark rings under his eyes, but he was resolute. "I know you," he said. "Finn's life was at stake. If I hadn't made the bargain, you would. I had to get in first."

To this I could say nothing. He was right, as usual. I knew from the moment the door opened what the cost would be. Redcaps know only blood.

I hugged him close. "I love you," I said.

From somewhere within the ring, I heard a cough. "Tha's verra touching. But the time's come tae pay up. I'm glad tae see ye've come."

There are stories. In the tale of Gawain and the Green Knight, the Fay threatens three times to behead Arthur's knight, and three times reprieves him for his honesty and courage. The lords and ladies amongst the Others are known to value such things.

There are stories. Tam Lin won free from a Queen of the Others by the strength of his true love, who held him fast though his shape was changed by Fay glamour to fire, to a serpent, to a dire beast. There are those of the Others who respect love.

Then there are the Redcaps.

Geoffrey stepped into the circle of toadstools. From a pool of shadows, Rory came forth, a long, wicked, rusty pike in one hand. He chuckled. "Ye may wish tae turn yer head, lassie," he said. "I cannae promise this will be quick, or pretty."

"I challenge," I said, in my strongest voice.

Rory stopped. Geoff turned and stared. I had not discussed this with him.

"I challenge," I cried again. "Blood for blood, a life for a life. If you can take my life, Rory Redcap, then you shall have us both and no crime on your head. But if I can take yours, then I walk free with my man and no punishment to follow. Will you bargain?"

The little Fay stared at me. In other circumstances, I would have enjoyed the incredulity on his craggy face. "Ye're mad, lass. I'm Rory Redcap. I've killed hundreds, nae, thousands o' strong men, and yer nowt but a skirted lass. This is nae challenge at all!"

"Do you cry yourself a coward, then?"

Rory hissed at that, and Geoff stepped back to the very edge of the ring, his eyes wide. "No one calls me a coward," said the Redcap. "I'll take yer challenge, lass, and make an orphan o' yer wee lad." He spun his pike menacingly so it growled and whooped in the chill morning breeze.

I laughed, and stepped into the circle bringing out my Glock. Firing two-handed, I put a full magazine into the Redcap, the roar of the gun filling the little clearing. Yet for each round I fired there came a sharp clang, and the Redcap's grin widened as he deflected each and every shot with his iron pike. "Yer on my soil, lass," he said. "Nae man's toy can reach me here. See the touch o' the Fay!" He pointed with his pike and I dodged instinctively, but I was not his target. In my grip, the steel and plastic of the Glock subsided, pitting and rusting and corroding to nothingness before my eyes. It was not simple glamour, but the touch of Time itself, and I remembered the old stories: how a year might pass on Earth in a single day spent in Faerie lands.

I dropped the remnants of the gun with a laugh, and brought my sword from over my shoulder into *chu-dan*, the middle guard. "You'll need more than tricks, Redcap," I said. "I'll bathe my steel in your blood and nail your cap above my mantel."

The Redcap chuckled, the sound like someone shaking an iron bucket full of gravel, and pointed at my blade. Then he frowned, and pointed again.

I laughed. "No," I said. "*This* blade was made in Japan eight hundred years ago, by a smith who learned from the *Tengu*. It is sharp enough to slice a whisper, hard enough to cleave steel, and proof against all your magics and tricks."

Rory growled, and advanced with his pike held low. "I'll have yon blade from yer cold hands," he said. "Yer still nowt but a lass."

He was closing on me too quickly. I wasn't ready for him yet. I danced aside, and moved across the ring. "You never asked my full name," I told him, and he paused, watching me. "It is MacCall, but that's only these few centuries past. Geoff tells me that long ago it was Mac Cumhail, and in his veins runs the blood of the great Finn, slayer of giants."

At this, the Redcap laughed aloud and touched his pike to his cap. "I met Finn Mac Cumhail once," he said, and looked across to Geoff. "A sight stronger than you, laddie." Turning back to me, he said: "So ye've married above yerself. What will ye, talk me to death?"

But the tremors were upon me now, and I could scarcely form words as my muscles writhed and my very bones shifted. "No," I managed to growl, my voice an octave lower than before. "Geoff . . . married above himself. *My* family . . . comes from Ulster." The heat rose in me, and even through the ringing in my ears, I heard my clothes split and tear. Somewhere close by Geoff cursed, and stumbled away into the hawthorns, but my enemy was close enough that I could smell his sweat and hear the blood in his veins. "Did you . . . ever meet the one they called . . . the Hound?"

Rory shifted his grip so he held his pike like a quarterstaff, and made to close with me. His eyes were wide, now, and I could smell the beginnings of fear in his rank sweat. "Cuchulainn of Ulster is dead three thousand years," he shouted, "An' soon enough ye with him." He dashed the pike at my head with the same speed that could deflect bullets.

I cut away the head of his weapon with a counter that was faster still.

"Shite," said the Redcap, looking at the bright steel where his pike ended.

"We're on . . . *your* soil, monster," I grated. "Here I can use . . . the gifts . . . of *my* blood."

My breath was a howl, my heartbeat a frenzied drumroll. The Redcap snarled and brought out a huge, ragged-edged knife. I laughed.

We fought.

♦

MUCH LATER, I staggered to the back of the house. There was an old horse-trough there, brimful of icy rainwater. I plunged myself into it again and again until the water stopped boiling and steaming, and I could see properly at last. I was naked, covered in bruises and scratches, but in my right hand I held the Masamune sword, and in my left I held a shapeless cloth cap, improbably scarlet in colour.

Geoff called down from the window above. "Is it safe?"

I looked up, and nodded wearily. "It's over. The battle-frenzy is gone. I'm done."

"Thought so," he said. "I'll unbolt the doors in a minute. Oh—the Internet is back up."

"Oh, good," I said. "Any word on Finn yet?"

"Clear," said Geoff. "There's more tests to come, but I think it worked. Would you like a cup of tea?"

"Not yet," I said. "I'm still hot through."

I sagged back against the trough, heedless of my nudity. The wracking, body-warping spasms of the battle-frenzy always left me exhausted. It would be hours before I cooled enough to bear clothing, days before I recovered my strength. "You should probably tell the agency what happened to the Glock," I said. Then I looked at my sword. "You should also ask them if they can source another blade. Sooner or later, the boy's going to need one."

"Right you are," said Geoff. He smiled down at me. "He'll be a monster-hunter for certain."

I blew him a kiss. "No question about it, love. It's in his blood."

THE FLOWERS
THAT BLOOM
WHERE BLOOD
TOUCHES EARTH

STEPHANIE GUNN

SOMETIMES, when I am dreaming, I tear fistfuls of hair from my scalp. When I wake, the blood-dotted strands are woven into a tight nest in the cradle of my palm and within the nest, there is a flower.

This morning, there is nothing in my palms but air, nothing left of the dream but the sour sweat that dampens my nightgown. Nothing to hide from Clara as she stirs from her fitful slumber.

I make my way to the washstand. There are feathers of frost clinging to the edges of the washbowl. I barely feel the chill as I dip a sponge.

"Another dream?" Clara asks. There is a rustle of sheets as she turns away to give me what privacy she can in our small room.

I strip off my nightgown, begin washing. "The same as always."

I have only ever told Clara scant details of the dream. In it, I am flying: light in a world of shadows, drifting on warm, gentle currents. I have no place to be, no *one* to be. I simply *am*. And I know that if I let go, I could drift on and on, free forever. There always comes a moment though, when I am floating further and further in the shadowed world, when the currents shift, bringing me a thread of scent. White sweetness cut with a pure, bright chill: asphodel.

Asphodel: my regrets follow you to the grave.

In that moment, I am given a choice: I can keep drifting, keep going out and out into whatever lies beyond the shadows, or I can grasp onto that thread of scent, and drag myself back to my body. Always I choose to go back. To return to the House, to return to Clara.

There is a creak of leather as Clara opens a book. It is Swedenborg's *Heaven and Hell*; I saw the volume next to Clara's Bible the previous day. I suspect that Clara's eyes are too weak to see the words printed on the page, but she knows the text of both books well enough to pretend.

We are both good at pretending, Clara and I.

"In Heaven, there will be gardens filled with every kind of flower that has ever existed," Clara says. "Can you imagine?"

I pull on my loose white gown, draw a comb through my pale hair. In the mirror above the washstand, I can see the supine form of Clara. Beside the candle on the chair next to the bed, a coin gleams. It is a rare thing to see it there—we are not allowed money, and have no need for it, for Mrs Fox supplies us with everything we require.

"Do you know," Clara says, "I almost feel well today."

She looks anything but. She is so pallid I can see the blue tracing of veins at her temples, and the bones of her skull press out against her skin. I pour clean water from the jug into a smaller bowl, bring it over to the bed and help Clara sponge her face and hands. Despite her words, even this small action costs her dearly, and when she is done, her breath comes hard.

"It will be like all the other times," she says between breaths. "The crisis will pass, and I will be well again. Spring always follows winter, and after the snow, the flowers always bloom."

I fetch her a clean nightgown, look out of the window as she changes. I can hear the butcher boys crying their wares from house to house, skipping over ours, of course. Across the road, I can see a small girl trudging along, a basket of flowers bowing her back into a weary curve.

This has been the longest consumptive crisis Clara has experienced. It has been weeks since she has been able to rise from bed, months since she has been able to manage the stairs. Over a year since she has been able to work a sitting.

By the time Clara bids me turn, the butcher boys' cries have faded, the flower girl gone from view. The skin in the hollow of Clara's throat draws in sharply as she fights for breath.

I gather our discarded nightgowns. Beneath the fust of sickness on Clara's gown, I can smell asphodel, belladonna, hemlock. Flowers of grief, flowers of death.

♦

Mrs Fox lays gloved hands on my shoulders.

"Welcome, seekers, to the House of the Lilies," she says.

Her voice is warm, but beneath the frills on my gown, her fingers dig hard into my flesh. She presses the sharp edges of her nails against my bones; dulled by her kid gloves, the pressure is hard enough to bruise, but not hard enough to break skin, nor to make me bleed.

Mrs Fox will not—*cannot*—waste my blood.

"Tonight in the Seeing Room, we are joined by the medium Virginia Lily," Mrs Fox continues. "Virginia has been fasting and meditating all day, and tonight she will part the veil, see into the beyond." She stands behind me, so I cannot see the pose she strikes, but I know it well enough: arms out, palms and face turned up to the Heavens. "Which of you wishes to *see*?"

In the dim light of the single candle, I can make out little of the room, but like Mrs Fox's theatrics, I know the space well enough. The walls are thickly plastered, the windows and door hung with heavy velvet. The wallpaper and curtains are claret in colour, so as to appear black in the dim light. Eleven chairs circle the room, the small lace-covered table I sit at set slightly apart. Two chairs are directly opposite me, with Mrs Fox behind.

A man moves, his spectacles reflecting the light as he stands. The woman beside him follows more slowly, jewels on her fingers catching greedily at the scant light. Mrs Fox waves them to my table, and they sit.

I will not be told anything about them, but as they seat themselves, the light of the candle shows me their story well enough. The woman's dress is edged with black crape, and she wears white lace at her throat: she is in mourning for a child. The dress is made from cheap fabric, but bought black, not dyed, and well-tailored: they will have paid handsomely.

Mrs Fox lays her hands on my shoulders again, lightly now. The man's eyes move from Mrs Fox to me, and I see the doubt in them. And why not? Of a certainty, I appear to him as nothing more than a lanky child in white, my pale hair tumbling loose down my back.

"Do you have an item belonging to the one you wish to contact?" Mrs Fox asks.

The woman draws a photograph from her purse, lays it on the white lace that stretches between us.

The child in the photograph is perhaps three or four years old. She reclines in a chair, a doll tucked by her side. Her hands are lax, her eyes closed. Impossible to tell if she was living or dead when the photograph was taken.

I lay my hands flat on the table, one on either side of the image. Beneath my palms, lace; beneath that, a thin layer of clean earth.

Mrs Fox snuffs the candle. The woman begins to weep. It is a ragged, tearing sound which reminds me all too much of the way my mother sounded on the nights she thought me sleeping. Those nights, she curled herself around a photograph, sobbed my sister's name over and over, as though she could bring her back to life with the force of her grief.

Mrs Fox settles her skirts: a signal that I am taking too long. I pull my attention back to the present, remind myself that I owe Mrs Fox my livelihood and my life. I close my eyes, focus on the beating of my heart, count: *one, two, three*. It is a well-practised cue, and my body relaxes automatically, head slumping forward, chin on my chest.

Behind my eyes, I can see my pulse: silver beating against blackness. Another moment, and my awareness expands; like a photograph being developed, the silver tracery of my veins emerges from the darkness. It looks something like the lace beneath my palms, but far more intricate, more beautiful than anything that could be spun with human hands.

It takes a thought, something like a *push*, and the silver lace rises towards my skin. It feels as though the inside of my body is expanding, and I cannot help the moan that rises as the pressure of it builds to pain. Just when I feel my skin will split open, something releases, and the silver lace is moving through my skin, becoming a mist as it touches the air.

I am on the edge of the dream. If I keep going, letting the silver rise and rise, I could float away, be free. It takes all of my will to rein in that desire, to keep the mist anchored in my body.

Mrs Fox clicks a heel and I open my eyes. The lace tablecloth and my gown are glowing in the pale light. On one of the rare occasions Mrs Fox has spoken directly to me, she told me that it looks something like the light cast by the stars on a clear, moonless night. I wouldn't know. All I ever see when I look up is cloud and smoke, or else the fog obscuring all.

Mrs Fox settles her skirts again. Once the light has been released, everything else comes without effort: I could shake this room to pieces with only a thought. But the sitters expect theatrics, and so I begin to sway in my chair, let my breath rasp in and out of my chest. I hate the latter, for it reminds me too much of Clara, but Mrs Fox insists.

Another shuffle of Mrs Fox's skirts and I still, allow the light to move away from me. In the corner is the spirit cabinet that Frances uses in her sittings; I avoid it, project the glow into empty space. It is a simple thing to arrange the light into the likeness of the child in the photograph, to make the 'manifestation' smile and wave.

Gasps from around the room, and the woman's sobs become more pained. A heavier tap of Mrs Fox's heel: this is too much. I loosen the illusion, make it look rougher, something like linen wrapped around a wooden doll.

I make the 'manifested spirit' move around the room, dancing and smiling, until Mrs Fox shifts her skirts again. It is time for the flowers.

Secreted in the collar of my gown is a long silver pin. Feigning the need to adjust my dress, I press my finger against the sharp end of the pin. One prick, one drop of blood. I always expect to see it flow forth as silver as the light, but the drop that falls on the lace is red, black in the thin light. It takes a moment for the blood to soak through to the earth beneath the cloth, and I glance up to ensure that the sitters are still enthralled by my illusion.

They are, all but one.

She—and I only presume that it *is* a she because she wears a dress, for there is little else of the feminine to her—is seated in the back of the room. Her hair hangs ragged to her shoulders, the almost white strands tangled and knotted. Even seated, I can tell that she is taller than the tallest man here. She wears no gloves, no hat. She alone is watching the place where my blood is soaking through the lace.

A scent like charred honey emerges, and then, where blood touched earth, there are flowers. The strange woman looks up at me, and her lips part. When her eyes meet mine, an odd sensation moves through me. Like the way the air feels in the moments before a storm breaks, except this storm is rolling deep into the darkness of me.

Mrs Fox is tapping her heel again—has been for some time, I think—and I drag my attention away from the strange woman. It hurts, as though I am pulling a tooth out, root and all. The woman and man at the table are weeping, each of them holding one of the 'spirit's' hands. I am thankful for Mrs Fox's training, for the illusion has not faded, even when my attention strayed. I make the 'spirit' kiss them both once, and then allow it to dissolve back into the silver mist.

I pull the light back close to my skin, and take advantage of the shifting shadows to slip the flowers from beneath the cloth, arrange them in my cupped palms. The harshness of my breathing is not feigned now, nor the way I droop in my seat: drawing the light back gets harder each time.

"A message from beyond," Mrs Fox declares. She places her hands on my shoulders again. Her fingers do not dig in, and I know that I have judged the flowers correctly. "Baby's breath for innocence and purity of heart, and a lily from the House itself. Your daughter is well and blessed in Heaven."

She produces a white ribbon from her sleeve, wraps the flowers and hands them to the couple. The scent of the lily catches, thick and choking, in my throat.

I pull the light back beneath my skin. It takes great effort and I am glad when Mrs Fox taps her heel, giving me the signal to slump over the table. It is one of her recent additions to our theatrics: a swooning medium makes it easy for her to clear the room, to ensure that no one lingers overlong.

The other girls tell me how they roll their eyes, fall boneless in their chairs. For me, none of it is feigned. My heart races, my skin feels hot and tight, my body too small to contain the roiling light.

The scent of the earth beneath the lace is soothing, and I take deep breaths as I listen to Mrs Fox lighting the candle. The man and woman thank her over and over, press more coins into her hands. One by one, the sitters file past me. It is forbidden to touch the medium, but I feel several of them reach out anyway, the heat of them brushing my skin. One such almost-touch brings that edge-of-a-storm feeling rolling through me again. In its wake, it is easier to keep the light contained.

When I finally look up, only Mrs Fox remains. The colours of her dress meld with the candlelight and shadow. The silk is the old-fashioned colour known as Dust of Ruins, the skirt trimmed with a band of black crape. The style of Mrs Fox's dress and her hair are as old-fashioned as the colour. She wears no decoration but for a locket pinned at her throat, jet carved into the shape of a lily.

She looks at me for a long time, expression unreadable, then turns and exits. Her footsteps move down the hallway, the door opens, closes. Her key clicks in the lock.

The doors are always locked when Mrs Fox leaves, and only she has the keys. It is to keep us safe, she says, to keep the Lilies unsullied by the world outside.

I make use of the spirit cabinet to change into the slate grey tea dress waiting there, moving carefully around the chair and ropes that Frances uses in her sittings. I bundle up my white dress and the tablecloth, sweep the table clear of earth.

My work done, I should leave, but instead I cross the room to the chair where the strange woman had been sitting. A fragrance lingers in the air, something like the bright green of new ferns, the foliage sliced through with a silver knife.

Fern: magic, fascination, shelter.

I breathe in deeply, and some of my exhaustion fades. For the first time since Mrs Fox brought me to the House, I wish that she lingered after sittings. Everyone who attends her private sittings is known to her, or vouched by someone well known. I want to ask her—no, I want to *demand* of her—who this woman is, why she smells like *home*.

◆

GIRLS SMILE AT me from the row of photographs on the back parlour mantelpiece. Each of them is arranged prettily on the arm of their new husband. Their cheeks are plump, their hair neatly pinned. They all bear an armful of bridal roses, their stems stripped of thorns.

Bridal rose: happy love.

Looking upon these women, I am acutely aware of the thinness of my body, the weight of my loose hair against my spine. Mrs Fox's canon for her perfect Lilies: sylph-like, unbound. Once upon a time, each of these women were moulded thus by Mrs Fox, all saved by her from lives in the workhouse or on the street. When they came of age, their service declared satisfactory, Mrs Fox made arrangements for them. They were given new names, introduced to good families, matches made. Within a year of them leaving the House, each was photographed thus, as a happy bride.

One day, I too will smile from that mantelpiece.

Frances enters the room, Rose buffeted in her wake. Though it is against Mrs Fox's rules, Frances has a scarlet sash pulled tight around her waist. The fabric strains, and I fear for the seams as she pulls two chairs together, reclines on one and props her boots on the other.

Frances fixes her eyes on me as she pulls a packet of boiled sweets from her pocket. Her hair is brassy, and I suspect that she has been at it with alum, honey and black sulphur again. The ends of her hair are canon pale—as the whole length was when she was younger—but the roots are dark, like shadows growing from her skin.

In contrast to Frances, Rose is the image of Mrs Fox's perfect Lily: slender as a reed, her hair so pale that it is almost white, her eyes clear blue. She carries a basket filled with pans and brushes and blacking for the grate. She kneels, strews old, clean tea leaves on the carpeting to catch the dust, and begins sweeping out the grate.

"I thought it was Frances' turn for the fires," I say to Rose.

Frances crunches a sweet between her teeth. "Rosie volunteered."

"It's good practice, it is," Rose says in her customary half-whisper. "When I marry, I want to be ready, I do. We might just have a maid of all work at first, and someone'll have to help." She coughs as ash plumes from the fireplace. "Besides, I have a sitting tomorrow, and I'm the one who'll need the fire, I will."

"*I* need the fire now," Frances says. "It's bloody cold."

Rose flushes at Frances' language. "I'll get you a warming pan for the bed when I'm finished with the fires."

I want to remind Rose that she is not Frances' servant, but it will be of no use. Frances always gets what she wants. I remind myself instead that Frances will come of age within a month, and none of us will have to deal with her again.

Frances crunches another sweet. "I'm close to a full materialisation," she says to me. "Mrs Fox says it's the best she's seen. Better even than bloody Florence Cook. Better than *you*."

Rose finishes with the fire, sweeps up the tea leaves and dust. When she stands she sways, coughs again. "It's not like Clara," she says quickly. "Just the dust." She picks up the basket. "I'd best get on with the rest of the fires."

Rose heads into the dining room, Frances on her heels. I move deeper into the house, towards the kitchen and scullery, where I find the twins. Gertrude is rinsing the day's tea leaves and Genevieve is elbow-deep in scummy water scrubbing the dinner pans. I set the white cloth and gown with the rest of the laundry to await the next wash day and sit down gratefully.

Supper waits for me: a bowl of watery vegetable soup and a sliver of dense bread. I've eaten the same every day since I moved to the House—Mrs Fox forbids us meat or milk—but the portions are even more miserable than usual.

"It's the same for all of us," Gertrude says. "Mrs Fox's orders. For which I believe we can thank Frances. I don't know how she manages to keep growing out, even with Rose giving her most of her food."

The soup is cold, the vegetables almost rancid, but I force it down. "Frances says she's close to a full manifestation."

Genevieve rolls her eyes. "I don't know why she bothers. No one has asked for her for weeks, and she'll be out of here soon enough."

"She says that it's better than Florence Cook," I say.

Genevieve makes a rude noise. "Katie King," she says, referring to the spirit guide the medium Florence Cook summons, "is nothing more than Florence's sister draped in linen, or else Florence herself."

"Do you know, I heard Frances talking to Rose about how she's planning on setting up her own salon once she leaves," Gertrude says. "She wants to keep working as a medium."

The noise Genevieve makes now is even more unladylike. "Who's going to pay *Frances* for anything? Other than the obvious. We all know where Mrs Fox found her." She elbows her twin, grins. Both of them came from the workhouse, same as Rose and Clara.

I focus on eating. Like Frances, I was living on the street when Mrs Fox found me. I sold flowers; Frances sold herself.

"Do you know," Gertrude says, "I think Frances really believes that she's channelling something."

A lump of potato sticks in my throat. "What . . . what if she is?"

"Then it's the madhouse she's set for, no husband or salon or anything else," Gertrude says. "It's just tricks. Even Rose knows that. Frances herself spent half the day in here yesterday practising swallowing linen and bringing it back up as 'ectoplasm'. How can she think that's anything real?"

My hands are pressed palm-down on either side of my bowl. My skin tingles, and I think of the silver lace beneath my skin. Am I, too, deluding myself?

I pocket my bread, head upstairs. My footsteps echo in the silence. Mrs Fox leases the houses on either side of us, leaves them empty in order to keep us undisturbed. Before Mrs Fox brought me to the House, I had never known silence. While my mother lived, there was always the sound of men coming and going, and her sobbing in between. After, on the street, the city was never silent, not for one moment. Always someone crying their wares, the sounds of horses and carriages, the cries of girls calling to potential customers.

At first, I had thought the silence here a balm. Now it feels like the darkness in Mrs Fox's beyond: a void that goes on and on, a thing which hungers for spirits and souls.

The upper floor of the house holds three bedrooms: the twins share the largest, their space always cluttered with wooden contraptions, wiring and the linen 'spirits' that they use in their sittings. Frances and Rose are in the next, and Clara and I in the smallest.

When I return upstairs, Clara is awake, bent over a notebook, her pen scratching softly at the page. In the candlelight, she is even more perfect a Lily than Rose, her hair almost translucent. The notebooks are supplied by Mrs Fox for Clara to practice her automatic writing—her speciality—but Clara confessed to me once that it is poetry that she writes on those pages, though she will show the verses to no one, not even me.

I wait until she blots the page, slips the book beneath her pillow. Only then do I offer her the bread from my pocket. It is a ritual from the first time she was ill, when the doctor tried starving out the illness. I know that she will not eat it now—she barely touches her toast and water—but I offer it all the same. If I keep walking the same steps, keep doing the same things I have always done, then Clara will keep being here as well.

I help Clara use the chamber pot, then change into my nightgown and slide into bed. Just before Clara snuffs the candle, I see the blood on her pillow, ill-concealed by a fold of the blanket.

In the darkness, Clara's hand finds mine. In her palm is the fat coin. She presses it into my hand, draws away.

"The doctor told me of a man named Livings," Clara says. "He runs a small salon down near the Foundling Hospital. They say he spent a year in Egypt studying some of the ancient ways, and that he can capture spirits in photographs. He can show you the faces of people you've forgotten."

Something leaps high inside me. I quash it down. "This money was to pay the doctor. For your medicine."

"It will not help me," Clara says. "The doctor himself refused payment, since he could not assist."

"You said this morning that you were feeling well."

"It happens sometimes like that, the doctor said. At this stage, even the medicine is nothing more than a salve."

"What about the water cure?" The words tumble over one another as I speak. "You have ever been Mrs Fox's favourite. I can talk to her in the morning—"

"Mrs Fox knows," Clara says quietly. "There is nothing more to be done. The coin will be of more use to you. This is what I want, Virginia. For you to see your mother. Please."

I rub my thumb around the edge of the coin. The metal picked up no warmth at all from contact with Clara's skin. "Even if I did agree, what use is a coin if I am locked in here?"

Her hand finds mine again. This time it is a key she presses into my hand, smooth on one side and rough on the other. "Locks always have keys."

"How?"

"Frances, of course. She loaned it to me readily enough when I asked. Even Frances is kind to the dying."

Tears prick at the corners of my eyes, and I feel something squeeze tight inside me. "You are not dying!"

Her hand presses against mine again, the coin and key between our palms. "I have been dying since the moment you met me, Virginia."

I can hear the effort the conversation has cost her in the heavy rasp of her breath. I want to ask her so much more, but I know that talking further will bring on another coughing fit. I know well how such a fit can end. I watched the blood flow and flow from my own mother's mouth, even as she cursed me with her last breath.

For Clara's sake, I make myself turn over, feign sleep. Clara will not sleep until she thinks I am. When her breathing finally slows, I make a tent of blankets around myself, release just enough of the light to illuminate the small space. The photograph that I slide out from beneath my pillow is one that Clara has seen many times before, a secret I have shown only to her. I have never shown Clara the silver light, though. I have trusted her with all else, but this—I fear too much what I would see in her eyes. I know what her Bible says about demons and witches, and I could not bear to have her turn away from me.

The photograph is worn and creased, one corner torn away entirely. There are three people captured in it, though you can only see two, the third face hidden beneath a swathe of black fabric. On my mother's lap, is a baby—me—hands and face indistinct smears of light. I often wonder if I was struggling towards, or away from my mother as the photograph was taken. Others would have had the image retaken, but not my mother. It was an expense that she could not afford, and I was not who she sought to capture.

My sister, Marguerite, sits in a chair beside my mother and me. She is a beautiful, frail girl on the cusp of womanhood, almost old enough to have her skirts fully lengthened. At first glance, anyone would think her to be alert, her eyes meeting the camera evenly. It is only when you look closer that you see the laxness of her hands, that the eyes which watch you are merely painted onto the photograph.

More tellingly, there are morning glories tucked into her sash.

Morning glories: flowers that bloom, wilt and drop from the vine within a day, a life cut short.

This is all that I have left of my family. My father unknown, my sister a corpse and my mother forever hidden from view. Time has eaten any memory I have of my mother's face, everything but the blood and the sound of her sobbing at night for her poor Marguerite, this photograph clutched to her bosom while I lay cold on the other side of the bed.

I slide the picture back beneath my pillow. I think of the couple at the sitting, the extra coins they had pressed into Mrs Fox's hands afterwards. I owe Mrs Fox, this is a certainty. But do I owe the people who come to the sittings, too? Enough to tell them the truth?

For beyond the silver lace and the light and the flowers born of blood and earth, I can see what Mrs Fox calls the beyond. And there are no choirs of angels, no spirits, no gardens, no God, not even any demons. There is only the cold world, and beyond, the endless, empty black that goes on and on forever.

◆

THE HOUSE IS silent as I make my way downstairs.

Clara woke this morning coughing and fevered after a restless night, bright blood on her lips and pillow. I helped her sponge her face, change her nightgown and the pillowcase. I averted my eyes as much as I could, but caught too many glimpses of her wasted body, thin skin stretched over brittle bone. I persuaded her to take some of her remaining laudanum, then sat with her until she fell into a fitful sleep.

I fear now that the doctor is right, that Clara does not have long for this world. The thought of her lost in that endless black is almost more than I can bear.

At the bottom of the stairs, I pause, take measure of where everyone is in the house. Mrs Fox and Rose are in the back parlour with Rose's new client. The twins are upstairs working on their tricks, and Frances is at work in the kitchen. I have an hour, perhaps, before anyone will notice me missing.

My heart thuds hard as I slide the key into the lock. A click and a step, and I am outside, the door locked again behind me. The air is thick with grey fog. It clings to my skin, weighs down the skirts of my gown. The last time I stood on this step there was an almost identical fog. I was in rags then, my only possession in the world my basket of flowers.

Every morning, I would rise from whatever corner I had managed to secure for the night, find a clear patch of earth where no one was watching. There, I would scratch my nails against my skin until I drew blood, let it patter down onto the earth. From the blood and earth flowers bloomed: violets and roses, baby's breath and poppies. I would scratch again and again until my basket was full. Exhausted from the summoning of flowers, I would drag myself around the streets as best I could, with barely any breath to call my wares. Some days I could do little but sit on a stoop, my body bowed around my basket. Mrs Fox found me thus one day, drawn by the brightness of my hair. When she brought me to the House, it was Clara who met me at the door that day, tall and slender and impossibly beautiful in her white gown.

A thin thread of green comes through the fog: ferns, and trailing vines. It reminds me of the strange woman from the sitting, and an echo of that edge-of-the-storm feeling rolls through me. Free of the House, I could seek her out. Right now, I could walk away from the House, never look back.

I glance up at the small window of my bedroom. I cannot leave Clara.

Calling on my old memories of the streets, I make my way to the Foundling Hospital. Here and there I take wrong turns where streets have sprung up where I remember none, and I am forced to backtrack. On one such occasion, I swing around a corner and collide with a small girl, in her hands a basket full of wilted flowers. She is thin and shivering, her hair a pale dirty gold and eyes pure blue. She says nothing, just kneels and begins to gather the flowers which have scattered over the path. I help her. The scent of rot is thick on the flowers: no one will buy these wares. There are bruises on the girl's thin arms, and her eyes dart about as we work; she is being watched.

The key is in my pocket. While the girl is looking away, I press my finger against its rough edge. It hurts more than the pin, but it suffices. Blood wells forth, falls onto the filthy cobblestones. It takes more effort than clean earth, and I am only able to bring forth a single red rose and a spray of violets. I gather them up, place them in the girl's basket.

"But—" she begins.

"If you go around by the park, you'll find more customers," I say.

I want to tell her that things will get better, that there will be happiness for her to look forward to. She takes a hesitant step towards me, and I quickly hurry away. I am not Mrs Fox, I cannot make anything better for her, or for anyone.

Eventually I find the place Clara had spoken of: a small salon marked by the carved figure of a pharaoh in the window. The door stands open, everything beyond dark. Propped up next to the pharaoh, a small sign invites seekers to enter.

That green scent twines around me again. The coin is heavy in my pocket. I should go back, confess to Mrs Fox, bid her have the doctor return. Or else find one myself, secure laudanum. I could tell Clara that I could not find the salon, or that the man Livings was not there. Then I think of how Clara had sounded when she had given me the coin. Clara wanted me to do this. To Clara, I cannot lie.

I step into the darkness.

The air is thick with something powdery and choking, but oddly without scent. One step, two, three, and then I am in a gas lit room. When I turn, I see that the darkness I passed through is nothing more than a cunning arrangement of velvet curtains.

A chair and stand are pushed against one whitewashed wall, before them a camera. A door stands opposite me, closed.

The door opens and a man appears. He wears an ill-fitting suit, a crimson turban askew on his head. He grasps at my arm, and as he draws me across the room, somehow the coin passes from my hand to his. He arranges me against the stand, affixes a clamp to the back of my neck.

"Stay still," he says.

I obey as best as I can as he ducks beneath the cloth.

The place where I cut my finger throbs. It seems to take forever, but finally the powder flashes and he reappears. He doesn't look at me as he pulls the tin plate out of the camera and hurries out of the room.

When the photographer returns, he unscrews the clamp, the metal pinching my skin. He thrusts the photograph into my hands, leaves the room again. In the photograph, my hands and face are slightly blurred, as though I had been shaking. Arranged in the chair beside me is a gauzy wisp: if you wanted badly enough, you could believe it a spirit.

It is only a swatch of linen, identical to that which Frances and the twins use, somehow transferred onto the photograph with me. It is only another trick.

I expect disappointment, but instead a laugh bubbles up. It's all tricks, there is nothing but the cold world and the darkness beyond.

A small noise, and I swallow my laughter, look up, expecting to see the man. It is not he who stands before me, but a tall, thin gentleman in a well-cut suit, face shaded by the brim of his hat.

Then he lifts the hat from his head. It is the strange woman from the sitting, garbed now as a man. Or is it a man, garbed then as a woman? I do not know, and the more I think on it, the more confused I feel.

"You may think of me as a woman, if it helps," the stranger says. Her voice is clear, slightly accented. She leans over to look at the photograph. "He is a fraud, no, this Livings? Clever, but not too clever. Tell me, who was it you sought to see?"

Her eyes fix on mine, unblinking. Her pupils are pinpricks, her irises so pale a blue that they are almost silver. Her eyes on mine, I find that I can do nothing but speak the truth.

"My mother," I say.

She looks at me for another long moment, and when I inhale the green fern fragrance of her, it is as soothing, as comforting, as the scent of clean earth.

Nestled in the folds of her white silk cravat is a diamond-tipped pin. She presses a fingertip to the sharp end, her eyes still on mine. A drop of her blood wells. I taste green in the back of my throat. She lets a single droplet of her blood fall onto the photograph. The scent of charred honey rises and silver light ripples over the picture. As it fades, I see that the image has changed.

It is now identical to the photograph of my mother, Marguerite, and I.

When I breathe in, I feel green go down into the depths of me, uncurling like smoke in the darkness. Tears prick at my eyes. "Is it another trick?" I ask.

"No tricks." She holds up her pricked finger. The small injury is already healing. "Do you wish to truly see?"

I can no more look away from her than will my heart to cease beating. "Who are you? *What* are you?"

She turns away then. "Someone who has been alone for a long time." When she looks back, I am surprised to see tears shimmering in her eyes. "I will force nothing upon you, Virginia. The choice is yours. You may walk away, if you wish, and I will follow you no longer."

I remember the green scent in the fog. "You were following me? You know my name?"

"I was . . . curious. I wanted to see."

Mrs Fox's voice echoes in my mind: *Who wishes to see?*

"How do I choose if I do not know what I am choosing?" I ask.

"How do any of us know? We simply choose a path, and then hope." Her voice is heavy with sorrow. "If we do not have hope, we do not have anything at all."

Hope. What hope have I ever had in my life?

What if I can *choose* it?

I hold out my hand. She takes it in hers, presses the tip of my finger against her cravat pin. The metal slides painlessly into my skin. A single drop of blood wells.

She presses my finger to the edge of the photograph. Unbidden, the silver lace rises to my skin. There is no pressure, no pain; it is as simple as breathing, the release of the silver light. The woman looks around in wonder, her expression like that of a child suddenly given her heart's desire. The mist plays over the photograph. I stare at the image of my mother, waiting for the black veil to be pulled back. Nothing changes.

I look up at the woman.

"Look again," she says.

When I look back, I see it: Marguerite's eyes are no longer painted on the photograph, but open in truth—open and *alive*. My mother is still hidden beneath the black veil, and I am still a blur of light, but Marguerite is *real*—alive and breathing in the frame of the photograph. She turns, looks at the babe who was me, and just once, she smiles.

Everything slots into place in my mind, as though a key has been slid into a lock, the door that had hidden all flung wide.

"She was my mother, wasn't she?" I ask. "Marguerite was my mother."

The silver light dances, shaping forms without my bidding. I see the woman I thought of as my mother, shadowed and indistinct, moving in and out of the room we had lived in. I see the men on her arm coming and going, the way they turned to Marguerite, the way my *grandmother* screamed at them, turned them out.

"She had no choice," the strange woman says. Her voice sounds far away, echoing as though she is speaking down a long, dark tunnel. "After her husband died, she had nothing, no way to put food in her daughter's mouth but to sell herself. She made herself only one promise—Marguerite would never be touched. Marguerite was going to be more than she was."

Shadows move through the light as men come and go, come and go. Not once do I see my grandmother clearly—always she is turned away, always in shadow. Only Marguerite is always perfectly in focus.

"But she could not always be there," the woman continues. "She had to leave sometimes, and all it took was one moment when Marguerite was alone."

A shadow moves across the light, advances on Marguerite. I close my eyes then. I do not want to see it. I smell roses, the bright copper of blood. The woman lays her hands on my shoulders, and I feel the light slip beneath my skin once more. When I open my eyes, the photograph shows only me and that wisp of linen masquerading as a spirit.

"I killed her. Birthing me killed her," I say. "That's why my mother—my grandmother—that's why she hated me so."

The woman looks at me, sympathy in her eyes. My finger is still bleeding. She presses her own finger against the cravat pin, touches her blood to the wound. It heals over immediately, as smooth as though the skin had never been broken.

"You can heal," I say. "Your blood. It can heal."

"*Our* blood," she says. "It can do many things, should you only wish it."

Our blood. My blood. *It can heal.*

My heart thuds hard against my ribs. I can heal Clara. I can make her well again.

I pull away from the woman, the photograph fluttering to the floor. She is still talking to me, shouting at me, but I do not hear a single word. I am already leaving, I am already *running* back home to Clara.

◆

THE HOUSE STANDS open.

I pause as I step over the threshold, aware of the odd scent of must in the house, of things old and decaying. Then I see the blood on the staircase, and I am running again.

A hand reaches out from the parlour—Gertrude, clutching at my arm. Genevieve and Rose are huddled together behind her, both of them pale. There is blood, black on all of their grey dresses.

"Is Clara—?" I ask. "Where is Mrs Fox? Where is Frances?"

"Mrs Fox has gone to fetch a doctor," Gertrude says. "Halfway through Rose's sitting, Clara started to scream. She dragged herself down the stairs, and there was so much blood . . . " She shakes her head. "Mrs Fox has not come back, nor the doctor. Frances said she was going to fetch them both, but I think she will not return. We carried Clara back upstairs, but we did not know what else to do. There's no more laudanum . . . "

I run upstairs.

Everything is red.

Clara's nightgown, the bedding, even a good part of the carpet, all swim in bright red. Clara herself lies in bed, her head on my pillow. Her books have been torn to shreds, pages scattered over the blankets, and my photograph is in her hands. On the scraps of paper, I see my own name, over and over.

For one horrible moment, I think that I am too late, but then her eyes flicker open.

"Virginia," she says, and her voice is barely a sound, more the sound of air whispering through wintering trees. "You came back."

I kneel down, heedless of the blood soaking into my skirts. I clasp her hand in mine; her skin is so cold. "I would not leave you, Clara."

She tries to smile, but the smile becomes a rictus, a cough following soon after, blood staining her lips afresh. I can hear the air whistling in her lungs. It sounds as though there is no flesh behind her ribs at all, only empty space that stretches on and on forever.

The key is still in my pocket. I press the rough edge hard against my finger, hard enough that I feel metal scrape bone. Pain shrieks through me, but I push it away. What is my pain, measured against Clara's death?

She has no strength to fight me as I touch my torn finger to her lips. For a long moment, nothing happens, and then Clara's breath catches. I feel something break inside of her, and then blood rushes in a torrent from her lips.

Panic seizes me, and not knowing what else to do, I summon the silver light, *pushing* it through my skin. A hundred small tears open up over my body from the force of it, my own blood welling and mingling with Clara's. I wrap Clara in the silver light, close my eyes, think: *heal, be well, be alive.*

Clara's breath moves against my skin, and I open my eyes. She is *well*, her cheeks plump and pink, the blood on her lips flaking away to reveal healthy skin beneath. She takes in a deep breath, another, another.

She is alive. She is well.

She clasps my hand, her eyes filling with tears. "Virginia, you're an angel. Why did you never tell me that you were an angel?"

I see myself reflected in her eyes, my face haloed with silver light. Tears well, the salt stinging the torn places on my cheeks. All this time, I have feared what Clara would say when she saw the silver light, but never have I dreamed that she would react like this.

One more deep breath, and another. And then the air catches in her throat. She coughs, and I tense, expecting blood, but what comes from between her lips is a flower. White, its scent sweet and chill. An asphodel.

Asphodel: my regrets follow you to the grave.

Clara tries to breathe, but another asphodel flower unfurls from her lips, and another and another, and then there is a stream of them coming forth from her.

I pull flowers from her mouth, reach down into her throat to tear more away. The more I remove, the more of them blossom, their scent a miasma that surrounds us. And she is choking, she is suffocating, she is *dying*, and there is nothing that I can do.

More and more of the asphodel bloom, pushing me away, until Clara is covered with them entirely, the bed becoming a bower that shivers as she struggles beneath the flowers.

She stills, but the asphodel continues to bloom, a carpet of them flooding from the blood-soaked bed, creeping across the floor. With a last tremor, the place where Clara had been subsides, and I realise that the roots of the asphodel are burrowing into her, making earth of her flesh.

When the flowers threaten to cover my slippers, I retreat, move back down the stairs. The whispering of unfurling asphodel follows me, the river of white blooms spilling down after me as I descend.

It is only when the screaming starts that I realise that I have not pulled the silver light back beneath my skin, that I am standing in full view of the parlour, that it is Rose and the twins screaming. I am only barely aware of them rushing past me, the flowers following them out into the street.

The silver light uncurls, tendrils of it extending like vines towards the photographs on the mantelpiece. I pull each of them from their frames, smear blood onto their surfaces.

The photographs change. Each of the women who had lived here as Lilies sits there dead and alone, nothing in their hands but broken, dead roses. I let the photographs fall the ground, where they are quickly covered by the carpet of asphodel.

Out on the street, the twins and Rose are nowhere to be seen. I look up in time to see the upper windows shatter, asphodels tumbling in a flood from the broken panes. Perhaps the roots will slide between the bricks of the House, eat away at the mortar until the whole thing tumbles down, becomes earth for the garden that Clara had spoken of.

I let the silver light unfurl into the street, let it show me the direction in which I must go. It indicates I should follow the thin thread of green, the scent of *home*.

My feet barely touch the ground as I begin to walk, the scent of asphodel trailing me all the way.

BLOODLINES

'Now go we in content
To liberty, and not to banishment.'
~William Shakespeare, *As You Like It*

OLD PROMISE, NEW BLOOD

ALAN BAXTER

I still think of myself as a twin, though it's been fourteen years since my father killed my brother. And after all this time, it still feels like a nightmare, some dark and twisted fantasy, yet it's an open wound that never heals. We were twelve when he sat us down on the threadbare sofa for a 'talk'. Twelve years old and inseparable, almost one person in two bodies.

He explained why one of us had to die. He talked of blood prices, old promises, stupid mistakes. He cried so hard. We'd never seen him cry before. But all we heard was, "One of you has to go." I can't understand why we didn't rage and scream, why we were so strangely calm. Unnaturally so. Maybe that's why it hurts more now than it did then. The agony of loss, injustice, those pains increase with every passing day, along with the resentment.

He sobbed as he told us how much he wished it were different, but if one didn't die we both would. We told him that was fine by us, we'd both go, but he wouldn't have it. "Someone *has* to survive," he said. "One, at least, has to cleanse the blood. Then it hasn't cost us everything." As if the cost wasn't immense in any case, regardless of any 'survivors'.

And then Simon had said, "It has to be me." He was the elder, by twenty minutes, and that made him the one. He looked at me. "Brothers, always and forever."

I railed against it, shouting and spitting incoherent denials, but our father simply nodded. He put a shaking hand under Simon's chin and said, "Thank you for not making me choose."

♦

As I WALK this darkened corridor my heart is strangely calm. My mind is still. All the doubt, all the planning, all the second-guessing, seems pointless now. Even if it's not the right thing, it's the only thing. There's no going back. I know my father wouldn't approve, but really, fuck him. Like I owe him any kind of allegiance.

I don't hate him, though sometimes I wish I could. Maybe that would be easier. I've lived a life furious with him, but hate is the wrong word to describe how I feel. I get it. He made a mistake. A terrible mistake that nearly cost him everything. And everyone makes mistakes.

The door at the end of the hall is deep red, as I'd been told to expect. I raise my hand to knock and I'm surprised to see it trembling despite my calmness. It shudders like I'm cold, or struck with a palsy. I grip my fingers into a tight fist and the shaking stops. I rap against the crimson wood: one, two, three. Pause for a three count and rap again: one, two, three. I wait. Nothing happens and a weight descends on my mind, everything crashing down around me with the realisation that it was all a joke, all pointless. I've been led along on a merry dance by magi with—

I jump as the door clicks open. A two inch gap of darkness appears inside the frame as the door drifts inwards and slows to a stop. I give it a gentle shove. It swings soundlessly all the way, a yawning blackness beyond that threatens to suck me in.

A sharp scratch and a flare and I wince as matchlight blossoms into being. Parts of the room resolve; armchairs, bookshelves, a desk, small tables, a standard lamp. In the middle of it all is a man so old he looks desiccated by age, his face stark yellow in the light of the flame. Deep wrinkles seem to squirm on his cheeks as he lowers the match to an oil lamp. Light flares brighter and he turns the wick down, the illumination settling to a soft glow that doesn't quite reach the edges and corners of the room, thick shadows left lurking on the periphery. He sinks into a chair and beckons me in with one crooked finger.

♦

SIMON'S BRAVERY THAT day still shames me. I never once offered to take his place. I shouted and screamed at him not to do it. But he understood it had to be done, there wasn't a choice in the matter. One of us had to go to save the other and I never offered my life for his.

I turned on my father. "Why can't it be you?" and he hung his head, tears spattering the knees of his worn jeans.

"I've offered," he said in a broken voice. "I've begged, but the deal is fixed. It was made when you two were born, before I knew you. I loved you both. From the moment I found out your mum was pregnant, I loved you. When we learned there were two of you, we had twice the love. But I didn't *know* you. And I . . . " He sobbed so hard the words were lost. He sniffed, drew breath, tried again. "Damn my soul, I loved her so much."

"Mum?" Simon asked, as I stared in disbelief.

Our father simply nodded, crying too hard to speak.

♦

I STAND BEFORE the old man, my eyes straining through the gloom for some kind of detail. I feel awkward, hands hanging limply at my sides. They are trembling again.

The man's eyes are rheumy, the lower lids wet and loose, hanging away from the eyeball, red and sore-looking. He nods almost imperceptibly. "You brought them?" he asks, his voice paper-thin with decades.

"Yes." I reach into my pocket and pull out the muslin-wrapped parcel, grubby with specks of mud still clinging to it. I hand it over.

The old man shifts back in his chair, shakes his head vigorously. "No, no, I can't touch them." He points to a sturdy walnut table beside him. "There. Unwrap it."

I lay the muslin down, fold back the sides to reveal the dirty, thin bones inside. My father's hand.

"Have any trouble getting them?" the old man asks.

I shake my head. The gesture is a lie, it had taken months to find his grave and weeks to plan the theft. I was almost caught, digging up the hard ground one frosty night, and nearly abandoned the operation as a result, only to return the next evening. But this old man doesn't need to know all that.

He leans forward, his face lowering over my father's bones until his nose almost brushes them, and sniffs. Three quick, short inhalations. He nods again and sits back. "And the other?"

I hand him the envelope with the money. More money than I've ever had before. Difficult as the bones had been to find and retrieve, this price had been harder.

He opens the envelope and peers inside, runs a thumb over the wad of bills. "Good. Pull up a chair."

◆

"SHE WASN'T KILLED in a car crash, was she?" Simon said as Dad cried. It wasn't really a question, the realisation hit us both with sudden surety. As Dad's tears soaked his knees, we knew we would soon be separated and that our mum hadn't died in an accident.

Our father shook his head, taking short, shallow breaths.

"That day we were picked up from school by Aunty Sue, when you told us Mum had had an accident," I said. "What really happened?"

He looked up at us for the first time since Simon had offered himself and nodded. We deserved the truth, his nod said, and he wouldn't shy away from it anymore. "She couldn't handle it." His voice gained strength with each word. "What I'd done, it pretty much destroyed her. For years we grappled with the decision, she fought with her hatred of me and her love for you. She endured my presence for your sake, but she never loved me, not after you were born." He paused, hitched a couple of ragged breaths. "We tried," he went on. "We searched for any possible way to save you both, even if it meant our lives, but there was no option. That day, when you were ten, she finally cracked. She couldn't bear the thought of what would happen. I tried to tell her she needed to get as much of you both as she could, that we owed you as much time and love and attention as we could possibly manage, but she . . . her mind . . . she broke inside.

"I got a call at work that day because the postman heard a car running in the garage when he knocked to deliver a parcel. The garage door was locked. He called emergency services, but it was all too late. Your mother had been in the car, a hose through the window from the exhaust, for hours." His sobs took over his voice again and he sank his face into his hands.

Simon and I exchanged a look and we both felt the loss of our mother more strongly than ever. The agony of losing her was fresh and tender. We were tormented by her pain at not being able to cope with our father's mistake. And we burned inside knowing she hadn't been able to stay with us until the end. We looked into each other's eyes, missing our mother and, for a while, hating our father. I don't know if Simon died still hating him, or if he'd found any kind of forgiveness. He didn't have long.

"I just loved her so much!" Dad said suddenly through his tears. "I loved her more than life, and she was dying, haemorrhaging as she gave birth, and the doctors started to panic." He rubbed his palms over his face like he was trying to drag the skin off. "I couldn't bear the thought of losing her and the doctors said I would. They could save you boys, they told me, but not your mother. And I wished, I wished so hard for her to live."

"And?" Simon's voice was hard and cold as ice.

Our father looked up, eyes red and haunted. "And it came to me. As the doctors worked, the room around me darkened and time froze, everything stilled like a photograph. And it stepped from between shadows. Like a man, but not entirely. Strange angles and shadows to its form. It was as if a beast lurked within, straining to get out. And it said, 'You really want her to live?' I thought I was dreaming. I thought I had gone mad, but I said, 'Yes! I want her to live!'"

He stood up, anger pulsing off him in waves as he paced the small room. "I was consumed with her loss. I loved you boys, but I didn't *know* you." His red eyes were wild. "'What price?' it said and I didn't understand. 'She could live,' it said, 'but I need to be paid. Blood for blood.' I stared at the creature. I didn't know what to do. It pointed over my shoulder at the frozen tableau of your mother in the fatal pain of childbirth and said, 'One of them, when they come of age.'" Our father collapsed back onto the sofa, gasping for breath between sobs of grief and rage. "And I said yes!"

◆

I PULL UP a wobbly dining chair and sit across the table from the old man, my father's finger bones on the wood between us. My hands are uncertain in my lap, but my heart and mind are still.

"Your father made a terrible deal," the old man says. "He played a dangerous game."

I nod, unsure what to say.

"And you play an even more dangerous one."

I nod again. I don't plan to lose my nerve now. Everyone is gone, I've been alone so long. My grief and pain have eaten me for years. We've been apart longer than we were ever together, Simon and I, but the pain won't go away. The scars won't heal. We were one person in two parts. Now I'm half a person.

"If this fails," the old man says, "he gets you all. I will not allow his presence into *my* life. I'll take no chances for you."

I shrug. "So be it." I'm pleased my voice sounds strong.

The old man stares at me for so long I start to shift uncomfortably on my seat. But I won't give in. He doesn't think I've agonised over this? I don't care now, whatever way it goes will be better than how it is. I need closure, even if that's a new hell. My father may not have been able to find a way, but I have. This option was never open to him. Simon's a part of me, after all. We shared blood in the womb, so much more than what my father gave to us at conception.

Eventually, the old man nods and stands from his chair. He opens a dresser drawer and takes out a piece of chalk. With slow, careful movements he starts marking the wooden floor around both our chairs with intricate sigils of a kind I haven't seen before. And, despite my father's warnings, despite his desperate plea that I leave the magic alone, I've seen a lot as I searched the shadows of this world for a way.

◆

"HOW LONG HAVE we got?" I asked our father and his eyes gave me all the answer I needed.

"He's there with you now," Simon said. "The Devil, sitting on your shoulder, waiting for me." He was always the smart one, Simon. Wise beyond his years. When I looked, I saw it too. A dark, cold smudge in the room. Not corporeal, but indisputably, defiantly there. We felt its mirth.

Dad shook his head. "Yes, he's here now. But there are things older and meaner in these worlds than the Devil, son," he said. "Hungrier and stronger. The kind of things that would bully the Devil in his own hell if they actually gave a shit about him." He vibrated with fear and grief.

We were both so calm, Simon and I. Every time I recall that horrible day, I can never understand how tranquil and accepting we were. I think it must have been some magic of our father's. Or maybe something as simple as a drug in our meal before he told us. I'll never know. But it was time and strangely we accepted that. The evidence was coldly present there with us, and it chilled me deeper than my bones.

Dad stood and led us down to the basement. I begged him not to do it, regardless of my calm acceptance. And Simon cried too, put his hand in mine and we gripped each other like we would never let go.

And I never once offered to go in his place.

In the cold basement, our father stood between us and the stairs, his face a mask of misery. "I've done so many things I shouldn't have," he told us. "Messed with forces and magics I should have left well alone, since well before you were conceived. I opened myself to this and it's cost us all so dearly. If there was another way, I promise I would have found it. But if it doesn't take one, it *will* take all. I tried to go in your place, Simon, I begged and pleaded, but nothing can break the deal. The only way for one of you to survive is for one of you to go and I am so very, very sorry. But one of you *must* survive. We can't let it take everything."

He began to cry again. I hated his tears.

And still I didn't offer to go in Simon's place.

◆

THE OLD MAN slumps back into his chair, the protections drawn. He unrolls a leather wrap, smooth and shiny with age, exposing an array of knives in stitched pockets, from a tiny switchblade to a wicked long machete. He hands me a small, ornate dagger, with jewels in the hilt. The lamplight reflects off the silver blade, glinting across our faces as I turn it over in my hands.

"You ready?" he asks.

It took me so long to find him, so long to find the ritual and someone willing and able to do it, that I've never been more ready. I just want this all to be over. One way or another. "Yes," I tell him.

"There's no going back," he says, his rheumy eyes serious. "Once this begins, once we call it in, there's nothing to do but let things play out."

I nervously twist the knifepoint between my fingers. "I know."

"If those aren't the right bones or . . . "

"I know," I say, a little more sharply than I mean to. "I'm sorry, sir, but I know. This is what I want."

"I tell you again, if it goes bad, you'll go. I won't chance myself. Yes?"

"Yes."

The old man sighs. "Then cut yourself, and every time I raise my hand, let one drop of blood touch those bones. And you'd better hope your blood is strong enough."

With a nod, I draw the blade across the side of my index finger. My hands are criss-crossed with scars already, from previous excursions into things my father expressly forbade I do, and from practising for this one. I can bleed myself like an expert. The old man starts chanting something. I recognise some of the words, some of the phrasing. I feel the old magic, knowledge older than history swelling into the room. This is rare and powerful stuff. The old man raises his hand, two fingers extended like a blessing, and I drip my blood onto my father's bones. The bones of the hand that shook on the deal twenty-six years ago in a delivery room soaked in my mother's blood. An arcane wind stirs between us.

♦

IN THE BASEMENT that terrible day, our father suddenly switched. Something took hold of him. I like to think it was his own will, that he was determined then to see the thing through without any more delay. But I think it was more likely the strength of that evil presence taking command. He drew himself up and sucked air into his lungs. Simon took me in an embrace I can still feel to this day, and held me tight. "Brothers," he whispered into my ear. "Always and forever."

"Always and forever," I whispered in return.

Grief already tore at my gut, yet that uncertain calmness persisted. I wanted to scream and rage, push our dad out of the way and run with Simon out into the world and never look back. But I knew, deep inside, without any doubt, that he was right. It would cost us both if we ran from this.

As Simon stepped back from our embrace Dad put one hand to his shoulder. His other hand held a large bowie knife. "I love you, son," he said. "I love you so much." And he gripped Simon's shoulder tightly and plunged the knife into my brother's chest.

Simon gasped, his eyes wide, and I screamed. Simon was torn away from me and a wound opened in my heart that has refused to heal ever since. I don't remember a life without the trauma raw inside me. Our father hugged my brother tightly against his body and Simon's gaze met mine, his cheek pressed against Dad's checked shirt. My scream withered away as I watched the light slip from Simon's eyes. "Always and forever," I whispered, as Dad lay Simon's body gently on the cold concrete floor.

I don't know how long we stayed like that, my father crying over Simon's corpse as I sat numb and frozen. All I can remember is an icy laughter that seemed to echo and bounce around us, sweeping up and back, dancing in a satiated glee that chills me every time I recall it. Eventually it drained from the room and my father stood and turned to me. "It's done," he said. "On your feet."

I struggled to stand, my legs like tissue paper. The grief, the misery, the sorrow in my father's eyes was horrible to behold, yet still the calmness soaked through me. Surely it had been some magic of his to protect me.

"Don't let the temptations of power distract you like they did me," he said, laying one bloody palm across my cheek. "No matter how much you think you can gain, no matter how powerful you think you can be, it's a game we mortals can never win. We're pawns in the frivolity of greater beings, nothing more."

I wasn't really sure what he meant, not then. I know now, since I didn't heed his advice, but then I simply nodded and said, "So it's over now?"

"You're the new beginning. It ends here and starts again with you. Fresh, untainted blood at last. Promise me you'll never go near anything unnatural again. Promise me! Don't make my mistakes!" Lost for words, I nodded as Dad stepped back, then pointed at Simon. "Never forget," he said, and drew the blade across his throat so quickly that for a moment I wasn't sure I'd really seen him do it. His eyes were wide, like he couldn't believe it himself, then his throat peeled open like a scarlet mouth, his lifeblood arcing across the space between us. I felt it splatter on the backs of my hands, across my face and neck, hot and thick. As I stared, he held my gaze with his and slowly crumpled to his knees and tipped facedown to the floor.

It was hours before I staggered from the house—the poor victim of a murder/suicide—into a life of foster homes, rage, abuse and arcane searching.

◆

THE WIND WHIPS widdershins around the room as the old man chants. His fingers raise and I drip blood onto the bones. It's pooling, spreading out like a flower blooming across the golden polished walnut surface of the table. I make a cut across my middle finger and switch, determined to control the bloodletting perfectly. My only active role in this ritual will not be the thing that lets us down.

I feel the presence rise and my father was right. Older and meaner than sin, pure malice strides through the space, drawing the shadows from the corners with it. Evil howls in the world and things start to shift, drawn towards some frozen abyss we've opened. From somewhere I feel my father again, for the first time since that basement when he left me all alone. He's still crying.

The evil bends and stretches and, for the first time in fourteen years, Simon is with me. I see the shades of my brother and my father, sweeping through the room, both with expressions of confusion and fear. I smile at Simon, still a boy of twelve and so bewildered. So innocent. My father is a ragged old man, bent under the weight of guilt and loss, even though he hasn't physically aged to my eye. I almost miss the magi raising his hand. Things shudder as I swing my fingers over the table and squeeze free a drop of blood.

The evil howls in anger and my brother is confused, uncertain, aching with such deep pain. *It's me!* I scream through the aether. *I've come to get you back!*

My father's presence rips through me, his grief palpable, but overwhelmed by his anger. *I told you not to!* he cries as he slides nearer to the icy chasm.

The old man signals, still muttering, and I drip my blood. *Fuck you, I owe you nothing!* I spit after him. He may not really deserve this, but Simon and I are brothers, always and forever. He should pay the price, not us.

The evil desperately clings to my brother, but loses its grip as my father slams into his place. It's screaming its anger, fury at a trade it didn't agree to.

"Now!" the old man shouts, and I drag the knife across my palm, clench my fist over my father's remains. Blood floods across the table, washing the bones into a strange pattern, like a sigil of separation. But something isn't working as it should. The connection doesn't sever, the evil still builds. My father is screaming, my brother cries in my mind and cold, furious malice crawls through the blood and enters my hand. The old man's voice goes up a notch in volume and desperation as he chants, his magic pushing against the rising evil, but it suddenly feels weak, insubstantial in the face of ancient malevolence.

You think to stand against me? a voice booms into my head, and my bowels turn to water. My mind freezes solid in panic. That anything can be so all-encompassing, so total and insurmountable, is staggering.

I've doomed us all.

♦

BACK THEN, AS I grew up and began the quest my father forbade, searching the dark corners of human existence for the magic, the connections, the secrets best left buried, one lesson stuck with me beyond all others. A woman in a bazaar in Morocco, whose face bore burn scarring that was hideous to behold, said to me, "Never try to renegotiate a bargain."

She taught me a lot, that old witch, and helped me along my journey, but perhaps the lesson that always stuck with me, the one that I chose to ignore, was the most important after all.

I'm a fool, like my father.

♦

THE PRESENCE CRAWLS through my blood lasciviously, tauntingly, making the most of my complete inability to do anything about it. Without words it makes sure I know what it will do to me for eternity, and to my father as well. And to Simon, as it has all along. I've done exactly what my father managed to prevent. For all his mistakes, this thing only got Simon. Now it has us all.

Then the malice howls in rage-filled denial and something slams ice through my arm at the elbow. Pain lances through me, from fingertips to shoulder, white lightning through mind to groin and back again. I rock back in my chair to see the old magi, his face twisted in desperation. In one hand he holds high his blood-soaked machete, in the other is my severed arm.

The evil screams its fury, but it and my father are carried away, swirling into the abyss.

The old man's machete is over my head, ready to sweep down and end me. "Is it gone?" he yells.

"I felt it go!" I shout back over the dying winds.

His eyes narrow, his intention to let that huge blade drop all too clear. "Truly gone from you?"

I'm weakening as the stump of my upper arm pumps my lifeblood across my lap, the table, the floor. I let my swimming mind search my body, to check that every trace of the damned thing is out. It took its time to toy with me and that was its downfall. All I can feel is myself, and something else, in the back of my mind, lost and confused, but not evil. "It's all gone," I say weakly.

As darkness closes in, the old man's mind sweeps over and through me, scrutinising. In the last dim moments of consciousness, I see his blade sink slowly to hang by his side.

♦

As I come to, the first thing I hear is the old man's rasping breath. He tourniquets the pumping stump of my arm, muttering incantations as he works. My severed arm lies on the floor by his chair, withered and blackened from what it briefly contained. Quite a price, I've paid, but worth it. The magi's magic as much as his first aid is keeping me alive. His eyes flick up from his work to meet mine. "You're strong," he says, respect evident in his voice.

"Stubborn is what I am," I tell him.

A flicker of a smile ghosts across his face. "It'll never leave you alone, you know. Not after that. It'll hound you forever, try to cajole you into a mistake, to exact its revenge. And you'd better be careful how you eventually die, if you don't want it to win in the end. One thing it certainly has is eternal patience. You have a hell of a burden to carry alone now."

I nod, and smile. "But I'm not alone."

The old man shakes his head slightly. "I suppose not. I hope it was worth it." He bandages the raw end of my arm and I realise his magic is dulling the pain for me. "You'll not have me caught up in all this. A man will be along in a moment and he'll drive you to a hospital and leave you there. You'd better come up with a good story to explain everything."

"Thank you." I mean it, I'm genuinely grateful to him.

Can you feel me, Simon? I think to myself.

His voice in my mind is lost, scared, still that of a twelve-year-old boy. A new agony lives in me. Simon's pain. *Jacob? Is that really you?*

Brothers, Simon, I tell him, as a burly man appears and lifts me like I weigh nothing, carries me from the magi's dim apartment. *Brothers, always and forever.*

THE MYSTERIOUS
MR MONTAGUE

JANE PERCIVAL

I never eat pork. It's not that I'm vegetarian, or Jewish or Muslim, it's all to do with something that happened in the 70s, when I was fifteen years old.

As a kid, I had a fascination with meat. I have an early memory of accompanying Mum to our local butcher's and being given a fat, pink saveloy. She lifted me up onto the counter and I sat there munching on the sausage, looking around wide-eyed. I liked the smell of meat and sawdust. There was a plastic ribbon curtain dividing the shop front from the rest of the premises, and I caught glimpses of strange shapes when the strips moved in the breeze.

My uncles, Eddie and John, owned a butcher shop in Kilbirnie. On a visit when I was about ten, they took me through to the back to show me the other two rooms—a workroom where they processed the meat, and a walk-in cool room. I wandered around, careful not to slip, absorbing every detail . . .

In the middle of the workroom there was a rectangular wooden block, scrubbed clean and scored with the marks of countless knives. There were also a couple of circular wooden chopping blocks; one had a small hatchet embedded in it. A range of gleaming knives and hacksaws hung from the left-hand wall. There were lidded bins containing mysterious pieces of raw flesh. Strings of pale sausages, looped like intestines, were hanging from the ceiling alongside fat black puddings. On the benches there were shag-pile carpets of tripe waiting to be trimmed, and a huddle of glossy sheep kidneys. Through another door was the cooler and I could see a row of carcasses hanging from huge hooks attached to the ceiling.

There was that 'fleshy-bloody' smell that I now identify with the butchering of meat. I didn't find it repelling. The floor was covered with sawdust, which added a subtle, pine smell to the room.

Later, when I was a teenager, I hung around long enough to be offered a job helping keep the workroom and cooler tidy, and sweeping up the sawdust. After a while, it became accepted that when I'd finished school I'd be taken on as my uncles' apprentice.

♦

ONE AFTERNOON, I was left alone to mind the shop while my uncles made their deliveries. I was fifteen and in my last year at college. In fact, I'd been trying to drop out for some time, but Mum had insisted I stay on until the end of the fifth form. It was just after 4.00 pm and quiet. Most of the housewives had finished their shopping for the day, and it was too soon for the after-work rush of people looking for a last minute chop or piece of steak for that night's tea. I was in the workroom, trimming some hard fat off a piece of brisket when I heard the ring of the front door bell. I returned to the shop, wiping my hands on my blue and white striped apron. The sprung door slammed shut behind me, but the guy didn't raise his eyes. He was looking intently at the various items displayed in front of the window.

He wasn't someone I'd served before and looked to be roughly the same age as my uncles, in his forties, I suppose, with the kind of thick hair that is dark but fading to silvery grey around the edges. He had olive skin and a neatly trimmed beard, and was wearing a grey three-quarter length woollen overcoat, despite it being a warm November afternoon. His shoes were a well-polished black and he wore matching leather gloves.

His glance rested on the tray of plump black puddings sitting on the counter.

"Do you make your own blood sausage?" His voice was smooth, with the merest hint of an accent.

"Of course. Well, not me, but my uncles do," I responded, thinking this was a stupid question. In those days, butchers didn't sell anything they hadn't made themselves. "It's their shop."

"And they are made using . . . pigs' blood?"

"Yes, and some barley and oats, herbs . . . " my voice trailed off. The guy had an odd look on his face. "Why?"

"Are your uncles . . . in?"

"No, they're out making deliveries. They'll be finished after 5.30 pm, but we'll be closing around then."

The man stood for a moment, tapping his fingers on the counter. He looked out the window then checked his watch, before turning towards me.

"I'm short of time today, but I'd like to talk to them about their methods." He withdrew a small, white rectangle from his wallet and placed it on the counter. "Can you give them my card?"

With those words, he left.

I watched him walk briskly along Kilbirnie Road until he'd disappeared from view, then retrieved the card from the counter. On it was inscribed 'Saul Montague' in black, with the word 'Facilitator' written below in a cursive script. There was a local phone number. I propped it up on the shelf behind the counter next to the jars of pickled onions, then immediately forgot about it.

It wasn't until I was sitting in class the following afternoon that I remembered the card. I felt bad that I hadn't given it to my uncles before finishing the previous day. Perhaps they'd found it already.

After school I hurried to the shop. Opening the door, I was relieved to see that the card was exactly where I'd left it. I went over and took it down from the shelf. Eddie was serving a woman with a couple of kids. When they'd left, I walked over to him.

"This guy came in yesterday and asked about black puddings. He was a bit odd, but said he'd be in touch with you. He left this."

Eddie read out the word 'Facilitator' then turned the card over. The reverse side was blank.

"Black pudding, did you say?" he queried. "Is that all?"

"Well, he asked if we made it ourselves and if it was made from pigs' blood. But that's all. Sorry I forgot to tell you yesterday."

I had barely finished speaking when the shop doorbell rang again and there he was. I glanced at my watch. It was just after 4.00 pm. Eddie looked at me with eyebrows raised and I nodded.

Montague went straight up to Eddie, "I see you have my card." He stepped forward and extended his gloved hand. Eddie wiped his palms on his apron, then shook hands with the man.

"I have a proposition for you," said Montague. "Is there anywhere we can talk without interruption?" He didn't acknowledge having met me the previous day, directing all his attention to my uncle. I could hear chopping sounds from the workroom.

"We can go to the back. My brother's out there, too. Are you able to mind the shop, Joe?" Eddie looked my way and it was then that the man turned and stared directly into my eyes. He had an odd expression on his face and didn't avert his gaze when I answered, "Sure."

They left me alone for a decent amount of time. Then the sprung door opened and all three came back into the shop. Montague walked through swiftly and left. Eddie and John stood by the window and watched as he walked down the road.

"Are you still okay in the shop?" asked John.

"Yep," I replied, and my uncles returned to the back room where I could hear them talking. Finally, my curiosity got the better of me and I went through.

"What did he want?" I asked.

John looked at Eddie before responding. "We're not exactly sure."

He explained that Montague had initially enquired about the black puddings; about how often we had deliveries of pigs' blood and how fresh it was, how many puddings it was likely to make, and so on. My uncles had at first thought that he wanted a regular supply of the puddings, perhaps to on-sell. But as the conversation had developed, Montague had seemed more interested in the blood itself.

"He asked us about supplying blood to him on a regular basis," added Eddie. "We said we'd think about it. He told us it would be worth our while, whatever that means. Anyway, he's coming back on Monday, after we've had time to think about it and to come up with some options."

As I helped my uncles with the end of day tidying up tasks, I couldn't help wondering about Montague; what exactly he wanted and what on earth he'd use the blood for. It was a Friday and I had a whole weekend to reflect on it.

◆

By Monday I was still thinking about him. It wasn't just the blood thing that had captured my attention, but the strangeness of Montague himself. After school, I hurried to the shop. Both John and Eddie were serving customers behind the counter. What I really wanted to know was whether Montague had returned and what had been decided, but I didn't know how to broach the question. In the end, I didn't need to. As with his previous two visits, he turned up at the shop just after 4.00 pm. I was sorting the different meats in the front-of-shop display and made an effort not to stare at him. When I finally raised my eyes, I was disconcerted to see that once again he was looking straight back at me. He had a very direct gaze. I quickly glanced away and focused on re-arranging the mock chicken legs.

Eddie and John finished their sales and ushered Montague through to the workroom. On his way past, Eddie looked at me, raising his eyebrows. I nodded back. The three spent a good twenty minutes talking. At one point, I stood by the sprung door, straining my ears. When I had to go through to fetch Mrs O'Grady's order, they were sitting around the desk where John worked on the accounts; they stopped talking when I came in. Avoiding eye contact, I collected the brown-paper parcel and hastily retreated. It all felt very secretive. Finally their discussion drew to a close and they came back into the shop. They shook hands and I could see that an agreement of some kind had been reached.

John turned to me. "Mr Montague here is going to be taking collection of some products from us. He has requested that you make the delivery to his premises in person, twice a week after school."

"Okay . . . " I said.

John went on, "He has a shed down by the bay. Can you go with him now so that you know where it is?"

I was surprised and looked at Eddie. "You go, Joe. It's not far away, it won't take long."

Montague was already half out the door. He barely acknowledged me, so I removed my apron and followed as he walked briskly down the street towards the harbour. In ten minutes, we were at the waterfront area where a scattering of small boats and yachts, and two or three fishing vessels were moored.

The slight curve of Evans Bay was dotted with small boatsheds and a couple of larger, covered dry docks. Seagulls wheeled overhead as we approached, and some kids were fishing further down the wharf. There was the tangy smell of salt water and rust. Barnacles clung to the wharf posts, just below the water line.

Montague led me to a boatshed positioned at the end of its own small jetty. Green paint was peeling from the walls in several places and the windows were grimy and didn't offer a glimpse of what was within. The door was shut tightly and locked securely with three large padlocks. Montague withdrew a decent-sized keyring from his coat pocket and, using a different key for each padlock, unlocked them. They were well-lubricated and opened easily.

"Wait here." He went into the boatshed and returned almost immediately with a one-gallon steel milk pail, complete with lid. He handed it to me. "This is what I want you to use. You can bring it here after 4.30 pm on the agreed days. I'll be here to collect it from you." He turned away.

"Mr Montague . . . "

"What is it, boy?"

"Nothing." He was locking up the door and raised his head to look at me.

"That's all right, then. I'll see you next Tuesday." He returned the keys to his pocket, turned, and walked away in the opposite direction.

Carrying the bucket, I made my way back to the shop. I knew I'd look stupid walking along the road with it and hoped that I didn't run into any of my classmates.

♦

READING THIS, YOU may well think that so far, my story is of no great interest, but it is difficult to convey in words the strangeness of Mr Montague himself. I was only fifteen; my mind was alive with ideas of adventure and strange happenings. I had recently been reading Edgar Allan Poe and Bram Stoker, and my brain was humming with questions and suspicions.

My uncles didn't really expand upon the arrangement they'd come to with Montague. And because of their reticence, I didn't raise it either. So it became something of a secret.

◆

WHEN THAT FIRST Tuesday came around, the pail was full and ready to be delivered when I arrived at the shop after school. The arrangement was that I would drop it off between 4.30 and 5.00 pm, which was fine by me. At 4.30 pm I collected the pail from the workroom—the blood was so fresh that the outside of the bucket was warm to the touch—then carried it down the road to Montague's boatshed. It was heavy and awkward to carry and kept bumping into the sides of my legs. I had to change hands several times and was left with red marks on my palms after the delivery. I could see that I'd have to find a different way to carry it if possible.

Montague was waiting outside as arranged. I greeted him, handed over the bucket then stood awkwardly, waiting for his response.

"Thank your uncles from me," was all he said. His look told me it was the end of the conversation so I headed off, but after a few steps I turned back.

"The bucket . . . I'll need it for the next delivery."

"I dropped off another at your uncles' shop. When you bring the next one, I can exchange it for an empty one."

"Oh." I headed back along the road. The sun was beginning to drop behind the hills and it was cool in the shade. When I looked back, the boatshed was in shadow, the door and windows tightly shut.

◆

DELIVERY DAYS WERE Tuesdays and Fridays. It was December and getting close to Christmas. School had closed for the year, and I was finished with it for good. John and Eddie had talked to Mum and it had been decided that I'd start work 'officially' in the third week of January. I still came in to the shop for a few hours each day, usually in the afternoons, and had attached a wooden crate to the front of an old bike for the blood deliveries. As long as I avoided bumps, this seemed to work okay. It wasn't long before my curiosity about what

Montague was up to got the better of me. I decided to do a bit of investigation of my own.

On the last Friday before Christmas, after delivering the blood and returning the empty pail to the shop, I quickly retraced my route on foot. It was summer and would still be light for a couple more hours. I ordered some fish and chips from the shop across the road from the wharves, then sat to eat them on a park bench in the adjacent children's playground, partly hidden from Montague's shed by a couple of straggly trees. A bunch of seagulls appeared as soon as they saw me and vied for a position at my feet. There I sat, partly in the shade of the trees, watching, savouring the hot, salty chips.

I didn't have to wait long. After about ten minutes the door to the boatshed opened and Montague came out. As usual, he was wearing his woollen overcoat, suit trousers and shiny black shoes. I could see him quite clearly through the vegetation. He'd closed the door and was about to lock the padlocks when he stopped, opened the door again, and peered in. He seemed to be talking to someone. This I didn't expect. I wondered who or what on earth was locked inside. It didn't make sense and I felt a prickling on my spine.

I sat there for a bit, not sure what to do next. I weighed up asking my uncles about him again, but knew there'd be no point. I finished my meal and shook out the paper. The gulls fought over the last scraps, and a cool breeze started up. I gazed northwards along the bay towards Wellington Harbour. The road wound around the suburbs and back towards Oriental Bay. I was almost certain that this was the way Montague had walked, but I wasn't one hundred percent sure. I had the feeling that he wouldn't be pleased to find me poking about near his boatshed . . . but after seeing him talk to someone behind those padlocked doors, I was more intrigued than ever. I decided to double-back along the road a bit, then turn around and walk back to the shed, as if I was arriving for the first time. That way, if Montague did reappear, he'd think I'd only just arrived. I was sure I could invent some reason or other to explain my presence.

Five minutes later I was on the wharf, surveying Montague's shed more closely. I realised that despite its run-down exterior, it was actually in really good shape. The items lying on the wharf around it—the heavy metal hooks, rusted chains, even an unravelling fishing net—now seemed contrived, as if added for effect. A shiny steel flue rose from the left front corner of the roof above the curling red paint of the corrugated iron. I surveyed the area. The kids fishing at the other end of the wharf were packing up their gear, and traffic was building up on Kilbirnie Road. At that very moment, the sun slipped behind Mt Victoria. Across Evans Bay, a golden light rose up the hills behind the Shelly Bay Air Force Base, leaving the harbour edge in dusky shade. A gust of cool wind swept along the wharf and the seagulls rose in unison and flew squawking into the last of the sunlight.

I walked around the three sides of the shed. The fourth side had a ramp leading down to the water. It was high tide and the water lapped halfway up the ramp. Unlike the remainder of the shed, the ramp was clearly in disrepair, its door nailed shut with battens. Someone had used white paint to roughly write the words 'The Larch' diagonally across it.

I was about to peer through one of the windows when I felt a hand grip my shoulder. I jumped involuntarily then half-turned.

"Looking for something?"

"I . . . " My face flushed hot with embarrassment.

"Have you ever heard the phrase 'curiosity killed the cat'?" Montague's accented voice was cool.

"Yes. But . . . that's all it was. I was just curious. I didn't mean any harm."

Still gripping my shoulder, Montague twisted me around to face him. With a frown on his face he slowly looked me up and down. My shoulder hurt and I was afraid. I was tall for my age, but Montague was taller, his figure imposing. I could sense a muscular frame beneath his coat. Of course, now I see that he was in the prime of life, but at the age of fifteen, anyone over thirty seemed old.

I was weighing up whether I could escape from his grasp when he finally spoke. "I was going to drag you back to your uncles, but perhaps you can be of use. Can I trust you, boy?"

"Yes. I—I think so."

His face relaxed a little. With a sigh he let go of my shoulder, giving me a small shove as he did so. "Well, we'd better have a talk. Inside."

He reached into his pocket and passed me his keys. "Open the locks. Use the three Yale keys."

With shaking hands, I tried to unlock the first padlock. After a couple of unsuccessful attempts, Montague took over. He indicated that I should go in first, but I was no longer that keen to see what was inside. I cast my eyes along the wharf, and across to the street beyond. There were no actual people, kids or otherwise, in sight—just cars driving past. No-one would hear if I called for help.

I turned the handle and pushed open the door.

♦

IT WAS DARK inside. The glass in the windows was opaque and little of the early evening light could penetrate. It was uncomfortably warm and I noticed the glow of a pot belly stove in the corner to the left of the door. Montague switched on the light.

The sight that met my eyes was totally unexpected. The interior had been completely refurbished. The walls and ceiling were shiny white, and the floor, also white, was tiled. The corner diagonally opposite had been partitioned off, the interior hidden by a single blue curtain hanging from a metal rod. I could hear the regular beep of a monitor of some kind, and there were several items of unfamiliar equipment in the room. One of the buckets was on the floor by the partition, empty. I looked around.

It reminded me of a hospital ward. The wall facing the harbour, where there once would have been large doors leading to the ramp, was completely sealed. A wide, waist-high bench ran around two-thirds of the room, into which a stainless steel double sink was set. There was a small, white refrigerator and a large wooden desk positioned against the sealed doors, and a couple of chrome and vinyl swivel chairs. The desk was stacked with a few books and some tidy piles of papers. I noticed an open spiral-bound diary, covered with lines of tight writing in black ink.

"What do you think?" Montague was looking for a reaction. I tried to remain calm, but he would have seen my surprise.

"What is this place for?" I couldn't help but ask the obvious. It was a lot to take in.

"This, dear boy, is my laboratory. It is equipped with the latest medical and scientific equipment. My work involves the study of life itself."

Our conversation was interrupted by the sound of coughing from beyond the blue curtain. As it died away, the beeping of the machine seemed even louder.

Montague scrutinised me. "I'm about to reveal something to you, boy. I want your word that what you are about to see will be kept between ourselves."

I looked him in the eye. "My name's Joe."

"I know your name. I want your word."

"You have it." It had been so easy to agree, but I hadn't known what I was agreeing to.

Upon this, he walked briskly to the curtain and drew it aside. I stepped closer and saw a high, single bed, made up with snowy white linen. Beneath the covers lay a young woman. A large, dull-green enamelled machine of some kind, set on casters, was positioned next to her supine form. A clear plastic tube rose up to the top of a shiny metal stand, then down again, all the way to the invalid. Halfway along the tube was a clear, plastic cylinder, three quarters filled with bright blood, which fed directly into a vein on her bare right forearm.

I had taken all this in with my first glance, but my eyes were drawn to the sleeping figure. She was tucked in securely, with only her right arm exposed. Although asleep, she appeared restless; her lips moved as if she was having a conversation in her dreams. A tangle of long, auburn hair spread across the pillow, framing her face. There were purple shadows under her eyes and translucent skin pulled tightly over her cheekbones. She didn't look well.

"What's wrong with her?" I asked.

"This is Maria. She has a . . . rare disease . . . and I am in the process of implementing a cure."

"If she's sick, shouldn't she be in hospital?"

"A hospital cannot help her, boy."

I looked back at Maria. I couldn't help thinking that there was something very wrong with the whole situation.

♦

MONTAGUE REPLACED THE curtain and walked to the other side of the room, indicating that I should sit down beside him. It was then that he offered me a job. He explained that he was run off his feet with collecting and delivering the various items associated with his projects and could use the help.

At first I refused, but he was very persuasive, explaining that it would only take a few hours a week, perhaps ten at the most. I could fit the errands around my butcher duties, once I started my apprenticeship. Additionally, he offered me a very good hourly rate. He reiterated that his work was sensitive and I understood that this wasn't the type of work I'd discuss with anyone else, not even my uncles.

And so it began. On Tuesdays when I dropped off the blood, he would tell me when he needed me to call by during the following week. On the occasions that he had an errand for me to run, he'd invite me in, but only briefly, and I didn't get another chance to see the girl, Maria, for many weeks. By then it was too late. As for the fresh pigs' blood, I felt certain it had everything to do with Maria. I often found myself wondering if she was still gravely ill, or if her health was improving.

After I'd been running Montague's errands for more than a month, he provided me with a set of the padlock keys, emphasising that they were only to be used in a case of *extreme* emergency. I realised that he trusted me.

♦

AROUND THE THIRD week in March, everything changed. It was a Tuesday evening and I turned up at the boatshed with the bucket of blood. When I arrived I was surprised to see that the padlocks were still in place. I knocked on the door, then looked around, to see if Montague had left a note, but there was nothing. I took out my keys, aware that my heart had begun to beat faster.

I pushed open the door. It was dark inside, and cooler than usual, the only glow coming from a lamp beyond the curtain. I turned on the lights, placed the bucket of blood on the bench, and walked over to the desk, looking over my shoulder, expecting Montague to show up at any moment. There wasn't a note there, either. By now my heart was racing and my one thought was that this was my chance to check on Maria.

With trepidation I walked over to the curtain and drew it back a little from the corner. There she was, propped up a little in the bed studying a picture book held in her left hand. She looked up, clearly startled to see me. I was struck by the colour of her eyes. They were a very dark brown, almost black, but with a ruby hue. Her skin had a pinkish tinge, as if she were feverish.

"Hi," I said. "I've brought the blood for Mr Montague. He's not here so I've left it on the bench."

She didn't say anything.

"You must be Maria. I'm Joe."

Maria's eyes were fixed on me, watching every movement. She seemed to be glued to the bed, with her right arm still attached to the transfusion tube. I was absolutely sure now that this was what it was.

There was no way to tell how much blood was left in the machine, but it appeared that it was fed in from the top through a stainless steel funnel-type arrangement. I noticed a small glass bottle of transparent liquid also feeding into the machine, inscribed with the hand-written words 'antigen suppressant'.

Maria opened her mouth as if to speak, but the effort must have been too much for her as she fell back upon her pillow, breathing in short gasps, her body trembling. I realised there was no point in asking her any more questions as my presence seemed to be making her agitated. She had started to quiver uncontrollably.

I wasn't sure what to do, so I scribbled a note on the back of an envelope and left it on Montague's desk. Other than that, I could only wait for him to get in touch with me. If nothing else, he'd need to give me the list of days he wanted me to come in for the next week. As I made my departure, turning off the lights on the way, I touched the pot belly. It was quite cold.

◆

WHEN THURSDAY ARRIVED and Montague still hadn't contacted me, I was starting to wonder. I decided to visit the boatshed during my lunch hour on the off-chance that he might be there.

When I drew nearer, my heart sank as I saw the padlocks were still in place. I let myself in. There was no sign that Montague had been back, and the air was stale and smelt of decay. I could hear the machine beeping urgently from the corner. Almost too afraid to look, I made my way over and drew aside the curtain.

Maria was lying in the bed, barely conscious. The transfusion tube had dried up and the entry point in her forearm was inflamed. The bottle of clear fluid feeding into the machine was empty. I stood there, paralysed with uncertainty. Finally, I wet a rag under the tap and wiped her brow, but she barely moved. The bucket of blood was still sitting on the bench where I'd left it. I lifted the lid and wasn't surprised to see that it had started to go bad. I emptied it into the sink and rinsed it out.

I went over to Montague's desk, hoping to find some clue as to what he was up to with Maria. My note was still there, of course. Sifting through his papers I noted that his correspondence was mostly associated with orders for medical supplies and an exchange of ethical ideas with (what I assumed was) a colleague in Germany. The spiral notepad was nowhere to be seen.

It was then that I noticed an old book Montague had left on his desk. It was lying open and had thick yellowing pages, with lines of ornate Gothic script. The page to the left had the heading, *'Blōd, Pigge and Seolf'*. On the right was a simple illustration depicting three figures—two men and a pig. One of the men was standing over the other, who was lying on a bed. The unfortunate pig was strapped to a bench alongside. It appeared that the pig's throat had been slit; the blood was squirting out and being collected in a container. I had no idea what it meant and quickly shut the book.

When I returned to Maria's bedside, her eyes were open, but she didn't seem aware of her surroundings. I decided to straighten up the bedding and, as I did, the sheets came away from the side of the bed. I pulled them back to smooth them out and was concerned to see that she was restrained by three leather belts, at the chest, waist and hips. Looking further, I noticed two red rubber tubes leading from beneath the hem of her simple white gown to a couple of bags similar in size and appearance to hot water bottles, tucked into a bracket at the end of the bed. They looked full. By this time, I was shaking all over. Then my eyes focused on the unfathomable. Maria's gown had risen up a little. Instead of feet peeping out below the hem, I saw two pig's trotters. I thought my heart would leap from my breast.

I quickly pulled the bedding back and tucked it in securely. It was time to leave; I had no idea what to do.

♦

THAT EVENING I went to the library to check the newspapers from the previous few days. I found what I was seeking on page three of the Wednesday edition of *The Evening Post*. It was a brief item about a man's body having been found washed up at Shelly Bay. It stated that the deceased was bearded, aged around forty to fifty and had been clad in a heavy woollen coat. There was no indication of wrong-doing and it was suspected that he'd fallen out of a boat or off a wharf and had been weighed down by the coat and had subsequently drowned. Police had requested that people come forward if they had any information.

The next day I told my uncles about Montague's non-appearance and the item in the newspaper, leaving out any mention of what I'd found in the boatshed. I needed time to think everything through. They suggested that if he still didn't show on Friday, we should contact the Police.

On Friday when I biked down to the shed with the fresh pigs' blood, I was almost certain it would be for the last time. I unlocked the door and was hit with an overpowering smell of stale bodily fluids. Horrible grunting noises were coming from the corner and I had to force myself to investigate.

When I pulled back the curtain, I saw that my worst fears had been realised. The creature that had once been Maria had diminished in size. The head and face were distorted. A few coarse, white whiskers had sprung up around its jowls and the teeth were exposed behind a scary grin. The tube had come away from its front leg—for a leg it clearly was—and the picture book was lying partly-chewed on the floor. The creature had been thrashing around on the bed and what was left of the beautiful auburn hair was a matted mess, most of it lying in tangled clumps on the pillow. The rubber tubes had disconnected and the bedding was badly soiled. The creature was emitting plaintive grunting noises and clearly wanted to escape. Its dark eyes looked at me wildly.

This time I knew what I had to do. It's not that I *wanted* to do it, but the creature was obviously in severe distress. God only knew what Montague had done to it during the course of his experiments.

♦

WITH A HEAVY heart, I left Montague's boatshed and made my way back to the shop. Once there I collected my new set of butchering knives, honing my best boning knife until it was razor sharp, before packing them up in my leather satchel. Then I walked back to the harbour, all the while thinking about the image in the old book I'd seen on Montague's desk.

It was a simple matter to dispatch Maria. She was already restrained, after all. Before attempting the task, I removed all the bedding from under her body and positioned the stainless steel bucket beneath the bed to collect the blood. As I gripped her head to hold it still and raised my knife, I swear that her eyes looked as human as they had before her body had reverted to its original self.

Before I left, I retrieved the old book from Montague's desk and screwed up the note I'd left for him. I put both into my satchel with the knives.

Later that day, I asked my uncles to sit themselves down, explaining that I had something serious to discuss with them. I updated them on how Montague had asked me to run errands for him, and how he'd been conducting experiments on a pig in that boatshed.

They weren't as surprised as they might have been. I suspected that Montague had been paying them *extremely* well and that despite their reservations, they'd appreciated the money. I also told them about how the poor pig had been strapped to a bed and neglected since Montague's disappearance. I then explained that I'd taken it upon myself to kill the poor animal and that I needed to dispose of the remains.

The three of us took the butcher's van down to the boatshed. I let my uncles in and they carried the carcass out to the back of the vehicle. John commented that it was a poor specimen of a pig, and would only be good for making sausages. I stuffed the bedding into a large plastic bag and we took the mattress, too, as there was a fair bit of blood on it. I locked up the shed for the last time.

◆

AND THAT SHOULD have been the end of the story.

After about a month had passed, I rang the police to report Montague as missing. A couple of constables came by to interview me, with my uncles sitting in. We showed them Montague's card and I explained that I had delivered blood to him twice weekly and that I sometimes ran other errands for him. I left out the bit about having access to his shed, or about seeing the pig. I told them that we hadn't seen sight or sound of Montague since sometime in February. That we'd had to throw out three buckets of perfectly good fresh blood that we hadn't been paid for.

After the interview, I accompanied the police to Evans Bay to show them the boatshed. They called for help and were able to break the locks on the door. Inside, the room was exactly as I'd left it. I could see that the constables were more than a little surprised at the interior. I stood by as they gaped, until one looked up, saw me, and told me I could go.

The police contacted me again a few days later. They felt certain that our description of Montague matched that of an unidentified person who'd been found drowned in the harbour in March. I feigned surprise. They thanked me for coming forward as they were glad to have that mystery solved. They were now hoping for information about his next of kin.

♦

Two months later, I had my final call from the police. They'd located Montague's next of kin, a sister in England. She had only just reported him missing after not having received any correspondence for a couple of months. They asked me if I'd ever seen anyone else with Montague.

"No. Never. Why?"

"It seems that Mr Montague was taking care of his niece, Maria. She had a serious ailment. He was apparently working on a cure and she had been placed in his care. Her mother is desperate to hear from her."

"Oh . . . " I said, my voice weak. "That's terrible."

"Yes. It is. You definitely didn't come across Maria?"

"No. I wouldn't have," I stammered. "I mean, I only made deliveries and ran the odd errand."

"That's a shame. We have no other leads. Well, it seems we are finished here. Ring us straight away if you do think of anything."

"Yes. Of course."

As I'd hung up the phone, I'd felt bile rise in my throat. That batch of pork sausages had been a great favourite with the customers.

♦ ♦ ♦

THE STONE AND
THE SHEATH

KELLY HOOLIHAN

AT the edges of the city, as far away as was convenient for the humans that lived there, there was a garbage dump. Piles of rotting food, cast-off plastics, rusting scraps of unidentifiable metal, and the everyday commodities that humans had to have, but no longer wanted, were discarded in large piles. One shifted. The movement was not unusual: things decayed, gravity snagged at precarious hold-outs, and bouts of wind and rain moulded the mounds. But this was no simple decomposition. It wasn't just material garbage that was stored here. Ambition and energy and devotion were thrown away every day, attached to physical things. The garbage heaved—the movement akin to the rise and fall of breathing—and sighed, and then something in its heart began to crawl forth. The newborn reached the surface, turned its simulacrum face to the sun, and keened out a call that spoke of desperation and pain and need.

In the distant city, a klaxon sounded.

♦

LILITH MYERS WAS nearly at the blood clinic when three burly guards stepped out from the side streets and surrounded her. She drew up at the sudden triangle of men, not bothering to hide her irritation. She was on her way to the clinic to do her duty to the government—why were they hassling her?

All three of the men were scanning the area in broad, suspicious sweeps, their eyes only stopping occasionally on the woman they were caging. Lilith didn't bother stepping back from the too-close guard, glaring up into his shaded face. The guard finally looked at her, frowning back in a mixture of concern and bother.

"Miss Myers?" he asked, as if every guard in the city didn't know the face of their only Stone, didn't know her schedule of blood donation at the clinic.

"Yes?" She tried to make it clear that she had things to do, that this delay in her day was unacceptable. In reality, she had no pressing plans for the afternoon, after her excess blood was drained away, but they didn't need to know that.

The guard leaned in closer, and even though Lilith wanted to move away from him, she didn't. She wasn't going to give any ground. "There has been an incident at the edge of town and we just wanted to make sure that you were safe," he said in a low voice.

She raised an eyebrow and spoke at in a measured tone. "Must be something pretty important for all three of you to be here." She paused significantly. "Right here. On this side walk. In my way."

The guard ignored the jibes. Likely they bounced right off his government-thickened skin and brain. He looked her in the eye, his face grave, and Lilith realised that it might actually be a real problem.

"A Sheath manifested in the landfill on the edge of the city and it slipped through our defences. We're not sure where it is." As he spoke, it became clear that his eyes wanted to continue scanning the area for the threat, but he fought the urge and kept them affixed on Lilith's face.

Lilith, for her part, was conflicted over this news. "Has it grabbed anyone yet?"

He shook his head. "By this point, they would normally have taken any random person in their quest for blood—this one seems to be playing a longer game than most, though. It's why we were worried about your safety."

Lilith knew the basics of Sheath existence—they were golems of a sort, living beings of trash thrust up from any pile of human refuse that was large enough. They were constructs, but because they came from garbage laced with the energy left by the people who threw it away, they had some knowledge of what they were missing out on. They also seemed to instinctively know that if they got enough blood into their inorganic systems, they would become flesh. It was this desperate dream that fuelled them. And Lilith had a theory that was more speculation than fact—that the blood of a Stone was worth far more to a Sheath than the blood of some regular person.

A Stone's magic was fairly minor: they produced more blood than other people and they healed quickly. Still, the government found the excess blood to be useful, and so Stones had mandated trips to the blood bank. Lilith didn't mind—the idea that her extra blood was helping people in need was a good one. She wished guards weren't involved, but the fact that they were here now, with a Sheath on the loose, was useful. She still chafed at their presence.

"Wouldn't it make more sense for most of you to be out there, looking for the Sheath?" There was a bite of irritation in her voice that she didn't bother covering up. They still surrounded her like a meat cage, far too close, and she wanted out as quickly as possible. Even the smallest increase in her breathing room would improve her mood. At her suggestion, they frowned, almost in unison, the same distaste rearranging their blocky features. She decided to try again. "I'm on my way to the clinic anyway, and there are always guards posted there. It's just a few streets over." She spoke conspiratorially, "I imagine the accolades for capturing the Sheath are pretty high."

The three faces ringing her were shifting gradually; ambition, concern, and confusion all trying to bloom in one single garden. She gave a weak smile. "How much trouble can I possibly get into between here and there?"

Lilith had never witnessed the thought process so clearly on someone's face before. Two of the guards began to leave slowly, turning to look back over their shoulders at her, but the one she had been talking to was more reticent.

"This is done for your own safety, as you well know," he said firmly.

"I know," she replied. When she brushed past him, he didn't stop her. "I'll be sure to wait at the clinic until the Sheath is captured."

◆

LIFE WAS PAIN.

THE SHEATH COULD feel all of its parts pulling in a hundred different directions, each one wanting to return to the home that had discarded it. It had to focus—to fight—to keep itself together. On top of its never-ending urge to fracture, it sensed the heartbeats of the townspeople, a steady *thump* all around it; it could almost hear the rush of blood. Oh, how it wanted that life-giving fluid, how it needed that flowing vitality, but it denied itself. Blood would make it whole, would end the pain, but it knew there was singular blood somewhere amongst these walls, and it would not begin the trip towards humanity until it was within reach.

Hidden in its alley, the Sheath felt a new pulse, one that spoke of strength and power. The construct leaned unobtrusively around the corner. There was the being—the one it needed—walking quickly along the concrete path. The Sheath knew the word Stone without knowing which piece of itself supplied the term. Its claws bit into the red bricks of the building it hid behind, leaving scratch marks, and the serrated edges of its metal teeth caught against each other. Light, and purpose, glinted from the green glass shards of its eyes. It slid forward in a clatter of refuse, snatching the flowing blood.

◆

LILITH WOKE TO a pounding head and a dry mouth. Cold leeched into her bones, untempered by the rags awkwardly cushioning her body. Attempting to move, she realised she was bound, rough rope tied around her wrists and ankles. She tried to wriggle free, but the bonds had been secured too well. She didn't open her eyes. Thinking back, she tried to work out what had happened. Last she knew, she'd been on her way to the clinic, walking quickly to make up for lost time spent with the guards. She'd been certain there was no real danger from the Sheath. Clearly, she'd been wrong, she didn't need to see the golem work that out.

Once the pain in her skull had eased slightly, she opened her eyes to take in her surroundings at a sideways angle. The room looked like an old basement, long abandoned, stone walls covered with mildew. The light washing through the room was murky and weak, filtering through a small, dirt-encrusted glass window set up high on the stone wall. The poor light hid much of the decay, but Lilith could smell mouldering cloth and gently rotting wood. Maybe that belonged to the Sheath. Her rag mattress seemed to be in somewhat better shape than she'd initially hoped. The back of her neck and her head ached from where she'd been grabbed, but the pain was already diminishing; her body healing itself. Trying to sit upright, she bit back a groan of pain.

Just as she managed to wriggle into a seated position, a clattering sound, like garbage shifting in a pile, reached her. Lilith froze, gaze flicking around the stone walls, trying to find the source of the noise. She considered screaming, but decided against it; she didn't want the Sheath to silence her, potentially permanently. Opening her eyes wide, so that she could get as much light into them as possible, she saw a shadowed movement in the corner across from her. As if sensing her appraisal, the hunched form unfolded, nearly filling the space from floor to ceiling.

Lilith leaned forward. "I see you."

The Sheath paused. Tingles shot through Lilith as she realised she had some level of power, even tied up. She shifted again, pulling discreetly against her bonds. There was a clatter of metal and a single spark sheared off, illuminating a jagged mouth.

"You shouldn't pull on those—they won't give." The voice was rusty and low, as if it had been pulled from a dark abyss; it made her think of loss given sound. A chill rushed down her spine.

Lilith's hands dropped to her lap. She tried to find the Sheath's eyes in the gloom. "What do you want from me?" Although she already knew the answer, she figured it was better to keep the creature talking. A distraction couldn't hurt. At least, she hoped it wouldn't.

"You know what I want, Stone."

Her stomach churned.

"So, are you going to get it over with?" She preferred not to die in some dank basement, but right now, it didn't really matter what she wanted. She wasn't exactly confident in the city guards' ability to find her. She'd rather die with dignity then become some Sheath's toy.

Shrouded in darkness within the safety of its corner, the Sheath made a noise that might have been thoughtful, and then stepped forward. Moving into the dim light, Lilith finally saw its true form, and her blood ran cold. It was bulky, its shoulders asymmetrical and broad. Much of the creature was cloaked in tattered fabric, a makeshift robe, a useless disguise if ever there was one. It clanked and clattered as it stepped closer, and she had a sense that it was mostly metal and plastic, hard garbage. Dry too, from the sound of its grinding movements. Its hands were wrapped in scraps of cloth, but Lilith could see that the fingers were metal and uneven, and she was willing to bet that they were sharp. As far as she could tell, its teeth were crafted of the same material, even though it had a rotting handkerchief wrapped around its head. And finally, she could make out its eyes. They were green glass and surprisingly smooth, glittering with an inner light. They gleamed down at her from under the brim of a rough hat, shockingly beautiful.

"I'm not going to kill you, Stone."

"No?" She pressed her back to the cold stone wall. She did not believe the Sheath at all.

It shook its cumbersome head. "No. A single bloodletting will not raise me to human." It stepped forward and leaned over her. "We will be together for a while, you and me."

♦

THE STONE'S BLOOD sang as it coursed through her veins, so close the Sheath had to fight to not fall upon her. The golem had thought it understood control when it had not preyed upon the townspeople, but this pull was so much worse. Resisting the urge, the Sheath simply stepped forward instead.

The Stone didn't flinch at its approach, and the Sheath admired her resolve. It took hold of her bound hands with care and watched as her fists clasped once before relaxing.

It was time.

The Sheath leaned forward and cut the skin of her forearm with one sharp, metal claw before bringing its mouth down. The Stone jerked in protest, but didn't make a sound. The Sheath had no human tongue, rather a piece of old leather, which pressed against the wound, lapping at the blood. As the powerful liquid filled the Sheath's mouth, it could feel the beginnings of change. The journey from refuse to refuser had begun.

It was careful not to take too much—it somehow knew about the Stone's healing ability, but it had no desire to push the woman's limits. The Stone was staring, steady and unblinking. Thoughtful almost. "Do you want me to let you know when my blood level is back up?" Her voice didn't tremble in the slightest. Were all Stones like this? So . . . accepting?

"What?" If it could blink in surprise, it would have.

"No one knows my blood better than me. I know when I'm full up and I can tell you about it."

"Why would you willingly help me?" The Sheath was curious. It knew it was hunted by other humans, had known its life was limited unless it could become flesh and bone. The Stone tilted her head and looked at it, and for a moment it felt oddly exposed.

"If I help, maybe you'll let me survive this." She moved her hands awkwardly. "I'd rather keep living, to be honest." She looked into its glass eyes. "Do you think that can be arranged?"

It turned away, dipping back into the shadows of the abandoned basement. "We shall see."

◆

WHILE BEING CUT open by metal claws and licked by leather was an unorthodox method, Lilith was relieved to have been drained of her excess blood. Her weekly trips to the clinic were internal battles—on one hand, she needed an outlet for her surplus blood, yet she had no love for the controlling atmosphere of the clinic. But she was happy to help people, even though she'd often wished that there was some alternate way to disperse her blood.

While her healing body slumped with relief, she knew she had to focus on escape. At the moment, the best way to accomplish that seemed to involve humouring the Sheath. She briefly wondered at the future possibility of two humans walking out of this basement together, but it seemed almost impossible. She'd never heard of a Stone surviving an encounter with a Sheath.

She could still see the Sheath's outline in the shadows. "Bringing me food would be helpful," she said, trying to sound neutral. A shiver passed over the creature, its garbage body rattling with the movement.

"Food?" The Sheath's voice was quietly bemused.

"Yes, food. Some juice or water would also be good." She thought a moment longer, tallying up what might be available in her immediate vicinity. "We'll need stuff for cleaning up too, since we're going to be together for a while. And maybe something else for restraints? This rope isn't great."

The Sheath cast a glittering glance. "We?"

Lilith shrugged as best she could. Her eyes were drawn to the shards of green glass that shone out of the darkness. "Do you have a name?"

The Sheath drew back slightly, rustling in the dark. "A name?"

Lilith was silent, thinking of something to call the creature. It didn't take long; there was only one thing about the creature that didn't remind her of rot or death. "I'm going to call you Glass." For a moment, Lilith though the Sheath might protest, but it shuddered again and bobbed lightly.

"Whatever you want, Stone."

"Lilith."

Glass paused, then dissolved into the shadows. "Whatever you want, Lilith."

◆

GLASS HAD A name now, though it wasn't sure how it felt about it. The Sheath only knew the basics of its appearance; metal and plastic, a leather tongue, rag coverings, glass eyes. Were its lenses really so special as to warrant naming? The Sheath considered stealing a mirror to verify its musings, but only for a moment. It was not going to endanger itself for vanity. Glass paused in an alley, wondering if gaining human conceit was a sign of true change.

Physical alterations had already begun to manifest across its metal frame, small but growing. Through twinges of burgeoning sensation, it knew the night was slightly chill. On its torso, a small patch of pale flesh let Glass know what fabric felt like. These physical feelings were all strange and uncomfortable, but this was the path Glass had chosen: it was the only option for a future. Glass ducked into a back alley and began its hunt for the Stone's supplies.

◆

IT WAS THE eighth time that Lilith awoke in the basement, but she was still briefly confused by her surroundings. Glass had recently taken its third feeding, which didn't help her muddled state— Lilith's blood level wasn't much lower than a non-Stone's, but it left her sleepy and slightly weak. The fact that her surroundings kept altering subtly didn't help, either. Glass had accommodated every one of Lilith's small requests. She was no longer bound by rope, instead she was chained to a timber post with shackles that the Sheath must have stolen from a guard post. They'd been padded with the soft cloth of someone's stolen laundry. She had a pillow, new bedding, and even a sheet that acted as a curtain, which could be drawn closed when she wanted.

She heard the rumble and creak of Glass' return and she considered rolling over and going back to sleep, but the Sheath called her name softly. No matter how quiet it was, she could always hear it clear as a bell.

"Lilith, are you awake?" Glass murmured again and she muttered an affirmative, twisting halfway out of the sheets. It seemed that Glass could hear her as well as she heard it, because it moved to her bedside, pulling the curtain aside. "I have fruit, Lilith."

Lilith sat up at once, fatigue forgotten. The sugar would help, of course, but she hadn't had anything quite so fresh since being captured. Getting the good stuff entailed more risk. It was an orange and the tangy scent hit her, making her mouth water. "Was it too much trouble?" she asked, stumbling slightly over her words in her eagerness.

Glass shook its head. "I got lucky. There's a whole bag of them actually, and the theft shouldn't point back to us—Sheaths don't need food."

Lilith considered this. "But do you? Need to eat now?"

Glass shifted uncomfortably and tried to cover it up by lowering itself to her bedding. "I'll worry about that." Then it began to peel the orange, Lilith watching as the sharp fingers that cut into her flesh every few days carefully removed the peel in a single coil. The citrus smell was overwhelming, and when Glass placed the first segment in her hands, she devoured it quickly. Glass made a rough grinding noise, and it took a moment for Lilith to realise it was a chuckle. She pulled back to look at it, gaping.

"What?" it asked, holding up another slice of orange. "I don't intend to feed you by hand, Stone."

"You laughed!" Lilith's tone was a mix of accusation and delight. Part of her was surprised at the happiness, but she'd grown . . . closer to Glass in the last week. She hadn't intended to, but it was too late now. There was something inherently sympathetic about Sheaths, and Glass had been nothing if not kind, despite holding her captive. "Have you *ever* laughed?"

Glass tilted its head in thought. "I have never found anything funny before." The Sheath gently handed over the rest of the orange and Lilith tore it apart, the juice running down her wrists and chin. Trickles ran over the healed cuts Glass had made for sustenance. Even the wound from the day before was only a faint pink line. Glass brought her more food and drink, these items less exciting, and moved to return to its dark corner.

"Wait!" she said, and Glass froze with a slight shudder. "Sit down for a second and tell me how you're doing." She surprised herself with that question.

Glass hesitated, then sat almost delicately back by her bed. "What do you want to know?"

Lilith bit into some dry bread and gestured, which only confused the Sheath. "Just . . . how are you doing? What's the change like?"

Glass shifted, appearing to think deeply. Lilith heard the rattle of its metal parts and the rustle of some unseen paper. "It is . . . unsettling. To be two things at once is a strange state." It paused. "I can't really describe it. Is being human strange to you?"

Lilith considered. "I suppose not. But I'm not exactly a typical human." She took another bite of bread. "Or maybe it's all completely strange and we're just strange together. I'll be sure to ask you when you're human."

Glass gave another little chuckle and moved to go. Lilith let it.

◆

IT WAS AFTER the fifth feeding that Glass realised it liked the sound of Lilith's voice. This was surprising, because it hadn't *liked* anything before. The feeling was not entirely pleasant. As the days passed, the feeling went beyond liking her voice—it *liked* Lilith, and that came with extra drives. Glass suddenly wanted her to like *it*, for her life to go well. For her to know happiness, whatever that emotion entailed. Somehow, it had changed its plans from simply wanting a human life, to ensuring she kept hers as well. So Glass decided that Lilith would live, and if that brought retribution down on its head, then so be it. Glass' self-preservation dimmed whenever she spoke.

That scared Glass.

The Sheath vowed to keep its distance from her, to protect itself, but when she requested its company, Glass was unable to ignore her. It was like trying to ignore a part of itself. It made Glass want to push harder, go faster, finish the change, quickly, but that would kill Lilith. So Glass hung back as best it could, which was not much at all, and hoped that by the time it was human, its fear and affection would have passed, or at the very least, begun to make sense.

♦

It HAD BEEN two and a half weeks since Lilith entered the basement, and the ninth feeding had just ended abruptly. For the first time post blood-letting, Lilith was still at higher blood levels than non-Stone humans. Glass had nearly thrown itself away from her, and was now crouching on the basement floor. As Lilith watched, a heave passed through the Sheath, something that seemed like a prelude to vomiting. She hadn't thought that Glass was far enough along in the process to react so . . . humanly. "Are you all right?"

Glass waved a hand dismissively, but didn't rise from its crouch. "Fine, I'm fine." Its voice was shakier than usual, and sounded less like loss. Lilith tried to step to its side, but the Sheath was out of range of her chain. The basement was silent except for the rattle of her shackles and its heavy shudders.

In the silence, Lilith felt something new; a building up of some non-physical pressure along her spine. It felt like the coursing of her own blood, but it seemed to be coming from *outside* of her body. Eyes wide, she realised she was feeling *Glass'* blood flow.

The Sheath was still huddled on the floor, so Lilith closed her eyes and focused. She could feel the platelets papering over the cut Glass had made on her left arm. As she breathed, she sensed the blood in her lungs taking in oxygen, felt it travel through arteries, her steady heartbeat running it all. She could also feel her blood coursing through a half-formed circulatory system, one that was still half-garbage. She felt every patch of flesh Glass had, every developing organ—they were all serviced by blood that was still hers. She felt the tongue that had developed almost as if it were in her own mouth, knew that Glass was repulsed by the taste of blood, and that its still-growing stomach rebelled against the liquid. She suddenly knew what it meant to be a Sheath, at least physically. Blood wove its way around trash that strained against its binding, garbage that only wanted to return to the humans who had cast it aside.

Lilith opened her eyes to see Glass doing no better than before. She recalled its meek acquiescence to her requests and decided to try something. "Glass, are you hungry?"

The Sheath managed to sit up some and shook its head. "I don't know, since I've never been hungry before. I don't think so, but I don't know." It sounded miserable and was slowly collapsing again even as it spoke.

"Eat something." Lilith kept her voice light but firm—it was the most direct order that she had given the Sheath.

"What?" Glass asked, but it shuddered as it spoke and clutched at its belly. Lilith noticed that two of the fingers on its left hand were flesh now, not shards of metal.

"Eat," she said again, and Glass crawled hesitantly towards the food store they had in the basement. "Try bread to start—it's bland and goes down easy."

A metal hand curled around a roll, slicing it into smaller pieces. It brought one of them to its mouth and carefully bit down. Glass' back was to Lilith, but she heard the noise it made as it tasted its first mouthful of food. It was something of a gasp and a cry, soft surprise and amazement all at once, and Glass' shoulders shook as it reached quickly for more. "Slow down!" Lilith called. Glass stilled instantly and she felt terrible, as if she had reprimanded an overenthusiastic child. "I don't want you to choke," she said, softer.

Glass' movements began again, but cautiously. It ate silently for a few minutes and Lilith felt the improvement in the Sheath as nutrients and energy were introduced to the semi-biological system. "Try water, too," she offered and it did, with greedy intensity. She let it go, let it feed itself on something other than her blood, and considered her options. She wondered if Glass would undo her shackles if she asked it to.

Freedom would be within easy reach.

But the victory felt hollow. Frowning, she realised that escape was not what she wanted—she couldn't leave Glass in this in-between state. But she had to know.

"Glass."

The Sheath turned from the food, green glass eyes gleaming in the dark. Now or never. "Come undo these shackles. Please."

Glass retook its feet, swaying slightly. "Why would I do that?" The Sheath's voice wasn't angry, just . . . tired. Lilith could see and feel the slight tremors that ran through the creature's body.

"I've been here for over half a month and have made no efforts to escape. I want to help you. If you undo my shackles, I promise to stay with you through this whole process. I *promise*." Lilith meant every word. But she had to know she was trusted in return.

Glass didn't hesitate. It stepped quickly to her side, pulling a key from its makeshift robe. Moments later, the shackles fell away with a clatter and Lilith rubbed gently at her wrists. They were unmarred, thanks to her Stone-abilities, but she needed to feel that it was real; that Glass trusted her enough to set her free. She doubted that the Sheath understood the potency of its gesture.

She gently probed at the Sheath's physical state, and decided on one more course of action. "Are you tired?"

Glass half-shook its head. "No, I don't—"

"You should at least lie down," she interrupted. Glass seemed like it might rebel for the first time, but then it lowered itself to the floor. Lilith gathered the extra bedding around it and gently tucked a blanket over the prone form. Glass grumbled, but didn't fight her. "Just relax," she said.

Glass had started breathing recently, though Lilith could still hear the rustle of paper in its chest cavity, and its breath slowly transitioned into the quiet measure of sleep. Lilith watched the sleeping Sheath and wondered what their next step was.

◆

GLASS DREAMED.

It didn't know how it understood what dreaming was, but it accepted this as fact. In its dream, it was human, fully human, and was walking amongst the others who lived in this town. No one regarded it with suspicion or fear or disgust—no one regarded it at all. It felt free; free of the pull from the myriad pieces of garbage that wanted to return home, free from the fear of being destroyed.

But most of all, it was free of pain.

In the midst of all this, Glass realised that there was a presence beside it, a force within it, and before the Sheath even turned, it knew it belonged to the Stone. Lilith walked at its side or, more accurately, Glass walked at hers. It could feel her hold on it, like a collar around Glass' neck, but the Sheath welcomed the weight.

◆

IT WAS TIME for the twelfth feeding. Past time actually, and Lilith was growing edgy with the excess blood in her system. Glass had spent most of the day avoiding her. Now it had settled down in its corner, hunched up and oblivious.

LILITH WAS DONE waiting. "Glass."

Glass huffed out a noise of acknowledgement.

"Glass, are you ready for the blood?"

The Sheath shook its head before it curled up tighter. Before Lilith could ask again, Glass began to cough. It still didn't have a complete set of lungs and the rustle of agitated paper filled the small space. Concern gripped Lilith. "Are you sick? Can Sheaths get sick?" She stood and strode briskly to its corner, even as Glass tried to wave her away with a feeble, half-human hand. There was a papery crunch under her foot. Looking down, she realised that the Sheath's violent coughing was causing it to shed some of the rubbish that filled its chest. Maybe it was the sign of lungs growing in.

Lilith went to take another step, but she paused, seeing the large city emblem on the crumpled letterhead under her foot. Leaning down, she realised that the trodden paper was rubbish from the blood clinic. Squatting down so that she could read the text, she froze. Her eyes swept the lines of fading print again, then a third time. The words finally began to sink in. Her bones felt cold. "Glass."

The Sheath must have sensed the change in her mood, but didn't respond. "Glass, it's time for you to feed."

Glass shook its head more vigorously. "I don't want to. It hurts."

Lilith swooped down to hiss in its new ear. She had to shock it into action. She couldn't let it give up now, not when they'd come so far. "What hurts? Turning from a Sheath to human? Why *wouldn't* it hurt?"

Glass gave a slight shake of its head.

"Do you want to live in this twilight, with the pain of being a Sheath and the pain of being a human?" Another shake. "Then it's time for you to take this blood."

Finally, Glass turned to look at her and Lilith saw that one of its striking glass eyes was gone, replaced by a human eye. But it was equally lovely, with the iris the same luminous green. She could see the worry and hesitation there, but she couldn't be gentle. Not with the letter she had just read.

"I've been helping you for over a month—it's time for you to help me a bit. I said I would stay with you and I will, but I need you for something. I need you to be strong." The hesitation faded and Lilith could see that she would get whatever assistance she asked for. She held out her forearm. "Drink."

Glass' brow furrowed, but it leaned over her wrist and bit with its mix of metal shards and human teeth. The skin broke easily, the pain sharp, and blood flooded the Sheath's mouth. It began to shiver, to buck, but Lilith kept up a litany of encouragement and comfort, and once she figured Glass had taken enough, she pulled away. Glass ran a wrist across its face to clean it as best it could. Its eye was glazed, distant, but it regained its focus quickly.

Lilith picked up the paper from the floor and held it where Glass could see it. "I need to see if there are more of these in your chest."

Glass' face contorted, but it pulled its robe open, revealing a mish-mash of plastic, aged wood, metal, and flesh. She could see the beginnings of a human ribcage, but within the cavity was a great explosion of paper with wet, pink flesh clinging to its edges.

"Will it hurt if I take some of them out?"

"I don't think so." Glass was craning its neck in an effort to see inside itself. "I'll let you know if it does."

Lilith reached in carefully and plucked out the pages. Maybe it would make Glass' transformation quicker, without all that paper in the way. The documents fluttered underneath her hands, and she got a peek at the heart that was blooming within the Sheath. Blood red and glass green, it beat in time with hers. Lilith looked away quickly, offering Glass privacy. The Sheath closed its robe and leaned over to look at the papers. "What do they say?"

Lilith spread them out on the floor, keeling on the ground before them. Some pieces were wet with borrowed blood and organ tissue, others dried and ripped. She read them twice before sitting back on her heels. She'd always been told that her blood was used to help the people who lived in her city; it went to the sick and the old and those unlucky enough to need blood transfusions. But these letters were largely shipment invoices, showing that the bulk of her blood was sent to a distant capital, so that it could be pumped into the veins of government officials. Somehow, old men were extending their lives and their rule through transfusing the blood of Stones from all over the land. Only a fraction went back to the common people, to the ill and the needy. One document had a waiting list of those who needed her blood, with a scant handful marked as having been treated with the miniscule amount of her blood that her city actually received. Anger boiled in her veins.

"I didn't give it to them. I gave it to the world. Not them." Lilith was shaking with rage. Fumbling through the pages, she saw another report, which had been stuck to the back of a damp sheet. This one, she read with growing horror, listed the number of Sheaths that had been destroyed the year before. She had never heard about any of these incidents and she realised it was because these Sheaths had never done anything to become noticed. She couldn't look at Glass; it would see the truth about all those newborn lives lost.

Glass grasped her by the shoulders, forced her to look it in the eye. "What do you want my help with?"

Lilith clenched her teeth and fists, trying to ignore the roar of blood in her ears. "To make a statement."

◆

DAWN WAS BREAKING and a klaxon sounded in the heart of the city. Lilith and Glass heard it loud and clear, even on the edge of town. A plume of smoke caught the sunlight and Lilith smiled grimly. Overnight, they'd snuck into the clinic and stolen all of the stored blood, leaving it out in the open in a nearby square. Then they'd set the clinic on fire. Lilith had cut her palm, using the crimson liquid to inscribe 'Blood for the People' onto the pale stone wall of the building. Glass had worked on the clinic's sign, cutting rough grooves into it with its remaining metal fingers. It carved what Lilith had dictated: 'Sheaths are Alive'. The only thing they had saved from the blaze was the shipping records, which were now tucked safely underneath her arm.

Glass stood beside her, looming over her, surveying their work. It looked at her out of the corner of its eye. "What do you want to do next?"

Lilith patted the folder under her arm. "There are some addresses in here that I would like to look into. What are your plans, Glass?" She was surprised at how light her voice was, how much better she felt.

Glass shrugged, casually. When had it learnt to be casual? "I think I go where you go."

Lilith looked up, eyebrow raised. "You think?"

Glass laughed, half scraping metal and half human flesh. "All right, how about this: I know."

Lilith nodded, satisfied, and the two of them turned their backs on the city of their birth. The rest of the world was waiting.

◆ ◆ ◆

LADY KILLER

ANTHONY PANEGYRES

" . . . we do not feel horror because we are haunted by a sphinx,
we dream a sphinx to explain the horror that we feel."
JORGE LUIS BORGES—RAGNAROK

THE CHILD

THE first time it happened I was eight years old and my hometown, Halls Head, was in its embryonic stage. Only eight houses lined either side of my lazy street and behind us was bush for miles around: banksias and scrub plants, punctuated by a shorter type of eucalypt, which I called brumby gums, after the horses in *The Man from Snowy River.*

On autumnal Sunday dawns, where I'd breathe visible puffs of air and pretend I was a fire-dragon, my father and I would go bush walking. I had spidery legs and arms, blond waves of hair, and a closed smile, which was apparently endearing to all. We'd find ourselves deep in the bush, but always maintained our sense of direction. It was something visceral, even when all we could see were stunted trees, shrubs and russet hues. We'd sneak up on mobs of boomers, who'd eventually spook and bound away. When the roos lost us, I'd peer through the dry scrub for the little people. I'd just read *The Hobbit,* but my eyes were not sharp enough to detect any Shire folk.

One Sunday, I discovered two orchids: rare delicate touches of colour amongst the sandy browns and motley greens of the bush. The first, a spider orchid, had a spindly flower, pink and white, favoured by most. But my second find was a cowslip. Small but rounder and more symmetrical, the same colour as my pet canary, Courage. It was the perfect flower. I uprooted it, scooping my cupped hands underneath to keep a pile of dirt, so the flower felt comfortable. I planted it in a little red clay pot and watered it for three days running.

It wilted.

♦

IT WAS A roasting November day and school lunchtime. Our teacher, Miss Lane, sat cross-legged on an outside bench observing me and two girls. I lifted their skirts up to peep underneath. They giggled, raised their skirts higher and shoved their frilly-knickered bottoms into my face. It was taboo, but Miss Lane was smiling and so were we. Lisa and Natasha both invited me to their birthday parties before the siren sounded.

I didn't return to the sweltering classroom—they weren't air-conditioned back then. Miss Lane went inside and I snuck away around the corner and strode across the oval towards the bush that enveloped the school.

I remember it still. Cicadas, crickets and grasshoppers trilled like children's popping toys. The land pulsated too, in a heavy heat-laden orgasm. I entered the bush, crunching dry thorny banksia foliage as I walked. Skinks scampered away before me, and there were the occasional scurrying sounds of other small animals in the undergrowth. The more I walked, the more I perspired. I grabbed a brumby gum leaf, crinkled it in my hand, and held it under my nose. The clean fragrance made me feel cooler. In the air, there was little visible movement besides sporadic wrens and scrub birds fluttering through the trees. But on the earth in the distance, I saw a whisper of yellow.

Cowslip.

I strode forward, despite my now clinging polo-shirt. There was another splash of yellow ahead—I'd never seen more than a single flower before. I began to jog to discover another at the foot of a blackboy.

A trail.

An orchid every dozen steps or so. I followed the yellow deep into the wild, deeper than I'd ever been.

The sky began to dim as I arrived at the path's end, exhausted. A glade opened up before me: a floor of flowers. All cowslips, I could discern them even in the now wan light. But something large stood in the centre; too still to be a roo. The only audible sound was my tread, which although gentle, regrettably hurt the orchids underfoot. The object ahead was substantial. A monument? I wondered whether the bush held such hidden riches. I advanced, noticing four great feline legs with paws shaded by two giant wings like those of the sea eagles that haunted the Peel Inlet, and a tail like that of a snake. I drew closer: fur, feathers, scales, and a head. A lady's head. Her eyes were closed. If I had been older, I would have found her seductive, but her lips were too thick, her nose too developed, her body too strong, and she possessed a round pair of breasts, which, for me at the time, were just fat, ugly, useless appendages.

Overhead, the first stars glittered. I reached out to stroke her fur, it felt like the hide of a roo I'd patted at a deer park, only much colder. Chilly fur on a baking day was a queer sensation—maybe that should have been warning enough to stay away. But I was eight and didn't understand heat conventions; all I knew was that she was cool and I was hot. I traced my fingers through the coat for respite.

Nothing happened at first. I didn't notice the pelt warm, but after a while, it felt hotter and obscurely rhythmic. That was the last I could remember as I fell asleep. The last I could recall before my nightmare began.

I awoke feeling a weight on my chest. My eyes opened and I found myself pinned by a paw, breasts dangling above my head. The pitiless face that eyed me felt ancient, yet I couldn't distinguish any age lines.

What have the Muses brought me to devour? Her accented voice was breathy, devoid of emotion. Although I didn't grasp every word, I sensed their meaning echoing through my mind.

"Why eat me?" Even then I was quick-thinking; the extraordinary tends not to astound some children, rather it draws them closer.

The Muses have delivered no riddle. She bent down and licked my face, like I'd seen lions lick their kill on documentaries. *So you must be a treat, a little taster.* Her sapphire tail glinted as it flicked contentedly.

I wriggled beneath her paw. She smiled, her violet eyes excited. It was the first sign of emotion I'd seen and it felt predatory. Her leg remained poised on top of me as I attempted anything and everything to free myself—I punched, scratched, even pinched. I sensed her disappointment as she removed her paw. I scrambled up and away, racing towards the glade's boundary. I felt a gush of wind behind me and then above. Before I reached the edge of the glade, she landed before me, wings flailing.

"There are bigger meals than me." I pointed towards school, which must have closed hours ago. I felt rotten—I was no dobber.

The beast-lady looked wistfully out from the glade's border. Like a dog motioning to open a door, she lifted a paw towards the direction of the school. I realised then that the creature couldn't move beyond the glade. Perhaps it guarded something, or had some hex on it?

A blood trade, two lives for yours.

A claw pricked my finger and her tongue lapped the droplet that bloomed there. My thoughts leapt—or rather dived—into depths unknown to a child of eight. Images were in my mind, and hers, too. *A couple of frilly-knickered girls.*

The beast-lady licked my face once more as she released me. *This is no trade. Your blood reveals your very nature, your fated sins, child. Your victims of betrayal will taste sweet. Your appetite will feed me whenever we both hunger.*

I fled through the bush, this time not stopping to appreciate the flowers. By the time I arrived home, I was faint. Mum swallowed me in her embrace and made me drink what seemed like litres of water. Dad called the police to say I'd returned, and after I'd eaten, he grounded me. "And from now on you're being picked up from school." Dad was furious—it was only a ten-minute walk, and yet I'd been gone hours.

I never mentioned my encounter with the beast-lady. By the next day, I wasn't convinced it had actually happened. I knew I had an active imagination.

The day after, the two girls, Lisa and Natasha, went missing. They disappeared at recess and their remains were found two days later. Bloody trails were discovered on leaves and bark, but there was no mention of cowslips or a glade. There were clues though, traces of me were found near the scene. I didn't know then that you left hints of your clothing as you moved, or hairs and prints in the bush.

Bloody clothes, strewn and torn apart—but not by human hands—meant I wasn't suspected. The evidence led to a large feline; fabric was flown overseas where forensic scientists endorsed the theory. There was rumour of a cat, the size of a mountain lion, sighted in Nannup, but that town was a three-hour drive away. Dogs, an Aboriginal tracker, volunteers and helicopters searched, but the largest animal anyone saw was a grandpa boomer.

THE ADOLESCENT

THE TOWN CHANGED. Fields, some fallow, others not, replaced my beloved bush. I was older by then, thirteen. Housing estates now bordered the school where the two girls went missing. I avoided yellow—watching Australia compete at almost anything, the Olympics, even one-day cricket, made me nauseous.

There were fewer roos to see, but at least nature of some sort was still available. Every Saturday, Dad and I would take the dinghy deep into the Peel Inlet. We'd wade out, and push the boat off and ride slowly in the still dawn water. My eyes were everywhere: they searched the small islets, where pelicans hooted; they scanned the surface for dolphins and the occasional seal; they inspected the shoreline for all manner of birds. As we travelled, I often dangled an arm over to enjoy the water splashing up and over my body.

After we anchored, my father would cast a line for fish or nets for crabs. I didn't like doing either and stole the least tasty fish in the catch—usually bony trumpeters—and fed them to the dolphins so I could stroke them as they swam by our boat. Often, these were simply polite-hellos; they would release the fish after receiving them.

Cormorants dove and I'd count the seconds before they resurfaced with a contented bob of the head. Great sea eagles with ivory chests perched regally on the long dead trees on the shores of river mouths. I knew all the birds: the terns and the gulls; the herons, the ibises and the egrets.

The return trip was similar. Our feet submerged into the mud as we pulled the boat to shore; my eyes captivated by the mudskippers hopping about.

I loved observing my father clean and gut the fish with that razor-sharp blade of his. Blood and innards spilled out in delicious cherry and cerise. I'd scoop up the driblets and feed them to the pelicans by hand as they waddled over.

I liked to read; in fact, I discovered the beast-lady during reading time in the library, in a book called *Bestiary*, the letters gold on the brown hardback. Opening it up, I felt like Ali Baba unearthing an unimaginable jewel. I brushed through the pages, reading wherever the pictures enthralled me. I came upon centaurs, basilisks, minotaurs and trolls, ogres, satyrs, dragons, and griffons. But my hands tightened on seeing the sphinx. I whacked the book down onto my lap, shut my eyes and then opened them with a resolve to read on. I didn't receive a riddle like Oedipus. Or did I? I began to wonder, replaying the nightmare through my mind. Apparently, sphinxes guarded things, Oedipus' foe a gate. Mine a glade? They did devour humans. That was evident in all the tales.

By sixteen, I'd wiped the event from my mind. It remained asleep, locked in some tenement cell of my consciousness. All the surface recalled was to avoid Greek myths and that I reviled yellow, even canaries. The rest of my time was consumed by Aussie Rules. I remained glued to every match—unless Hawthorn or the Eagles competed. I played a pretty mean game too—burying into packs and winning the hardball with the tenacity of a tiger-quoll.

Later that year, I discovered my manhood in the form of Lorenza Torre. She was tasty. Honey-coloured skin, the type you could lick all night, and buoyant caramel tresses. Lorenza was on exchange from Italy, and a synchronised swimmer. I learnt that synchronised swimmers had bodies I'd suicide for. Lorenza's accent awakened a xenophilic appetite that's never left me. She sat behind me in history, mincing her words in a fashion I found endearing. We'd bonded through our comparison of Mr Durkin's moustache to Stalin's.

I got Lorenza's number from her friend at recess in the canteen line and phoned that same afternoon. We chatted (I can't remember about what) for an hour and 'Ls' were crammed all over the post-it paper near the phone before I eventually spat it out: "Want to hang out some time?"

"Sure," she replied.

At school, I only saw her in history class and my voice would quaver. At best, all I could conjure was a frail, 'Hi'. But she invited me over one night when her host family was out for dinner. Outside, the air was moist and had that fresh smell of undergrowth, while inside her room—pink doona and all—it smelled of carpet, and teddy bears and chick perfume. Lorenza played me the latest Italian CDs. I liked bits and pieces of the corny pop, but pretended to enjoy every song. We tried to dance, me with my pendulum moves, slipping my hands around her waist. She copied me, and then our hands strayed. Her mouth opened for my first kiss and I almost gagged as her tongue entered. But soon after, we were lip and tongue wrestling. I flipped back the quilt and we snuck under it, touching each other underneath our clothes, fingers trickling over each other's skin. I nibbled on her lips. I nibbled on her breasts. Our lips were sore by the time I had to go, as were her nipples. By the front door I grabbed her hair and pashed her Hollywood style in the cool evening air, before leaving for my walk home in the dark.

My eyes gradually adjusted to the leering shadows. A new footy, a Burley, lay right there in the middle of the street. It began to roll away from me on a tangent. I chased, but whenever I closed in, it sped off again, sometimes tumbling, sometimes bouncing erratically, sometimes skipping just beyond my reach. I pursued it down along the asphalt and then off the street as it took a turn and bounced over a wire fence. I scrambled over. It travelled right through a copse of banksias and brumby gums, snapping twigs in its path, and onto the fields of the golf course. It avoided the sand bunkers, cruised around the ponds until it raced away on the green. My eyes hunted solely for the ball on the long, dark fairway. I should have looked up. I should have been alarmed by the peculiarity. The footy hurtled into something immense in the middle of a rounded green.

I should have realised.

I should have run.

But then her paws held me close to her breasts like I was her cherished infant.

Thank the Muses. My feeder, I've been so hungry of late. She whipped her scaled tail and it stung my earlobe, puncturing it. Blood oozed out. Her tongue left an affectionate trail of saliva over my right ear. *Your blood tastes of future sin.*

I didn't think of escape, instead I thought of Lorenza.

What was I to do? She came to mind.

Stay for a while, my feeder.

I found myself caressing her fur, touching her breasts like I'd touched Lorenza's, and stroking her hair. I slept there in the park, the sphinx my blanket.

◆

I AWOKE AT home not knowing how I got there. I thought of the sphinx flying me, but she seemed to be guarding the green with the same sentinel manner she had the glade, years before.

Mum knocked and entered, her face in its usual morning-puffy state. I was still clothed under the sheets, eyes matted with sleep. The cops had arrived. She was sure it must be some mistake, but they intended to escort me to the station.

They let me go, even though evidence of me—traces of clothes, and hairs—were found thickly laden at the scene, like some overpowering *parfum*, along with bloody shreds of Lorenza's clothing.

They couldn't pin her disappearance on me, but one tubby hirsute man at the station tried. Drawing his jowls near my face, breath stinking of raw chicken, he spouted all the clichés. "I'm watching you, boy. Don't think you'll get away with this shit. It's only a matter of time."

Thankfully, there was a patch of feline hair among the *panthera*-sized prints.

THE ADULT

I STUDIED ZOOLOGY at the University of Western Australia. Although I had not abandoned my love of nature, I never watched footy again and took to reading *The Guardian*—no Aussie Rules news in those pages. I still had a taste for women and 'toured' Greece and Italy, Malta and Egypt, Germany, Hong Kong, Israel, and Serbia. In truth, I had a craving for something exotic and toffee-coloured, like a North Indian or Latin American. I fucked all over the place: in fire escapes, empty construction sites, library shelves in shadowy hours, toilets, lecture theatres and tutorial rooms, beaches, muddy river banks and parks. I lived up to my new nickname, Lady Killer. Maybe it was in my nature, in my fated blood?

Like so many mammalogists, I headed for the vast continent of Africa as soon as I could. My passions roamed from the spotted hyena, to the handsome bongo, to the pangolin: an armoured animal which ripped open ant and termite mounds, it's hunched bipedal walk more at home in the realms of *The Dark Crystal* than Earth.

I was working with a filmmaker on a documentary concerning my current favourite, the Cape buffalo. We had three jeeps camped around a muddy waterhole, focusing on an aggressive group of old bulls that had retired from the herd. It was the arid season and everything was the colour of dry wheat, aside from the sunken greys around the water's periphery, where I dared not step. One of the photographers had already been sucked into the quagmire up to his knees, before being hauled out.

Shaparna was in the jeep with me, a passionate and sporty North Indian, with a studded nose, flawless cappuccino skin and those long-lashed sub-continent eyes that were both bright and sad. At times they'd widen cheekily and invitingly. She crossed her legs and laid her dirt-caked boots on the dashboard. Something about the casualness of it all made me hunger to reach out a hand and lay it on her khaki working trousers.

But I had a loyal fiancée, Rosa, back in South Africa. She'd read deep into the dead of night, and always had some interest; presently, it was jazz. Breakfasts of late were accompanied by the rhythms of Ella Fitzgerald and Billie Holiday. It really fired me up. I told Rosa everything.

Well, almost everything.

I never spoke of the sphinx or the blood that bound us.

Three lionesses lapped up the water nearby; fierce muscles flexing beneath almost diaphanous coats. The cameramen readied for the bulls' arrival. Old bachelor bulls frequently had a short fuse and enjoyed tormenting their potential predators. These were no exception. They trotted haughtily, flaunting bustling chests while headed straight for the lionesses, who hissed and growled, flashing their canines in retreat. One lioness sank into the mire. Sharpana's long fingers reached for my hand excitedly. A bull, Old Heracles, bore down on the lion and savaged it with a horn, lifting it out of the sludge with a toss of its head. The wounded lioness snarled as it landed in the mud, rolling away before gingerly clambering off after her pride.

When it was over, Sharpana still clenched my hand.

Her lips that night were as soft as I'd dreamt, and her mouth tasted of cinnamon.

♦

IT WASN'T THE allure of an orchid or a travelling ball, but an okapi that led me astray that year. I was on the plains of the Serengeti collecting dung samples from a spotted hyena clan. As for my debauchery, I'd broken up with Rosa and moved in with Sharpana, who I married. But after a while, too much of anything—even cinnamon—becomes tasteless and dull.

I was depositing the scatological samples into my jeep when I saw him. It was odd, you don't find okapi on the plains and even in the jungle they're such a retiring type. I drew my binoculars. He was striking, flanks painted entirely white, continuing down his legs in ivory stripes, as if a painter had taken to him with a thick brush. The rest of his body was a dark iron-brown, two small giraffe-like knob-horns protruded from his head.

This time, I couldn't ignore the ambiguity. The okapi was as enticing as an exorbitant chocolate truffle. *Sphinx,* I thought. But then again, what if it wasn't the sphinx's lure, but a freak of nature? What if there were okapis in the Serengeti? I leapt into the jeep, but he stayed tantalisingly out of reach—even when I was roaring across the plains in top gear. The thrums from the engine reflected my active mind: perhaps part of me wanted to again come across the sphinx? For all I knew, I may have been insane and conjured up my own mythological vision.

Three deaths already. *Lady Killer.* The name shimmered about my mind.

As I trailed the okapi through sandy grass, around the occasional *kopje,* and acacia, the lowering sun and dusty air smeared the sky with the juice of blood oranges and tamarinds. The plains appeared endless, but after a while we began to descend. The grass thinned and then disappeared as the okapi advanced along the mudflats, to eventually stop, glancing now and then over its shoulder at me. Fearing that my vehicle would become bogged if I went further, I ground to a halt and jumped out. I realised that I was being led as I watched my boots submerge into a centimetre or two of reeking mud with every stride. The okapi had vanished; *she* stirred in front of me. I was in her territory—her sphere of muck on the flats.

I approached and patted her flanks.

Thank Hera, you came.

The acrid smell exuding from the mire dissipated as I massaged her hide, running my hands tenderly through tufts of hair. I felt slow, heavy, percussive purrs vibrating through my fingers. I reigned in all my thoughts and locked my mind on the sphinx. I would prevent myself from feeding her—I did my best not to stare at her breasts.

I need sustenance. It's been a while since they've sent you.

I patted her flanks. I couldn't fathom her gaze, somewhere between fondness and fear. Her front paw crept behind me and drew me near.

Feed me.

Feigning nonchalance, I continued to stroke.

Feed me. Claws flashed from sheaths. I remained mute and kept kneading.

Empty your mind, I told myself. A claw brushed my face, not breaking the skin.

Now.

I didn't reply. My heart quickened. One hand clenched. *Remain still,* I told myself, but it suddenly felt like a chill winter's day, when the icy breeze tears through your clothes and invades your bones. My teeth rattled briefly and I shuddered.

One paw held my back, and with the other she raked a claw down under the tender skin just beneath my eye, along my left cheek to the bottom of my jaw. My skin felt dry before the liquid gushed, drenching the side of my face. I managed to stay firm, vacant, until her tongue began lapping up my blood with invasive, rough strokes. *It is not your fault. Your blood is wrought in sin, wrought by fate. Feed me.*

Maybe she was wrong? Wasn't it my choice to satisfy my nature, my lust?

Her paw moved portentously to my opposite cheek, a claw pressed firmly over my now closed eyelid.

I suppose I saw myself as heroic, I'd wiped my mind of Sharpana and my ex, Rosa. I gave up a stranger's face instead. A bank teller, freckled and arrogant. I didn't even know her name.

I woke alone, lying in the muck.

♦

I SCANNED THE papers after that. Days later, I discovered the woman's name on the TV. Sophie Haines, mauled by a wild cat, most likely a lion. Nobody had witnessed the event. Search parties swarmed all over seeking a rogue animal. Sophie had been a widow with two children, Simon and Peter. Both attended elementary school.

I no longer considered her a stranger.

THE OLD MAN

SHARPANA SUFFERED ME, my unconfessed guilt, my anger and even my philandering—until she burst in when my hand was up the babysitter's top. Divorce was worse than I thought.

After the mudflats, the thought of the wild left a plunging sensation in my stomach. I never again travelled to national parks and reserves unaccompanied, and found that besides my son, few wished to travel with me.

I was no longer a Lady Killer, but rather the Invisible Man; my once wavy hair was scant, white and wiry, I was skeletal thin and limped on an arthritic right knee that kept me up on winter nights. I tried to remain a decent father and think I was to a point; I introduced Nanda to wildlife and he became a vet. But I can't take any real credit for my son's achievements. He turned out well thanks to Sharpana.

My head was embroiled in books. I still submitted to *The Zoological Journal,* but my main passion was fiction, all types and any genre. The pages and words were really my only company, I brought them with me everywhere: on the bus and train, to restaurants and cafes. I found even that friendship damaging of late. I'd become a conceited critic. A real prick. Nothing seemed right: the flow of words, their sounds as they unravelled across the pages; writing was either too fresh or too old or a vulgar cross-breed of both. Authors were too cerebral or egotistical, shallow became deep, and vice-versa.

I thought I had read my final three books during the week before I left: *The Fan Man, God Bless You, Mr Rosewater,* and *A Man in the High Castle,* randomly chosen from an insurmountable reading-list.

Just this morning, I'd left a letter on the table. The black ink, puddled in places, informed that I've left everything to my son and that I wished him a long and hopefully meaningful life. I stated that I didn't have long to live: an inoperable brain tumour, which spanned across the cerebral cortex. Cowardly fabricated details, but they did add a sense of authenticity.

I'd decided to head out alone. No more lady-killing. This time, no body would suffice but mine.

I drove through the rubble and sheets of a shantytown. Kids who had little else but chalk and balls played hopping games on the side streets. I passed through the locked fortresses and empty streets of those with plenty. I pulled out onto the old road near the coast, but not close enough that you could actually view the ocean. There was only shrub and scrubland, a speckled demented landscape as far as I could see.

The seat cushioned my back and the air-con cooled me. Liberated, I flew along with the pedal to the floor. I'd taken the road because hardly anyone took it these days since the new freeway had been built. Its painted lines were long eroded, blurring the two lanes into one.

I sped, passing through a stunted terrain where only stunted animals could survive. Scrub-birds, hovering falcons, rodents, reptiles and a droning army of insects. Then, in the distance, like an apparition, a long-haired figure stood in the middle of the road. I braked too sharply on seeing her. The car skidded and the wheel locked as I drew near. She stayed motionless as I spun in a circle towards her. Closer and closer the car screeched as I lifted my foot off the brake and released my hands from the wheel, leaving both our lives to the hands of fate.

The car careened to a stop. The woman stood mere centimetres from the bonnet, staring at me through those long lashes. Sharpana.

But she was the Sharpana of our early days; the Sharpana of the safari. There was no sign of the light bulge that had settled around her waist, or of the skin sagging slightly beneath her chin; and her eyes were not mournful, but still held some light.

This time I was not tricked or curious. A pitiful enticement compared to our past encounters. It wasn't a magical rush of colour to a child; or the mystical dance of a ball to an adolescent; or the lure of an exotic animal to a young man. I confess that I felt disappointed by the certainty.

The lure stared at me as I left the car and then she walked off into the scrubland in sandals, oblivious to all the dangers that lay there. Now and then she turned with an attractive sweep of her mane to see that I followed. How I loathed myself in recent years for the way I had treated Sharpana. I would have knelt for a dramatic apology, except I knew the body in front of me was only a creation of the sphinx.

My knee creaked and throbbed as I stomped to alert any snakes. Large wasps hovered around, skittishly flying this way and that, and flies hung thickly around bushes that stank of carrion. Tiny winged insects with grub-like bodies annoyed me the most; they tickled my arm hairs and I squashed them in my fingers in what seemed like the hundreds. I passed my hands constantly over my scalp to wipe the irritants away as I pursued her trail down a slight slope, remembering that taste of cinnamon. Soon we could not be seen from the road.

She stood there in the sand and spinifex and tufts of scrub.

Muses, how could you bring me this?

Her mind felt altered: desperate, disturbed.

What could he bring me? Who would follow him? Old, alone, bitter. There is no nourishment in that emaciated husk. How could he feed me?

"Take me," I said, almost prostrating myself before her. Despite just seeing Sharpana, my mind was clear: no lady-killing. The scar the sphinx had left me burned like ice down the side of my face.

She protested, wailing in my mind. I moved closer and found myself patting her fur rhythmically, like I was calming a distressed child, all the while whispering: "Take me." I developed an erection. It was intense, forcing against my pants like hot iron. I hadn't had one in years.

You are of no use! She cried as I continued to caress her fur.

Reaching up, I began to touch her breasts. If they were closer I would have traced my tongue all over them. Her movement slowed. The paw that had sliced my face open with ease years ago now lifted feebly in an attempt to force me away.

Muses! She called to them desperately, while gradually cooling beneath my fingers.

My cock still burned: "Take me," I repeated.

Things appeared in a pool around her: cowslips, with wilted petals, burst up from the earth; flat footballs rolled rather than bounced this way and that; an emaciated okapi stood staring at me listlessly; Sharpana crawled around on the ground, searching, like a deranged patient.

Then they all vanished.

She cried softly in a final appeal to the Muses before turning cold beneath my hands, a lost statue once more. I came against the material of my trousers as she froze. Afterwards, I sat on the dirt; a mien of emotional intricacies: self-disgust merged with confusion and relief. Lady killers, both of us. I don't know whether I was more repulsed by her actions over time or mine.

This land was more isolated than the bush surrounding my primary school. I couldn't help but wonder how long it would be before another lady killer awakened her.

CRIMINALITIES

'It will have blood, they say;
blood will have blood.'
~William Shakespeare, *Macbeth*

A RED MIST

MARTIN LIVINGS

SAHRO leaned against the doorframe and examined the living room of the old house. It might have even been a beautiful house, once upon a time, with its high ceilings and original features that would have been a real estate agent's wet dream. It should have been occupied by an elderly couple who'd bought it soon after they'd married, or perhaps by a pair of high-income earners who'd decided to move out of the inner city to the northern suburbs of Melbourne to raise a family.

Instead, it was a squat.

The large living room was almost entirely bare, with dark and dirty wooden floorboards stretching to every wall. The only light filtered through a large, greasy window on one side; the glass thick and uneven, causing weird refractions and patterns of light on the floor and walls. The air in the room was alive with dust, which glimmered with a reddish hue in the sunlight. There was an old-fashioned fireplace, clearly not used for decades, its bricks blackened with past fires, and beside it, an old axe, probably used to chop wood in the backyard once upon a time. If they'd brought it inside to prevent it from rusting, they'd failed miserably. The walls were covered in patchy, peeling wallpaper. The wooden floorboards creaked and bowed beneath their feet. And the smell . . . oh, the smell . . .

Sahro sighed tiredly. Her gloved hands were tucked in the pockets of her coveralls, idly fingering the half-empty pack of cigarettes there. She wished she could remove her mask, have a smoke, relax a little. She saw houses like this far too much in her line of work: the old and abandoned. It somehow echoed a faded memory from her childhood home town in Somalia, a lifetime ago and half a world away. There had been caves nearby, which her superstitious parents had always warned her about visiting, claiming they were haunted by evil spirits that would bewitch and confuse her with illusions and lies, all while hiding in the shadows. She'd gone, of course, always a wilful child, and found nothing but stone and dirt; no spirits, no illusions. Those caves had been abandoned for centuries, millennia, but they didn't feel empty to Sahro. Quite the opposite, in fact. The lonely years filled them.

Houses like this always felt the same. But she didn't let that affect her. She wasn't a little girl anymore. She was a cleaner now. It's who she was, what she did. And she had a job to do.

She looked around more closely. Near the fireplace was a small writing desk with some books on it, and a tattered but comfortable-looking upholstered wooden chair, furniture that had clearly been picked up off the side of the road during the annual hard rubbish collection. The couch in the middle of the room—the main reason she was here—had probably been obtained the same way, once someone's pride and joy, now junk. Like this whole house. But nobody would touch it now. Never again.

The man's body had apparently almost completely decomposed, the flesh stripped away by months of neglect; beetles and maggots and myriad other small creatures having feasted on him, undisturbed, uninterrupted. The body and its colonies were gone now, thankfully. The remains themselves had been removed by the police earlier, of course, but you could see his outline on the ruined fabric of the faded brown couch, the rotting stain almost black in the dim sunlight.

"Christ on a bike," Ted gasped, as he put his tray of cleaning materials down by the doorway. His voice sounded wet through his mask, like he was trying to swallow something. Half her age and a head taller than her, with his pale skin and red hair, Ted was easily the whitest man Sahro had ever known, and considering she lived in Australia now, that was no small feat. They couldn't have been more dissimilar if they'd planned it that way. But the young man was hard-working and never complained. Well, not too much. Both were good qualities to have in their business.

Sahro shook her head a little, sighed. "Man up, Ted. Sooner or later you're going to get used to this."

"I bloody hope not," he growled.

Sahro hoped not too, but would never admit to doing so. Her poor parents, may their souls rest in peace, would have been horrified by her chosen career. Well, not so much chosen as fallen into; cleaning work was easy to come by after her divorce, and forensic cleaning seemed a logical extension of that. It was harder work but much better pay and fewer hours. Plus Alexander, her ex-husband, would have hated it. To her perversely pragmatic heart, it had seemed like a win-win.

She put her own tray down next to the couch—stocked with the usual stuff like bleach and detergents, as well as other cleaners, like methylated spirits and acetone, plus a sizable array of sponges, brushes, scourers and rags—and took a closer look at it. Down its front, two uneven black streams told Sahro the entire story in a glance.

"Slit wrists," she said in a matter-of-fact tone, then looked down at the floorboards and frowned. "Not much blood, all things considered." She thought back to the details the police had provided her. Harold Fulham, forty-three, of no fixed abode. They didn't know how long he'd been squatting here before he'd killed himself; the house itself had been empty for decades, the convoluted result of a disputed will, which Sahro's cynical soul was certain had put a lot of lawyers' children through school.

Ted glanced at the stains, then was distracted by something else on the floor. He walked over and knelt down. "Sah?" he asked, voice weak.

"What is it?"

He pointed at the floor. "Is this . . . I mean, is it . . . ?"

An old large kitchen knife lay there, a few feet away from the ruined couch. Its blade was stained a deep brown. For a heartbeat, Sahro saw what Ted saw. An implement of death, stained with dried blood. Then she blinked and laughed.

"It's just rust, Ted," she assured him. "The police would have taken whatever Mister Fulham used to kill himself. Evidence."

"Oh yeah," he replied with a shrug, face turning a splotchy red. "My bad."

She shook her head, then turned and looked closer at the spot where Harold Fulham had died and rotted. Her heart sank. "Ted?"

"Yeah?"

"I think we have a problem."

Ted walked over and looked where Sahro was looking.

"Oh shit."

The floorboards at the base of the couch were uneven and cracked, with almost a finger-width of space between each plank in places.

"I think I know why there's not much blood," Sahro said grimly. "It's mostly gone under the floor."

"Ah, crap," Ted swore. "That's gonna be a bitch to clean. What do you reckon is under there?"

"Not a clue," Sahro admitted. "Dirt?"

Ted straightened. "Dirt would be good," he said. "We could just cover it up. Nobody would be the wiser."

"Ted," Sahro admonished the younger man, "that's not very professional."

"Hell with professional," he replied. "This place gives me the heebies."

"Heebies?" Sahro asked, raising an eyebrow inside her goggles.

"Yeah, you know. Heebie jeebies. The willies." He sighed. "It makes me nervous."

"Ah." She nodded. "'Heebie jeebies'. I like it."

"Still coming across colloquialisms you haven't heard before, hey?"

Sahro laughed. "Every day in this country!" Then she became serious. "We'll have to find an access point into the floor."

"I think we walked past one in the hallway," Ted said.

"Really?" Sahro hadn't noticed it. She was always amazed by Ted's keen eyes. For her, the job was just a job. Clean it up and get the hell out. Ted, though, he seemed to take a close interest in everything around him, always examining the house, the surroundings. *Looking for clues*, he'd called it when she'd asked about it on their first job together. *Every person deserves to be understood. Even the dead ones.* It was probably why he'd never really gotten used to the job. He was just too involved, too invested, every single time.

"Yep," he replied, and pointed back over his shoulder. "Looked pretty small, though."

She looked at him, up and down his unwieldy six foot frame, then sighed. "I guess I'm going down, then?"

"You must be psychic, Sah."

"I must be." She looked at Ted. "What will you be doing while I'm down there? Cleaning? Or looking for clues?"

Ted grinned.

"I thought so."

While Ted walked over to the writing desk, Sahro turned and headed back to the entry hall. Just as Ted had said, there was a panel cut into the floorboards there. Not big, but big enough for her. One of the boards had a small round brass handle with inset hinges that were flush to the floor. She flipped the handle up and removed the board with effort, the wood swollen in place. She realised nobody had been down there for years. The other boards came out easily enough once the initial panel was removed. She placed them aside and looked into the gloom below.

"*Sharmuutaa ku dhashay*," she grumbled. She fumbled in her pocket, past the half-empty packet of cigarettes and the single butt she'd put there, and grabbed her lighter. It was a Zippo that she'd bought herself with her first pay from cleaning, an indulgence to celebrate her new life, or perhaps to commiserate the loss of the old, it didn't really matter which. She flicked it open and lit it, a little clumsily with her gloves on, then held it carefully down into the darkness. All she could see was black dirt.

She climbed into the hatch. It was deeper than she expected, deep enough that she could scuffle upright on her knees without hitting her head. Something between a basement and a crawlspace. She looked around, saw the wooden joists holding up the floorboards above her head, swathed in thick curtains of opaque cobwebs that, thankfully, seemed spider-free. The foundations of the house were made of rough stone, and between them, Sahro could see where the living area was, thin lines of sunlight painting the dirt with dim zebra stripes. The ground was peppered with chunks of old brick, clearly left over from the original construction of the house. There was even more red dust down here, hanging suspended in the strips of light like a million crimson fairies. She shuffled forward, prepared to see an awful puddle of congealed blood, a cleaner's nightmare made terrible reality. Sighing, she remembered she'd left her shovel in the car.

But the flickering light of her Zippo didn't reveal a mound of biohazard waste. Instead of dirt and blood, what she saw was a small field of dark red mushrooms covering the entire area beneath the living room. They were of various sizes, some grown large and swollen, others struggling, but there wasn't a square inch of the space that wasn't occupied by the crimson fungi. Above them, the shimmering ruby-coloured dust hung thick in the air, slowly circulating with the slight airflow that intruded underneath the house, drifting gradually upwards. It was such an incongruous sight, so strange and unlikely, that Sahro just knelt there and looked, mouth agape under her mask. It took her several seconds to realise there was a grim pattern to the growth of the mushrooms, and several seconds longer to understand what that meant. When she did, her breath caught in her throat.

The largest mushrooms were directly beneath the couch. Where the blood had fallen.

"Sah?" Ted's voice came from above, but somehow, through the floorboards and Ted's mask, it seemed very far away. A lifetime and half a world, in fact. Sahro felt like she was back in the caves she'd explored; she was a child again, confused and small. Lost. Unwelcome.

"Sah?" Ted called again, and this time she shook herself out of her light trance. She suddenly noticed her lighter getting hot enough to almost melt the plastic of her gloves. She doused it for the moment.

"Uh, yes?" she called back.

"You won't believe what I found up here!"

She laughed without humour at that. "Try me."

"A scrapbook." Ted's voice was suddenly clearer. She sighed; he'd probably taken his mask and goggles off to read the book, knowing him. Him and his clues. "Looks like this Harold guy did some research on this house. And it ain't pretty."

She ignited her lighter again and looked over the mushrooms through the haze of dust. In a strange way, they were *pretty*. The red mist near her lighter moved more frantically, some incandescing briefly, caught alight in the flame. "What do you mean?"

"Well, he's not the first person to kill himself here," Ted explained distantly. "I see newspaper stories going back ten, fifteen years.

Mainly squatters, a few brief tenants. Suicides, murders, murder-suicides . . . no wonder no-one lives here!"

Sahro didn't respond, just looked at the mushrooms. They appeared to be healthy, thriving, in fact. She wondered how many people had fed them. How much blood had flowed through the floorboards. She wondered what had come first; the blood or the mushrooms. Curiously, barely aware that she was doing it, she reached out with one gloved finger and touched the nearest one.

The mushroom burst like a puffball, sending a dense cloud of crimson powder straight into her face. Sahro yelped and fell over backwards, the lighter falling from her hand and going out. Blackness rushed in, and she felt her mask twist sideways, its edge caught on the rubble strewn over the ground. It was damned lucky she didn't hit her head. She tried to yell again, but there was something in her mouth, in her lungs. She coughed, choked. A metallic taste, sharp and acrid, filled her mouth. She gasped and coughed, choking for a moment before catching her breath. Over her ragged breathing and pounding heart, she could hear Ted's voice.

"Sah? Sahro? Are you okay? What's happening down there?"

"I'm all right, Ted," she replied through oddly numb lips, the bitter taste of the powder still lingering on them. She straightened her mask, got to her knees in the shadows. "Just had a little scare." She scrambled blindly in the dirt for her lighter, found it, and re-lit it.

The space beneath the living room was completely filled with the red mist. Sahro could see it drifting upwards, through the floorboards, disappearing into the room above. She watched for long seconds, dumbfounded by just how much dust could come from one small mushroom. It seemed unreal, like a terrible dream.

She shook her head, and turned and made her way back to the hatch in the hallway floor. She climbed out, doused and pocketed the lighter out of sheer reflex, and glanced into the living room. It was filled with the crimson dust now, the entire room tinted red, as if she was inside a blood vessel. Ted was kneeling by the couch, his back to Sahro, his mask and goggles on the floor as she'd suspected. He didn't seem to notice her, or the dust for that matter.

"Ted?"

He stood and turned, faced her. She gasped and took a reflexive step backwards, her heart pounding. Ted's bare face was covered in open sores, thin, watery blood oozing from each of them. Twin streams of blood ran from his eyes, streaking his cheeks like war-paint. His nose and ears were also bleeding. Sahro's mind just couldn't take it in, kept catching on it like a loose thread on a nail, unravelling the years. She was a teenager again, in her tiny house in Somalia, watching her parents die in front of her over three screaming weeks. The disease had consumed them whole, taken them away, body and soul. By the end, they didn't know who she was, just that she was the cause of their suffering. The mess they'd left behind when the men in hazard suits had carted their limp, bloody bodies away unceremoniously had been unbelievable. She'd left the house with them, never to return.

The disease hadn't just taken their lives, it had taken hers. She'd married a man she barely knew, because her father was no longer there to take care of her. She'd moved to another country, a strange place where she didn't speak the language, a place where her skin made her an outcast, all because her husband wished it. When he'd divorced her three years later, she'd been left alone, no friends, no family. A foreigner, alien and isolated. Small, like a little girl in a big cave. All because of the illness, the bleeding fever.

And now she was seeing it again.

"No," she breathed, terrified at how tiny her voice sounded, how young, how vulnerable. She staggered backwards. "No . . . "

Ted looked at her, confusion clouding his bloody eyes. "You?" he asked softly. He took a step towards Sahro. She took another stumbling step away.

"Ted, please," she sobbed. "You're sick. You need to see a doctor."

"Why are you here?" Ted didn't seem to hear her. His eyes were fixed on her face, but somehow she knew they weren't, not really. "Why did you do it?"

"Do what, Ted? What are you talking about?"

Ted raised his right hand, and for the first time Sahro noticed that it wasn't empty. Her attention had been so fixed on the weeping sores across Ted's face that she hadn't even seen the knife they'd found earlier. But she saw it now. The rust on its blade looked more like blood than ever.

He took another step forward. "Why did you do it?" he asked, and there was a wet break in his voice, a barely contained sob. "Why?"

"Ted . . . " Sahro tried to sound calm, but her voice was shaking wildly, blood pounding at her temples. She glanced around the room, never really taking her eyes off the lanky redhead, off the bloody lesions across his skin, disease oozing from them. "Ted, please . . . "

"*Why???*" Ted screamed. He charged at her, knife raised.

Sahro ducked to one side and rolled across the floor. She saw the mist alter in her wake, whorls and eddies of red dust spiralling through the air. She hit the fireplace with her back, and her vision went redder still from the pain. Something clattered to the floor beside her, and she scrambled to her feet, her hand automatically grabbing at the object. It took her a few seconds to realise what it was.

The axe.

She held it out in front of her, both hands together, waving it back and forth like a club. Ted didn't even seem to notice. He started striding towards her, knife still raised. His red-stained eyes never left her face, and they were filled with death and pain, nothing else.

"Not even a note!" he wailed, tears and blood running down his cheeks freely now. "Why, Peter? *Why???*"

"Ted . . . "

He was on Sahro with a speed that took her completely by surprise. The heavy axe fell from her hands as her back hit the floor, the breath knocked out of her. Ted straddled her while she wheezed for breath. He took the knife in both hands and held it above his head, the rusty tip pointing down. The blade shook in the air, surrounded by the mist.

"Ted," she gasped. "Ted . . . clues . . . "

The knife stayed where it was. A look of confusion crossed Ted's bloodied, pox-ridden face, his eyes suddenly unsure, darting. They found Sahro's, and she saw recognition deep within them. He looked down at her, blinked a few times.

"Sah?" he asked in a small, frightened voice.

"Ted," she replied as gently as she could. She tried to smile, but all she could see was the disease on his skin, so virulent, so deadly. She had to get away from him, but his weight pinned her to the crooked floorboards.

"Sah?" he repeated, and his tears flowed again. "Sah? Oh God, no . . . "

He lowered the knife, then put it to his own throat.

"Ted, no!" Sahro yelled. She thrashed to get out from underneath him, but was helpless as she watched him slice into the soft flesh of his neck.

Blood gouted from the wound, splashing across Sahro's goggles, mask and chest, blinding her. She bellowed, a wordless cry filled with shock and fear, and found a strength she never knew she had. Dragging at reserves deep inside herself, she shoved Ted off her and onto the floor beside her. She scrambled to her knees, eyes closed hard, wiping the blood from her goggles, clearing her vision.

Ted lay on the floor, the knife discarded next to his open, limp hand. The gash in his neck bubbled with every ragged breath he took, each one shallower than the last. His eyes rolled up into his head. She looked at him, trying to understand what she saw, what was there. Or, more accurately, what wasn't there.

The disease. Ted's face, even paler than usual, was splattered with his own blood from his wound, but apart from that, there were no weeping sores, no purple discolouration. No sign of the illness. Sahro reached out to him, but stopped, her hand hovering in the air, in the mist. She looked at it, and a new fear rushed into her veins, filling her until there was nothing left, not even loneliness.

Through her clear plastic gloves, she could see that the back of her hand was diseased. The same open sores she'd seen on Ted were now on her own flesh, the same sores she'd seen on her parents' bodies in the days and weeks before their awful deaths. Blood wept from angry, split blisters, staining the inside of the gloves pink.

"No . . . " Her voice was barely more than a whisper. Her hand moved of its own accord, away from Ted's prone body, towards his open hand. Towards the knife. She picked it up and held it to her eyes, looking at it closely. It was covered in Ted's fresh blood now, So much blood. She could imagine it seeping between the cracks in the floorboards, imagine the mushrooms below leaning towards the red rain, thirstily drinking it, taking strength. But wanting more, always wanting more. Always.

Carefully, crimson tears filling her eyes, Sahro placed the blade against her diseased wrist. She couldn't die like that, not like her *aabaha* and *hooyo*. Not like that. She looked at her hand, at her wrist, the sores opening up so fast that she could actually see them move, like hungry mouths begging to be fed, bloody maws wanting nothing but death. She closed her eyes, trying to remember a prayer from her childhood, any prayer, but she couldn't. All she could remember was that cave, and her parents' warning.

Evil spirits, lies and illusions.

Sahro opened her eyes again, frowning. She looked at Ted, at his pale face, free of sores and blemishes. Free of disease. Her frown deepened.

"No." This time her voice wasn't small, wasn't vulnerable. It was *her* voice, the voice of a woman who'd overcome a thousand obstacles just to be there. "No," she said again, stronger still.

The knife fell to the floor, forgotten. She looked around her, could see the tiny crimson spores from the mushrooms filling the room. They'd been there all along, she realised, even before she'd touched the mushroom beneath the floorboards. So much dust in the air, in her lungs. In Ted's lungs. In Harold Fulham's, in the weeks or months before his death.

Lies and illusions. Illusions and lies. Heebie jeebies.

She knelt down and grabbed a rag from her cleaning tray where she'd left it beside the couch, then balled it up and pressed it to Ted's neck, to the awful wound there. "Hold it in place, Ted," she ordered him. "Put pressure on it." He didn't seem to understand at first, so she grabbed his hands and moved them to the makeshift bandage. He hesitated, then pressed against the blood-soaked rag as hard as he could manage. She quickly yanked her own mask and goggles off, ripping the elastic out of them, before tying it around the makeshift bandage as best she could. She flashed what she hoped was a comforting smile at him, then turned and looked through her cleaning tray again.

Sahro breathed in and out deeply, let more of the red spores enter her lungs. She didn't care, they couldn't hurt her, not anymore. She'd survived a hell of a lot worse than this. She grabbed the bottle of acetone and spun the child-proof lid off with practised ease, then grabbed another rag and shoved it into the bottle, gave it a quick shake, then put it aside.

She scrambled across to where the axe had fallen and picked it up. It felt solid in her hands, her diseased hands. No, she told herself, not diseased. Lies and illusions. She stood up, hefted the axe, then slammed its blunt, rusty head into the floorboards just in front of the couch. It took four hard swings to crack them open enough for her to bend over and tear a few boards up, the rotten wood snapping wetly, easier than she expected. Beneath her feet, she could see the mushrooms in their lush underfloor field. She imagined them flinching away from the wan misty sunbeams that had been released into their midst, hissing like the *dhegdheer* legends of her homeland. She grinned without humour, a bloodied berserker grin. Picking up the acetone with one hand, she then reached into her pocket and pulled out her Zippo. She lit the rag and hurled the bottle through the hole.

The glass bottle didn't shatter on the ground. It didn't need to. A heartbeat later, the acetone exploded and sprayed liquid fire all over the mushrooms, which burst into flames instantly. In the air above them, she could see a million scintillations as the red mist also caught alight, tiny galaxies igniting and dying in an instant. In a matter of seconds, everything below the floor was burning.

A few seconds later, so was the floor itself.

"*Hooyadeed wasto,*" Sahro cursed under her breath. She grabbed Ted underneath his shoulders and dragged him out of the burning living room, down the hallway, out of the house, the fire catching around them as she went. She hauled him until they were on the footpath outside the front fence. Then she sat him up against the van, sat down beside him, and fished the packet of cigarettes out of her pocket. She waved it at Ted's pale face, eyebrows raised. He shook his head weakly, so she took one out for herself and lit it. Her fingers were no longer bleeding within the gloves. She was exhausted, yet strangely elated, the last dregs of adrenaline in her veins making its fading presence known through the beginnings of a pounding headache.

"Help's coming," she assured him, and indeed, she could already hear people shouting, alarmed neighbours and passers-by. A couple of people standing in the neighbour's yard were talking frantically into their mobile phones. They'd certainly have some questions to answer later, she and Ted, but for the moment, Sahro was more than happy to just sit and smoke and watch the house burn, a strange contented smile on her face.

Lies and illusions, she thought, *hidden within the shadows.* She just wished she could tell her poor parents they were right, after all. But most importantly, she wanted to tell them that sometimes the best way to defeat such danger was through a cleansing fire, one bright enough to burn the shadows away.

Now that's what Sahro called clean.

◆　◆　◆

SEEING RED

S. ZANNE

AFTER that night, he dreamed in shades of blood.

From the bright, fresh wetness of crimson, scarlet, and vermillion, down to the darkest, drying shades of maroon and burgundy verging on black. Every night it was the same, no deviation allotted to his sleeping cerebrum.

Always the same woman and always the same claret colours.

Her hair was the one aberration from the sanguine-hued norm of his dreams, not that the red didn't try to saturate that, as well. All that rich, wet colour made her hair glow, just the hint of firelight streaking her black tresses, framing her exotic, almond-shaped eyes, which were set over slashing cheekbones. The radiance tinted her flesh with a faint flush, giving a virginal glow to her nearly nude form, except for the blood-dark hand prints that covered each of her breasts. These prints played at coyness by camouflaging her dusky nipples, giving the impression of cover though the rest of her lay bared to his view.

Her only adornment was a rope of black pearls coiled around the length of her throat, the strands draping elegantly between her blood-painted breasts. She played with that necklace constantly, running the beads between her fingers; the slide of the pearls over her taut skin would tease her nipples into hardness. She would absently tug on the strands until it dented her delicate skin, but she paid him no mind.

He was nothing.

Who she was he didn't know, but she was there in his dreams every night. She had been there since that evening so long ago, when he had accidently cut himself after hearing another one of his parents' endless arguments from the next room. Fascinated, he had played with the edges of the cut, watching the blood flow faster from the wound. Then he had added another—and another. As the blood swirled down the length of his arm and dotted the floor, he had felt the great burden of being so young and ineffectual lift from his shoulders.

No one cared about him, and it felt good not to care in return.

She was his first flash of memory when he awoke in the hospital, the only distinct image in his hazy, hallucination-driven world, and he wondered if his blood had been enough, but she did not deign to answer. She remained a distant and beautiful idol, and more than slightly terrifying. But he fell in love with her all the same, a dog's loyalty to its master. She was the gruesome yet beautiful sun to his distant earth, something he could not touch, that would kill him even if he could.

But still he worshipped her. He wanted to clothe her in garnet, give her rubies to dangle from her ears and around her neck, the jewellery so long it would spill across her breasts, blood red and sinuous—as if her throat had been cut.

As he grew older, he would wake from these dreams, longing hot and hard in his heart and in his dick. He felt too ashamed to strip himself as he did when he imagined other girls, so he would proceed through his morning with the evidence of his arousal lying thick and heavy beneath his trousers. He may not know her name or who she was, but he had always known what she wanted from that first moment, and relief wasn't it.

So he gave her what gifts he could. He started small in his attempts to please her, with the lizards and frogs he could catch down by the creek, or the baby birds that fell from the nests hidden in the boughs above. When that did not seem to be enough, he increased his efforts to include larger offerings—a hungry stray or a neighbour's curious pet. And when he was done, he would hang them up high where he was sure she would see them. Each night after, he dreamed of her studying his sacrifices, hands dancing beneath the blood that continued to drip from the still-warm carcasses—how she would caress the length of the rope that kept the bodies bound at eye level.

But he felt she remained unsatisfied, for he still received no piece nor parcel of her attentions.

His behaviour did not remain unnoticed for long, and soon he was forced to share his thoughts and feelings with a psychologist—a tightly buttoned, older gentleman whose expression lay hidden by the brush of bristly hair above his lip. The doctor asked about that early 'accident', and he never felt he was lying when he insisted it was nothing more. It was through that glorious bit of mischance that he had met *her*, and that made it less of an 'accident' and more of a blessing of fate.

What bothered him at the time was that he couldn't read the man easily, the mobility of the psychologist's mouth too well shielded to give any clues as to his mood. Not that it mattered all that much. Just by looking at the man, he could tell the psychologist would be of no interest to her—too desiccated to hold her attentions; he had no vitality to offer her. He faced no competition here. The man's steadiness of features hinted that he lacked the desire to see and to understand her wonder.

Though he tried to keep her a secret, he had yet to build walls capable of keeping others from picking apart his random utterances and piecing together their own tales. He realised his mistake when the doctor asked if his imaginary friend had told him to do these things—these terrible, hurtful things—eyebrows raised over the rim of his glasses and his intense gaze pinning him in place.

He hastened to reassure the doctor that she hadn't told him to do anything. He was beneath her notice.

It was only when he eavesdropped on the conversations between his parents and the doctor, and began to hear murmurs of schizophrenia and institutionalisation, that he knew he had to work harder to keep her to himself. He did not mind; he had always hated the idea of sharing her anyway. Especially with a non-believer.

She disappeared from his conversations after that. He no longer referenced her in such familiar ways and her face disappeared from the doodles on the edges of his notebooks. She was relegated to nothing more than a passing dream, some childhood terror that he had adjusted to over time, and there was nothing more for his parents, or his doctors, to worry about.

It just made him more cautious.

So he became even more careful in his collecting over the years, choosing only those who wouldn't be missed and placing them where they were sure not to be found—the homeless hiding in the alleys or the prostitute strolling alone along the darkened docks. These still did not seem to please her as he had hoped they might, and he wondered if she would prefer something a little more . . . noticeable.

And it worked. She'd even smiled when she had seen the offering of the little boy, body suspended with rope, wrists and throat slashed to release the torrent of innocent life. She noticed, but so did the authorities.

He could feel them getting closer by the day, and he knew he couldn't take her down with him. He had done what he could to please her, and had failed. Now he had to set her free to find someone else.

♦

As HE LAY in the bathtub, looking up at her shimmering shape from his cocoon of pink-stained water, he realised her full wonder. He could feel her fingers trail along the rope tied to the showerhead as if they were skimming along the length of his dick, the cord around his throat keeping the arousal thrumming through his veins, even as he bled out into the rapidly cooling water.

Her pearl necklace was a shock of cold as it dragged across his cock, the strands of it spilling into the water just as he had done only moments before. Her touch burned to the depths of his soul as her hand came to rest upon his sternum, her fingers brushing through the sparse hair dusting his chest, his blood collecting around her fingertips as if wanting to be absorbed into her flesh.

She was more vibrant outside of the confines of his own head, even if she hadn't quite attained the full vitality of corporeal form. Her eyes were a bright obsidian, her skin a rich caramel. Perhaps as he was leaving this life, he was becoming more like her—something floating in the ether between here and there. Something that might one day achieve the same elegant grandness she possessed within the wisps of dreams. Perhaps he would one day visit some unsuspecting soul and bring the same wonder into their lives.

His heartbeat stumbled in its tempered rhythm as if trying to reach for the caress of her palm, hope kindling within him. She had come to bless him, to welcome him into her world.

It was time.

He had given her his allegiance; he had given her his devotion.

And he had given her his heart.

He had not realised those last words had escaped past the tightness wrapped around his throat until a vulpine smile spread across her beautiful face. She leaned close, and he wished he had the strength to lean forward to touch his mouth to hers, though he would never dare to presume. Not after so long.

Her delicate hand, braced against his chest, sunk beneath his cooling flesh, fingers disappearing from view. He could feel the warmth of her grip around his heart as she took his pledge, pleasure radiating in warm waves from her solidifying form. He felt no pain in those final moments, the emptiness of the cavity that once held his organ brimming full of love for her.

His heart looked so dirty and small within her grasp, but as she cupped it in her palm, he felt more than he was, than he had ever been, even as her prophet.

As his vision started to grey, he saw her thrust her hand into her chest, the flesh peeling away as she deposited his paltry offering within her own ribcage, settling it carefully amongst the others that rested inside. The skin sealed closed, as smooth as water stilling over a pond, and left only a fresh bloody handprint as proof he'd been inside her. Though the mark slowly faded, leaving her flesh as flawless as before, he knew that part of him would remain within her forever.

Then she leaned in, one hand clutching the strands of pearls encasing her throat, the other wrapped around the rope holding him in place. Her breath warmed his already cooling flesh as she whispered in benediction, her lips nearly touching his. It took several precious seconds for his brain to translate the words, the language far older than any he knew. But as the bathwater turned a deeper shade of scarlet and his breaths came with more effort, the consonants and vowels fell into something familiar, and at last he knew he had pleased her.

Finally, after all this time.

THE TENDERNESS
OF MONSTERS

PAUL STARKEY

LARRY Drake haphazardly parked his little rental Toyota on the road outside the apartment building. The only free space was a loading zone marked with hatched yellow lines, all the others were taken by patrol cars or white CSI vans, and he didn't have time to walk a block and a half to get back to the building. Almost immediately, a young patrolman came running up to tell him he couldn't park there. A flash of his badge soon changed the cop's attitude.

The crime scene was on the third floor, and there was no lift, so he clambered up the stairs, his knees creaking almost as much as the warped wooden steps. Yellow crime scene tape hung limply from one side of the dented doorframe. Drake paused, his gaze roaming up and down the hall, noting an expensive if worn carpet, freshly painted cream walls, and the other doors shut tightly against the crime that had taken place. He had to step back to let a couple of CSIs exit the apartment, their arms full of gear, and their white plastic suits noisy as they walked by him.

Inside, the apartment was neat, tidy, and well-furnished, with an astringent chemical smell hanging oppressively in the air. Only one person was left inside, a woman, her dirty blonde hair tied up in a no-nonsense pony tail. She was standing in the bedroom with her back to him, her attention focused on the double bed with its rumpled sheets. Her shoulders tensed slightly, and he figured she'd heard him enter the room.

"Can I help you?" she asked, turning slowly towards him. To most observers, the move would have been casual. He saw the flick of her jacket though, as she made the pistol holstered behind her right hip more accessible.

Drake pulled out his badge, flicked it open. "FBI. I'm looking for the officer in charge."

She cast her glance about the room, widened her eyes as if in surprise, and then smiled. "That'll be me," she said at last. He instantly warmed to her—he appreciated attitude. She continued, "Detective Catherine Van Brugen, Midleif PD." She didn't offer her hand. "And you are?"

She was young, but Christ, they all were these days. She wore scruffy jeans and a leather jacket, and several errant locks of blonde hair had already escaped the pony tail she'd confined them to. She wore the bare minimum of makeup, further hinting at a no-nonsense nature, and her nose was crooked. Whether she'd broken it during childhood or the line of duty was anyone's guess. She seemed like the perfect avatar for this city; pretty, but in need of a makeover.

He held out his badge to her. "Larry Drake."

She took the badge. Raising an eyebrow she read, "Assistant Special Agent-in-Charge Larry Drake." She raised her blue eyes to meet his. "If your job title was any longer, you wouldn't be able to fit it all on."

He laughed politely. He saw her size him up, knew what she'd be thinking. Drake was a Fed through and through: he wore an off-the-shelf suit—crumpled from the flight he'd taken to get here—with a neat fifties-style haircut. Drake knew he looked older than he was, his bloodshot eyes were surrounded by thin lines, his skin stamped with liver spots. He slumped like he had the weight of the world resting on his shoulders, and sometimes he felt like he was carrying around the damned globe. But someone had to.

She handed his badge back. "What can I do you for?"

"I'm hoping to assist in your investigation; I believe you may be dealing with a serial killer, one I've been tracking for several years."

Van Brugen frowned. "Hate to waste your time, Agent Drake . . . "

"Larry, please."

"Larry. I'm guessing someone at the precinct got their wires crossed."

"Excuse me?"

"You're in town following up on the murder of Elena Garcia, body dumped in the alley behind Tenth Street, though she must have been killed elsewhere, since she'd suffered extensive blood loss and there were only a few drops at the scene. I'm not on that case." She gestured towards the bed. "This is a rape investigation, and my victim's very much alive."

Drake smiled, almost with relief. "There's no mistake, your man is my man." He glanced around and noted a grey upholstered chair in the lounge. He headed towards it, Van Brugen following him. "Do you mind?" he asked, sitting down with an audible sigh before she had a chance to answer. He began rubbing his right knee. "Your victim is aged between twenty-one and twenty-seven, she's blonde, *naturally* blonde, and she'll have brown eyes. She lives alone and probably works as an administrator or a secretary, though she could be a teacher.

"She came home last night and found no evidence of a break-in, but at some point during the evening, while she was cooking, or running a bath, someone snuck up on her and jabbed a needle in her arm. She was injected with pentobarbital. Once she was knocked out, he brought her into the bedroom and assaulted her. If he tied her up, he used silk ribbons, and after he was done, he tucked her up in bed and dialled 911 on her phone, then he left. Am I right?"

Van Brugen stared at him for a few seconds. "Tox screen will take some time, so I have no idea what he slipped her. As for the rest; victim is Kelsey Hendricks, twenty-five, natural blonde with hazel eyes. She lives alone and she's a paralegal. He got her while she was cooking, don't know if he tied her up, but we found a stray ribbon under the bed. He tucked her up afterwards and called 911 just like you said. Dispatch sent a car round and found her front door wide open and her asleep in bed."

Drake saw Van Brugen glance back towards the bedroom. "I have to say, *if* he is a serial killer, he's a weird one. Serial rapist maybe, but he seemed to go out of his way not to harm her." She wrinkled her nose in disgust

Drake leaned forward, elbows on his protesting knees. "He doesn't kill the girls he rapes, except by accident, but the other woman, what was her name, Eleanor . . . "

"*Elena* Garcia."

"He has two methods of attack; they fulfil different needs for him. If Elena suffered extensive blood loss, then he'll have killed her, I've no doubt about that."

Van Brugen shook her head, a tuft of hair worming its way free. "So you're saying this guy preys on two types of victims, the women he kills and the women he rapes?"

Drake stood, wincing as he did so. "No. He has one type, just one, women like Kelsey. The others, the ones he kills, they're irrelevant, chosen at random, all ethnicities, men and women."

"I'm sorry, Agent . . . Larry . . . but that's a weird pathology, it doesn't make a lot of sense."

He smiled wearily. "Tell me about it, that's what's made him so hard to catch. Hell, sometimes I have a hard time convincing anyone he's even real."

♦

"So how long have you been after this guy?" Van Brugen asked.

Drake ran a hand through his hair, then dropped it back into his lap. "A long time. Too long."

Van Brugen had co-opted the young patrolman—the one who'd been keen to have Drake move his car—to drive Drake's hired Toyota and luggage back to his motel. Drake was riding in the detective's car, a grey Chevy Impala. It was three years old, but looked suspiciously like it hadn't been washed since the day it drove off the forecourt.

He was staring out the window, intrigued by the city. On the one hand, it was banally generic. Uninspired architecture, the same nationwide outlets found in every city in America, but every so often he saw something odd; a gaggle of what looked like Japanese schoolgirls on bicycles, oddly shaped mailboxes—no two alike—that looked like modern art sculptures, and more fifties-style automobiles than he'd seen anywhere outside of an old movie. Then there was the graffiti, it was all tags and text. There were several instances of it, sprayed on walls or boarded up shopfronts, but he didn't recognise the language; it almost reminded him of Egyptian hieroglyphics.

Every town has its quirks, he mused. He faced Van Brugen. "I almost got him nine months ago in Nebraska. The local PD found his second rape victim just as I touched down, and the trail went cold pretty quick."

"And the MO is always the same?"

"Pretty much. In Lincoln, it was two murders, two rapes. Each rape within forty-eight hours of a murder. Murder, rape, murder, rape. In October 2012, he was in Mobile, Alabama, exactly the same MO, but before that it was New York, April 2011; three murders and two rapes."

"What prompted the variation?"

"Sheer bad luck. The second girl had a reaction to the Pentobarbital. She had a heart attack before the police found her."

He watched Van Brugen's hands tighten on the steering wheel. "And before that?"

"2010, Jackson, Mississippi, two murders and two rapes. Before that you have to go back to 2007, Mesquite, Texas, one rape and one murder. He got interrupted just as he was about to attack his second victim—murder victim that is. I guess it spooked him, so he quit town."

"Three year gap," said Van Brugen. "Could he have been inside at the time?"

"It's possible. It's more likely that there were other crimes that just didn't flag up with the Bureau. The further back you go, the more gaps there are in the timeline. Prior to Mesquite, there were two murders and two rapes in Pasadena in '99."

"An eight year gap?" Van Brugen cast a scowl his way. He'd seen that kind of frown before, and he knew she was starting to wonder about his story. He also knew that frown was only going to deepen.

"Like I say, I expect there are other instances I haven't heard about. Prior to Pasadena there was Cleveland in '96, but before that you have to go all the way back to 1988, Las Vegas." She was back staring at the road, but he saw her face in profile. She was glowering. There was no use putting it off any longer. "The earliest incidents I've been able to track down took place in Duluth in 1975."

She slammed on the brakes and swerved over to the side of the road. A horn honked behind and then to the side of them as an angry motorist shot past. She flipped a finger dismissively towards the irritated driver, but then quickly turned in her seat to face Drake.

"1975? We're talking about a man who's committed upwards of twenty murders and rapes in forty years. You realise even if he was a teenager when he started, he's got to be knocking on sixty now, yet if anything, he only seems to be getting more prolific."

"I appreciate how it sounds."

She raised her left eyebrow. "Do you? I can see why you've had trouble convincing people of this."

"I have evidence. I didn't make these crimes up."

"So? I've been a cop a long time, I know how easy it is to make the evidence fit a theory, to get so bogged down in wanting to catch a perp that you try to fit round pegs into square holes."

Finally, his calm demeanour shifted. "Frankly, I've been an agent a lot longer than you've been a cop, and I know the dangers of looking for patterns where none exist, but the similarities in these cases can't be ignored. The almost caring treatment of the girls he assaults, the viciousness of the murders, the fact that the bodies have always suffered massive exsanguination, the fact that the primary murder scenes were never found . . . "

That got a reaction. "Really?"

"Really," he confirmed. "Never once."

She looked at him for a minute. "Okay, that's a little weird."

"Weird enough to ensure you'll help me?" he asked.

She grinned, pulled the car back onto the road. "No, but weird enough to let you buy me coffee and tell me more."

♦

DRAKE FOLLOWED VAN Brugen into a café called The Coven. At least, that's what he'd thought the place was called, but after they entered he realised it must have been Cavern and he'd misread it. Certainly the café had a cave-like feel to it, although despite the dim lighting and low ceiling, it was a welcoming place.

They took a corner table and a waitress dressed all in black, with an unfortunately large wart on the side of her nose, delivered them coffees and Danishes. He tried not to stare at the wart.

"Best pecan Danish in Midleif," Van Brugen said, but Drake was only half-listening; he was watching the waitress' receding back. Van Brugen laughed, picking up a Danish. "The wart's a fake."

He looked back at her, pretending innocence. "Huh?"

She took a bite of her Danish and smiled; sugar crested her upper lip like a dusting of ice. "The wart, people expect a bit of theatricality in a place called The Coven."

So he'd been right after all. His eyesight was still good, even if various other bits of his anatomy were letting him down.

Van Brugen seemed to take pity on him and changed the topic. "So, do you know much about Midleif?"

He took a tentative nibble of his pastry, which was quickly followed up by a larger bite. It really was delicious, the nutty flavour melting on his tongue. "To be honest," he mumbled as he chewed, "I never even knew this place existed, until a few days ago."

Van Brugen clasped a hand to her chest and looked hurt. Then she laughed. "We get that a lot. So what do you know now?"

He reached into his jacket and removed the folded-up tourism pamphlet he'd picked up earlier. He showed her the front cover, which featured the silhouette of a windmill. "I know that Midleif is the hundredth biggest city in America."

She shook her head. "Sorry to ruin your illusions, that info's twenty years out of date; we're closer to the hundred and twentieth now, only that doesn't look as good on the cover of a tour guide."

He flipped open the pamphlet. "Next you'll be telling me that Windmill Park doesn't exist anymore?"

"Oh, it's still there, and it still has four working windmills."

"Says here there were originally twenty?"

She nodded. "Built by Obadiah Trench in 1935. He hoped to power most of central Midleif by wind generated electricity."

"Sounds ahead of his time."

"He was, but he was also an idiot. He thought he'd got the land for a steal, but there was a reason it was cheap. While he was building his windmills, several local property tycoons were building big-ass skyscrapers right across the street. They acted as the world's best windbreak, and Obadiah Trench died penniless."

"Sad story." He looked down once more. "Muller's Department Store?"

"That's still here."

"I'd like to visit," he said, then quoted the guide: "'Reminiscent of Dracula's castle or the Addams Family mansion, this triumph of gothic architecture remains as fascinating today as when the doors first opened in 1924. Admire its towers, buttresses and gargoyles from the outside, then roam its four floors, which stock the very best merchandise at affordable prices'."

He looked up. She was chuckling, but her mirth soon bled away. "Tell me more about our guy, do you have a description? A name?"

"I have aliases." Drake returned the pamphlet to his pocket. "He likes to call himself Ray or Roy, sometimes Alvin, and he uses the surnames Hollis or Hollister."

"How original."

"It seems to work for him. He tends to set up shop in the seedier parts of town; I got those names from a variety of cheap motels over the years." He shrugged. "The ones that kept records, at least."

Catherine—or Katy, which she preferred—finished her coffee and set the mug down on the table with a soft clink, and looked at FBI Agent Drake. She wondered if he was here officially, or on his own recognisance. She quickly considered calling the local field office to check up on Drake, but decided against it. His evidence was slim yet compelling; there *had* been a brutal murder, there *was* an exsanguinated body, and there *was* a rape. She very much wanted to meet this Roy/Ray/Alvin.

"Don't worry, we'll get him," she said. "He's really picked the wrong city to mess with." She saw an almost pitiful look in Drake's eyes, as if he thought it was just the kind of bravado he expected from a two-bit cop in a two-bit city.

Drake didn't say anything though, just let her mouth-off. He was the epitome of the 'old pro'; he had no wedding band, he was obsessed with the case . . . she knew he would pursue this killer till he dropped. And Katy figured he may not have much time left; the way his hands trembled, the sunken eyes . . . she just *knew* he wasn't long for this world. Maybe she could help him catch the perp.

"We could canvass motels?" he suggested.

She shook her head. "Midleif has a large transient population; we probably have more cheap dives per square mile than most cities. Even if I drafted in a few dozen uniforms, it'd take days to canvass them all."

He looked crestfallen. "We don't have days. If he follows his usual pattern, there'll be another murder inside of twenty-four hours, and another rape soon after." He'd put the Danish down half-eaten and pushed the plate away from him. She frowned; he'd seemed to like the pastry, but lacked appetite.

"There's one other thing we can try," Drake said.

"Shoot."

"He tends to frequent red light districts."

Katy shrugged. "I have a few confidential informants who are hookers but, like I said, we have a large transient population. One new," she paused, "*face* isn't going to be that noticeable to a working girl."

"Trust me, our guy's memorable."

"Well, in that case, congratulations." She stood up, slapped a five dollar bill down on the table. "You're going to get to see Windmill Park, if nothing else."

♦

DRAKE WAS GENUINELY impressed when Van Brugen parked the Impala outside what she advised was the north entrance to Windmill Park. He'd expected a cramped patch of land not big enough to swing a cat, but the park actually looked extensive enough that you could swing a pride of lions if you were so inclined.

The four windmills stood in haphazard formation. Three were relatively close together, although it was clear there were gaps where their fellows had once stood. The fourth was some distance away, its sails pointed in the opposite direction, as if shunning the others. Around the windmills was the usual paraphernalia you found in most parks. Picnicking families, dog walking couples, jogging fools . . . and kids, lots of kids; either playing on jungle gyms and swing sets, or just racing around on the grass chasing Frisbees. Drake felt a pang of regret.

"It looks like a nice place," he said, feeling silly at his nostalgia.

"It is," said Van Brugen, slamming her car door, "at least during the day, and so long as you keep away from some of the adjacent side streets." She smiled. "Which is what we're not going to do; we're heading over to Millers Avenue."

The road running parallel to the park didn't look too bad; a few rundown shops with a few rough-looking denizens, but hardly Hell's Kitchen. Millers Avenue was different; it was replete with the kind of invisible filth that hovers in the air, a miasma of destitution and desperation, mixed with the scents of marijuana and sweat. They'd gone barely two strides before he felt a sudden urge to take a shower. Cars were parked on kerbs out the front of bars and shopfronts, making the avenue feel even more claustrophobic. The buildings were tall, yet somehow flimsy, casting the avenue in deep shadow. He walked on, fearing that the buildings may collapse if the breeze picked up, raining debris on their heads at any moment.

The people they passed wore dead-eyed stares set above hollowed-out cheeks, their emaciated bodies draped in thin and skimpy clothing. He'd seen that look far too many times in far too many towns. Women—and a few guys, too—who'd dropped so low that the only thing of value they had left were their bodies. Despite the air of desperation, there were plenty of takers; acne-pocked young men eager to pop their cherry, old married guys who barely lifted their eyes from the pavement, as if it didn't matter what the girl looked like, they were just eager to get off the street. There were pimps too; men in flashy outfits who stared back at passers-by with the certainty that they were untouchable, that they were *The Man*. Pathetic little kings ruling their wretched little kingdoms. Back in the day, he'd have made a point, busted a few heads, tried to encourage the girls to get off the streets, get off the drugs. He'd been nobler then. Not to mention a damn sight more naïve.

The one positive thing he could say about Millers Avenue was that business was booming. There might be a recession in most of America, but there were no going out of business signs or boarded-up shopfronts here. Music emanated from multiple bars, and every 'hotel' had one hundred percent occupancy, even if the rooms were the 'by the hour' variety.

Drake was glad of the comforting weight of the pistol in his shoulder holster, glad too of Van Brugen's company. They were just about to enter a bar when a bum appeared out of nowhere and made a beeline for Van Brugen. "Katy, Katy, Katy . . . ." He mumbled, eyes wide as he shambled towards them.

Drake tensed, expecting trouble, but Van Brugen smiled at the ragged old man. "Hello, Bob. How's things?"

Bob shrugged. He wore a poncho made out of garbage bags and smelt worse than the alley. He looked like he might be a hundred years old, but could have been closer to eighty. The streets weren't kind to their inhabitants. "So-so. Still waiting to get my letter back from the president."

"I'm sure it'll be here soon." She glanced at Drake. "Bob's an old friend, best informant I've ever had."

"Damn straight," said Bob. "Pleased to meet you." Drake was grateful Bob didn't offer to shake hands. "Old friend, you heard her, right?" Drake noted Bob barely had any teeth left.

"Old friend," agreed Drake.

"Since school." Bob smiled at Van Brugen. "She was the prettiest girl in my class," he said wistfully.

Drake forced a smile. "I'm sure she was."

Van Brugen was rooting around in her jacket pocket. "Now, Bob, I'm going to need for you to stake out the St Francis shelter for me again, I'm still sure they're a Mafia front. Can you do that?" She handed him a dollar bill.

Bob straightened and saluted her. "Aye-aye, Captain." Without another word, he turned and shambled away.

Van Brugen shook her head. "Lovely guy, but mad as a box of frogs." She gestured to the door. "Ready?"

"As I'll ever be."

♦

"WAS HE INTO anything weird?" Agent Drake asked, notepad out and at the ready.

Jill—"Just Jill" she insisted, when Katy had pressed for a surname—was the fourth working girl they'd talked to. One of her CIs, a bartender nicknamed Puck, suggested they talk to four girls who'd mouthed off about weird clients in the last couple of days.

The first three hadn't proven much use. One was so stoned she could barely remember her own name, let alone anything else, and the other two, as it turned out, had been talking about regular johns who'd just gotten a little kinkier of late.

But they might have just hit pay dirt with Jill.

"Weird? I'll say. I mean, you get a vibe about a guy in this job, a sixth sense, like Spider-Man, you know?" She snorted at her own joke. "Well, my sixth sense was warning me off this guy something bad." She shrugged. "I needed to score, though. Sometimes you gotta take a chance, right?"

The offhand way she talked about risking her life for a few bucks made Katy's stomach clench. Back when she'd started walking the beat, girls like Jill—and despite her haggard look, she guessed Jill was still a teenager—had given her sleepless nights. Not anymore. It wasn't because she'd hardened so much she didn't care, she just understood now that people had to play the hand they were dealt, and that you couldn't play it for them. All she could do was offer the occasional helping hand, like ensuring the Bobs of this world got a decent night's sleep once in a while. Nickel and dime nobility, but it was all she had.

"So what was weird about him?" asked Drake.

"Everything," said Jill, pointedly addressing Katy and ignoring Drake. "He was pale, I mean *really* pale, like he was sick, and he smelled kinda fusty, you know, like those . . . what do they call 'em, those things old ladies stick in their closets?"

"Mothballs," Katy suggested.

"Yeah, he smelled like them, like he'd been hanging in the wardrobe a long time." Another snort. "He was skinny too, dressed like a dumb hick, and his clothes were hanging off him." She shook her head. "He gave off this vibe though, you know, like he was more dangerous than he looked. Like the rube thing was just camouflage."

Katy cast a quick glance to her left. Drake was nodding.

"You brought him back here?" she asked.

Jill shrugged. "Either that or do him in the alley. Sure, we came back here."

'Here' was a single room above a bar. Somehow someone had levered a double bed and a wardrobe inside the room, though the wardrobe was missing its doors. A handful of outfits dangled from hangers inside, none of them very substantial. They seemed to match Jill's current outfit: hot pants with a halter top that revealed tattoos up both arms. It was possible that Jill simply liked ink, but Katy thought it more likely she was covering up track marks. Jill had short black hair, but over on the dresser was a blonde wig that looked like someone's dead pet rat.

"So what happened next?" asked Drake.

Jill rolled her eyes at him. "You can't be *that* old. What do you think happened next?"

Drake seemed to ignore the sarcasm, and fiddled with his notepad. "I'm guessing he couldn't get it up?"

Jill frowned, caught by surprise. "Yeah, that's right. Only he *really* couldn't get it up. I mean a lotta guys, 'specially the older ones—no offence—they have trouble, but I can usually get some kind of reaction, even if they're still too limp to be much good. But this guy?" She shook her head. "Nothing, floppy like a dead fish, cold as one, too."

"Did he get angry, threaten you in any way?" asked Katy.

"No, that was the weirdest thing about it. I played around with him for a while, you know, used all my tricks, and then I got worried. Sometimes guys who can't get it up, they blame a girl, but him . . . " She shook her head. "He was creepy about it, actually smiled, as if he was glad he couldn't get it up. That scared me, I mean, a guy gets angry I know how to deal, offer a full refund, suggest another girl, or you take a few slaps. Ain't nice, but a guy's gotta get it out of his system. He just stood looking at me for a minute, then pulled his pants up and left, didn't even ask for a refund."

"Did you get a name?"

"I didn't ask."

"Okay then, would you be willing to sit down with a sketch artist for us?"

Jill's face contorted. "I dunno . . . "

Even as she was trying to weasel out of having to go downtown, Drake was reaching into his jacket pocket. Katy almost expected him to pull out the Midleif Tour guide again, but it seemed to be a crumpled mugshot.

"Is this the guy?"

Jill took the piece of paper. Katy saw recognition light up her tired gaze. "Yeah."

"Do you recall anything else?" Finally, they seemed to be getting somewhere.

"Nah . . . oh, wait. Just one thing, he had a Grim's shopping bag."

Katy's eyes locked on the photograph and anger stirred within her. She'd ask Drake about it, and his lack of information, later. But for now, they had a lead . . .

◆

THEY DIDN'T SPEAK on the way back to the car. When they got in, Van Brugen put her key in the ignition, but didn't start the engine. For a handful of seconds she just stared out of the window, watching windmill sails turn languidly in the breeze.

"Why do I get the feeling I've pissed you off?"

Her head snapped sideways. "What do you think, Mr Assistant Special Agent-in-Charge? I don't like being taken for a patsy."

"I wasn't . . . "

"You have a name and a face," she snapped. "You gave me some bullshit about aliases but you know who he is. You have a *picture*."

For a moment he just sat there. "I wasn't playing you," he said finally. "It's just that, well, what I know can be a little hard to swallow. I thought it best to take things slow."

Van Brugen narrowed her eyes. "You patronising bastard."

He laughed. "Quite the reverse, I just didn't want you to think I was nuts."

"You going to show me then?"

"Okay." He withdrew the folded-up paper from his pocket, but even as she reached for it, he held onto it. "Just one thing. Whether you believe me or not, he's still out there, and he's dangerous. You can call me a fruitcake, call me all the names under the sun, just don't kick me out of the car. We can still nail this son of a bitch."

She glared at him for a few seconds, then she nodded and he let her take the paper.

He knew what she was looking at, had memorised the image long ago. It was a black and white mugshot, the subject a skinny guy, with a face so thin and angular that it reminded him of knife blades. The old-fashioned board he was holding identified the date as October 15, 1970, and detailed that he'd been arrested by the Minneapolis police.

There was a reference number, and below it, a name: Raymond Alvin Holliston.

"I guess we know where he gets his aliases from," she muttered. Drake's heart stuttered in what might have been relief.

He saw her eyes drop to the bottom of the photograph, still reading the board. Van Brugen's eyes widened when she saw the date of birth: January 2, 1941. She glanced up. "Your guy's in his seventies?"

"Yes, I suppose he would be."

But Jill had recognised the guy, not a hint of hesitation.

Van Brugen waved the mugshot in the air. "Okay then, let's be clear on this. I can see two alternatives. Either our guy is this man's son, or you're telling me he uses the best wrinkle cream ever invented."

Drake didn't bother holding back a chuckle. "The latter."

"Somehow, I knew you were going to say that." She sighed. "Okay, it makes sense now, the exsanguinated bodies, the ageless killer; we're looking for a vampire, right?"

"So you believe me?" Drake asked.

The idea of monsters was a bit hard for most cops to deal with.

"I'm trying to," Van Brugen said.

"Okay, so yes, I think our guy is a vampire, but not in the traditional sense. He doesn't age, and I don't think he drinks the blood of his victims for sustenance. I think the blood is for something else ... I ... " He hated this bit, wondered why he was even bothering. She was going to toss him out of the car in a minute anyway.

She turned the photo over in her hands. "He needs the blood so he can get an erection, right?"

That startled him. "Yes, but how ... "

Van Brugen shrugged. "It all adds up. Blood flow can cause erectile dysfunction, so I hear." She winked at that. "We have an eye-witness who tells us our guy can't get a hard-on, tells us our guy is white as a sheet, and then we have a man who brutally kills, drains people of their blood, then a few hours later goes out and rapes women. You don't have to be a detective to put two and two together."

"No," he said, on the back foot now. He was in unfamiliar territory. Before now, he'd either managed to keep the more fantastical elements of the case under wraps, or he'd been kicked to the kerb for being a wacko. "I'm surprised you're taking this so calmly."

"Well, Midleif's not your average city; and my grandmother had Romany blood in her. Besides," and she smiled slyly, "like you say, even if you're a lunatic, this guy is still out there. A lead suggested by a madman is still preferable to no lead at all."

"Thanks." He smiled. "I think."

"And this explains the lack of a primary kill site—for all we know, the spot where the victims were found *could* have been the primary. So, do you have a crucifix or a wooden stake in your shoulder holster?"

He shifted uncomfortably in his seat. "Just my service-issue Glock." He knew he'd have questioned his own sanity, if he'd started packing crosses and garlic.

"Well then, let's hope bullets work." She turned the ignition key. "I know where to go next, at least."

"Grim's?"

She nodded. "There used to be a chain of convenience stores across Midleif owned by the Grimalkin family. One by one, they all closed. There's just one branch of Grimalkin's left, on the corner of Third and Haxan." She was grinning as she shifted the car into drive. "There's only one hotel nearby. I think we've got him."

♦

THE HOTEL WAS old and cheap, yet despite this, it was clean and well-maintained. A Ray Hollis was booked into room 206 and, as far as the desk clerk was aware, he was there now.

Drake felt almost giddy as they approached the room. All his aches and pains seemed to have receded; even the agony caused by the cancer in his gut had eased. It was adrenalin he knew, a temporary respite, but he didn't care. Once he took down Raymond Alvin Holliston, it wouldn't matter very much. He had a very special date planned with a bottle of Kentucky bourbon and his nine millimetre Glock.

The hotel creaked and groaned around them. They saw no other guests on their journey to room 206.

There'd been no discussion of backup, both of them eager to get this done. After all, how could they explain the call to dispatch? 'Please send backup, we have a vampire on the loose?' Without a word needing to be spoken, they took position on either side of the door and drew their weapons.

"Before we do this, let's just get our story straight," she whispered. "We knocked, identified ourselves, and we heard signs he was trying to escape, so we went in. Sound good?"

"Sounds perfect." He narrowed his eyes. "We're not taking him alive, right?"

Van Brugen shook her head. "If you're right, he's already dead."

"Touché."

There was no knock, no warning. She stepped back and kicked the door open. They went in fast, Drake first, Van Brugen behind him; he went left, she right.

The room was dark, dusty. The odour of mothballs permeated the air.

Drake knew something was wrong even before he heard the sound of something crashing to the floor behind him. He turned fast on his heels, too fast, his head spinning as the room blurred. Van Brugen was lying on the floor, unmoving. Eyes searching frantically, he saw Raymond Alvin Holliston. The man was naked, his flesh so shockingly white it almost seemed to glow. His feet were affixed to the faded paintwork above the doorway, like he was a spider, leaving the rest of his body suspended in the air. In his right hand was a syringe.

Drake started to raise his gun, but he was too slow. Or perhaps, his brain consoled him in those final few seconds, Raymond Alvin Holliston was just too fast. Like a swimmer kicking off from the side of the pool, the killer sprang towards him. Holliston's mouth gaped impossibly wide. Wolfish fangs erupted from the man's gums, and Drake had just enough time to realise that he'd failed, before everything went dark.

♦

KATY AWOKE TO find herself staring at a nicotine-stained ceiling. Her head throbbed in protest, the pain reminding her that the bastard had jabbed her with Pentobarbital before trussing her up.

She tilted her head to assess her body, but knew that she was partially naked. Her shirt had been ripped open, her bra missing in action. Her jeans were around her ankles, and though her panties were still in place, she knew they wouldn't be for long. This was just Holliston prolonging his pleasure.

Katy couldn't see the ribbons securing her ankles, but she could see the ones that fixed each wrist to the metal framed bed. The silken material looked fragile, but had been tied tight enough that she had no room to manoeuvre, and could do little except wave her hands uselessly. Anger—and disgust—pounded through her veins, washing away the drug and its effects.

The sounds of slurping reached her then, the greedy guzzling reminding her of a parched man who had been given his first taste of water in months. She turned her head to the sound, realising she was still in room 206. She let her gaze skip over the two figures against the wall. She needed a plan.

She couldn't see Drake's Glock, but spotted her pistol, a Ruger SR45, its matt black surface vivid against the pale carpet. Her phone, and one she assumed was Drake's, lay nearby. She stared at the pistol, gauging the distance. Then she looked back at the figures.

Holliston was plastered against Drake, his mouth pressed to the FBI agent's throat. The killer was naked, his skin pale, but even as she watched, she saw it begin to glow with a rosy hue. Drake was still, his body limp and empty of life.

She shouted, "Hey, asshole!"

Holliston's shoulders twitched, and he paused his slurping, but he didn't look round. When she said nothing more, he resumed drinking, though she could tell the process was near its end. There couldn't be much blood left.

Holliston then stepped back from the wall. Katy could see Drake's body, slumped against the wall, eyes wide and lifeless, his skin almost blue. There was a raw wound in his neck, though there were only a few flecks of blood to mark the outer edges of the laceration.

Holliston turned to face her. He looked exactly the same as the mugshot, although his features were tinted with stolen colour, and his face wore a smear of crimson blood across his jaw. He had an erection, throbbing purple and red.

She wasn't his type, but guessed expediency would make up for her imperfections.

"You shouldn't be awake," said Holliston.

"What can I say? I have a strong constitution."

He grunted.

Katy shook her head. "Seriously, asshole, you really picked the wrong city this time."

He cocked his head to one side, reminding her of a confused bird. He shook his unease away, and stepped towards her. His penis bobbed with the movement, and she might have laughed if she wasn't tied to a bed. Holliston didn't seem able to look her in the eye, his gaze instead directed a few inches to her side. "I'll give you another shot," he said. "It'll be easier that way."

"Easier for you?" she asked, when he turned his back and walked to the dresser.

He paused. "I'm not a monster," he whispered. "I wasn't always like this, but the blood . . . I need it." He started moving again. "I'm not a monster," he repeated. He reached the dresser, which had a syringe and a small bottle perched atop.

Enough pissing about, Katy, she told herself.

She let her glamour drop.

The spell she so carefully wore didn't just make her appear younger, it changed her physically as well. When the magic was released, she became the old woman she really was, her body withering and shrinking to its true form. The agony of arthritis washed over her in wave after painful wave, along with a whole host of other torments, but her wrists wasted away as muscle shrank beneath the skin, and the ribbons that had been taut grew loose and she was free.

Holliston still had his back to her as he refilled the syringe. Quietly, she clambered off the bed. He hesitated at the sound of creaking bedsprings, but didn't turn around, apparently confident in the secureness of his bindings. Katy bent with effort, and picked up the Ruger. As she straightened, something twanged in her back, and she winced ruefully. Old age could be a bitch. Clicking off the safety, she saw Holliston's spine lock, but before he could turn, she fired a single round through the small of his back, the snub nosed .45 slug tearing through his spine.

He screamed and dropped like a sack of potatoes, landing on his back, which made him cry out again. He lay there, unable to move, screaming, while Katy pulled her jeans up—she had to hold them tight with one hand because they were too loose now— and fastened the few buttons left on her shirt. Feeling better, she hobbled over to Holliston.

She grinned at his almost childlike confusion. Where he expected a young blonde, he found a withered old woman standing over him. "Like I said, you picked the wrong fucking town, sonny."

"I . . . I don't . . . I'm not a monster!"

Katy chuckled, the sound crackly with age. "I know a Romany curse when I see one, and I can guess why someone cast it, though it was a blessed stupid thing to do, all things considered. Magic might have made you a killer, but I'm willing to guess you were a raping SOB long before then."

"I . . . I . . . wait . . . no . . . "

She'd had enough. There were ten rounds left in the Ruger. She put three of them into his groin, vaporising flesh and splattering the carpet beneath with Larry Drake's blood. She let him scream for almost a minute before she emptied the rest of the magazine into his face. Katy had to make certain he wouldn't come back again and to do that, she'd need to cast a binding spell. She hoped the other residents at the motel would keep quiet for as long as she needed. Once she was done, she'd restore her glamour and call it in.

"First things first, though," she muttered.

♦

LARRY DRAKE WAS surprised to open his eyes. His vision was blurry, and he could only just make out the haggard old woman, despite the fact her face was just a few inches away. He was cold too, freezing, yet he wasn't shivering.

"I'm alive?" His words were so slurred he almost didn't recognise them as his own.

"For the moment," said the old woman. "I'm afraid it's only temporary, though."

Something about the voice was recognisable. He frowned. "Van Brugen?"

The old woman nodded. Her nose was still crooked.

"I don't understand?"

"Don't you? If you can believe in vampires, why not witches? You see Bob wasn't kidding when he said we were kids together, and I wasn't lying when I said I'd been a cop a long time."

He blinked. "Why?" he gasped. It took a huge effort just to utter the single word.

"Why'd I bring you back?"

He nodded.

"Because you're a decent man, and I didn't like the idea of you heading into the great beyond thinking you'd failed. We got him, we got Raymond Alvin Holliston. He's dead and he won't be coming back, he'll never hurt anyone else." She smiled gently and she brushed a lock of hair from his eyes. "You can rest easy now, job done."

He frowned. "How . . . long?"

"Not long," she said softly.

"Shame."

"Why?"

"Wanted to see . . . Muller's Department store."

Van Brugen chuckled. "You haven't missed much. It's nowhere near as impressive as the tour guide suggests. Besides, it's overpriced and . . . " She stopped talking.

Larry Drake could no longer hear her.

Katy gently closed his eyes and stood up, reasserting her glamour as she did so. She groaned in relief as age and pain melted away, but a crushing fatigue almost floored her. Magic like that demanded a price. "I hope you make it to a better place," she whispered.

She stepped over Holliston's body. "You, on the other hand, can go to hell." The binding spell didn't take long; she had everything she needed. Then she snatched up her phone. "This is Van Brugen, there's been a shooting at Hopkinson Inn, backup required. One officer is down." Looking at Drake, she shook her head sadly, although no one else could see. "No, no need for paramedics. Yeah, I'll hold . . . "

◆ ◆ ◆

AZIMUTH

PETE KEMPSHALL

"SHOULDN'T it be *more* . . . ?"

"What? Mystic?" Blum chuckled, a wet sound that rose from his chest and bubbled in his throat. "Say 'abracadabra' if it makes you feel better. Actually, don't. Too easy to guess."

My face flushed. "What does it even mean?"

"How the devil should I know? That's the point, my boy." He paused. "Look, the word itself is insignificant. It's like a password, a security code. It has to be something you can remember, but that no one else can guess or use by mistake. You don't want someone else setting them free, before the job's done, do you?"

"I suppose not."

"You suppose right. Try it."

"What?"

"The word. Try it for size."

I stared at him, and he held the look, one eyebrow raised expectantly.

"All right." I took a breath.

"Azimuth."

◆

FORBES TAKES THE envelope and tucks it into the pocket of his long, white coat. We've been at these little acts of midnight commerce for long enough now that he doesn't feel the need to check the contents—I've got nothing to gain from cheating him, and he's got too much to lose from cheating me. That's the climate in which our transactions take place—if not in a spirit of trust, then in open acknowledgement of our needs.

"So, who are you here for?" he asks, turning smartly on his heel and leading the way to the refrigerated area.

"Lucy Turnbull."

"Oh, *her*." He pushes open a set of double doors, and strides into the chill beyond, leaving the rubberised portals to swing back in my face. I put up my hands to stop them, and slip through the gap after him. "Mutilation, decapitation . . . Good choice. One for the connoisseur. Thought you'd have been in for her sooner, actually." He chortles.

My fists bunch. "I've just been busy. And I knew you'd hold on to a sample for me."

Forbes's grunt blossoms white in the freezing air. "Nothing to do with me." The room is lined on both sides with small drawers, no bigger than post office boxes. "If your old mates were any good at their jobs, she'd be long gone by now." He smiles so widely I think the top of his head might fall off. "Lucky for you, they couldn't detect a fart in a shoebox."

He sucks his teeth in a way that makes me want to kick them out. Once, I'd have felt bad about thinking that, but I spend more than enough time staring at the ceiling feeling bad as it is.

He locates the right drawer with unerring efficiency. There are hundreds of the small chiller units—thousands, perhaps—and none of them are identified by name. For all that he's a money-grubbing opportunist with zero professional ethics, I feel a grudging admiration for the way he can identify an individual case from its serial number alone. Everyone has to have one talent, right?

He pops open the door and extracts the test tube. "I've not got any slides made up," he says. "Give me a couple of minutes and I'll fix you one."

"No problem."

"You know, I've been meaning to ask for a while . . . " He pauses. "You know, if that's . . . ?"

"It's fine. Go for it."

He indicates the small glass vial, with its red-black contents. "The slides. What exactly do you do with them? Do you, like, pour some wine, and get them out and look at them or something? Like Dexter?"

I hesitate. The prevailing opinion, after I left the force—after Alicia Connor—was that I'd turned in my sanity with my badge. If I tell Forbes the truth, I'll be in a padded cell so fast my feet won't touch the ground.

So I shrug. "Or something."

◆

IT'S A SPECIAL *kind of hell, to be trapped in a hot metal box with nothing but your guilt and a handgun.*

One mistake was all it had taken to put me there. One transposed number, the difference between admissible and inadmissible. The difference between me leaving the courtroom with justice done, and me sitting in my car outside Trevor Ramsay's house, staring at the Glock in my lap and agonising over who I'd be best served to fire it at, him or me.

Or him then me.

The force had dropped me like a shit-covered doughnut. 'Medical leave', they called it, a valid enough concern at the balance of my mind, but everyone knew to read between the lines. It was my fault Ramsay had walked. And that meant it was my fault Alicia Connor was dead.

The day had topped 40 degrees and the night brought no relief, not even a breath of wind through my rolled-down windows. But the heat was keeping people indoors, and in the four hours I'd sat there, waiting for Ramsay to get home and wondering just what I'd do when he did, I'd seen no one.

I almost didn't spot Ramsay. It was only when the screech of the flywire door snapped me from my inner blackness that I was able to focus and spot his silhouette entering the house.

I waited a couple of minutes, then popped the door and stepped into the street.

I don't remember walking to the front porch. One instant I was in the road, the next I was on the deck, shrouded by the bilious yellow light from Ramsay's window, peering in.

He sat in front of the TV, one of those trays on his lap—the ones that have the cushion built into the base to make them stable while you eat. He forked pasta into his face from a bowl, occasionally supplementing his mouthful with a swig from a moisture-marbled can of lager.

Just like any single thirtysomething chilling after work. Normality incarnate.

I raised the gun and aimed through the glass.

I'd spent more than a decade as a cop, and in all that time I'd rarely had cause to draw my weapon. But on the occasions that I had, it had never felt so heavy, never shaken so much in my grip as it did then. If I'd pulled the trigger, the shot could have gone anywhere, could have taken Ramsay in the side of the head or just as easily blown out the light bulb above it.

I lowered my arm and turned back towards the street. I'd only be needing one bullet after all.

♦

NOW AND AGAIN, I still feel like a fraud. This kind of gig, you need the silver salvers, the golden chalices carved with arcane symbols, right? Sitting at my kitchen table, scrawling on a paper plate with a Sharpie . . . It's hardly Doctor Strange.

"You're not doing this for show," Blum had explained when he'd shown me the ropes. "No one's going to be watching, there's going to be no one to impress. What counts is the intent, not the materials. Get your mind right and you could pull this off scrawling with mud on a hubcap."

I'd settled on picnicware because it was cheap. My deal with Forbes eats up most of my cash; custom-made magic crockery doesn't enter into it.

The runes take me a little under five minutes: when I was starting out, it was closer to fifteen, assuming I didn't stuff up and have to start again. Don't get me wrong, I'm very careful, I took my lessons seriously. If there's one thing Blum stressed it was that the slightest slip, the smallest variance of line, and I could summon, well, something a whole lot nastier than what I was aiming for.

"They're out there," he'd told me. "Waiting for an opening. That's why you shouldn't rush, my boy. They're patient. So must you be."

I inscribe the last line, then reach for the envelope Forbes gave me.

I've known Forbes a while, from back when I was in and out of his lab in an official capacity. When I renewed our acquaintance as a private citizen, I told him I was a collector of murder memorabilia, something his thinly veiled desire to supplement his income made him all too ready to believe. (Seriously, I thought I'd have to work harder to get him to buy into the arrangement. He practically tore my arm off.) Accordingly, he'd cocooned the slide in bubble wrap— no one wants their prize exhibit broken before they get it home.

I unwrap the small glass rectangle and snap it, displacing the cover slip and exposing the dried blood beneath. Once I've placed the fragments on the plate, in the centre of the inked symbols, I pick up the knife.

You'd think, after all I've seen, that I wouldn't be quite so squeamish, but it's different when it's your own blood. I screw up my courage and nick my thumb, wincing at the brief, sharp pain. Holding the wound over the plate, I allow three fat drops to spatter onto it, then I stick my thumb in my mouth, sucking like a sulky toddler. It never stops the bleeding, but it's something I've always done, from that first time under Blum's tutelage to today. It's part of the ritual now. My signature move.

I pick up the plate and lay it in the sink before dousing the whole paraphernalia in lighter fluid and reaching for the matchbox. I get a flame first strike, and drop it on the plate. There's a hollow *whoomf* and the flames leap up at me.

Feeling their heat on my face, I close my eyes and think of the word.

Despite the fire, a chill ripples through me, the hairs rising on my arms . . .

"Where am I?"

I open my eyes, turn towards the voice, and begin to explain.

♦

MAYBE I SHOULD *have kept walking, returned to my car and finished it.*

I didn't.

From the house came a clatter, hollow and metallic: a beer can, dropped on the floor. I don't know why that made me turn round and look, it's not like it's an uncommon sound.

Ramsay sat, just as he'd been when I'd turned away, except . . . except now he wasn't staring at the TV. It was like he was staring through it. And he was shaking. Hard.

He still had his fork in his hand, loaded with pasta, but raised no higher than halfway from the bowl. As the tremors wracked him, strands of spaghetti came loose and fell, missing the bowl and plopping instead on the tray, on his legs, down his t-shirt.

With a stiff motion, he flicked his wrist, dislodging from the utensil all that remained of the food. Then, with infinite, painful slowness, he raised the fork to his eye, and started to push.

I tried to look away as he eased the tines into himself, God knows I tried. All I can think of now is that the same desire in me to see him pay for his crimes ensured I bore witness.

Why didn't he scream?

Ramsay continued to push, thick fluids trickling down his cheek now, off his chin, and all the while he made no sound. Then, meeting some final resistance, he stopped, and lowered his hand. The fork stayed where it was.

What happened next . . . You remember that fad for subliminal messages on TV, right? The way film editors would sometimes splice a random frame into a show, an image that had nothing to do with what you were watching, and that passed by so swiftly, you only registered it subconsciously? For one fleeting moment—one 'frame'—it seemed to me that Ramsay wasn't alone. That standing by his side, leaning down as if whispering in his ear, was a young woman.

Then in a blink she was gone, and Ramsay bent at the waist and head-butted the arm of his chair.

I staggered, my breathing fast and ragged, legs too weak to support me. I'd have collapsed, been found there by the police, in shock, a few feet from the body of the killer I'd failed to send to jail, if a hand hadn't tugged at my arm.

"We need to get out of here."

It was only when we were in my car—him driving, me in the passenger seat, enervated—that I took the time to really see him.

He had to be sixty, hunched over the wheel like Barry Humphries in an Einstein fright wig. Whereas I was still numb, there was an air of excitement about the man, crackling from him like he'd been plugged into the mains.

I concentrated on my words. "Who are—?"

"Blum," he said, chopping me off mid-question. "Daniel Blum. No need to introduce yourself, I know who you are, Aaron. Know why you were there, too."

I gaped at him, my mind unable to keep pace with what I'd seen, with what was happening now.

"You couldn't go through with it, I noticed," Blum said, turning into the bend ahead. "Good. No need anyway, I had it all under control. Well, not me exactly, but you know what I mean."

"No . . . no, I—"

"You saw her, didn't you?'

"I saw . . . "

"Who? Who did you see?"

"I can't have . . . "

"Who did you see?"

"Alicia. Alicia Connor."

If he hadn't been steering, I'd have sworn he'd have clapped his hands together with joy. Instead he stiffened abruptly, struck by a thought. "Oh my word, I nearly forgot!" He closed his eyes, as if he was standing stock still in an empty room rather than flouting the speed limit on a residential street. And in a voice so soft it was almost lost to the noise of the engine, he said:

"Azimuth."

◆

THE SIGHT OF her face is unsettling. Sure, I've seen it on the news, in the school photo that accompanied all the reports, from the first trickles of concern that she'd gone missing to the horror and outrage when she was found. The parts that *were* found. Looking at her now, there's nothing left of the wide-eyed innocence in that photograph. Agreed, her face is the same, but there's something in her eyes, something deeper; older.

Then again, being dead for a week is going to change you.

I spend a short while dancing around the main points so as not to freak her out. Number one, you're dead. Number two, I brought you back. Number three, it's not permanent. But she *doesn't* freak out. Not even close. I've brought back kids before, they all want their mums, their dads, their teddy bears, for God's sake. But Lucy here? Not a flicker.

It unsettles me, so I cut to the chase. "Do you remember who did this to you?"

She looks at me with those cold eyes. "Oh yes."

"Can you take me to him?"

She doesn't answer. She just turns and heads for the door.

♦

"You brought her back."

"I did."

"How?" Sitting in the squint-bright light of the burger bar, drinking abysmal coffee at two in the morning, none of it seemed real enough to properly disturb me. That came later.

Blum wiffled his fingers in front of his face. "Magic. You don't believe me," he said, without missing a beat.

"I saw her. But . . . "

"You're pleased, aren't you?"

"I'm sorry?"

"With the way it turned out." Blum tore open another sachet of sweetener and tipped the contents into his polystyrene cup. As he stirred, I realised this was the fourth or fifth packet he'd used, but I had yet to see him drink. I wondered if that made him smarter than he looked, using the coffee as a prop, a distraction rather than a beverage. He certainly made no attempt to taste it. "You went there to kill Ramsay, and you couldn't. Now he's dead, and you got to keep your hands clean." He reached for another sachet. "You're welcome, by the way."

"You do this . . . ?"

"A lot? Yes. I bring back the souls of the wronged to exact justice on those who wronged them. I can't say it pays the bills, but the job satisfaction is top drawer."

"How long?"

"Oh decades, my dear boy. Hundreds of times. I'm something of an unsung hero."

"So why show yourself now?"

Blum removed the plastic stirrer from his cup, stared into the swirling vortex of brown liquid. And he told me.

◆

WE PASS THE house—a two-storey new-build in the sprawl north of Joondalup—and park in the shadows around the corner. I look across at Lucy, but she's already out of the car. No need to open the door.

It's a strange feeling, playing chauffeur to the dead. Your logic rebels against it: they're ghosts, can't they just appear where they need to be?

"They're tied to your soul until you release them," Blum had explained when I'd voiced my surprise for the first time. "It's like a piece of elastic, it can only stretch so far before they snap back. They'll be able to sense whoever killed them, no matter who they are or how far away, but the onus of transportation? That's part of our service."

"So they can't find their own way?"

Blum had chuckled. "Not unless you cut the elastic, my boy. You've got to remember, your blood mixed with theirs, binds irrevocably. You say the word to perform the summoning, and until you say the word again, you're stuck with them. And vice versa."

Of course, that makes it difficult. It means I have to attend the scene while a returnee fulfils its mission. But Blum had an answer for that, too.

"Keeps you honest, my boy. If you have to watch it happen every time, you never get blasé about it."

I step out of the car and walk the short distance back and around the corner. Lucy is waiting by the garden path. There's no one around, but even if there were, the most anyone would see of her was that same 'subliminal flash' I saw years ago at Ramsay's house. Your average passer-by wouldn't even see that.

Lucy turns in silence and drifts up the path. There's still something about her that doesn't jibe. Not all spirits are chatty when you bring them back, although a lot are—some of them you end up wishing you could kill all over again, just to shut them up. But there's an oppressive feeling about Lucy's quietness, a brooding quality that belies her age. It weighs on my mind as I stop at the mailbox and peer inside. There's a single letter, uncollected, addressed to a Josh Hathaway. Names, Blum told me, are also part of the accountability incumbent on us. They ensure we don't become too detached. That our souls don't callous over.

For me, there's more to it.

Spirits have no substance, they can't act directly against their killers. Physically, they can't harm anyone, so they coerce, they persuade, like Alicia did to Ramsay. The flipside is that after a certain point, they don't need me. So long as I'm close enough for the 'elastic' not to snap back, I can leave them to it. It's not like they need me to knock on the door for them.

But I want to see. I *need* to see. I need to be able to go to bed at night and close my eyes and know justice has been done. And not think of when it wasn't.

So no, I don't need to knock. But I do anyway.

◆

"Why me?" I asked.

It was one of those summer days when Kings Park seemed to have more people than blades of grass, from dating couples to families, all out in force to enjoy the sunshine. By comparison, we made a strange pair, me in my t-shirt and shorts, Blum in the kind of padded anorak more common to a British winter than the height of the Perth heat. Nothing seemed to touch him though, not heat nor cold, like he was somehow above it all.

He struck off up the slope towards the DNA Tower, and said nothing until we were halfway up the grassy rise. When he did speak, his voice was quiet. Serious.

"You still feel it, don't you, Adrian?"

"Aaron. Feel what?"

"Why do you want to do this? Why do you want me to teach you?"

"Because you asked me to."

"No. Why do you want to learn? What do you get out of it?"

"Justice," I said without hesitation.

"I don't believe you."

I stopped dead, and he walked on a pace or two before realising and turning back. "Justice is a by-product, my boy," he said. "You don't want justice. You want the same thing I wanted when I started." He waited for me to say something, and when I didn't, added, "When I brought my son back."

I couldn't hold his gaze then. My eyes drifted to the twisted white double helix of the tower dominating the hilltop ahead. I could make out the figures of the people climbing its myriad steps, those who'd reached the top and stood pointing and gawking, and it felt like they were pointing and gawking at me . . . As if they knew, just like Blum knew.

"You've been letting it fester," he went on. "The trick is to make it work for you. To use it to do some good. The kind of magic I practise—the kind you'll practise—is all about will. What you're carrying around with you . . . it can make your will stronger. And it can make you more willing to pay the price."

"Price?"

"What do you think it is that's killing me?"

I hesitated. From the moment back in that fast food joint that he'd told me he was dying, that he wanted me to fill his shoes, the subject had been studiously avoided. "I assumed cancer."

Blum's smile was thin. "Tell me, have you ever been so foolish as to lick a frozen metal pole?"

The change of direction was so absurd, my laugh escaped before I could stop it. "In Perth?"

Blum shrugged. "But you are aware of what happens if you do?"

"Your tongue sticks to the pole, and if you try to pull it away—"

"You lose a layer of skin. It's the same thing here. Blood magic is an intensely personal endeavour. Your blood is entirely unique, an utterly individual physical and cosmic marker. When you use it to bring back a spirit, in order to stay on our plane, the spirit bonds to your very soul, until you release it."

"Okay."

"And when you do release it . . . It's like your soul is a tongue and the spirit the pole. You rip."

"You lose part of your soul?"

"Irretrievably. I've cast this spell . . . oh, so many times. And every time I've done it, another piece of me has been lost.

"I'm not dying from cancer, Aaron. I'm dying from having my immortal self torn to pieces."

♦

"WHO THE FUCK are you?" The man who opens the door— Hathaway, I presume—is in his mid-forties, short hair greying into a salt-and-pepper tone more pronounced on the sideburns valancing his face. He's a couple of inches shorter than me, but radiates belligerence. "What do you wa—?"

Before he can finish, the air beside me shifts, a physical sensation that tickles every inch of my exposed skin. The eyes of the man in the doorway widen in shock. And then something strange happens.

Now, I've done this dozens of times, I've seen it all. Some have screamed, some fainted dead away. Most run. Hathaway . . . Hathaway is furious.

"What the fuck have you done?" he asks, like I've not been paying attention and put diesel in an unleaded engine, instead of conjuring up the ghost of the girl he put in the ground.

In answer, Lucy's shade lunges, howling, fingers extended, ready to gouge, claw, scratch . . .

She hits something, something I can't even see. It reminds me of a bird that's failed to spot there's a window in its flight path, smacking into the glass and dropping dazed to the ground.

Hathaway points at the floor. A chalk line delineates the boundary of inside the house and out. Sigils, of the same kind I use on my paper plates, run parallel to it.

He sneers. "Not my first rodeo, fucker."

It's as if my brain has switched down a gear or two—I'll get there in the end, but I can't maintain the speed needed to keep up.

Lucy turns from the doorway, howling like she's being dragged through the gates of hell itself. She flickers, vanishes.

"Try all you like," Hathaway shouts at the empty air. "The whole place is sealed." He looks at me again, fury in his eyes. "You fucking amateur. Do you have any fucking idea who you brought back? *What* you brought back?"

"You killed her," I say, and step towards him. My fists are clenched, I'm going to flatten the bastard.

"She was already dead, you idiot. It killed her the second it abducted her."

"What the hell do you mean, 'it'?"

"Dorthamas," he says, and his voice softens, the edge disappearing. Like he understands suddenly that I *don't* understand.

The air shifts again, and Lucy strikes. She roars like a gale, rushing through the doorway where before she's been barred. The force of her takes Hathaway in the chest and he barrels over backwards, landing heavily.

The thought screams into my head.

How did she knock him down?

Hathaway pushes himself up on his elbows, but she's on him like a shot. Like smoke pluming back down a chimney, she pours into his nose, steadily at first then picking up pace until the very last wisps of her are gone.

I have just enough time to cover my face before his head explodes.

When I look again, she's standing there, pristine against the gore-stippled walls and floor. The smile on her face is no longer cold. It's hungry.

"Thank you," she says. Her eyes flit to the floor in front of me. I look down.

The thin white line between inside and out has a gap in it, smeared vague on the wooden boards. I lift up my foot, check the bottom of my shoe.

Chalk dust.

"Time for your reward," Lucy says. "Hold still."

I feel the building pressure inside my head, fight to focus, and the word pops free, like a cork from a bottle.

"Azimuth."

The expression on the dead girl's face changes, she quivers in equal parts rage and frustration.

"Soon," she says.

And she's gone.

But by that point, I'm already running.

♦

I DIALLED WITH *a shaking hand, the dream of Alicia hanging around me, miasmic.*

"Do you have any idea of the time, dear boy?"

"I'll do it," I said.

"You're sure?"

"I can't . . . I have to do something."

"But you understand the sacrifice?"

"Yes. Yes, I understand. Please. Teach me."

On the other end of the line, he sighed. I couldn't tell if it was satisfaction or resignation. "We'll begin in the morning. There's much to cover and I don't think I have a great deal of time."

"I can manage on the basics, can't I?"

"Well yes, but this is not a world for the ignorant, my boy, not if—"

"Blum," I said. "If you stop now—right now—and let me take over, will it—?"

"Save me?" Even without seeing him I knew he was shaking his head. "Too much of me is already gone. I might not die, not properly. My personality, my presence . . . It'll be like being dead." I thought of him in the park, how the heat didn't seem to affect him; how he got my name wrong; how he forgot how many sugars he'd put in his coffee. *"That's why we can't waste time . . . my memory."*

Tears welled in my eyes. *"You already said that."*

Silence down the line, then he burst out laughing. *"Just for that we start early. Be here at six."*

♦

THE DRIVE HOME is a nightmare. I'm shaking so hard it feels like my bones will break. Every time I look in the rear-view, I expect to see her sitting there. It should be a baseless fear—the rules are that once the shade has completed its unfinished business, and it's released by its summoner, it returns to the afterlife. If it didn't, we'd be hip deep in ghosts.

Lucy's business *is* finished, I dismissed her, she should be gone. But then there's that single word, resounding inside my head, a promise—a threat—I'm utterly unequipped to face.

"Soon."

Whatever's happened to Lucy's shade, I know beyond even the smallest doubt, she's still out there.

By the time I get home, I've calmed down enough to piece some of it together. I head straight to the back room and prise up the floorboards, retrieve the books Blum left me, and set to work filling in the gaps. A nervous couple of hours later, and I think I've got the facts.

There's no point questioning if Hathaway was right. I've seen the evidence with my own eyes. Lucy Turnbull was possessed. One of the things Blum warned me about—a 'patient entity'—must have found some way through to our world, and taken her body as its vehicle.

The more I read, the more it becomes clear to me. Lucy's murder had attracted me because of its brutality. Whoever could flay the skin off a thirteen-year-old girl's chest, decapitate her and keep the head; that was exactly the kind of sick fucker deserving of my attention. Without the facts, I blundered in, made a mistake and—

I think of Alicia Connor, and ice crystallises around my heart.

Knowing that Hathaway wasn't a thrill killer, the details of the mutilation take on new significance. He wasn't taking a trophy when he removed Lucy's skin, her head. He was *concealing* what he was up to.

It takes a while for me to find what I'm looking for—a binding rune. Hathaway would have had to carve it into Lucy to keep the demon trapped inside her while he . . . I imagine that if someone digs up Hathaway's garden, they'll find Lucy's burned skull. Brutal, savage even, but according to the books Blum left me, it's the only way to be sure. By all rights, the entity should have been lost in limbo for centuries.

Except I summoned Lucy back when she wasn't really Lucy any more.

I gave it a lifeline.

It's easy enough to find the rune Hathaway must have used, it's right there in the books. Each ward is tailored to a particular demon, and Hathaway was good enough to give me a name before he died: Dorthamas. Flicking through the pages, I read up on it: Lord of Deceit, apparently, but what really floats its boat is inflicting pain. Apparently, it's very good at it. Even better, when given a physical form to work from. Hathaway must have known the swathe of destruction the thing would leave, even in a little girl's body.

And then I understand.

"*Soon.*"

I feel a surge of panic, a desperate, futile wish that Blum was still here to tell me what to do, because it's all clear to me now. I know what's coming.

Dorthamas isn't coming to kill me. It's coming to take me. It needs a new host, and thanks to my blood magic, our essences are already linked. Dorthamas has a foot in the door, all it has to do is push. Standard magical protection will be completely useless. It'll be the easiest possession ever.

I'm low-hanging fruit. And unless I can think of something to do about it, I'll be plucked.

♦

IT TAKES ME most of the night to prepare. When I finally get home, and seal the entrances with chalk lines, I'm tired, stinking and hurting. I switch on the TV, allowing the sights and sounds to wash over me. The news cycles already have the story, the main stations latching on to it with grim alacrity.

The feeling of intoxication I experience is only partly due to the scotch, which I hit like a speeding train the moment I sit down. The smell of the booze scarcely masks the other, pungent smell that hangs around me no matter how often I wash my hands. I swig from the bottle rather than sip, I've been half-drunk for most of the evening anyway—I needed the whisky to counteract my usual squeamishness. By now there's only the occasional dull throb to suggest I'm any different, physically.

Just so long as I don't look down, I can ignore it.

It can't be long now—Dorthamas and I are joined, I can feel it coming. I take another belt from the bottle, and focus again on the screen.

I jerk awake. The room has grown cold, bitterly so, and I shudder. I know that outside, the night is still humid, sweltering. The change is local to this room.

It's starting.

The TV flickers, burps static, then the picture resolves itself into the rolling news coverage again.

"Hello, Aaron."

She—it—stands in the kitchen doorway, arms hanging loose at her sides. "Ready to go?"

I get to my feet, wobbling from the booze and the sudden flare of pain in my chest. "The chalk lines didn't work then."

"They're only any good if I'm not invited in. And I own part of your soul, Aaron. It's like an access-all-areas pass."

"How about if I asked you to fuck off?"

Lucy shivers with delight. "Oooh," she says, "You're adorable. I could just eat you up."

She flies at me, leering and triumphant, and I manage an instinctive step backwards before she hits me, hard, like a shoulder charge from a footballer three times her size. I go down, flat on my back, and can only watch, dazed, as she ebbs and swirls into the same smoke that destroyed Hathaway.

Then she's in me.

My vision goes black, all I can hear is the ragged panting of my breath. Then my eyes clear and she's standing next to me, puzzled. Angry. "What have you—?"

I fumble with the buttons on my shirt. My fingers feel thick and unresponsive, but I get the fastenings undone and draw open the garment, like curtains parting on opening night.

The bandages across my torso are stained red, the wounds beneath stubbornly refusing to scab.

"It's the same one Hathaway carved into your chest to keep you in," I say, lurching to my feet. "Figured it would keep you out, too."

"It won't be enough," she spits. "I already have part of your soul." A lick of the lips. "It tastes wonderful."

"Make the most of it. You want any more, you'll have to fight for it."

"Oh, your little rune might work if I didn't have a foothold already. Now it's just an inconvenience." She tilts her head, quizzical. "You're really going to make me fight?"

"You'd better believe it."

"I see. You realise that would cause you as much pain as me?"

"You could give up. Spare yourself the grief."

She laughs, a high, melodic sound. "I don't think so. I'm stronger than you in every regard, Aaron, I'll own you eventually. I'm just keen to get started." A moment's thought and she says, "I tell you what, how about I make you a deal?"

"You've got nothing to offer me."

"Oh, but I do," she says. "We're joined by blood, Aaron, I know exactly what you want. What you need." The cold in the room seems to deepen. "It never helped your mentor, you know."

"What the hell are you talking about?"

"All the guilt he felt over his son. 'Oh, if only I'd taken him to school that day instead of making him walk.' The whiny bastard carried that around until the day he died. All those victims he brought back to enact 'justice', all they did was tear up his soul." She shakes her head. "You're the same, you're in denial. This isn't justice, Aaron. It's atonement."

I watch her, as if frozen to the spot, unable to speak, thinking of what Blum said the night we met. Knowing that he lied . . .

"The job satisfaction is top drawer."

"But you'll never really atone, Aaron. No matter how many times you cast your spell, no matter how many little bites of your soul you sacrifice to the magic, it'll never be enough. Because for as long as you live, there'll be the nights when it comes to you in your sleep and drags you awake and reminds you that Alicia Connor died because you were incompetent. Deny it all you like, punish yourself til your head spins, it'll keep eating at you.

"And you know the best thing? All that noble self-sacrifice, everything you've done since you met Blum, that's just made it worse. Hathaway was one of the good guys, I could never have got to him if you hadn't wiped out part of the chalk line. Plus, you brought me back. I'd still be banished to the outer void if not for your blood magic. But now I'm back and I'll take your body and I'll kill and kill and kill.

"And it's all your fault. Again."

The rune in my chest burns with cold fire, seems to weigh tonnes, crushing my heart. I choke on my words.

She's right.

"So here's the deal." She sits down in my armchair, makes a show of wriggling around until she's comfortable even though we both know she can't feel anything. "When I take your body—and I will take it—there's the problem of what to do with your soul. Now normally, I'd consume it. Surround it and absorb it so that there's nothing left. That's what I offer you."

"Eating my soul?"

"If you like. Or you could look on it as my granting you oblivion."

I see it then, the deal. Let her in and she'll destroy me utterly, beyond any hope of existence in this world or any other. Unable to feel anything ever again.

She's offering me absolute, final peace.

"Or, you can fight me. In that case, I'll keep you on," she says. "Just enough of your soul to *feel*, enslaved inside your body as I drive it around. As I bathe in blood. And I'll make you watch, Aaron. All of it. You think you feel guilt now? Defy me, I'll give you guilt everlasting."

She holds her hands out, palms open, a 'take it or leave it' gesture.

I'm shaking; she already knows my decision. "How? How do I let you in? The rune . . . "

She shrugs. "The rune's just a spell, Aaron, it's empowered by your will. All you have to do is will it to stop working."

I take in a deep breath. All these years, all this hurt. "It's over, isn't it?"

"Let me in, Aaron. No more pain. I promise."

I close my eyes and will away my protection.

She rushes into me like an icy flood, and despite her promise, the pain is excruciating. Every cell of my body catches light, flares with bright, inescapable agony.

Then it's done.

"There," I hear my voice say. "All better." My body reaches for the bottle of scotch. It takes a long pull, and I imagine the burning sensation down my throat. Imagine it because I can't feel it. Because it's not my body any more.

"You know the secret of good mystics?" Dorthamas asks.

Tell me.

"Research. Learning. Kudos to you on discovering the protection rune, but I can't help feeling you dropped the ball."

I did?

"Well, if you'd done your homework properly, you'd have known what people call me." My voice trembles with laughter. "The Lord of Deceit. I don't make deals, Aaron. I break them." Another swig of booze I can't taste. "I think I *will* keep you around for a while. It might be nice to have some company."

I thought you might.

"And you still took the deal? More atonement, is it? I've known some self-flagellating basket cases in my time, Aaron, but you're something else."

Ha. Have I got news for you . . .

"I'm all ears."

No, really. Check the TV.

"Why would I—?"

It's on now. Watch.

I feel Dorthamas switch its attention to the screen. A reporter is talking into camera, behind her a building in flames. Half a dozen high-pressure water jets are being directed at it by fire crews, but the blaze is out of control.

"So what?" Dorthamas says. Deep in its being, I feel a twinge. Uncertainty.

The building. You know what it is?

Dorthamas scans the screen, reads the scrolling bar of information along the bottom of the news feed. "A storage facility."

It's where they keep the evidence in cold cases. Biological material.

"Again, so what?"

You smell that?

Dorthamas twitches my nose, notices at last the odour lurking under the scotch fumes, the one no amount of soap could shift from my hands. "Petrol?"

The TV. Look harder.

I sense his eyes—my eyes—examining the scene.

You were right, you know.

"What?"

I'll never be able to atone for Alicia Connors. No matter how many little pieces of my soul I sacrifice.

It's seen them now. The news camera pans across the scene and just for a second, catches the spray paint on the ground beside the building.

"What was that?" There's an edge to my voice now.

But what if I could save hundreds of lives by stopping you? Wouldn't that balance the books?

"Was that a sigil—?"

What if instead of giving up hundreds of little pieces of my soul, I make one lump payment?

"What have you done?"

Blood samples, Dorthamas. That building's full of them. Hundreds. Thousands. Mine too. All burning together.

All those souls, joined to mine. Joined to yours too, now. Until I let them go.

"But that'll tear us both to—"

Yes. Yes, it will.

I feel it try to disengage from me, flee my body, but I've refocused my will on the rune in my chest. The door's locked.

Too late, Dorthamas.

And I say the word.

♦

GIL FAVORY LAUGHED so hard that a fine spray of beer escaped his lips. When the moment had passed, he wiped his mouth and took another belt from the bottle. His favourite show on the box, a cold brew . . . It didn't get much better than this.

With Andrea it had been like serving time. She'd virtually banned him from going out at all, had capped him at one beer a night. When she was being really spiteful, she'd hide the bottle opener. Yeah, she'd let him watch TV, but even that had the sense of a grudging privilege that she could revoke at a moment's notice. Every time he looked over his shoulder at her, sitting behind him in the corner under that lamp, she'd had her nose in a book. But Gil knew—he *knew*—that once he was facing the screen again, she'd be watching him, searching for some transgression on which to pounce. And of course, if the volume on the TV crept up too loud, or Gil chuckled too hard, he'd hear her, a single 'tut' and an exasperated shushing noise.

Now and again, a neighbour would ask him if the police had made any progress, if they were any nearer to catching Andrea's mugger. Her killer. And Gil would cast his eyes to the ground, shake his head. "Not yet," he'd say. "But there's always hope."

The sitcom paused for a newsbreak—another one of those bodies with the head blown off in the burbs—so Gil got up and wandered to the fridge for another drink. Popping the cap from the beer, he raised it in a silent toast to the cops, and took a long, luxuriant pull from the bottle.

Back in the lounge room, the commercials were wrapping up, and Gil flumped back into his chair, digging in for the long haul. He reached his free hand for the remote and jacked up the sound. The laugh track boomed around the room, Gil supplementing it with his own guffaws. He got so carried away that he didn't even notice to begin with, the noise from over his shoulder. It was only when his mirth properly subsided that he recognised it for what it was, that low, irritated sibilance building pressure in his skull . . .

"Shhhhhhhhhhhh."

♦ ♦ ♦

THE CITY

'What is the city but the people?'
~William Shakespeare, *The Tragedy of Coriolanus*

THE TANGLED
STREETS

KATHLEEN JENNINGS

"ARIADNE Winter?"

The woman standing over Aria was narrow and dark, yet the bulky vest, numerous belts, and the square and mysterious holsters that police everywhere seemed to find necessary, made her loom in the hospital corridor. She was carrying Aria's shoulder bag, her silhouette shadowed in front of the empty windows, which the flickering fluorescent tubes turned into mirrors. Beyond them, Aria was dimly aware, the city spread out under the night.

The policewoman's uniform was not quite the right shade of blue, and the embroidered state logo with its wreath of green leaves rising like wings around it was unfamiliar. Little differences from home, but enough to have been discomforting even if there had not been a glint of knowledge in the woman's eyes. The badge on her right sleeve read "Gray".

"You shouldn't have shot him," said Aria, her voice fraying. She picked nervously at the edge of the bandage a paramedic had fastened around her forearm.

"He followed you through the . . . perimeter," said the policewoman coolly. "And he had a knife." The latter, Aria thought, was more of an excuse than anything else. The woman returned the shoulder bag to Aria, whose fingers clenched around the straps. Officer Gray then perched on the lip of the orange plastic bucket seat opposite hers. Any natural ease the policewoman might have had was obstructed by the belts and vest of her uniform. Aria, powerless and embarrassed, looked down at her own arm. The edge of the bandage was already unravelling.

"Do you want to know what the surgeon said, seeing what we'd brought in with you?"

Aria waited.

"'Tell those bloody northerners I'm not a necromancer'."

Aria, to hide her surprise and weariness, looked down at her own hands, still filthy with dirt and blood and ink.

"Neither am I," she said in a low voice.

Officer Gray's black eyebrows drew together. "What, exactly, *are* you?"

Aria raised her palms up, helpless. She saw the policewoman's shoulders tense at the movement, and let her hands fall back to her lap. "I'm not anything—I'm just Ariadne Winter." She had another, a proper name, but there was no call to give it. "This was meant to be a holiday. I want to go home." To her shame, she burst into tears.

Officer Gray waited, unmoved. When Aria's tears resolved into hiccoughs, the police officer said, "There are borders in cities. Boundaries some of the authorities know about, and walk, and watch, as far as we can. Old crimes still under investigation, old punishments. Old budgetary constraints. Most people don't know about them; never find them. But you aren't a regular tourist. You walked right out of the middle of them."

"I am a tourist," said Aria. "At least, I was trying to be."

The officer waited in silence and Aria, anxious to fill it, hoping to trade the facts for an explanation, began to tell her story.

◆

ARIADNE WINTER LIKED to spend her holidays wandering. In consequence, that afternoon she had lost herself. That, of course, was the charm and purpose of walking alone through an unfamiliar city, between quaint crowded terraces built for colder winters, under trees where there was no guilt in not knowing their names, beneath birds whose accents had changed.

She was not alarmed. She was, however, aware of an enchantment in these streets stronger than the mere play of light on brown leaves and powerlines. It was not like the weighty glamour of the city centre below, where the earliest buildings stood small and proud between mirrored towers, and where something marvellous always seemed on the verge of happening, but long ago and to someone else—the recurring dream of momentous events that haunts old architecture and steep stone stairs.

What Aria felt here was immediate and alive. It was not entirely welcoming, but she let the streets lead her past sweet decaying terrace houses and sun-spangled alleys, nameless garden-plants and tiny cafe-galleries. She was a visitor here, this city's magic could have no greater interest in her than she did in it, and evening was still a long way off.

With her small shoulder bag striking her hip, she trotted happily around an unsigned corner, following only her own inclination or a whim of the wind, and found herself in the unexpected broad turn of a lane. It was wider than the street off which it branched, but utterly quiet. There were no cars crouched waiting along its kerbs. Fallen leaves lay curled motionless, golden as glass in the unshifting sun; no birds sang.

One side of the lane was formed by the brick walls of back gardens. The other side had a stone wall, stained moss-grey. At the point where the lane curved back to the street perched a set of solid, high metal gates. They were patterned with dull-pointed crowns and heavy-headed lions, plated with coppery light. A sign beside them stated they were Private Property, and warned against trespassing.

"Curious," said Aria. It was not the sudden antiqued splendour that intrigued her so much as the lack of any magical overlay. Whatever enchantment she had felt shifting in the streets beyond had fallen still here. Her palms itched with her desire to look for a crack in the gate and peer through. She glanced furtively around and realised she was not alone.

A man was standing on the narrow sidewalk opposite. He wore a slim silver suit, and held a phone to his ear, listening. He did not face her directly, but he wore dark glasses. Aria could not tell whether he was watching her. There was a nervous, bitter twist to his mouth. He shut his phone without speaking into it, and Aria felt his attention alight on her.

"Hello," she said, reminding herself that she had nothing to feel guilty about yet, that intention was not a crime and that she had only wanted to look, which was not trespassing. Then, because he was dressed as if he belonged in a many-windowed office tower, she asked, "Are you lost, too?"

"Telephones don't work inside," he said, his voice soured with dissatisfaction. His hair was very pale and spiked, although it was feathered with late afternoon light. If he had spoken with a hint of arrogance, Aria wouldn't have liked him at all—as it was, she reserved judgement.

"Do you work here?" She gestured at the gate, although it looked like the sort of place that might have security guards, or a maid, gardeners, maybe even caterers; people who wore uniforms, not suits. "What do you do?"

"Lull people into a false sense of security," said the man. Aria decided he must be a lawyer. He tilted his head back towards the sky. "You should get back to wherever you're from. Before dark."

"Oh, I will," said Aria, cheerfully. She had a healthy respect for the night-side of cities, even those which weren't her own. "I'm never *permanently* lost. And night's hours away—I know where I'm staying."

He took off his glasses and cleaned them with the lining of his jacket. He had pale eyebrows and bleached-blue, worried eyes. He put his glasses back on. "It falls faster than you'd think."

Aria shifted her shoulder bag, then smiled. He was so brittle and stylish, yet there was no sarcasm in his tone.

"Are you . . . warning me?"

He hesitated—and she wished she could see his eyes again—then said, "Eventually, everyone stays lost."

Aria held up her hands. "Peace!" she laughed. "I'm just sightseeing. I didn't mean to step on any toes, so I'll wander out again."

"It's not as simple as that, Ariadne Winter," he said. "The streets are a web."

"Oh," said Aria. A great deal now made sense: the silent building perched behind the gates like a fat spider crouching at the centre of its silk. This man, watching out for her. Not a lawyer, then, but someone who knew a little of the patterns of the world.

"What is the web strung to catch?" she asked, since she could as easily leave a question unasked as she could leave a street unexplored. "And how did you know my name?"

But she could see from the set of his jaw that the second query answered the first and a thrill—not quite of fear, not yet—ran across her shoulders.

"I'm on holidays," she said, as if that should be a talisman. "And I'm just me. Why catch me?"

The man shrugged. "Maybe they were starved for a Winter. Maybe you're worth something. Maybe you can do something clever. You found your way to this lane, after all. You shouldn't have been able to do that. The *others* have gone out into the streets looking for you. I have to go back inside, I've been away too long. You could come in with me, if you like, and ask."

For the first time there was mockery in his voice, and that was more of a warning to Aria, who suspected she did not know enough to be properly afraid.

"You come with me," she shot back. "You know the way."

"I've done what I can," he said. "I don't dislike you; I don't know you. Whatever you are, I don't think it would be good for you to enter. And if you are something . . . different"—again, that sour twist of his mouth—"it might not be good for anyone else, either."

Aria hated to run scared, or be thought gullible. Maybe this was something they did to tourists here. Or perhaps her cousins, who were remarkable, and who teased her kindly, had arranged this as a prank, although their tricks were not usually distinguished by subtlety. What decided her, in the end, was that if this was a joke, the man did not seem to be enjoying it.

"Walk away, Ariadne Winter," he said.

"Just like that?"

His glasses reflected the sky darkly. "No," he sighed. "Probably not."

Aria nodded. She gripped the strap of her shoulder bag and walked around the bow of the lane—past the gates with their soft-edged lions, features blurred by time or art. She kicked through the coins of leaves (chestnut? box? the freedom of not knowing had lost some of its appeal) out into the blue shadow of the terrace on the corner.

And arrived back at the other end of the lane.

"Oh! That's not fair!"

The man had crossed to the gate and lifted one silver-sleeved arm to open it, but stopped with his hand still raised.

"You're in a loop," he said. Aria had not noticed the spark of hope in his voice before, but she could tell now that it had gone.

"Then I'll just have to run at it," she said. She sprinted back to the corner, and leaped as she reached the road. For a moment, she saw the red darkness of her eyelids closed against the sun, and then she was out on the street in the bright afternoon. She stopped just before two women with Pekingese dogs walked by, and realised the man had not said what *sort* of people were combing the streets for her. She lingered for a moment on the street corner, feeling obviously from out of town, then turned and ran back into the lane, up to the gates. The man had opened a smaller door set into the large ones. Through it, Aria glimpsed cool green trees.

"Come with me!" she said.

He spun around. "I saw you get out," he said, and then his voice dropped to a whisper. "Why did you come back?"

"You said—" began Aria excitedly, and he put his hand abruptly over her mouth. His skin was dry, and scratched slightly against her lips. He shut the little gate, bringing out of it a last gust of breeze that smelled like air-conditioning, all ice and pines. He took off his glasses again, his pale eyes tired and the lines in his face too deep.

"Sound carries," he said.

"So does fear," whispered Aria, moving his hand away. The bones of his long fingers felt frail. "You warned me because you're afraid, and not just for me—you said yourself you don't know me. So you're afraid for yourself. Why do you stay?"

"It's too late for me. I can't leave."

"Why not?"

"I can't travel in and out at will. We who live here do not have an entirely uncomfortable life, Ariadne Winter. There are ways to survive, even to thrive after a fashion, but I cannot believe you would choose it."

"You can't know that. The only reason you would think so is because *you* wouldn't choose it."

"I cannot leave."

"I can," said Aria. She held out her hand.

"I would slow you, and we will not go unnoticed."

"Then we'll run," she suggested. She reached down and took his cool, papery hand. She hoped he was alive; it would make this difficult if he was not. She knew of paper-men and straw-men, but they were never weary like him, and rarely kind.

"What's your name?" she asked.

"Jeremy Lantern," he said, as if it were of little importance. She could tell it was not truly his name, but if he had another it crouched tiny and distant and unreachable to her.

She nodded, then ran, towing Jeremy through the blinding light to the end of the lane, and there they jumped.

It was as if they were drowning in treacle, in black molasses that let no light through, only a warm brown darkness. *We'll be trapped here,* thought Aria, her panic slow as syrup. *We'll be vanished, or become a trick of the light, or be suspended, and people will think we are living statues and throw coins at us forever.* Gradually she extended her free hand, and felt the darkness toughen beneath her fingers, like a membrane.

It's a wall, she thought, and then, *No, it's a border.* She pushed weakly at it with her fingernails. Behind her, Jeremy was slipping away. She tightened her grip on his hand, and tore out into the world.

The light was like a knife. They tumbled, stunned and reeling, into the crisp afternoon, fell against a street sign, and each other, and gasped at the sharp air. Jeremy had grown even paler.

There was no sign of the barrier. Light and a breeze winked in the lane. Aria put her forehead against the shoulder of Jeremy's suit—the fabric still clean and unwrinkled—and took a steadying breath.

"You should not have been able to do that." Jeremy's voice shook. "I didn't expect . . . "

"I told you we'd be fine," said Aria, her brightness brittle in her own ears. She straightened and stepped away from him. "Coming?"

Aria saw her reflection in his dark glasses. "I think . . . " he stumbled to a stop. "I think I will."

He sounded surprised, and Aria wondered if there had just been a test, and what it had been, and who had passed it.

"You can always go back," she suggested.

"Don't tempt me," said Jeremy tightly. He let go of her hand. "We'd best hurry."

Aria recalled the gradual climb to this street. She looked at Jeremy for guidance, but he shook his head, so she led them down the footpath. Aria was good at retracing her steps—an advantage for someone who liked to wander—and she did so now, glimpsing a familiar terrace-garden here, unpainted shutters romantic in the slanting light there. Across that way was a building she had noted because it was grown over with a profusion of leafless vines (she had wondered if it was ivy, and if ivy lost its foliage).

Jeremy walked a little closer than necessary, as if to keep her within arm's reach. She did not mind. The air was pleasantly cool. Nothing threatened them. Few people passed nearby, and the traffic was desultory.

"We've been walking downhill since we left the lane," said Jeremy.

"Yes. Not steeply, though."

"Try and point uphill," said Jeremy. He sounded tired.

Aria turned. They were only a few metres below a crest in the road.

"It's another loop," he said. "Like the lane."

"No," said Aria. "It's something else. We haven't been here yet. I'd have remembered that red door."

"Doors change."

"Oh, shut up," said Aria, with forced cheerfulness, and saw Jeremy's shoulders relax slightly. "This isn't like the lane."

Yet it was undeniable that, however far they had walked, they were no nearer the bottom of the hill. She tried to guess where to go next, and felt what familiarity had been there lurch and evaporate.

"The lane was still, closed," she said. "Here, things are shifting to keep us inside. And once we know what's happening, we can fix it. Look—did they have maps there, inside? Or paintings of these streets or the hills? Any sort of picture of the place?"

"Maps of the world," said Jeremy. "And big inlaid globes." He showed the height of them with his hand.

Aspirational, thought Aria with an inward shudder. "No street directories?"

"Not that I ever saw," said Jeremy. "They had spoken direction in the cars."

Aria wondered if any voice could talk them out of this. She tried to bring up a map on her phone. It stuttered and failed. Jeremy's was no better.

"I need paper and a pen."

Jeremy produced a sleek silver pen and a slender pocketknife from inside his jacket. After an investigation of his remaining pockets he replaced the knife and said, "I only have this. No paper."

Aria hunted in her shoulder bag and found a narrow receipt from a cafe, too small for her sprawling handwriting. "It looks like we're staying in one spot," she said. "But we aren't, we know that. We keep moving—it's just that we aren't getting anywhere." She drew a line across the paper and folded it tightly. "Maybe it's like—this is the map, and this," she unfolded it in concertina steps, "is what is happening. The street unfolds into more lanes and terraces and walls. Does that make any sense?"

"Yes," said Jeremy. He took the tiny piece of folded paper and held it so that they were looking at the stacked layers end-on. "You're saying the closed map is the map on your phone, and the navigation system, but we don't have access to them. We've been sent deeper. But wouldn't someone notice the suburb is so much larger than it should be?"

"Maybe it has reflections," said Aria. "Or variations, or shadows. Or maybe it's exactly what you said: deeper, and if we'd scratched the paint on a blue door back when we started we would have found the mark had gone through to the red paint on this red door, here."

"An endlessly refracting prison," said Jeremy slowly.

"Prism," Aria corrected.

"You're implying there's a way out."

"Damn it, Jeremy!" She ran her hands through her hair and glared at him. "I'm making this up as I go, okay?"

Jeremy blinked, a rapid movement of his almost translucent eyelids. "Really?"

Aria felt a flush of shame. "Yes, really. I've never been lost-lost before. It's the only sort of talent I have—not being lost—and I don't like not being able to use it."

"Ariadne Winter," he said sadly, changing the topic. "Why take that name? Doesn't Winter stand for despair?"

"That's summer," said Aria, surprised in her turn. "Decadence and despair. Autumn's resignation and Spring is carelessness. People always get them wrong." Most of her cousins went by the name of Spring, outside family circles. "Winter is baseless optimism. Where there's life, there's hope." She wanted to ask him in return why he went by Lantern, but she had an idea. "Are you certain you haven't got any more paper?"

A further search revealed no more paper, the gutters were inconveniently litter-free, and Aria was growing uncomfortable about the thought of who and what might be in the silent houses. The sunlight shifted and sank. Dogs barked on other streets, or on this street in other times.

Aria pushed one sleeve up above her elbow. "It's about maps, I think," she said. "I hope. If you've got a map, you've got some sort of power over the land, or power to get over it. You get into its head, or it gets into yours. So we'll draw our own map and follow it out."

"And that will work?"

I'm losing him again, she thought. *He'll slip back to that lane, and I won't let him. Not unless he wants to, and he doesn't, I'm sure.*

"Absolutely!" she said, inventing. "Think about who makes maps, and why. They're all about ownership or escape." She opened the pen and made a mark on her forearm. "This is where we are. This is the street with the red door, and we turned here, and here . . . " She closed her eyes and thought back to the lane, and to the shape of the streets she had walked before then. She was used to proceeding based on recognition rather than actual reconstruction. She marked the map out hastily while the ink dried cold on her arm.

"They've realised I'm gone," said Jeremy. "Listen."

"I'm listening," said Aria, but she was trying to remember how the streets had bent and turned, wondering if she was crazy and why her heart was beating so fast.

There was a low grinding sound under the earth, growing into a directionless panic. She looked up at Jeremy's frightened eyes.

"I thought we'd be out before now," he said. "They must have come back from searching and found the lane open and—"

"And you gone?"

"If I go back, I could delay them. You've got a chance."

"More than I had to begin with? Jeremy, how much of a chance do you think I have?"

"Not much."

"Do you think I'll have more chance without help?"

"What help?" asked Jeremy listlessly. "I just didn't want your blood on my hands. What's behind those gates, it will suck you dry."

Aria thought of his paper-dry fingers, his colourless face. "Vampires?" she hazarded.

"No. A power. A hunger. A large and formless beast." He closed his eyes for a moment. "Like a cat, but dropping blood like roses. It collects what it needs or thinks it can use. Power and strength and hope." He opened his eyes again. "Telling you to run was the only thing I could think of."

"Then let's go," said Aria, holding up her arm. The map was drawn poorly and in haste, but it would have to do. "We have our map, the sun's going down and I'd rather not run alone."

They ran, and the dogs of the folded streets were barking. The sky flickered, and as they followed the path she'd drawn, Aria finally worked out what caused the loop. When they ran through the long shadows, she could see the towers of the city centre below, and beyond them, the tiled roofs and chimneys. When they ran into sunlight, there was no city. They were travelling in and out of times.

"Jeremy!" she gasped, caught between alarm and discovery, for she had guessed correctly. The streets and years were nested in upon themselves.

"I see it," answered Jeremy grimly. "I just hope you get us out on the right side of things."

The evening's shadows gathered, coiling blue out of gardens and side streets. Aria saw them from the corner of her eye, but paid little attention until one brushed her sleeve, and the fabric jerked and tore. She felt a scratch like a thorn against her upper arm and discovered new speed, but Jeremy was already outpacing her.

"Where to?" he managed.

She held up her arm, trying to look at the map without stumbling. "Turn right. There's a little laneway . . . " Even as she said it, she knew she had not remembered a lane here. The pen must have skipped as she drew her map, yet as she looked ahead she saw that the houses did not meet along the street.

Jeremy, who did not know there was not meant to be a laneway, plunged into the gap between two terrace houses. It was barely wider than his shoulders. Aria dived after, and ran into him. They stumbled to a halt and both looked back in time to see a sleek black car slide past the entrance. The stinging shadows lifted like leaves in its wake. Aria did not ask Jeremy whether it was one of *their* cars.

The laneway rose steep and cold between windowless walls, then tipped them down again, spilling them from between the houses. Now they were amid trees, thickly overgrown gardens and a spearheaded fence which staggered identically on each side, as if it had been split to let the pathway through.

"Do you know where this comes out?" gasped Jeremy.

"No, but I don't think *they'll* know either." He kept running, and Aria held up a hand. "Stop, let me breathe."

"There'll be time for that."

"Stop!"

Jeremy stumbled to a walk and Aria doubled over to catch her breath, then sank down to sit on the path, uncapping the pen. She examined her arm.

"Your shoulder is bleeding," said Jeremy, squatting next to her.

"I think—*think*—we should come out onto a street with cafes, and then there's a church, so there must be a churchyard—we can cut through that."

She could not really remember a churchyard, but she had not remembered the lane either. She did not want to think, just now, that she might be able to create these things. It was enough to be able to open a way through.

"A graveyard?" said Jeremy uncomfortably.

"No," said Aria, who had been about to add little crosses to mark the headstones. "Just a gate and some grass and stairs down to a street below." She was sure she had climbed a hill before she became aware of the brooding tension over these streets. If they could only get down again, they might be safe.

She held up her hand and Jeremy pulled her to her feet. He touched her shoulder and she winced. "Shadows can get into your blood," he said. "You don't know where they've been."

Aria didn't reply. She already felt light-headed from running. There were sparks in her mind, falling dots of light. "Then you have to stay with me. I'll probably need you to carry me to a doctor, once we're out. And then I want you to explain all this." Jeremy frowned at her as if she had hurt herself deliberately, to trap him into an escape he wasn't sure he wanted.

At the end of the pathway they paused to check the street was clear, before darting across to the old stone church. Where trees broke the light, the building was solid enough, but in the patches of unshadowed, afternoon sun the golden-grey stone was barely visible. There was, at least, a yard next to the church, just as she had drawn it, even the two gravestones she had marked before she changed her mind.

"They've found the lane," said Jeremy. Behind them, shadow was filling it, spilling slowly down. It oozed between the half-fences and out, to pool in the gutter before rising to flow over the road. It was the same colour as the dark windows on that smooth, silent car.

"We're almost out," said Aria. "See, there over the trees? The city is solid. The city is now." She felt sick, her legs ached and she didn't think she could run any further, let alone invent new paths to run on.

Gripping Jeremy's hand, she limped determinedly through the churchyard towards the wall, which should have topped a fall to the street below, with its busy evening traffic and pedestrians shouting or slouching along the footpath.

She had been right, at least, about this being the edge of the domain, but although she kept a brave face for Jeremy's sake, she knew they had reached it too late. Shadows were seeping through the trees, creeping between the headstones, and they called to her, to the heaviness that was spreading through her arm and neck and shoulder, slowing her down until all she wanted was to sink into cool dreams.

One way or the other, it would soon be sunset. The light was red-golden. It caught and dazzled on the leaves. She would have sat down, save that Jeremy had an arm around her ribs and wouldn't let her.

"You're stronger than you look," she murmured. That seemed important. Something about lulling. Reluctant, brittle Jeremy Lantern—she did not want to trust her weight to him, yet she rested her head on his chest, feeling the feather-thin angle of his collarbone even through his jacket, and yawned. "This has been a very strange holiday."

The shadows coalesced. They ran together like ink and rose into a form. When Aria blinked, she saw the afterimage of a crowd, but when she opened her eyes again there was only a single figure, a woman shaped of indigo and delft china.

"Who is that?" whispered Aria.

"That is them," said Jeremy calmly. "And also it, the creature bleeding roses."

"I thought you said it was a beast."

"Why?" asked Jeremy, in mild surprise. "What do you see?"

"Come," said the woman (or beast, or multitude) and held out something like hands. She moved no faster than the creeping of night.

Aria turned her head slowly. She saw the wall at the end of the churchyard, just behind them, but when she tried to remember what was beyond it, she could only think of an eternity of ocean, sighing like stars.

Jeremy was speaking to the woman. "I'll come back with you. But you don't need her. She isn't what you think she is," he said.

"No," said the woman. Her voice—if it was a woman, if it was a voice—was deep and liquid, rippling like oil. "She is more, and shall be ours, even as you are, Lantern. The shadows already have her."

"Even as I am," echoed Jeremy. His hand tightened on Aria's waist, and then he turned and kissed her. She parted her lips in surprise. His other hand on her hurt shoulder felt almost warm, although it shook a little, and for the first time since she had climbed to these tangled streets, she felt safe.

Then a thin thread of pain lanced out from her shoulder, striking through the fog of her thoughts, sharp as a wire, brittle as a shard of glass. *He belongs to the creature*, she told herself. *This is his job. He told me. Lulling into a false sense of security. He's trying to kill me, or send me to sleep, and I'm not sure it isn't the same thing in the end.*

"I want to go home," she murmured.

"This is home," said the figure. "Ask Jeremy. He is full of the shadows of this place, and neither knows nor needs another refuge."

The light through the trees turned Aria's world into wheeling suns, and leaning against Jeremy's thin shoulder, she felt quite certain that the figure was both utterly right and terribly mistaken. Or perhaps, she mused, she was confusing the figure for herself. Jeremy had said the shadows would get into her blood.

"We had not expected him to be taken in by the lies of a Winter," the woman went on.

"You know me better than that," said Jeremy humbly, but Aria could feel his words and his heartbeat shake in his chest. "I wanted to test her to see if she could do what you—what *we*—hoped. She has a good memory, but that is all. The Winter blood is thin in her. She's nothing."

"That's harsh," murmured Aria. But her memories were shifting. The ocean of night was receding, even as she felt Jeremy grow cold, as if he had drawn the shadows out of her with that kiss. But her head was clearing too slowly. Each thought she tried to pull free clung stickily to the next.

"Look at her," said Jeremy. There was a blue tinge to his neck and jaw.

"We have, carefully," said the figure. "Did you really think you could seduce us into believing your lies, or that she could help you leave us? That you could live without us, hollow boy? These are my streets, Jeremy Lantern. My walls."

"But they aren't, are they?" said Aria, muzzily. "There's nothing of you in them. You have to travel along the roads, and stay between the walls."

"Hush," whispered Jeremy, but Aria was still too sleepy to feel afraid, and while there was some light she would struggle to survive.

"It's a trap, isn't it?" she said conversationally.

"No!" said Jeremy.

"I'm not talking to you," said Aria, straightening. She looked down at the map on her arm and said to the woman, "It's a maze, all these streets. A prison-labyrinth. You're stuck here digging deeper and deeper, running in circles years-thick and never getting away. And you don't have a red thread, or even a map you can follow out of it."

"We need no map!" snapped the woman.

Aria rubbed at the ink on her arm. It didn't smudge. "It's permanent," she said to Jeremy, accusingly. She could feel him growing cold as evening, and leaned closer, not grudging him what warmth she could offer.

The figure advanced, shadows roiling around it like skirts, licking forward across the thin grass as if sniffing out the echo of the line Aria had drawn. "We shall have our red thread soon enough, map-reader," it said. "And it will lead us to all the world."

"She's not a map-reader," said Jeremy, although there was little point left in denying it or in defending Aria now.

"She's a world-reader," said the woman, scornful of Jeremy even as her shadows stretched forward like hunger.

"But I'm neither," said Aria, wonderingly. She took hold of Jeremy's sleeve. "I didn't have a map at all, so I must be a map-maker, a world-maker." It occurred to her this would give her cousins pause, but the thought and the cousins seemed dim and far away. "I drew a path for us from the heart of your rat's nest, all the way to the wall that keeps you in."

"It keeps us all in," said the woman, amused.

Aria took Jeremy's pen out of her pocket. They had retreated and the wall pressed against the back of her legs, its stone rough and clammy. Carefully, for her hand shook, she finished drawing on her arm: a gate in the wall, and tiny lines for the stairs leading out into freedom. She did not look up until she had finished drawing.

Then she glanced to the side and saw that there in the wall, camouflaged by the angle of the stones, and the blood-red light of sunset, was a rusted metal gate, set a little ajar, and the top of a set of stairs worn concave with age and use.

"Come on Jeremy," she said, trying to keep her voice steady.

"Run," said Jeremy, but Aria dragged him after her through the gate and into the shadows between the wall and the stone balustrade.

"No!" cried Jeremy. "Let me go. Someone must stop it getting out!"

"How?" panted Aria. "You? How can you lull her asleep when you're so afraid? You had lost that battle before I came."

And you must be half-afraid of me, she realised sadly, *or else you would have lulled me to sleep and I would be dreaming now.* "Who has kept her in this long, Jeremy? Who was strong enough to trap her?"

Jeremy did not answer. Aria towed him down the stairs, and they were not simply stairs she had invented, but stairs that existed on their own and had been used by others—cracked and patched with cement, old and mossy and stinking of urine, cigarette-ends, and freedom.

Darkness spilled after them, with a viscous, probing swiftness. It bellied and grew, swelling above the walls as if still confined by them, forcing its way through the gate, darkening the edges of Aria's sight.

Aria and Jeremy scrambled down to the street, and fled out of the shadows of the stairs, into the sunset light. Straight into the arms of two police, who pushed them aside, eyes and weapons trained on the gate.

"After all this time?" said the woman—the multitude, the beast—from the shadows at the top of the wall. "After all these years, you are all that are sent to stop me?" Laughter shook the mortar between the stones and inky tendrils leaked down. "Have they forgotten me and left the door so poorly guarded?"

"The gate," shouted Jeremy. "Close the gate!"

Aria scrubbed uselessly at the indelible lines on her arm.

"The red thread," she murmured. "Jeremy, give me your knife!" The paths were only ink, after all. Surely blood was more powerful.

Jeremy pulled out his knife. He held Aria's wrist and she closed her eyes, bracing against the swift cold blade, as he sliced across her arm through the path they had followed, or made. Through the stairs, and her skin.

A man shouted, "Stop!"

She realised, later, it must have been one of the police. It was followed by a noise like falling stones. When she opened her eyes, there was far too much blood for the thin throbbing pain in her arm. Jeremy was curled in it. Night poured out of his chest: a spreading darkness of shadows that faded like smoke, while blood spread and stayed.

"Back away," said the policeman.

"No, no, no!" whispered Aria. She had her hands on Jeremy's chest, and scarlet welled out between her fingers. Hands were trying to lift her away, but she had something more important to do.

"Stop the shadows," she told the owner of the arms. "That's what you're here for, isn't it? That's all he was trying to do."

But Jeremy had succeeded. The air was clearing, the shadows were simply the shades of evening, and her own blood running down her arm dissolved the streets and alleys she had drawn. Nothing extraordinary would come down the stairs now.

"Can you reroute death?" she asked the evening, the distant lights and sirens. Her own blood throbbed to the sounds.

"Don't try," whispered Jeremy. "You'll get us both lost." She felt him try to force her to acquiesce, but he was too weak. The desire to sit and watch him die faded with Jeremy's strength.

Whatever of himself he had saved and hidden from the creature in the maze had not withstood that single bullet. Brittle Jeremy Lantern.

"You're losing your touch," she told him. "And you're still alive, so all's not lost."

"It will be soon," murmured Jeremy. "There are larger mazes than those streets, and darker labyrinths." His heartbeat fluttered under her fingers like a bird's wings.

A red thread through a maze, thought Aria, and because it was all she had, she drew with their mingled blood on Jeremy's chest a new path: a tangled maze to keep life in for just a little longer.

◆

THE DOCTOR, SHORT and gingery, regarded Aria narrowly when Officer Gray brought her in to the theatre. It was late at night, but even so, very few people seemed to be on this floor. The doors were poorly signed. Not so much a secret wing as an unobtrusive one. Hidden by being unremarkable, like boundaries in a city, and families in the world.

"This is Doctor Payne," said Officer Gray.

"My own name," said the doctor, drily, as if used to mockery and the hint of a smirk in the policewoman's voice. "Do you know who this is?"

Jeremy lay on the table, at once too pale and too bloodied under the unnatural light. His shirt had been cut away and his eyes were almost entirely closed.

"He told me his name is Jeremy Lantern," said Aria. "It isn't his real, own name. Whatever that is, I think it's been hidden for a long time."

"Do you now?" said the docto, with a voice like sand. "Frankly, it was a good shot, he should be dead, and I'm not a miracle-worker. But between your devilry, Miss Winter, and whatever your Mr Lantern did with his name, he hasn't quite died. Not that I'd say he's alive. Look at this." The doctor's hand, powdery in its translucent glove, touched Jeremy's shoulder and brought away a piece of him—a shard, like broken porcelain.

Aria wanted to hide her face against someone's shoulder, but the policewoman was the only candidate and she was not a comforting presence.

"Our friend here doesn't seem to be showing up on any records," continued the doctor, glancing once at Officer Gray for confirmation. "It happens. Stray bodies get dragged in more often than you'd think, although usually they aren't so well dressed." The remains of Jeremy's silvery suit were dark with drying blood.

"From what I understand," the doctor went on, "you're likely to be the only one who cares whether he lives or dies. And the only one to raise a stink about it, which is all you people seem to be good for. That's why you're here. Oh, don't look alarmed, I'm a doctor. Do no harm, and so on. Open the window, Claudia, just in case."

Officer Gray complied. There was a crisp wind, and to Aria the traffic sounded very heavy for so late. She sensed it moving through the night, up to starlit mountains or along the shore of a moonless sea.

The doctor opened Jeremy's chest, lifting the cold skin away as if it were dead leaves and snapping open the ribs like pale twigs. Aria, lightheaded, leaned against the door. Officer Gray was watching the procedure with sardonic interest and folded arms. The doctor's gloved hands reached into the cavity of Jeremy's chest, lifted out something small and grey and set it on the bed. It sat on the blue sheets for a moment as if stunned, then shook itself—a tiny bird, bedraggled and forlorn.

Aria straightened. "Jeremy?" she whispered. But if it was Jeremy, it gave no sign that it knew her.

"I haven't seen this before," said the doctor, with professional interest. "Chances are, if this is him, it's been locked away so long it doesn't even know itself anymore."

The bird shook out its wings, hopped to the edge of the bed, and then flew. For a horrible moment it battered about the room, maddened by light and partial freedom. Then it found the open window and was gone.

The doctor turned away as if Aria was not there, and drew the sheet up over the empty body. It was already collapsing in on itself. "I wish more of them would have the decency to clean up after themselves. A logistical nightmare. Vampires, now, they're tidy. I like vampires."

The police officer put her hand comfortlessly on Aria's shoulder.

"Time for you to go home, Ariadne Winter, before someone with a bigger budget takes an interest in you."

"What about those tangled streets?" whispered Aria. "And the shadow woman, and all of it?"

"That's our problem," said Officer Gray. But Aria knew that was not true. She was growing too aware of the pulsing night beyond the windows, the shape of the city, the stark presence of those prison-streets. She could have pointed to them blindfolded. Her own warm, small northern city, her family, her quarrelling laughing cousins: those all felt very distant, compared to the near urgency of questions to be answered, trees to learn the names of, a grey bird to find.

Jeremy had been right, Aria had lost them both. For better or worse, she had knotted her own life to this city, and those streets. She had already, so carelessly, come home.

◆　◆　◆

IN THE HEART
OF THE CITY

REBECCA FUNG

THE novelty of walking to work had long lost its shine. At first I had enjoyed it, embraced it even. It was good to feel my legs pumping along the pavement instead of hearing my toes tapping impatiently as I waited for a bus that was running twenty minutes late. In fact, it had been the unreliable bus service that had motivated me to walk to work. On the worst days, I'd figured that I could have made it halfway there by the time the stupid bus arrived. So I had begun. At first, there was a real sense of achievement. I could feel the whole energy of the city pulsing beneath my feet, and I'd smile, because my job helped keep that vitality flowing. My offices were at BloodSystems, in the heart of Harmille. Every beat I felt under the pavement was a reminder of why I did what I did.

As the weeks progressed, I started to think less of the steady thump-thump-thump beneath the soles of my feet and more about the litter on the sidewalk. I flinched at the bunches of cigarette butts that were scattered wherever my shoes hit the ground, and kicked away the greasy food wrappings that invariably found themselves caught under my heels. I noticed broken plastic containers oozing thick strawberry milkshake onto grey concrete, which I would expertly navigate around. I didn't see why people needed to be such pigs.

But the worst part of the walk wasn't the rubbish I traipsed around.

It was the hobos.

The largest group of hobos clustered on a street corner I passed. Usually a couple of them were asleep, even in the middle of the day, but the rest would call out to me. Sometimes the group was larger, sometimes smaller, but they were always there, as reliable as the city skyscrapers themselves.

"Got a dollar? Spare change? Spare food? Lovely weather, gotta dollar? Feed a hungry man, miss? God be with you! God be with you!"

A stench radiated from them, but it was more than the foul odour of people who hadn't washed in months. It was the smell of desperation and poverty. I held my head high and pretended not to notice them, though I wasn't fooling anyone. Not myself and not them. How could anyone not see the little crowd? As the weeks progressed, they grew bolder. They began to move in on me.

"Got a dollar? Got some food? I haven't eaten in days. It's for me and me kid, I gotta kid, I been out here for weeks, you look a nice lady. I could shine your shoes, gimme a coin?"

I quickened my step and tensed before sucking in a breath and wrapping my arms around my torso. I felt that by compressing my body, I'd become invisible to these disgusting creatures. But their dark gazes searched me. I felt their little beady eyes all over me, like flies buzzing all over my body.

Ugh.

But I made it past them. It was growing harder and harder to ignore the hobos; I wanted to scream at them, harangue them into nothingness, and yet I didn't want to linger near them. It was so much easier to avoid them and pretend they didn't exist. I broke into a little trot once I was a safe distance away.

I finally reached the office. The aroma of the old and desperate still clung to me; that hobo-stink had soaked into every item of my clothing. I scraped my shoes carefully on the doormat before I walked in, hoping the flowers at the front desk would hide the smell.

"You're late, Ivy," said Jordan, sitting smugly at her desk, inspecting her long, perfectly manicured nails.

I checked my watch. "Only four and a half minutes."

"It'll affect your bloodbar."

"Oh, come *on* . . . "

"Rules are rules," sing-songed Jordan, smiling as she typed. "I don't make them."

"The *bitch*." I threw my bag onto my workstation, knocking aside a small stack of brochures, and switched on the computer. The little icon showing my bloodbar flickered an alert, letting me know I was below the acceptable level. That mean bloodsucker. Jordan was well aware she could use her discretion when it came to adding or removing points from people's bloodbars; but she loved to wield her power, especially over the other girls in her work area.

Especially over me.

Everyone at BloodSystems had a bloodbar. It was company policy that all employees show their commitment to BloodSystems—not just through arriving at work on time, or putting in their eight hours, or attending work functions—and the usual way was through the donation of blood. The bloodbar was set so we all had to donate a minimum amount each week.

We could earn extra bloodbar points for outstanding work on projects or by managing to recruit blood sources from outside, but it was very difficult. If you gained points, you didn't have to give as much of your own blood. On the other hand, thanks to inflexible bloodbar officers like Jordan Wexley, it was also really easy to lose bloodbar points and have to give more than the minimum amount. The more points you lost, the more blood they could take. Of course, they couldn't take so much that you'd die or anything, but they could take more than enough.

I needed to get my bloodbar up before it was assessed. I *hated* having to give blood. Every drop that was sucked out of my body made me feel like I was being drained of my own life. I could deal with the absolute minimum being taken as one of the necessary evils of my cushy job, but anything more? I shuddered. I had one day, I calculated, to get myself some extra points.

It was hard to work, with Jordan humming so smugly to herself as she typed. She kept sending sidelong glances my way, while turning her perfectly maintained bun of hair to the side if I even tried to catch her eye. Jordan always had an excellent bloodbar status. I had to figure out how she did it. I had to get one like hers. I tried to concentrate on my work, but I was only halfway through one of my articles when a pop-up came up on my computer, letting me know that I was wanted in the donations office.

◆

"I NEED MORE time," I babbled. "I can get my bloodbar up."

"I'm afraid that we do the assessments for your department today. Now, please step on the scales, Ivy." The doctor acted cool and detached. He probably heard pleas like mine every day.

"But it's not my usual day. Aren't you early? I would usually have one extra . . . "

"We changed the schedule. Good, you seem to be maintaining your weight. Please, lie down." He waved at the sterile hospital bed next to the scales. I stood still, staring blankly at the mattress. The doctor gave me a not-so gentle shove towards the bed. Snapping on a pair of latex gloves, the doctor then wheeled over a tray of medical equipment. He stared at me until I lay down. My skin crawled as the crisp, starchy sheets met my back.

"Didn't Jordan Wexley notify you? There was a need to change some people's schedules to fit in with the time-tabling. It should be in your email. Now, please hold out your arm. I'm going to take your blood pressure first. Very nice. A little high, but not out of range. Your bloodbar is not impressive, Ivy, but then that's going to make a very nice donation for the central unit."

I gulped. "Are you taking more than last time?"

"Just a little. Nothing to be afraid of, your weight can handle it. Just hold still."

The doctor wrapped a tourniquet around my left bicep. Then he held out the needle. After all this time, or maybe because of all these times, I hated needles. He prodded my inner elbow, searching for a vein, before plunging the needle into my arm. I yelped. I always do that, almost out of habit.

"I feel sick," I moaned. "You're killing me."

"Don't be silly, Ivy. It's just a little blood. You have plenty. I've calculated how much I can take without affecting your health." His gloved finger pointed at his computer screen. It showed a series of numbers I didn't understand.

"Vampire!"

He didn't respond, just robotically made some notes. "This donation is for the greater good of the city, a contribution to its life and heart, so that we all may thrive." He was quoting the BloodSystems handbook.

I started to feel light-headed. I didn't want the damned handbook quoted at me. I helped write the bloody thing. "Get that stupid needle out of my arm. You've taken enough," I demanded.

"Not quite. Against your bloodbar score, we need to take a little more."

I felt as if my soul was being drained into the blood bag. *One, two, three, four*, I started to count, *surely you won't want more. Five, six, seven, eight, this syringe I hate hate hate! Nine, ten . . .*

He withdrew the needle. I stared at the plump, bloated bag. All that blood, it had once been pumping through my veins, keeping me alive, and now it would pump through the city. I should feel wonder. I'd be able to sense my blood under my feet as I walked to work. Instead, I wanted to snatch the bag and pour the blood back into my vein; the blood was *mine*. I got this feeling every time I saw my donation. It was surreal. Intellectually, I knew that blood kept the city alive, but it seemed so different when I was sitting there, actually giving it. My blood would light the street lamps, drive the trams and enable my emails to whiz through the aether to their destinations. I was doing a *good thing*, I told myself.

"For the benefit of humanity and society, one person's blood is the blood of all our fellow human beings in the city of Harmille," said the doctor. That was a passage I had assisted in writing— Promotional BloodSystems Donations Brochure 44, page 23. I stuck my tongue out at him.

He sighed. "You are being absolutely impractical. Thousands of people give blood every day. The city would not function if they did not. You write brochures as part of your job, encouraging people to donate. And look at the way you're behaving!"

I couldn't take my eyes off that dark red stuff in the bag. "I feel sick," I whispered.

"Go and have a bite to eat. It'll make you feel better. And from the way you've been going, I'll probably see you next week."

◆

"YOU SWITCHED MY schedules on purpose," I accused Jordan.

"Don't be so dramatic, Ivy. Everything has to be so dramatic with you. Someone had to switch. It was merely . . . convenient."

"You knew," I said, holding the little bandage on my arm. "Now I've given two batches and it hasn't even been seven days."

"A loss for the individual is a win for the whole city," said Jordan.

"How do you do it? I never see you give blood. I suppose you cheat the system, give yourself a whole bunch of points for nothing."

Jordan laughed. "If only it were that simple. I have to play by the rules, just like everyone else, Ivy. By the way, I'll give you a tip—stop arriving at work late." Then she handed me the little brochure on bloodbar statuses. "Some light reading when you're finished with those propaganda pamphlets you pump out over there."

I nibbled on a beef roll at my desk and attempted to read Jordan's brochure. I always tried to eat meat after I've given blood. I've been told it's good for getting iron and protein back in your body straight after it's been drained away. But even if there were no health benefits whatsoever, I enjoyed the sense of power it gave me. I liked the juxtaposition; if the company took blood from me, I would sink my teeth into something rich and red and bloody myself. Rare roast beef or lamb was the best. I want to taste the red juices running into my mouth and feel myself filling up with blood again.

My arm ached. The doctor always said he calculated a safe amount to take from me, but I didn't trust him. My limb felt weak. Maybe one day it would drop off with all the forced donations. I had to think of a way to keep my bloodbar up and not give away so much. Maybe no blood at all. It wasn't wrong, I told myself. Plenty of other people happily contributed; they were keeping the city running. What did it matter if just one little person opted out? Besides, not everyone was suited to blood donation. It just wasn't in their personality. I contributed in other ways; I wrote pamphlets, very good pamphlets, I reminded myself.

With the little strength I had, I flipped over the pages in the brochure. There was a section on crediting points to your bloodbar: if an employee found someone who'd donate in their name, it counted towards their status. The donor would lose any personal benefits associated with donation—such as tax breaks or welfare credits—but the employee's bloodbar status would benefit.

Jordan probably had a bunch of willing relatives who donated in her name, I guessed; a doting mother, father or siblings. I had none of these. I would have to find someone whom I could use.

♦

"GOT A DOLLAR miss? Spare change? Spare us something, anything?" The repugnant faces called out to me. But this time, I didn't hasten away at their desperate odour. Today, I didn't just smell poverty. I scented opportunity.

"Yeah, I have something." I beckoned to one of them. Tried to give a welcoming smile as one approached me. I couldn't bear, yet, to take any of those . . . those things . . . by the hand. "Let's go for a walk, I'll get you something."

"You gonna buy me a burger?"

"Yes," I lied.

The other hobos laughed and sighed in turn and one of them yelled, "Lucky!"

The hobo who came with me was a grubby man with a long unkempt beard, but otherwise I thought of him as faceless. He would not be remembered, not by the other hobos or by myself. And just as well.

"Is this where you get a burger?" he whined.

I wished he would shut up, but I needed his compliance, at least for now. Leading him towards my workplace, we entered through the back gate. "It's just through here," I said, when I saw his face scrunch in scepticism. "It's one of those burger vans."

I scanned myself in, and an attendant nodded at me from behind a small desk in the entrance corridor. He wrinkled his nose at the smell of the hobo, and I could see him forcing himself not to comment.

"Is he a donation?" the attendant asked.

"Yes, he's with me. I'm an employee. He's donating. Can you credit my bloodbar?" I rattled off my identification number, and the attendant entered it into a computer.

"What the hell's happening? Where's the burgers? I don't see no van." The hobo was looking around the foyer, fidgeting.

"Just go along with this nice man," I soothed. "He'll take care of you."

The attendant flinched. He watched the grubby, twitching fingers of the hobo warily. "Is he a full donation or is he just donating a vial? You haven't specified."

What was the difference? I couldn't remember that in Jordan's brochure. My confusion must have been obvious, because the attendant said, "The full donation's bigger."

"Does it mean more credit to my bloodbar?"

"Lots more."

I smiled in relief. The hobo gave me an uncertain grin back. It made my skin itch. "Then he's giving a full donation."

The attendant nodded and two uniformed men appeared from a side door. The men grabbed the hobo, wrenching his arms behind his back so fast it left me blinking. The sound of clicks reached me, and I realised they'd put him in handcuffs. He began to bellow in protest, trying to shrug them off. The attendant calmly walked over and tucked a sack over his head. My jaw dropped. The uniformed men began to drag him off.

"I'm sorry you had to see that," the attendant frowned. "I hope he wasn't close to you. But sometimes the donations try to . . . change their mind." He squirted the contents from a little pump pack of hand sanitiser, then rubbed some into his palms.

I shook my head slowly, still-watching the hobo being carried off down the corridor towards the double doors. How could he even think that . . . that *thing* . . . was in any way related to me?

"Good. Well, it's nice for you. Your bloodbar is in very good shape, very good indeed." The attendant smiled, a bright expression. "Congratulations, Ivy Hannigan. You've done a wonderful thing for the city. Can you feel it?"

I tried not to notice the hobo's still kicking feet being dragged along the corridor, or hear the sounds of protest he made. I finally grasped what they meant by a full donation. At least his misery would be over soon, I thought. And really, he was of better use feeding the city rather than feeding off it. What did he do all day but moan and beg? I was doing everyone a favour. Yes, a favour.

The attendant nodded at me. "You feel it, too."

Yes, I could feel the pulse of the city below my feet. It was particularly strong here.

"It's because we're close to where it's happening," he said. "When we obtain a new catch, I can always hear the city responding."

◆

THE NEXT DAY when I walked to work, the hobos seemed subdued. They didn't scream as loudly for money this time. "He never came back. He went off for a burger and didn't come back. Where did he go?" One of the hobos took a step forward, arms out, as if to touch me. I hurried back. "You were the one he went with, weren't you? You, lady?"

Their voices sounded like scared squawks. Ignore them, I told myself. Just keep walking. Turning my head to the side, I strode away, pretending they didn't exist.

I walked to the office, and took a seat at my desk, where the little electronic reminder of my bloodbar score cheered me immensely.

Of course, the high point score could not last forever. It needed to be maintained, especially since it was so easy for points to be deducted; Jordan penalised me for every slight infraction. It didn't take me long to find myself returning to the group of hobos, leading another away with a vague promise of food. They were a restless and sad group. The worry they had over the disappearance of the first hobo had been replaced by the more pressing concerns of food, drink and money.

Soon though, I wasn't content with keeping ahead of a donation; I wanted my score to be safe, without the threat of it dropping. So I lured another hobo, then another. My bloodbar went up and up and I couldn't help smiling more broadly each day, seeing it soar so high. I sometimes wore little disguises—scarves, coats, hats and such—so the hobos wouldn't realise it was the same person coming to their group, leading one of them away never to return. They weren't masterful disguises, but the hobos were so hungry and needy that when I offered food or held out money—promising it in exchange for a mystery 'errand'—it was easy for them to rationalise away the need for caution. I think some might have suspected something, but they came anyway. The idea of a burger or a few notes was too tempting.

Jordan began to look at me strangely; how did I manage to increase my bloodbar so quickly? My soaring bloodbar became office gossip, and even the doctor made some comments about it. I needed to stop, or my secret would be out. But it was so difficult, once I'd started. Seeing my bloodbar so high made me feel safe, and when I wasn't doing anything about it, I felt empty. Like all my blood had been drained away.

I hadn't donated a hobo in several weeks. My bloodbar had been dropping since my last gifted contribution, and I was desperate to see my bloodbar soar. I went back to the dwindling hobo group. There were two sitting together.

"Come on," I said, beckoning to one. "Don't waste time."

"Where did the others go? Where's everyone else?" This hobo wouldn't be so easy. He was more suspicious than the others had been, or perhaps he'd grown that way over the months as he noticed others disappear.

"Come with me and I'll show you," I said. At least I wasn't lying.

"It ain't good. I feel it ain't good. Don't go," said the other hobo. He drew away from me too, and I could feel my chances slipping away. An electric frisson of panic went through me, zapping through my body. It seemed to centre in my arm. I needed my arm. It needed its blood.

The hobos shook their heads at me and backed away, moving behind the park bench they'd been camping on. Enraged, I grabbed my high heel and hurled it at one of them. It caught him in the forehead. Blood welled. The heel had pierced him. Staggering, the hobo keeled over and his precious donation started to drip onto the packed dirt ground.

"Whatcha done? Whatcha done?" screamed the other hobo.

"I'm sorry, I'm so sorry," I said, waving my hands frantically, but inside, I was worried. I'd wasted his blood, watching as it formed a puddle on the ground.

"Help me then, help me take him somewhere," I commanded. The other hobo nodded, too stunned to do anything but obey. I pretended concern over the injured man, repeating how sorry I was, and that I was just so stressed with work and I was *just trying so hard* to help people like him. The man nodded, assisting me to half-drag the dazed victim through the streets. Worry lines marred the hobo's forehead, growing more pronounced as we approached the rear gate at BloodSystems.

"I work here, they have doctors."

The hobo nodded, and helped me drag the half-conscious man into the small entrance corridor.

"Two today?" the attendant asked with a smile. He frowned though, when he saw the wound on the injured hobo's head. I worried that he'd deduct points from my bloodbar because of it.

I gave a shaky smile. "Two."

◆

I HAD RUN out of hobos. Would it have mattered though, if there had been a few more? I hadn't been able to pluck the last two off the street as if they were naïve vagrants. But it was immaterial. I needed blood.

No, the city needed blood, I reminded myself. A BloodSystems pamphlet lay on my kitchen table, reminding me of my duty. Every good citizen should contribute. Every employee must contribute.

If I didn't donate soon, my bloodbar would be unacceptable. It was an ongoing cycle. For a few days, or a week or two if I were lucky, I'd get my credit up and stay on top of the world. But then things would happen; I'd run late, I'd miss a meeting, or I'd just do *something* that caused Jordan to dock my bloodbar status. And then I'd be worrying all over again.

I held out my arm. There used to be a few little dots, right there, where the doctor from the donations office would eagerly jab me, draining out my lifeblood to feed to the city. I hadn't had to give blood in well over three months, and the little wounds on my arms had healed themselves. I could hardly remember them ever looking so pristine. I wanted them to stay that way.

That needle would never touch me again, I vowed. I'd just have to find blood elsewhere. I picked up the pamphlet. "It is every citizen of Harmille's duty to contribute to the life of the city, the city that gives them their livelihood; the city that gives them their life . . . " I wasn't going to shirk my duty; I just wouldn't offer the donation from my own body. There was nothing in the pamphlet that said there was only way to give.

I walked over to my window. There were so many people striding around the city. People full of blood. One of them would be my contribution. I didn't care who. It didn't matter. From my apartment, they all looked the same. Little dark creatures, moving around on the grey cement below, like dots rearranging themselves on a computer screen. I tried to look for a pattern or sequence in their movements, but they just moved randomly, some edging out of my field of vision as other little dots appeared. But that's all they were, I reminded myself. Little dots, with blood inside them. Nothing more. And one little dot would be just as good as any other.

There was a knife in the kitchen. I laid it out and thought of what else I might need. A piece of rope? Something hard and long? A stick or a club would be good, but I had nothing, I didn't play hockey or baseball or golf, which would have yielded me a helpful instrument. But there was a long, sturdy umbrella in my stand with a usefully pointed tip. I'd take that.

What sort of blood hunter goes out armed with an umbrella, a kitchen knife and a small piece of rope? But that's all I had. It would have to make do. Somewhere deep down, I knew I was ridiculous: a hunter with a pathetic set of tools.

But I was also desperate.

It's amazing how much of a motivation desperation was. I didn't know why the hobos hadn't achieved more with that cloying sense surrounding them.

I reasoned that I couldn't just knock down anyone in the street, though it would have made things easier. The law frowned upon murders, assaults and kidnappings, even if it was for the benefit of Harmille. What mattered was not getting caught.

So I'd have to go somewhere a little out of the way, out of the very centre of the city, in some dark area where there would be fewer people and less monitoring. Then a little bop with my umbrella and . . . well, I hadn't thought it through after that. I'd work something out, though.

I caught a glimpse of my face in a shop window as I walked towards my unknown target. There was enough light from a street lamp to see myself, but I hardly recognised the woman staring back at me. Her features were grey and hard, and I saw two black eyes glaring from a non-descript face.

You're barely human any more. You're a demon.

The stranger should have shocked me into running back to my apartment, but a clear voice in my head said, *Does that mean I don't have to give blood anymore? Do demons have to give blood?*

All that mattered now was getting a body, a donation. If I was going to be a demon, then so be it. I could feel my expression grow cold and I knew my face was turning greyer.

I walked further away from the city centre until the people—the little black dots I'd seen from the window, I reminded myself—were fewer and fewer. I chose one at random to follow. The dot moved at a fairly brisk pace, and I quickened my pace to keep up with it. It turned down a street, then into an alley, and I thought to myself, when do I strike? Then it turned to look at me. I brought the umbrella down hard, and heard a crack. The dot fell over.

I stood there, panting, fingers gripping the handle of the umbrella so hard that my knuckles were white. There, that wasn't so difficult, was it? The body on the ground let out a low moan. I'd need that rope now. As I tied up its legs, I muttered to myself. How was I going to get it back to BloodSystems?

"So you're a Feeder, too," said a voice. "I thought I might find you here."

I looked up to find Jordan Wexley standing behind me. Or, what seemed to be Jordan Wexley, but her face was grey and drawn. I could only just make out her features; but I recognised that voice of hers. She wasn't cloaked in the heavy makeup she usually wore to work; she looked just like me.

"Jordan? Is that you?"

"Of course it's me. Is this where you usually find blood?"

I shook my head slowly.

"You've been doing this for a few months now, haven't you, Ivy? I've been watching your face at work. I've noticed your bloodbar. You shouldn't give yourself away so easily. And you really shouldn't hunt in such obvious areas. Don't you know anything?"

"I know I have to keep my bloodbar up, and you're not helping," I said.

"Relax," said Jordan. "You're one of us now." She beckoned at the shadows, and a handful of cloaked figures emerged. They were tall and grey and non-descript; they'd fade into the smog and concrete walls if I didn't look carefully. The only thing that really stood out about them was their black eyes. "Help Ivy with her catch. Take it to be credited to Ivy's bloodbar."

I stood, rope dangling from one hand, umbrella from the other. "Who are these people?" I asked.

"We're all Feeders. We all hunt to feed Harmille, just as you've done," said Jordan.

"I'm hunting for myself," I said. "You're creepy. I just wanted something to keep my bloodbar up. That's all. I don't want to join any weird clubs or anything."

Jordan shook her head. "Maybe you don't get to choose. Don't you know what happens to that body, and the blood, once you've caught it? Don't you know where it all goes?"

"Of course I know where the blood goes. There's a processor plant. The factory. The engineers ... " My voice trailed off. As

I spoke, I realised I knew nothing. Jordan's eyes grew wide with incredulity. I was just parroting propaganda, straight out of the pamphlets again. I knew no more than what BloodSystems told the public.

Jordan shook her head. "You haven't figured it out yet, have you? How long have you worked at BloodSystems, Ivy? I thought you knew, especially since you were hunting like me. I thought you had decided to become a Feeder. When I saw your face becoming," she shrugged, "you know."

"What are you talking about?" I didn't know what this Feeder stuff was about. But I knew what she meant by my face. I knew I was fading to a smoggy grey, just like her.

"Let's go for a ride," said Jordan.

"Just tell me." I dropped the umbrella to the ground.

Jordan shook her head, and pointed at the discarded make-shift weapon. "Get in and I'll show you."

I didn't like Jordan any more than I ever had, but she obviously knew something I didn't. She'd always known more about BloodSystems than I did. I had hated it, just like I hated her, but I wanted to know, too.

We drove in silence for a long time. "Where the hell are we going?" I asked. It was the same dark grey look that all of the city had, but I didn't recognise the buildings or streets. Here, the road was wide and the traffic was light. There was hardly anyone around at all. I couldn't see a single pedestrian. "Where are we?"

"How much of the city have you seen, Ivy? Do you ever come out here, to the edges?"

"I like to stay in the centre. Where everything's happening," I said.

Jordan laughed softly. "That's what I prefer, too. The heart of the city." She stopped and parked the car. "But I want to show you something. Come with me."

We got out of the car. Strange, that I never thought of what the edge of the city was like. In my mind it sprawled on forever, but of course, that wasn't true. I knew Harmille wasn't that big; the dimensions and population were in one of my pamphlets.

The buildings out here were lower and not so close together. I figured that would mean I'd see a lot more light flooding on to the streets, but the world was just as dull as it was on my way to work. Jordan walked down the street and was approaching a brick wall, strangely graffiti-less. I blinked. How had I not seen this before on our approach? The wall stretched right along the road, cutting it off. Did it enclose the city?

"Touch it," said Jordan. She put her hand against the bricks. I stretched my palm flat against the surface, and started. It was warm, and it . . . pulsed. My fingers became wet; the wall was slightly moist.

"There's blood in the wall?" I whispered.

"There's blood everywhere," said Jordan. "All around us, in the city."

I kept my hand there. The wall felt like a thick rubbery skin. As I examined it, I began to see more, as if part of my mind was awakening. I realised that a complex maze of blood vessels flowed under its surface. I could feel the ridges in the skin of those tubes carrying the blood, pumping it around, keeping the wall warm, and keeping everything inside it warm, including us.

"It's alive, and we're inside it," I said.

"Him," said Jordan. "Harmille. His name is Harmille."

"Harmille, my city," I repeated, and I stroked the skin several times.

We walked back to the car. The memory of my hand on the internal wall of the city—I still couldn't think of it as anything but 'the city', it was far too difficult to think of Harmille as 'him'— was hot in my brain. I kept looking at my hand and recalling the sensations, as if I'd never touched a living being before. Well, I'd certainly never touched one on that scale.

"When I decided to become a Feeder, it was because I fell in love with Harmille," Jordan was saying as she drove back into the city, back towards BloodSystems. "How can you not help but love a creature who gives every part of its inside for every moment of your life? The grey is inevitable. It's what helps us Feeders blend in to the cityscape. Unfortunately, Harmille needs food, but not everyone wants to be his sustenance."

"Everyone needs to make sacrifices. Everyone must contribute," I said. It was one of the pamphlet lines I'd penned. Jordan nodded and smiled.

Jordan stopped the car outside the back entrance; towards where I'd led countless hobos. She led me to the door, opened it and waved me through. Together we walked down the corridor, past the double doors the hobos had disappeared into, and then down a series of stairs. She led me into the room where the most important work of Harmille took place.

"This is where they send the blood, to feed him. To make sure Harmille lives forever."

It was dimly lit but as I walked closer, I could see more clearly. I could sense the pulsing under my feet, pounding against my legs harder than I'd ever felt before, drawing me in. Then I could see it. A huge lump of flesh suspended in the centre of the room, exactly how I was not sure. By thin wires? Held up on some transparent platform?

We were in the centre of the city. The flesh heaved in and out, processing the blood fed to it. There were tangles of veins and arteries—masses of pipes carrying red fluid—falling from the lump of flesh, leading the blood away and pushing it in. People in uniforms stood near the large tubes, measuring and taking notes; someone was injecting a pipe leading into Harmille's heart with another batch of blood.

"Keep going, old boy," said the man. "You greedy little bugger." Then he laughed softly and patted the artery. "All right, Harmille. I'll give you one more treat, but I want those street lights glowing for us extra brightly, and a bit faster internet wouldn't go astray. See if you like this." He selected another syringe and pushed the needle into the pipe and slowly let the contents drain into Harmille. "Hey, easy does it! You don't enjoy it so much if you gulp it all down like that!"

Harmille gave a little sigh of contentment and I felt the pulse beneath my feet strengthen and gain clarity and rhythm.

The man looked towards Jordan and me, and smiled warmly. "Come on over. He loves you, you know. He loves us all. That's why we'd do anything for him."

"Anything at all," I agreed, walking over. It was the most incredible thing I'd seen in my life.

This was the heart of the city.

◆ ◆ ◆

LIFEBLOOD OF THE CITY

LYN THORNE-ALDER

IT was raining when they phoned the body in.

Tick, thought Ellen, picturing a gear moving one cog forward. *Tick*, as the cook of the diner stood shouting into the phone, the cord stretched all the way from the office so he could stare at the body as he yelled at the emergency line. *Tock,* as he gave in and went back into the shelter of the kitchen, still shouting into the phone. The clock had been started.

Ellen watched from her hiding place as the rain fell, a thin drizzle that was just enough to coat every surface in a kind of slimy dreariness. The cook came out again, ten or fifteen minutes later, still shouting into his phone. The busboy followed, looked at the dead girl dripping with rain and as grey as the sky, and went back inside, looking a bit grey himself. The restaurant owner appeared soon after, swearing into his cellular phone, and quickly retreated to the bright light of the kitchen.

The rain was picking up. It was a good night to leave a body, a bad night to find one. Any evidence that might have been left on site—she tried to be careful, but *she* was human—should be washed away. The cops wouldn't want to venture out in this either; they would take their time getting here and rush once they arrived.

Twenty minutes. Thirty. Ellen didn't mind waiting. Thirty-six minutes later, the beat cops arrived with the ME. They looked tired already and the junior cop had a nasty bruise fanning across her face. Ellen, unseen in her hiding place, smiled. *Tick,* she thought, *tick, tick, tock.* The gears were in place and the machine well and truly started.

As she'd expected, the investigation at the site was quick, cursory, and, above all, damp. They knew it was a dump site; any moron could figure that out. There was no blood, no sign of a struggle, and no clothes. They 'knew' the killer was long gone: the cook had first found the body an hour ago, and it was already ice-cold—had been like that, they assumed, before the rain chilled it. There was little to do but snap pictures, pack up the corpse, and get out of the rain.

Ellen waited until after they'd left, long enough to make sure they weren't coming back—long enough for the cook and the busboy to get bored with loitering and close the back door—and then a little bit longer. But she had work to do and couldn't wait any longer.

Ellen slipped out of her hiding place and brushed the garbage off her jeans and raincoat. There were more pieces of the machine to find, and with the gears already in motion, she'd better do it quickly.

Tick, tick, tock.

♦

"WHAT CAN YOU tell me?" Officer Kira Baranek was pacing, circling the body on its slab in slow, measured steps, the sound echoing in the morgue.

"It's a body." Dr Pittman was not known for having an amazingly creative sense of humour. "Female, mid-twenties, Caucasian. Probably brunette before they shaved all her hair off. No visible trauma, no ligature marks, and she appears to have died of exsanguination." The ME picked up the corpse's hand to show the officer the needle marks, just in the crook of the elbow.

"Somebody wanted this girl very, very dead, but didn't want to hurt her in the meantime."

"Why shave her hair, then?" Kira's hand brushed the air near the corpse's head. "And recently."

"Maybe they wanted it for whatever their ritual was. Maybe they wanted to dehumanise her. Maybe it just got in the way." Dr Pittman shrugged. "I'm still working on the ID. We have a pile of missing persons' cases."

♦

TICK.

This piece, so close to the end, had been the hardest to find. Ellen slotted the man into the machine, one limb at a time, finishing with the neck and head, settling the new cog against his pads. He looked as if he was sleeping, surrounded by steel as shining and cold as the moon. In fact, all the human parts looked as if they were sleeping: bald and naked, their capsules spanning the concrete length of the warehouse floor. Tubes filled with blood ran from their bodies, arching towards a wall full of thicker glass tubes. From these, gravity lowered the blood down into jars and then more mechanisms forced the blood into her employer's complicated laboratory setup of beakers, pipes and small blue flames. They were all cogs in the machine, their faces peaceful in their slumber.

She slid a needle into the cog's soft flesh, the attached plastic tube snaking up into the collection system. There was a specific order to things, a procedure—a formula. Everything had to go properly; just as the body she dumped had to be removed before she could insert the second-last piece of the machine. Her employer insisted on order, and Ellen was in no place to argue with her boss.

She rapped the tube once with a fingernail—her own little rite, not part of the greater scheme, but permitted anyway—and then tapped the cog on the shoulder. Heavily sedated, he was past caring already, but it grounded her in what she was doing.

Ellen stepped away from the new component. Everything was in place, slotted in properly and connected to the system. Ellen threw the lever that started the gears moving again, *tick, tick, tock*. This place had been a factory once, when the city shone and the money poured in, when human labour and human love moved the gears. Ellen hadn't been born then, but her employer would sometimes wax poetic about the steel mills, about the factories of old, when everything moved like a perfect shining machine.

And now it all would move like that again.

The blood pumped like a metronome through the tubes, through the glass and into the beakers. If Ellen held her hand just right, she could pretend it was dripping down her fingers and onto her arm, coating her the way it coated the insides of the tubes. Sometimes she stood there for hours, just watching the blood drip down her hands.

Now she'd inserted the penultimate piece, the machine was almost complete. It would do, finally, what it had been built to do so many decades ago; ticking and clicking away, powered by all that blood. According to Ellen's employer, it would change the world—it would make magic. She turned out the lights and left the machine to tick and click to itself, like a machine ought to. She had errands to run.

♦

"IT'S A MYSTERY." Kira Baranek shoved the file away from herself and kicked back against her chair. Her partner, McEvans, three months from retirement and already checked out, didn't even look up from her magazine. Kira continued, "The girl doesn't match any missing persons in the last twenty years, not anywhere in the state, and I checked New York and Pennsylvania, too. I can't find another case with an MO like this in the last fifty years. And with no ID, I've got no motive."

"Box her up and put her with the rest of them. The Archives people need something to play with when they get bored." McEvans deigned to look up from her magazine long enough to relay this sage advice. "She's probably a nobody, anyway—nobody looking for her, nobody cares, nobody to worry—"

The phone ringing cut her off abruptly. McEvans stared at the thing as if it had done her a personal offense.

Kira grabbed it like a lifeline. "Baranek here."

"Officer Baranek. This is Sergeant Marje Allise. Say my name to your partner over there."

Obediently, Kira repeated the name. "McEvans? Sergeant Marje Allise?"

McEvans went from pale to ashen, dropping her magazine as if it was on fire. "Do whatever she says."

"I see your partner hasn't forgotten everything she learned in the Academy. Very good. Officer Baranek, you are going to go talk to Donald Neskaran, on East Avenue. You are going to ask him about the missing person. Take a photograph, or a nice artist's rendering. And then you are going to ask the coroner to go over the young lady's body one more time, with a microscope if need be. There's something she's missing."

Out of the corner of her eye, McEvans was making desperate and entirely vague gestures with both hands. "Yes, ma'am. I'm sorry, ma'am, what precinct do you work for?"

"That's irrelevant at the moment, Officer. Tell your captain I gave you these orders, and he won't argue with me."

Kira took a deep breath. "I feel like Dr Pittman isn't the only one who's missing something here, ma'am."

"She's not. But you'll figure it out fast enough. Donald Neskaran. East Avenue. He won't be hard to find."

The phone went dead.

◆

"THANK YOU, MR Connors. I'm sure you'll be richly rewarded." Ellen hung up the phone and looked through her day planner, neatly checking off coded items. Broken cog, discarded. New cog, acquired. Phone calls one through three, made. And she still had time for a lunch break.

Her office looked out over the factory floor. She had gotten very good at not looking, the way she had gotten very good at thinking about *cogs* and *gears*, about the way the machine ticked and clicked and not about what the individual pieces actually were. But as a rare ray of sunlight broke through the clouds and stabbed through the tall windows, Ellen caught a glimpse of the blood, bright as the sun itself, dripping ever downwards like a living rainfall, like rust on the sides of buildings that bled slowly towards the sidewalk.

She swallowed hard and scheduled a meeting over her lunch hour. She could get more work done that way, anyway. She had another cog to dispose of, from the looks of things. And her employer would want—

She picked up the phone before it had finished its first ring. "Yes, ma'am. Ellen here."

Her heart had started pounding the minute her fingers touched the headset. She didn't bother to try to hide it. When her employer spoke, she did manage to muffle a small keening whine, but only through years of practice.

"Is everything in place?" It should sound like a normal human voice, like a normal woman's voice. It never did. It never had, except the once, and Ellen had been very drunk and very upset at the time.

"Everything is in order, ma'am. I acquired the last—the last piece." She had been more than a little relieved to find that she wasn't herself the last piece. She had wondered, for many years, why her employer had pulled her from her dire situation; for what purpose she'd been saved. Since then, Ellen and her boss had pulled so many from similar situations, and they had all bled out into the machine.

"Very good. I'll start on the final distillation tomorrow night, then. I imagine there will be a few dump jobs before then, of course."

She could feel a nosebleed beginning. Blood, it always came back to blood. "Yes, ma'am." She fumbled for a handkerchief with one hand. "And the police?"

"They're not going to do anything, as long as you did your job properly. And I'm sure you did your job, didn't you, Ellen?"

Something escaped Ellen's throat, an animal sound, the last gasp of the dying. "Yes, ma'am," she managed. "The body was dumped with no identification. And I find it unlikely they will figure her out in time." She dabbed at her nose with the handkerchief. "I was going to take care of one of those disposals now, ma'am."

It amused her employer. It always did. The chuckle felt like small splinters of broken glass. "Of course. Get on with you, Ellen, and I will see to the ritual."

"Thank you, ma'am." Like a thousand times before, Ellen thought about asking, *what is the ritual?* Why were they doing this?

But the blood was trickling down her face and catching on her lip, and she thought she might vomit if she tried to speak. She waited for her employer's line to click off to hang up. She made it to the bathroom before her knees gave way.

◆

"Stories are the lifeblood of the city, Officer Baranek. Stories flow, you know. They follow the path of least resistance, like any fluid—blood or water, oil or wine."

Donald Neskaran turned out to be a man in his late eighties, wizened, but still healthy, his hair gone silver, living in the fanciest apartment Kira Baranek had ever seen. The name *Sergeant Marje Allise* had opened the door for Kira, and a brief description of the body had gotten her a seat in his living room.

After that, however, it had all been stories. And they might be the lifeblood of the city, but that didn't mean they were pumping life into Kira's investigation. Mr Neskaran had been telling her about the heyday of the city and all of his dead friends for at least half an hour.

Still, when she'd told the Captain that Sergeant Allise had given her an assignment, the Captain had said *do whatever the Sergeant wants.* If the mysterious Sergeant wanted her to listen to an old man tell stories about his glory days, Kira was not going to argue. She was too junior for arguing.

"Least resistance, sir?" she tried. He hadn't been steerable so far, but she just might not have found the right levers.

"So I tell you a story. If you don't like it—if you're fighting it—you're not likely to remember it or tell it again. But if it strikes a note with you, you'll tell your partner and maybe your husband, someone at the water cooler, or the girl who cuts your hair."

Kira didn't have a husband and she rarely talked at the water cooler, but she understood the point. "So stories have life . . . ?"

"And they can be dammed, clogged, stopped, the same as any other fluid. What happens if I tell you a story, and then somebody shoots you on the way home?"

"My partner has to collect the body and call my father?"

"And to that story . . . ?"

"Well, I guess I don't tell anyone." Kira nodded slowly. "A dead end. Are you saying this woman died so she didn't tell a story?"

◆

EVERYTHING AND EVERYONE told stories. Ellen flipped through the newspaper, looking for the sort of tales she could use. Not the big ones—the big ones drew attention. Murder, robbery, fires; they drew people like moths to a flame. *If it bleeds, it leads.*

But there were little stories that were no less powerful. The man who had been volunteering at the hospital every Saturday for twenty years. The women planting gardens in vacant lots. The fire-woman who'd been on the job five years.

They moved the city in small but noticeable ways, and so they moved the machine as well.

If Ellen had been the sort to make visible notes, she would have circled several tiny articles, on the back pages, in the Society section, parts of the obits. As it was, since her job and her employer discouraged leaving evidence behind, she closed the newspaper and dropped it down the trash chute. Fire would take care of the rest, as it so often did.

Small blue flames flickered down on the factory floor. Ellen turned her head so that she could see the laboratory space out of the corner of her eye. It didn't do to look at some things directly; it didn't do to get caught looking at all.

Her employer was down there, working on the blood. It flowed and boiled, bubbled and spat, steamed and trickled up into one tube and down into another. A light blue flame spat from the widest flask. She should not be able to smell it from here, but nevertheless, Ellen thought she caught a whiff of something like mould, something dank and unpleasant.

A light on her board was flickering rapidly: another cog in the machine was beginning to fail. With relief, Ellen turned away from the laboratory. She would likely have a body to move. From the looks of her boards, this would not be the last one for the night, either. When her employer began to light the burners, the machine was pushed past its limits and parts started to fail. But that wouldn't matter anymore. They would be done soon. Done, and Ellen would not need to find any more parts to feed to the machine.

♦

"THERE ARE ALWAYS people dying because of stories," the old man sighed. "That woman, other women, men, so many people." He stared towards the window, and for a moment Kira worried he was having a senile moment. "On the shelf, there. The photo album, Officer Baranek."

"Sir?"

"If you don't mind? The stories I have to tell are fantastical in nature, but I believe if you see the photo album, you may believe. Of course, Marje sent you. Marje has always believed, and she has good taste in people. I've been working with her for a very long time, you know."

"Sure." The photo album was easy to pick out in the shelf of old almanacs and older *National Geographic* magazines; its leather cover smelled like old men and creaked under Kira's fingers. She handed it to Mr Neskaran and took her seat again.

The old man flipped the book open. "I told you my friends died. They do that, you know, old men. And I'm old—nothing to call the police about. But these men weren't old, not when they died."

The pages were full of photos and newspaper clippings, small obituaries and larger articles. Kira peered, reading upside down as the old man told his stories.

"Carver Ellison. John Martin. Sammy Olsen. Died of depression, died of a heart attack, died of alcohol poisoning." He kept flipping. "Jack Taylor, oh, he was the best. And Jonah Goldblum. That man could make a factory *run*. Both dead. Killed himself, they said Jack did. And Jonah, nobody ever really looked."

His eyes met Kira's, and they were clear and bright with tears. "They were young men with everything to live for. They were wealthy, or climbing that ladder. They had young ladies or they had families. They were *good people*. So you tell me, Officer Baranek, why does a man in the prime of his life, the day before his wedding, put a bullet in his brain?"

"People do things for mysterious reasons . . . " It was the trained answer. *Nobody knows why someone steps in front of a train.* Kira had given it before, and hated it every time.

"Very mysterious, in this case." For some reason, Mr Neskaran looked pleased. He kept flipping. "Judith Frank. Cassius Mortimer. Deborah Carner. All my friends. All ready to turn the world on its end, all ready to make the world of steel and automobiles into something spectacular. The lifeblood of the city, some would say."

He put his finger on one yellowed obituary. "That was 1970, when Deborah Carter was found in the river. She was the last of us to go—and one of the best and brightest, too. She had *spine*, that woman did."

The photo album closed with a thump. "And then there was nobody left to hold it all together. Corruption sank in, and just plain incompetence. We were going to set the world on fire—and instead, those of us who survived just slowly drifted into the ashes."

He wheezed softly. "The *svartálfr* killed them all, the Iron Beast. They were the steel of the city, and it destroyed them." One liver-spotted hand flung out towards the window. "And now what do we have? Rust. Nothing but rust and dust, ha." The laugh was almost a sob. "Rust and dust and more rust. And your bloodless corpse— just like the rest of the city."

"Thank you for your time, Mr Neskaran." Kira rose to her feet. This was getting out of hand. "I'll let Sergeant Allise know that you were very helpful."

"I'm not crazy!" His fist slammed down on the album, cracking the leather. "I'm not a crazy old man, I can see it in your eyes. Listen! I've been studying this for decades. Just listen, will you?"

"I've listened, sir, it's just—"

"It sounds mad, obviously. But look into it a little more. Look into it, I dare you. And you'll find the Iron Beast."

◆

IT WAS RAINING again. This alleyway was dirtier than the last, the buildings streaked with dirt and mould. The restaurant to one side had been closed for years and the pawn shop on the other side assiduously minded its own business. The cog wouldn't be found for hours, possibly days. And this time, that was how Ellen wanted it. She left the broken part face-down on the dripping pavement. It didn't matter anymore.

Her employer was still hard at work when she returned. Ellen cleaned herself up before waiting in the doorway of the laboratory to be noticed.

Her employer never looked up. "Is it functioning properly again?"

Ellen dabbed a handkerchief to her nose before the blood could start. It did not do to leak in front of the boss. "Everything is slotted into place, ma'am."

"And yet it is producing very slowly."

It was hard to keep up a conversation with your back to someone, harder when that someone was so essential to your own survival. Ellen turned around, head down. "I believe many of the pieces are worn out, ma'am."

"They wear out so quickly these days. But I'm so close." The blood in the beakers bubbled and spat. Her employer poked the largest beaker with a pipette. "It seems like the metal in them has gotten thinner, over the years."

Metal, Ellen had learned, meant something different to her employer than it did to humans. She cleared her throat, because it seemed that she was expected to answer.

"The city is thinner, I think? It's rusty, where it used to shine. At least, that's what I've heard people say."

"It is." Somewhere below the headache suddenly splitting her skull, Ellen heard satisfaction. "Like the pieces of the machine, there. It wears itself out."

Ellen swallowed bile. "As you say, ma'am. I believe another piece is failing you."

"They always do." The pipette stabbed into the blood. "Everyone always does."

"I'll just take care of that, then." Ellen slipped away before her nose could start to bleed in earnest.

♦

THE RADIO SQUAWKED while Kira was on her way back from Donald Neskaran's place: three bodies found, dumps, all in separate corners of the city. She picked up the radio on a hunch. "Baranek here. I've got the one on Broadway and Court. If Dr Pittman's going out, send her to the one over on South and Main, please. She knows what to look for, if I'm right."

There was a lengthy pause, probably while the dispatcher considered what a junior officer was doing parcelling out orders. Following the hunch that had gotten her this far, Kira played the only card she had. "I'm working a case for Sergeant Allise."

"Marje Allise? Right. You want Pittman at the South and Main. Who's gonna get the one over on Goodman and Bay?"

"That's up to you. I'd say send McEvans . . . "

"But she's a short-timer, right. I've got it." Suddenly she was the dispatcher's best friend. "Good luck out there. I hear it's raining cats and dogs."

"Maybe a lion or two." *Or a beast, an Iron Beast.* Donald Neskaran's stories were swimming around in Kira's head. *Svartálfr.* Iron Beast. Some sort of creature stealing the energy out of the city's best and brightest. Fairy tales, if you were reading out of Grimm's darkest pages. But on a night like this, with the rain pouring down and the moon hidden behind clouds, when even the rust looked like blood in the streetlights—on a night like this, you could find yourself believing just about anything.

"Man, if there's a lion out there, he's one sad kitty. Bring that body in, Baranek. I'll tell the seat-warmers to get some coffee heated up for you. Hero's welcome—there might even be some crullers from Tomasino's."

"I am *not* turning into a cop stereotype. I'll be in soon." Kira was smiling. It was a bad time to be smiling, but she was doing it anyway. You had to take your moments where you could find them, in a city like this.

◆

THERE WERE THREE more components to be disposed of when Ellen returned to the factory. The blood was still trickling through the tubes, thinner now, dripping rather than flowing. The fires were still burning. In the back of the lab, her employer was still working. Soft chanting made the glass shiver and sent piercing pains through Ellen's left temple.

"We are almost there. Come here, child, I need a little of what you so freely lose around me. We are almost there."

Her nose had started bleeding again. Any mouse would run away, any squirrel, any rabbit, would flee the scene, flee the city. But Ellen could no more leave than she could cut off her own arm. She walked towards the beakers. Was this the time?

"I won't need any more pieces, not this late in the game. You'll have to dump the broken ones, of course. Aah, you've always had such nice blood. Such metal in it, shining like gold." Her employer giggled as her pipette dove in to steal a few bright red drops. "Gold, gold. Such silly creatures, hunting after gold when iron has always been where the power is."

Ellen's employer looked human. Glanced out of the corner of the eye, she looked like a stout woman in her middle age, her hair steel-grey and her skin ruddy. On bad days, Ellen told herself that she had been fooled when she signed the contract; that she'd thought she was making a deal with a human, with a *person*. Most days, she knew better. Most days, she understood that she had made an arrangement with a being so old it predated evil.

"I am so close." The drops of Ellen's blood went into the smallest beaker. "There. Deal with the broken bits, that's a dear."

"Ma'am." Ellen fled. There were more pieces to deal with, and she had managed to avoid becoming one of them for another night.

♦

"Baranek?" The radio kept calling her. "Officer, we've got another body. This one's down in the numbered streets."

"One of mine?" The radio kept calling her, over and over again. Another body. Another bloodless grey thing. Another photograph in the rain, another crime scene that was nothing more than a dump location. Kira had been running in a spiral around the city since before sunset, and it was nearly dawn.

"'Fraid so. If it's not one of yours, we've got a vampire or something going on. Sixth, over where it hits Culver."

"Can Dr Pittman make it?"

"She's up to her elbows in corpses and not exactly pleased with you."

"Somehow, I am not surprised." She finished her diner coffee and started the car up again. "On my way."

The roads were nearly empty, this time of night, and nobody who was out wanted to get in the way of a cop. She made her turns, left and then left again. If she focused on the road, she didn't imagine the bodies stacked up, piled to Pittman's elbows.

Left and then left . . . Kira turned her radio off and took another left. She really was spiralling. Something about that suited her sense of the dramatic. Ever turning inwards, twisting through the rust-stained streets of this corpse of a city, a spiral of death.

Kira had made two phone calls—one to Sergeant Allise, and one to Donald Neskaran. She'd contemplated calling McEvans but decided, in the end, just to ask Allise to relay a message if everything went wrong.

"The Iron Beast doesn't feed on blood." Neskaran had sounded so tired on the phone. "It draws energy from life, from vitality. What it needs blood for—that's a different story. I've been researching the creature for so long and I'm still not certain. It harvests it, I think. It's looking for something."

Sergeant Allise had been both less helpful and more. "If Neskaran is right and this is a *svartálfr*, you have to stop it before it's done. Do what you have to, and I'll clear the road for you."

Kira drove into the old heart of the city, where factory buildings stood like skeletons against the sky, a monument to Neskaran's dead friends and all their lost ambition. This had gone beyond a *lead* and into crazy land, but, even knowing that, she kept driving, following an old man's nightmare and a trail of corpses laid out like a sick Yellow Brick Road. *We're off to see the wizard . . .*

She wondered, wildly, if *svartálfar* cast spells. Wouldn't that be a way to go out? *Deceased appears to have been killed by a fireball . . .*

A blonde woman slipped into one of the abandoned factory buildings, her hair sharp and nearly white in the streetlights. Kira fishtailed the car to a stop and dove out. The corpse could wait.

♦

THE COP WAS right behind her. Ellen darted through the building, slamming doors, leaving a dripping trail of water behind her. There were so few components left in the machine. She had never seen her employer run it so long or so quickly. Maybe that 'keystone' really had been the crucial piece? It was down to him now, either way. The remaining lights on the board were flickering and dying, all but his.

"Some people have so much life." Her employer's voice ripped across Ellen's nerves, leaving stabbing pains in its wake. "Like this one, like you. They give up so much more vitality, so much more True Iron. I'm almost there."

The *svartálfr* had been *almost there* for as long as Ellen could remember. But there was something in the shuddering tones of her voice that made it sound so much more imminent this time. "Ma'am?"

"You've been so good to me. Such a good little human, and so much more alive now than when you came here. But it's time. The machine must go on."

"Ma'am?" Panic pinned Ellen to the spot. After all this time?

Her employer's grip took over when movement proved impossible. "I need three more grains of True Iron. The keystone won't be able to manufacture it in time. Put in yoke with two others, you ought to survive the process."

"But—" Her employer guided Ellen into the machine, one limb at a time and then then her neck and head, before slotting the needle home. "But," she tried, as the sedative took hold. "There's only two of us."

The door slammed open. Ellen blinked away blurriness and pain, forcing her eyes to focus. The cop. The lady officer, gun drawn.

"I thought she might send someone." The chuckle Ellen's employer made ripped into her ears. This close, she could feel an eardrum rupture. "Too late. Too late by half. Stupid thing never learned that cogs from one machine—"

The *svartálfr* strode towards the cop. A shot sounded, and another. The slot next to Ellen swung open.

"—can be used in another."

As Ellen's eyes closed, grunts and curses reached her ears. Soon though, silence descended as the sedative took effect on the policewoman.

Then, almost as if she imagined it, that horrible rasping voice filled her mind.

"Three more grains to go."

♦   ♦   ♦

UNNAMED CHILDREN

JOANNE ANDERTON

THE Ward looked like she had been pulled apart from the inside out. Her abdomen had ruptured, her legs cracked, and the tips of her fingers were torn clean off. Her simple grey dress was dark with blood, so much it had dyed the cloth a kind of purple, almost a pretty colour in the physician's warmly lit office. She was strung by her elbows on a shiny silver rack. Her limbs were convulsing, ruined fingers wiggling, loose-hanging ankles spinning, even the tubes dangling out of her gut slithered like living snakes.

Helena baulked at the sight of her, and would have turned to leave if the door hadn't closed firmly behind her.

"Please." The physician stood behind a wooden desk, bare but for a single file, which was ominously crisp, white, and new. He gestured to two chairs in front of the desk. "Sit."

Helena guided her daughter into one of the chairs. "What's wrong with the Ward, Mummy?" Ursula whispered.

"I'm afraid we have encountered an irregularity with your daughter's donation," the physician said. Helena hated physicians.

She hated their white cloaks with the red-rimmed hoods, she loathed the petty cruelty of their invasive hands. The smell of incense, permeating the office, was unable to hide the stench of boiling blood, making her sick to the stomach. The very sight of the file made her want to scream.

Instead, she took a calm breath and asked, "What do you mean?"

"There's no doubt." The physician gestured to the broken Ward. "Every donation is tracked and the evidence is clear to see. Your daughter's blood did this."

"But that's impossible." An old panic was rising within her, one she thought she'd left behind long ago. "Ursula was examined before she gave her first donation. The nurses didn't find anything wrong."

"Errors such as this only present themselves at the donation stage." The physician opened the file and began flicking through sheets of paper. Diagrams, charts. Crooked blood-letting circles and runes so powerful they seemed to shimmer on the page. "It's difficult explain to a lay person such as yourself. Let's just say that blood is life. It is the fuel that drives the Wards. Your daughter's blood has . . . too much life. It breaks the engine."

This couldn't be happening. They were going to take her daughter away. Again.

"She will need to be quarantined, and you will all require additional testing."

"Mummy?" Ursula gripped her sleeve. Her voice wobbled, fearful.

"But she's only six," Helena whispered, and placed a protective hand over her daughter's small fingers. "That's not fair."

"Old enough to donate, so her blood must be up to standard." The physician scowled at her across the top of gold-rimmed spectacles. "Everyone must contribute to the running of the city."

Helena lowered her gaze. The city demanded its sacrifices. Some harsher than others.

♦

HELENA HAD NO mementos from her time in the Home, except for the ones she wore on her skin. If she had her way, she'd get rid of the memories too, but it was not that simple. She wasn't a Ward, with a blank mind ready to be rewritten at will.

Harry had never questioned her scars. He'd seemed happy enough to believe her stories of delicate skin and recalcitrant blood vessels. After all, he'd seen her donate, knew it was difficult to find a vein and that she bruised purple flowers at the first prick of the needle. But he eyed them now, as she dressed. Patterns of stars on the inside of her arms, tracks like footprints on the back of her thighs. She pulled long sleeves and stockings over them, hiding her past beneath paisley print and opaque nylon.

"Did they say it could run in the family?" he asked, again.

"They just want to be sure," she said.

"No one from my side has ever visited the Clinic."

He must think she'd been sent to the Clinic too, and that's where the scars came from.

She couldn't tell him about the Home. She'd been only a girl, but old enough to get herself into the kind of trouble that required a polite, nine-month withdrawal from civilised society. She wouldn't ever forget the small, cell-like room, with its cement floor and single cracked window. Or lying curled in a ball beneath a single, green sheet while a Ward without a face drained blood from her arm. Her payment, in return for board and the necessary medical attention.

Her time in the Home had taught her that physicians were cruel. They treated the girls in their care like laboratory rats. But the Wards without faces were kind. She never understood why. The cells were cold, the sheets inadequate, but more than one had given her the dress from its back as a blanket. Rough, grey material warmed by the Ward's runic machinery. They were faceless, hairless, their flesh plump and round like a child's, flushed pink and riddled with tiny maintenance tattoos. Why did the Wards care when they had no heart? Why give up a dress when it could not feel the cold?

"What about your family?" Harry refused to let it go. "Do you remember anything? I know you were only young when your parents died, but what about before then? Your grandparents, cousins? You should tell them. It might help cure Ursula."

Helena closed her eyes. "I've never been to the Clinic," she said, after a moment.

She did not mention the Home.

◆

THEY RODE THE light rail to the Clinic, and Harry refused to meet her eye the whole way. Helena held Adam's hand and tried not to take it personally. She kept her son distracted by pointing out the city as they rattled through it. Look at the Ward crew dangling by precarious ropes to polish the windows of tall buildings. See that sweetshop, can't you just taste the coils of multicoloured candy? Sugar melts at one-hundred and sixty degrees you know, but the Wards roll it by hand. Yes, let's stop on the way home, we'll need something sweet. Next time, we should buy some for Ursula.

The Ward driving the carriage wore a small blue conductor's hat perched on a beehive of red curls, and a permanent red-lipped smile. She announced each station in a chirpy, sing-song voice that could be heard clearly even at the very back seats. They rattled to a stop at the end of the line, and Helena and her family disembarked in the shadow of the Clinic. The Ward gave Adam a little wave before jerking the lever to fold the doors closed.

The Clinic was an ugly block of a building, square and grey and perched at the edge of the river. The sky above them was a perfect blue, but the light from the sun couldn't seem to get through here. A cold wind twined up from the water, twisting around crumbling sandstone walls and rattling through boarded-up windows. Colonial-era buildings were squashed close together like stained teeth, each of them equally unsavoury. An old man slumbered in the doorway of a closed-up sex worker shop. Dusty, lifeless Wards hung naked in its windows. Another place with a black door seemed to sell blood-letting tools: needles, candles, chalk and ash. There were runes of protection etched into every corner. Gnarled fig trees soiled the street with their fruit and ripped at the plumbing with their roots. Everywhere the scent of incense and blood hung like smoke. It made Helena feel ill. It brought back memories she could not bury.

Somewhere, in this rubbish-littered warren, was the Home.

The streets were quiet here, and empty. No traffic, no people. No tall glass buildings it took scores of Wards to build, no bustling office-workers, no food-stalls, no delightfully manicured parks. They'd left that behind. This was the oldest part of the city, abandoned by all except nurses, physicians, the homeless and the desperate. Who would choose to live or work beside the contaminated and the shameful?

"Everyone will know," Harry said, voice little more than a whisper, as the light rail disappeared around the corner. "News travels fast."

"It's just a mistake," Helena said. "Soon, they'll release her. And everything will go back to normal." But she could already feel the stench creeping into her clothing, dirtying her.

Something shifted in the shadow of an alleyway, a narrow stretch of darkness between two leaning townhouses. The ghost of a face, cracked glass eyes reflecting the hazy streetlights, pale long-fingered hands wrapped around stone, and the edge of a grey sleeve.

"Let's get this over with," Harry said. "We need to get out of here as soon as possible."

It was bright inside the Clinic. Harsh, sanitised light beamed down on them from long globes in the ceiling. The floor was cement. The walls white tiles. Too familiar. Helena swallowed an urge to be sick as a nurse led them to meet with the physician. The nurse's white sleeves were rolled up to reveal blood-splattered plastic gloves, and protective runes were tattooed into his forearms just below the elbow. His face was hidden behind a fitted red mask. He took them to a room with three chairs, with Ursula on the other side of a one-way mirror.

Helena ran over to the glass, dragging Adam behind her. Harry hesitated by the door.

"Mummy?" Adam pressed his free hand against the mirror; Helena refused to let go of the other one. "It's Ursula! What's she doing?"

Ursula knelt in the middle of the room, crayon in hand, scribbling red all over butcher's paper. She had only been in the Clinic for three days, but already it had taken its toll. Her hair had been shaved, and she was hooked up to three drips, each at a different point in her arm. Terrible bruises ran their way across her skin; little pinpricks of blossoming blue and yellow flowers, trailing down her arms, across her scalp, her neck and back.

"Ursula?" Adam smacked the transparent wall with the palm of his hand. "Ursula?"

"She cannot hear you, or see you. She does not know you are here."

Helena turned. The physician entered the room, several more nurses in his wake.

"Let me see her," Helena spat the words out. "Let me hold her. She's my daughter."

"She's in quarantine." The physician was unmoved. "And tests will continue until the nature of her contamination can be determined." The nurses spread out like predators to surround them. "You saw what her blood did to the Ward, so you know why this is necessary. Any contamination must be removed from the city, before it has a chance to spread. Now, will you all submit to be tested? We must be certain you have not been affected too."

"That's why we're here." Harry, to his credit, was pale.

The nurses sketched temporary circles in thick white chalk, lit half-burned candles, poured piles of ash. Helena couldn't help but wonder if they'd bought them from the shop up the road.

Adam was the worst of it. He sat in the chair like he was told, ever the good boy. The nurse promised him a lollipop, so he began to educate the man on the melting point of sugar. It didn't last long. The first few needles were a betrayal Helena felt in her very bones. When he started to cry, they strapped him down.

Helena kept her eyes on Ursula. There were runes etched into the little plastic bands wrapped around her wrists, and she wondered what they were for. Not protection, it was too late for that. Her daughter's blood was already impure. Was it to give her strength to survive this ordeal? Was it to numb the pain?

The nurse struggled to find a stable vein in Helena's arms. When he finally managed, her blood came slowly, reluctantly.

They did not stop for candy on the long ride home.

♦

HER NAME WASN'T always Helena. She'd changed it, when she was released back into the world, so there would be no history of her shameful past. Except for the one she remembered.

The boy who'd said he loved her had whispered a different name when he'd held her so close. Nothing remained of that girl, and the baby they made between them, except scars.

But Ursula's absence brought it all back. The simple act of stripping Adam's bed summoned unwanted memories, of standing in a doorway as two Wards without faces wrung blood from empty sheets. They'd never wasted a single drop. They'd hummed, faintly, as they worked, a sound as sad as tears. It was made by the blood boiling deep within their chests, the engine of magic and stone that gave them movement.

Behind her, more girls had watched, all pale as ghosts, thin but for their protruding bellies. Fear had hung heavily around them. All they ever saw of birth was the blood it left behind. All they ever heard was the screaming. There were never any babies.

If Helena closed her eyes, the girls would be there, behind her, watching her make her son's bed. They never really left.

"Where do you go?" Harry asked, returning her back to the present.

Helena emerged from the past slowly, like swimming to the surface of a deep dark pond.

"I'm right here," she finally answered, tucking in the corners. Ursula's room remained untouched, the door closed, as though some invisible contagion hovered in the air.

"Are you?" Her husband didn't look her in the eye. "When you get like that I feel like you're hiding something from me. I feel like you're not even here."

Helena sat on the edge of her bed and listened to the clink and clatter of Harry pouring himself another drink. The girl she'd been back then had a different name. One her husband would never know.

♦

A FLASH OF light caught her eye, and Helena paused at the bottom of the Clinic steps. Something sparkled in the darkness of the alleyway. She leaned in, and the smell of the river wrapped around her, thick and carried on a cold breeze.

The Ward with the broken eyes was still there. She was propped up against one wall, legs stretched out on the slimy cement, almost lost in a pile of rubbish. She was not alone. A second Ward crouched beside her, and this one had all her features scratched out. Even in the dark Helena could tell it was done with a pen, dug deeply into warm, artificial skin.

They were both watching her. The flash she'd seen was morning sunlight, caught on a shattered iris.

The nurses were surprised to see her. It had been over a week since the testing, and the rest of her family appeared to be in the clear. She wasn't actually required to return. But Helena wasn't about to leave her daughter here, all alone. Harry might be able to bury himself in his son's wellbeing, fussing over him to the point of blindness—

"We don't feed him enough red meat."

"He needs blueberries and Echinacea. They have it in tablets now. It's much cheaper."

"Red clover, twenty-times strength. It's what the physicians themselves use. Impossible to get. But I know a guy who knows a guy."

—but Helena could not forget her daughter.

She must be lonely. She must be weak, and hurting.

The nurses left her to watch her daughter sleep, on the other side of the one-way mirror, hooked up to drips and surrounded by piles of ash and small runic circles.

Helena lost all track of time. Every so often, a nurse entered the room on the other side. One placed a crystal on Ursula's pale forehead and made notes as the clear diamond facets gradually clouded. Another drew charcoal diagrams around the bruises on Ursula's arms. A third took only the smallest pinprick of blood from her index finger, and dripped it into one of the ash piles. It bubbled sluggishly, the reaction quickly dying. The nurse nodded, and Helena's heart seemed to jump. Maybe that was a good sign.

Ursula hardly moved the whole time.

Eventually, Helena decided they had forgotten she was there.

Back stiff and her legs aching, she stood and crept quietly out of the room. Her daughter was just on the other side. She glanced up and down the empty corridor. Ursula must be close. Just one look. Just one touch.

But the insides of the Clinic were guarded by security runes, and without the nurses to guide her, Helena could not find her way. Where she thought she'd find her daughter, she found the Ward instead.

She was still hung up on her silver rack, forearms dangling loosely. If anything, she looked worse. She was still spasming, but the jerking movements had grown sluggish, tired. New holes dotted her skin, round and bloodless, and more of her anatomy had been extracted. Muscles the colour of mud, blue veins the texture of plastic, shards of steel and chunks of brick wound through it all.

The Wards were built from the city itself. And bound to it.

"Hello Helena," she said. "I remember you." The Ward smiled, even as her head rolled. They always smiled, no matter what was being done to them. Happy to serve the city that gave them life, in any way it required. "You are the mother."

Helena glanced at the fresh holes. "They're testing Ursula's blood on you."

"Oh yes, of course." The Ward chuckled gently, the sound humming out of her open chest. "The initial error broke me. What else can I do?" She glanced up at her torn fingers. "I cannot even lay bricks, like this. I bend, and everything falls out. I grip, and the stones slip right through my hands. This is my task, now."

"Does it hurt?" Helena couldn't shake a feeling of guilt. Maybe if she'd fed Ursula more blueberries . . .

"We do not know what you mean by pain," the Ward answered. "I feel the blood tear its way inside me. It undoes the spells that bind me together, it upsets the balance that initiates breathing, and it burns the runes that facilitate thought. If that is pain, then yes. But this is what the city asks of me now. They will test me, over and over, until your daughter is cured. If she is cured."

If hung in the room like a weight, but Helena asked, "And then what will happen to you?"

"I will be discarded. Because I am not useful anymore."

If she is cured.

What would happen to Ursula, if they could not cure her? To live in the city you must contribute to the city, and donate blood to the Wards who make it run. No free ride. No comfort without sacrifice.

"I will be returned to the city. The pipes that make my legs belong in an office block. The cement that forms my lungs yearns for the footpath it was torn from. The blood that gives us life will be spilled into the river and washed of all its impurities. And the flesh, the bones—" her eyes were terrible and Helena shrunk from them "—you know where they have come from. And you know where they will return."

◆

THE STREET OUTSIDE the Clinic smelled like the river as Helena remembered it. Sewage and storm water. Mangroves and mud. Incense and blood. The scent used to leak in through her cell window. In her blood-drained deliriums she'd imagined it as fingers, tangling in her hair.

The river washed everything away, all the dirt and the impurities, the used blood, the useless blood, all of it out to sea.

It was darker outside than when she went in, darker than it should have been. Helena glanced up at the clouds, low and boiling through heavy branches. The pavement seemed to steam in humid anticipation. The air felt alive.

The Wards were standing in the lane. Watching her.

"What about you?" Helena approached them. Her words didn't echo, but were sucked up by the darkness instead. "What use could the city possibly have for you?"

They held her gaze for a moment longer, before retreating in silence.

Helena followed. "Answer me!" she cried. "Look at you, you're useless too!" The alley was so dark even the storm clouds were obscured. "Why can you remain and my daughter—my daughter—"

The passage opened up to an empty and cracked street. A rusted fence. An overgrown patch of grass. Behind it all, a ruin overlooking the filthy water.

Helena knew this place. But in her memories the lawn was manicured, the fence painted green, the building tall and imposing. Was it really that long ago? The other side of Harry, Ursula, and Adam.

The Wards shuffled across the street, into the ruin, heads turned at unnatural angles so they could stare at her the whole time.

Helena's breath caught in her throat as she followed them through an empty doorway, to a stained and muddy foyer. The admissions desk was little more than firewood. The steel-mesh doors that had imprisoned unwed, pregnant girls like criminals now lay against the wall and played host to creeping vines with crisp white flowers.

There were Wards everywhere. Broken, every one. Cracked faces, missing limbs, ruined torsos held together with sticks and duct tape. They watched her, humming. And everywhere, the smell of blood, boiling. The sound of its hiss and pop.

A single Ward without a face stood behind the admissions desk.

Ancient, stooping, its grey dress torn and growing mould. One twisted foot, one missing hand. And no face. Just smooth and white where the rest had features. Hairless. Pale. It raised its stump and gestured to Helena.

Outside the rain came hammering down, and lightning flickered through shattered windows. Leaks pooled into little puddles on the uneven tiles.

The Ward without a face led Helena down hauntingly familiar corridors. Only this time, the girls that ghosted them were Wards. They peered from cell-like rooms, still furnished with the rusted frames of ancient beds, a single basin, a single toilet. Succulents grew from the cracked porcelain bowls.

The doors out the back had always been locked, but now they were flung open, one shuddering on rusted hinges, the other lying in pieces in the overgrown grass. Helena stood in the doorway. The Home loomed on the top of a small hill, the land sloping down in a tangle of rubble and weeds.

The city will find a use for you.

The Wards had always been kind to her. They had no faces, no mouths. But still, they had warned her in the only way they could.

Heavy rain beat down on the top of her head as Helena stepped out into the yard. It rushed like waterfalls down cliffs of rubble and weeds.

The last time she was here it was a sunny day, hot on her skin through the thin medical gown. Two Wards had guided her out of the Home, and down the steep slope. The weeds had snagged on her hem and rough stones cut into her feet. They'd taken her to somewhere hidden in the shadow of ancient figs, ringed by crumbling sandstone walls. Flat, empty, and smelling of ash.

A safety fence had been erected around the yard—corrugated iron sheets and steel mesh. It broke up the view into segments like paintings on a wall. Helena peered through them, one at a time. The river snaked around the edges of the city, water the colour of scuffed metal. The great fig trees had been cut down. All that remained of them were mangled stumps, tables for beer bottles and a couple of burned bongs, accompanied by rotting, unwanted sofas.

There were signs bolted to the fence warning about the sewerage drain. These had been ignored, and a door-shaped hole cut into the mesh to access it. Helena bent to climb through. The drain had obviously been sealed shut at some time in the past, but the cement was chipped away, the steel bars bolted to the manhole pried loose, and the cover removed.

Water rushed somewhere in the sewer, as Helena peered in. Wherever it was, it hadn't washed the bones away.

Tiny, discarded bodies, unwanted and dumped one on top of the other. Each one incomplete, plundered for parts. So many more than the last time she stood here—just a girl, scared and pregnant and shunned by the world. There were more bones than she could ever hope to count, any sense of individuality lost in the haphazard pile.

They peered up at her, white skulls and empty black eyes. Some were so pale, so clean, she could only imagine they were new.

The deep sound of humming echoed through her bones. Helena looked up. The Wards congregated on the hill, they peered from the cracked widows of the ruined Home, they squeezed through even the tiniest break in the fence.

Once, the Wards without a face had taken her here, and tried to warn her in their silent, muzzled way.

Feeling numb beneath the sound of so many broken machines, Helena nodded.

She knew then. Ursula wasn't getting any better. Soon, the physicians would give up. And if she couldn't donate blood to fuel the Wards then, well, the city would find another use for her.

But Helena couldn't let that happen to her daughter.

Not again.

♦

SHE'D TRIED TO escape, the night she went into labour. Through all the pain, and the blood, and the weakness in her drained body, she crawled on shuddering hands and knees down the halls. The smell of the river seemed to thicken around her, slowing her down.

She made it as far as the lawn out the front, before the physicians found her.

They did not let her hold the baby.

She was released two days later, small and cold and shivering, young and torn but healing. Her debt paid. She rode the light rail with her silent parents, already planning to change her name and lie about her family. She would never speak of the child.

She met Harry five years later, and married him almost immediately. Ursula took her time in coming, and when she finally held her daughter, Helena had promised them both, *never again.*

♦

SHE SPENT ALL night scrubbing, but Helena couldn't remove the muck from under her fingernails. Her hands were red as she held

Adam's tightly. The alleyway beside the Clinic was empty. The light rail rattled away, the streets quiet in its absence.

Adam clutched a present for his sister. It was almost as big as he was and too large for him to carry effectively, but he'd insisted. "When can Ursula come home?" he asked, voice hushed.

"Soon," Helena said, after a moment, even though she knew home was somewhere they could never return to.

"You shouldn't be taking him to that place," Harry had said, when she'd kissed his cheek to say goodbye. "You're obsessed. It's unhealthy." He smelled of whiskey and resentment.

"She's your daughter, too," Helena said, without any real enthusiasm. She knew she couldn't change his mind.

"No blood of mine."

He reminded her of her father.

Helena followed a nurse down the Clinic's corridors, though she knew the way by now. The man left them in the usual observation room. Ursula, on the other side of the mirror, lay tucked into her bed but not sleeping. Her face was white, her sunken eyes lost in deep shadows. Not much strength left.

"Is she getting better?" Helena asked, her mouth so dry it felt like she was talking around cotton wool.

The nurse turned to her, face hidden behind his impassive red mask. "The tests are helping."

It was a lie, of course. This was never about Ursula.

"Can I give her this?" Adam struggled to hold up his present, and the breath caught in Helena's throat. For a moment, the room seemed to freeze. The nurse looked down at the gift in Adam's hand. Long, wrapped in tissue paper, and decidedly doll-shaped. Adam looked into the nurse's scary red face with open trust, and confidence.

The nurse left the room without answering. When Adam glanced back over his shoulder at her, puzzled, Helena crouched to his level. "We will just have to give it to her ourselves," she said.

"When?"

"Soon."

They waited. Helena picked at the mud beneath her nails.

The nurse returned twice. Once, simply to check on them. Again, to bring water for Helena and juice for Adam. She did not let him drink it.

"Now," she whispered, as the door clicked gently closed.

They crept into the corridor. Adam, unsure but always willing to do as he was told, clutched the present to his chest. Helena watched the back of the nurse as he disappeared behind a set of large locked doors, then ducked across and into the broken Ward's lonely room.

She appeared to have been sleeping, her tics gentle and much reduced, but lifted her head as Helena closed the door. "You smell of dirt," the Ward said, her voice even harder to hear than usual. "And bone. And stone." She looked down at the present in Adam's hand. "What do you bring with you?"

"Stay very still," Helena whispered to her son. "And quiet. No matter what happens." He nodded, and she took the present from him. Carefully, she unwrapped it. One layer at a time.

It could have been a Ward child, if such a thing existed. Head a tiny baby skull, plucked from the sewer mud, wrapped in cloth with eyes drawn in permanent marker. Arms of fence-wire, fingers of screws. Legs made of more unwanted bone, tied together with hair from Helena's own head. Its body was sewn from the dilapidated couches, and stuffed with stones from the Home's ruins.

"City stone and human bone," the Ward whispered.

"All she needs is blood," Helena said.

The ancient Ward without a face had built the doll in the middle of a surreal circle. No ash, no chalk, no candles. Nothing but Wards, broken bodies clasped to form the circle lines, the ground vibrating with their deep and echoing hum, steam rising from the heat of their blood-boiling engines. They used their broken limbs to draw runes Helena did not recognise.

It wasn't for blood-letting, because the doll had no blood yet to let. But it seemed to be a transfer of life, nonetheless.

The Ward understood. "You will need to do it," she said. "I cannot command my own hands anymore."

"Don't watch," Helena told Adam, as she tugged at the exposed tubes peeking out of the Ward's arm.

"Take it all," the Ward whispered, as Helena broke the plastic, and hot blood began to pump sluggishly across her hands. "Leave me empty."

"But—"

The Ward shook her head. "The city finds a use for us all, but gives us little choice in the matter. I would rather this one is mine."

Helena opened the front of the doll and held it beneath the Ward's bleeding arm. Her blood—Ursula's blood—splashed across the gathered stones. It burned through the oddly shaped runes. It slid down the bodies of unnamed and unwanted children, splattered the stones from a lost and terrible place, and bubbled through the mud shoved into every last corner.

The doll soaked the Ward dry, before jerking into movement. Her stones rattled, her fingers jangled, her drawn-on eyes blinked.

Shaking, Helena put her down. She skittered along on her bone-stump feet, running out of the room and into the corridor. Wild and smoking with the unruly energy of Ursula's blood.

"Hurry," the Ward slumped. "Our magic is borrowed. Second hand spells, altered runes. My kind has given her what life they can, but she has no engine. Your daughter's blood will not boil forever."

Helena grabbed the tissue paper in one hand, and Adam with the other, and ran after the Ward child. She led them straight to Ursula's room, impervious to the security runes. Like she knew the way.

Adam let out a happy little cry, and ran to his sister's bed. Helena allowed herself a kiss on her daughter's forehead, but knew they didn't have time. A nurse could appear at any moment. She pulled the needles from Ursula's arms, and lifted her. She'd only been here a few weeks, but she was already so thin. Light as air.

Adam helped wrap his sister in the tissue paper as the Ward child scrambled into her bed. They wrapped her tightly, and she was somehow even smaller. So silent and quiet. Just like a doll.

Helena stood, and tucked the Ward child into her daughter's bed, drawing the single thin sheet right under her chin. The doll was flush with Ursula's blood, her face like a mask, her eyes not her own. For a moment, Helena wavered. Could she really abandon this nameless child—built from so many unwanted children—even to save Ursula? Then the doll whispered with Ursula's mouth—

Never again. Remember?

—and Helena bent to give her the kiss she had so long been denied.

She picked up Ursula, quiet and motionless and wrapped in paper, and left the room. The door locked behind them.

The nurse who led them out didn't cast the large, tissue-wrapped doll a second glance.

Ursula only started to move again when they left the Clinic. She groaned, and Helena tore at the paper around her face. Her stick-like body shuddered back into life, and she pressed dry lips to Helena's cheek.

"Mummy," she breathed.

Helena held both her children close: Ursula balanced on one hip, her bony arms wrapped loosely around Helena's neck, Adam's hand held tightly in her own. She turned them away from the light rail, from home, and the city, and walked toward the river instead.

It washed everything away, clean and out to sea.

ABOUT THE CONTRIBUTORS

JOANNE Anderton cooks up speculative fiction stories for adults, young adults, anyone who likes their worlds a little different. She sprinkles a pinch of science fiction to spice up her fantasy, and thinks horror adds flavour to just about everything. Her adult science fiction/fantasy novels have been published by Angry Robot Books and Fablecroft Publishing. Her short story collection, *The Bone Chime Song and Other Stories* was published by Fablecroft Publishing. It won the Aurealis Award for best collection, and the Australian Shadows Award for best collected work. You can find her online at http://joanneanderton.com.

ALAN Baxter is a British-Australian author who writes dark fantasy, horror and sci-fi, rides a motorcycle and loves his dog. He also teaches Kung Fu. He lives among dairy paddocks on the beautiful south coast of NSW, Australia, with his wife, son, dog and cat. He's the award-winning author of six novels and over sixty short stories and novellas. So far. Read extracts from his novels, a novella and short stories at his website—www.warriorscribe.com—or find him on Twitter @AlanBaxter and Facebook, and feel free to tell him what you think. About anything.

NATHAN Burrage's short fiction has appeared in a range of Australian publications including *Aurealis, Orb, Australian Dark Fantasy & Horror #2 and The Workers' Paradise anthology.* A graduate of Clarion South (2005), his debut novel, *Fivefold*, was released by Random House and translated into Russian. Nathan lives in Sydney with his wife and two daughters. Occasional updates surface at www.nathanburrage.com

DIRK Flinthart lives in Uttermost Taswegia where he raises children, teaches martial arts, and broods meaningfully in his lair. He is the author of . . . err . . . many short stories, and has received the occasional award for them. Look out for an anthology of his short works coming soon, as well as the long-awaited sequel to his novel *Path of Night.* Also, look out for snakes and other dangerous wildlife. It's a valuable tip.

REBECCA Fung is a legal editor based in Sydney, Australia. She has long had a love affair with books and will read almost anything— one of the crucial skills of a legal editor where you have to find the fun in hundreds of pages of footnotes and reading 'Ibid' over and over again. She writes fiction of all sorts, from weird humour, to fantasy, sci-fi (often with a dark edge), outright horror and even lighter children's stories. She has been published in *Midnight Echo, Trysts of Fate, Voluted Tales* and EGM Shorts, and has been a regular contributor to the *Demonic Visions* anthology series. Her horror has appeared in several other anthologies including *Between the Cracks (Sirens Call) Daylight Dims 2* (Stealth Fiction) and *Witches Stitches and Bitches* (Evil Girlfriend Media). Her children's stories have appeared in *Once Upon a Christmas* (Christmas Press) and *Zoo-thology* (Prints Charming).

STEPHANIE Gunn is a Ditmar-nominated writer of speculative fiction. In another life, she was a (mad) scientist, but now spends her time writing and reviewing. Her short stories have appeared in anthologies such as *Bloodstones, Epilogue, Grants Pass* and *Kisses by Clockwork.* She is currently at work on several contemporary fantasy novels and too many shorter works for her own good. She lives in Perth with her son and husband and requisite fluffy cat (and too many books). You can find her online at www.stephaniegunn.

com

KELLY Hoolihan is a marine biologist who lives and works on the gulf coast of Mississippi. She has been previously published in *HWA Poetry Showcase Volume 1* (2014) and in *Gothic Blue Book 4: The Folklore Edition* (2014). She is also co-host of the podcasts 'Coolihans' and 'Horror and a Half'.

KATHLEEN Jennings is a writer (and illustrator) from Brisbane, Australia. Her short stories and comics have appeared in such publications as *Lady Churchill's Rosebud Wristlet* and the Candlewick anthologies *Steampunk* and *Monstrous Affections*. Some of Kathleen's thoughts (but mostly her art) can be found at http://tanaudel.wordpress.com.

PETE Kempshall is a writer and editor living in Perth, Western Australia. His stories have been published in Australia by Ticonderoga Publications, Twelfth Planet Press and ASIM, and internationally by the likes of Big Finish, Morrigan Books, Dark Quest Books and Apex Publications. He has been shortlisted for a variety of awards, including Ditmar, Aurealis and Australian Shadows awards.

PERTH-BASED writer Martin Livings has had over eighty short stories in a variety of magazines and anthologies. His first novel, *Carnies*, first published by Hachette Livre in 2006, was nominated for both the Aurealis and Ditmar awards, and has since been republished by Cohesion Press. http://www.martinlivings.com

SEANAN McGuire was born in Martinez, California, and raised in a wide variety of locations, most of which boasted some sort of dangerous native wildlife. Despite her almost magnetic attraction to anything venomous, she somehow managed to survive long enough to acquire a typewriter, a reasonable grasp of the English language, and the desire to combine the two. Seanan is the author of the *October Daye* urban fantasies, the *InCryptid* urban fantasies, and several other works both stand-alone and in trilogies or duologies. In case that wasn't enough, she also writes under the pseudonym 'Mira Grant'. For details on her work as Mira, check out www.MiraGrant.com. Seanan was the winner of the 2010 John

W. Campbell Award for Best New Writer, and her novel Feed (as Mira Grant) was named as one of Publishers Weekly's Best Books of 2010. In 2013 she became the first person ever to appear five times on the same Hugo Ballot.

THIS will be the fourth year running that Perth short story writer, Anthony Panegyres has had a story published in a Ticonderoga anthology. The previous three were in *The Year's Best Australian Fantasy & Horror 2011, Dreaming of Djinn* and *Kisses by Clockwork*. Since 2011, Panegyres, a PhD candidate at UWA, has been an Aurealis Award Finalist for Best Fantasy Short Story, and has had stories published in Australia's premier literary journals (*Meanjin* and twice in *Overland*) as well as several anthologies including *The Best Australian Stories 2014*.

JANE Percival lives on the Kaipara Harbour, north-west of Auckland, New Zealand. On a typical day she juggles gardening, household tasks and writing; a good day being one where she manages to write for a couple of hours, garden for a couple of hours, cook up something yummy for tea, and walk at least 10,000 steps. She particularly enjoys writing speculative fiction and has been published in *Fiction on the Web, In Flash Frontier,* and *Micro Madness*.

PAUL Starkey lives in Nottingham England, but has no knowledge of the whereabouts of Robin Hood. He's been writing for many years and has been published in both the UK and the USA. To date, he has written five novels and has self-published the novels *City of Caves* and *Safe House* and a short story collection, *The Devils of Amber Street*. In 2015, he was commissioned by Abaddon Books to write a novella scheduled to be published in the autumn. He blogs regularly at https://werewolvesonthemoon.wordpress.com

ITS a long way from a rural homestead to an urban noir landscape, but Lyn Thorne-Alder has travelled the distance there and back again enough times to know the route. Lyn grew up on a steady diet of fantasy and sci-fi: Piers Anthony, Robert A. Heinlein, Mercedes Lackey, as well as movies like Mad Max and Conan the Barbarian. She likes to say "It all began with the winged cat-people": a make-believe scenario inspired by fantasy novels and Voltron cartoons, which led to her first-ever novel attempt. Thirty years later, the cat-people are still flying. From rural to urban fantasy and back to rural: Lyn Thorne-Alder currently lives in the Finger Lakes with her husband and a handful of politically-minded cats. An oenophile, bibliophile, and lover of the outdoors, Lyn enjoys gardening, hiking, various crafts, reading and, of course, writing. To learn more about Lyn Thorne-Alder, please visit http://lynthornealder.com/.

CALL her Zanne. She lives in beautiful, sunny Southern California, which is ironic since she tends to avoid the sun like it might incinerate her on the spot. While her colleagues often refer to her job as zoo-keeping, the technical title is actually middle school teacher. She has two published novellas, *Misfit Prophets Beneath a Bankrupt Sky* and *1KRV5*. Her short stories include "Persephone Is Bleeding" in *Hungry Hearts* and "Drawing Dead" in *Of Heaven and Hell*.

STORY ACKNOWLEDGEMENTS

ALL STORIES APPEAR HERE

FOR THE FIRST TIME.

ABOUT THE EDITOR

AMANDA Pillar is an award-winning editor and author who lives in Victoria, Australia, with her husband and two cats, Saxon and Lilith. Amanda has had numerous short stories published and has co-edited the fiction anthologies *Voices* (2008), *Grants Pass* (2009), *The Phantom Queen Awakes* (2010), *Scenes from the Second Storey* (2010), *Ishtar* (2011) and *Damnation and Dames* (2012). Her first solo anthology was published by Ticonderoga Publications, titled *Bloodstones* (2012) and you've just read (hopefully) the fantastic sequel, *Bloodlines*! Amanda's first novel, *Graced*, was published by Momentum in 2015. In her day job, she works as an archaeologist.

AVAILABLE FROM TICONDEROGA PUBLICATIONS

WWW.TICONDEROGAPUBLICATIONS.COM

LIMITED HARDCOVER EDITIONS

978-0-9806288-1-4 The Infernal BY Kim Wilkins
978-1-921857-54-6 Black-Winged Angels BY Angela Slatter

EBOOKS

978-0-9803531-5-0 Ghost Seas BY Steven Utley
978-1-921857-93-5 The Girl With No Hands BY Angela Slatter
978-1-921857-99-7 Dead RED Heart ED Russell B. Farr
978-1-921857-94-2 More Scary Kisses ED Liz Grzyb
978-0-9807813-5-9 Heliotrope BY Justina Robson
978-1-921857-36-2 Dreaming of Djinn ED Liz Grzyb
978-1-921857-40-9 Prickle Moon BY Juliet Marillier
978-1-921857-92-8 The Year of Ancient Ghosts BY Kim Wilkins
978-1-921857-28-7 Bloodstones ED Amanda Pillar
978-1-921857-04-1 Damnation and Dames ED Liz Grzyb & Amanda Pillar
978-1-921857-31-7 Midnight and Moonshine BY Lisa L. Hannett & Angela Slatter
978-1-921857-44-7 The Bride Price BY Cat Sparks
978-1-921857-60-7 Everything is a Graveyard BY Jason Fischer
978-1-921857-64-5 The Assassin of Nara BY R.J. Ashby
978-1-921857-78-2 Death at the Blue Elephant BY Janeen Webb
978-1-921857-82-9 The Emerald Key BY Christine Daigle & Stewart Sternberg
978-1-921857-57-7 Kisses by Clockwork ED Liz Grzyb
978-1-925212-06-8 Angel Dust ED Liz Grzyb
978-1-925212-17-4 The Finest Ass in the Universe BY Anna Tambour
978-1-925212-37-2 Hear Me Roar ED Liz Grzyb
978-1-921857-38-9 Bloodlines ED Amanda Pillar

THE YEAR'S BEST AUSTRALIAN FANTASY & HORROR SERIES
EDITED BY LIZ GRZYB & TALIE HELENE

978-0-9807813-8-0 Year's Best Australian Fantasy & Horror 2010 (hc)
978-0-9807813-9-7 Year's Best Australian Fantasy & Horror 2010 (tpb)
978-0-921057-98-0 Year's Best Australian Fantasy & Horror 2010 (ebook)
978-0-921057-13-3 Year's Best Australian Fantasy & Horror 2011 (hc)
978-0-921057-14-0 Year's Best Australian Fantasy & Horror 2011 (tpb)
978-0-921057-15-7 Year's Best Australian Fantasy & Horror 2010 (ebook)
978-0-921057-48-5 Year's Best Australian Fantasy & Horror 2012 (hc)
978-0-921057-49-2 Year's Best Australian Fantasy & Horror 2012 (tpb)
978-0-921057-50-8 Year's Best Australian Fantasy & Horror 2010 (ebook)
978-0-921057-72-0 Year's Best Australian Fantasy & Horror 2013 (hc)
978-0-921057-73-7 Year's Best Australian Fantasy & Horror 2013 (tpb)
978-0-921057-74-4 Year's Best Australian Fantasy & Horror 2010 (ebook)
978-0-925212-18-1 Year's Best Australian Fantasy & Horror 2014 (hc)
978-0-925212-19-8 Year's Best Australian Fantasy & Horror 2014 (tpb)
978-0-925212-20-4 Year's Best Australian Fantasy & Horror 2010 (ebook)

THANK YOU

The publisher would sincerely like to thank:

Elizabeth Grzyb, Amanda Pillar, Joanne Anderton, Alan Baxter, Nathan Burrage, Dirk Flinthart, Rebecca Fung, Stephanie Gunn, Kelly Hoolihan, Kathleen Jennings, Pete Kempshall, Martin Livings, Seanan McGuire, Anthony Panegyres, Jane Percival, Paul Starkey, Lyn Thorne-Alder, S. Zanne, Kaaron Warren, Cat Sparks, Lisa L. Hannett, Donna Maree Hanson, Robert Hood, Pete Kempshall, Penelope Love, Nicole Murphy, Angela Slatter, Karen Brooks, Jeremy G. Byrne, Felicity Dowker, Kim Wilkins, Marianne de Pierres, Jonathan Strahan, Peter McNamara, Ellen Datlow, Grant Stone, Sean Williams, Simon Brown, Garth Nix, David Cake, Simon Oxwell, Grant Watson, Sue Manning, Steven Utley, Lewis Shiner, Bill Congreve, Jack Dann, Janeen Webb, Lucy Sussex, Stephen Dedman, the Mt Lawley Mafia, the Nedlands Yakuza, Angela Challis, Shane Jiraiya Cummings, Kate Williams, Kathryn Linge, Andrew Williams, Al Chan, Alisa and Tehani, Mel & Phil, Hayley Lane, Georgina Walpole, Rushelle Lister, everyone we've missed . . .

. . . and you.

in memory of
Eve Johnson
Sara Douglass
Steven Utley
Brian Clarke

www.ingramcontent.com/pod-product-compliance
Lightning Source LLC
Chambersburg PA
CBHW021208250626
47155CB00008B/2729